THE CRITICS RAVE ABOUT SIMON CLARK!

"This guy Simon Clark is something special. It's time to find out what you've been missing."

—*Hellnotes*

"Not since I discovered Clive Barker have I enjoyed horror so much."

—*Nightfall*

"One of the best contemporary British horror writers. Watch this man climb to Horror Heaven!"

—*Deathrealm*

"Clark may be the single most important writer to emerge on the British horror scene in the '90s."

—*The Dark Side*

"Clark is worth seeking out."

—*Fear*

"Clark has carved a niche in the blood-curdling genre which is second to none."

—*Focus*

"A master of eerie thrills."

—Richard Laymon, author of
In the Dark

"A superb new horror writer."

—*Manchester Evening News*

"Clark writes with compelling characterization and indelible imagery."

—*DarkEcho*

"Simon Clark is not an author to let you down—the blood doesn't flow through his text so much as pump arterially into the reader's face."

—*SFX*

DEATHSTRIKE!

The Beast struck.

Richard looked back over his shoulder.

With an almighty crash the wall they'd just come through bulged inward. As if that vast expanse of cream-colored stone had just become as soft as a curtain. It bulged . . . bulged . . . splitting cracks appeared. The noise began. A constant thundering like a mighty waterfall as blocks of stone heavier than a man could actually lift poured down, smashing wooden pews, statues, lecterns, tables.

Richard moved backwards, unable to take his eyes from the terrible sight. Rubble cascaded onto the stone heads of statues, shattering them, then crashed down onto the human heads below, bursting them like raw eggs.

Screams pierced the thunderous rumble; people ran. In panic some ran into the destruction; falling timbers broke grown men like toys.

Crash.

Stained-glass windows punched inwards, in clouds of streaming colored fragments. Richard looked up. They seemed to hang forever there, a hundred feet above his head, twinkling shards of glass in brilliant reds, blues, greens, yellows; then he realized they were falling. He threw himself under the shelter of a lectern as ten thousand slivers of glass pelted down.

A wave of screams filled the building as the shards of glass buried themselves deep into necks and hands and faces.

Other *Leisure* books by Simon Clark:
DARKNESS DEMANDS
BLOOD CRAZY
NAILED BY THE HEART

DARKER

SIMON CLARK

LEISURE BOOKS NEW YORK CITY

*For Alex and Helen Clark, my children,
in recognition of their inspiration and patience*

A LEISURE BOOK®

January 2002

Published by

Dorchester Publishing Co., Inc.
276 Fifth Avenue
New York, NY 10001

First published in the United Kingdom in 1996 by Hodder and Stoughton

ISBN 0-8439-4962-7

Printed in the United States of America.

Visit us on the web at www.dorchesterpub.com.

DARKER

Part One

"Those who have once been intoxicated with power, and have derived any kind of emolument from it, can never willingly abandon it."

—Edmund Burke

Chapter One

Whatever Happened to Rosemary Snow?

Do you want power?

   More precisely, do you want power over people?

   Do you want the power to command someone to die for you?

   And for that power to be so absolute, so complete, that they not only die for you willingly, they go to their deaths so full of joy, so full of pride that they cry out your name with their final breath.

   Do you want that kind of power?

   Do you?

Tuesday afternoon. A quiet country road. 57 hours left.

Do you want power?

   When the stranger asked Rosemary the question she looked up at him, startled. It was as if he'd read her mind.

   Rosemary Snow: long black hair down to the small of her back; one small birthmark on her left cheek; a shy sixteen-year-old, still holding onto her virginity with a grip that would have been the envy of a professional wrestler.

   She sat on a roadside bench. The June sun, hot enough to melt road tar into sticky black pools, turned cars into ghosts in the rippling heat haze. The meat pie she was eating disgusted her, tasting like pulped cardboard and pepper. It had only been sheer brutal hunger that had driven her to buy it from the crappy service station down the road. Rosemary Snow would have sold her soul for a burger from a drive-thru McDonald's.

   As she picked off scabs of burnt pastry to feed the sparrows hopping around her feet, the man pulled up in the BMW. The car was so perfectly white it looked as if it had been molded from icing sugar. Without a shred of hesitation its driver wound down the window and began talking to her as if he'd known her all his life.

And, in a way, Rosemary Snow felt as if he had.

He was, she guessed, in his late thirties with the good looks of someone who might have been a pop star once: his brown hair had been brushed rather than combed; she'd describe his grin as boyish and relaxed. But it was his eyes that were the most striking feature. If you looked in a mirror, placed a finger on the edge of each eye and pulled gently down it would give the same effect as those downturned eyes that Rosemary found she couldn't stop gazing into. They were gentle eyes that told her: *This is a man who cares deeply about people in trouble*.

People just like Rosemary Snow.

"The devil nicked your tongue?" he asked cheerfully. "Come on, you can tell me."

The question had been: DO YOU WANT POWER?

"Yes." Rosemary answered so decisively that it surprised her. "That's exactly what I want."

That wasn't the only thing she did to surprise herself. When the stranger asked her to get into the car she did just that.

Tuesday night. The Manchester road. 49 hours left.

"Why are you driving so fast?" Rosemary asked.

"Because I need to get where I'm going quickly. Does it frighten you?"

"No."

Which was true. She knew he was in complete control of the white BMW as it flashed along the mountainside roads like a missile.

The only question that Rosemary asked herself now was: *Where is he taking me?*

Wednesday morning. A coastal road. 37 hours left.

The only breaks in the driving were brief stops at service stations. Twice they stopped for him to sleep. Then he'd sleep in the reclined driver's seat for precisely one hour.

Sometimes she wondered with a feeling that she couldn't decide was a thrill or panic whether he'd stop the car in a remote spot and order her to take off her clothes. Nothing she could do would prevent what might happen then.

Chapter Two

Faster

Wednesday night. A forest road. 27 hours left.

"Rosemary. Why did you run away from home?"

Before he'd asked the question she had been lulled into hypnotic half-sleep by the rhythmic sound of the tires on the road. She sat up straight, blinking. A dozen reasons powerful enough to make any sane person quit their home at a full-blooded run streamed through her head.

It had started after her parents' divorce, when her mother took her to live in a bleak industrial town. Her new school smelled like a filthy public lavatory, and its pupils must surely have been recruited straight from hell.

Rosemary wasn't fat, short, or spotty; she didn't break wind incontinently in the middle of prayers. But God in His infinite wisdom had seen fit to inflict upon her a birthmark on the left cheek. A shiny, fresh pink, like a scab picked off too soon, it was a letter Z shape. It wasn't particularly big; she could hide it beneath make-up or even a cat's-tail of her long black hair. But the demons at school grabbed at it like starving men at a chunk of bread.

When she walked along school corridors she always heard the same sound.

ZZZ—ZZZZ . . .

After three years of this she couldn't even look at a bee buzzing innocently around the garden without feeling a sickening clutch in her stomach.

ZZZ—ZZZZ . . .

"Watch out. Here comes Red Zed," they'd chant. "Red Zed, you wouldn't BEE-lieve what we're reading today. It's Shakespeare. Have you heard of Shakespeare, Red Zed?"

She'd look miserably down at the desk.

"Read some Shakespeare for Red Zed. To *BEE* or not to *BEE*, that is the question." Another favorite was: "Guess what? Red Zed asked me to be her friend. I told her to buzz off."

Then her mother stabbed her in the back. With a year—a full 365 heart-rending days—before she could leave school, for good, her mother remarried. She didn't mind her stepfather (he was remote and polite), it was his daughter, Jane. She attended the same school as Rosemary. Jane was streetwise and popular. And she led the other girls in the Bumble Bee chase.

At least for three years Rosemary had been able to escape the endless ZZZ-ing at hometime.

Now she went to bed with the same "ZZZ" coming through the bedroom wall, followed by a chuckle that went on and on until it turned into hiccuping laughter that she could hear no matter how hard she pressed the pillow to her ear.

Instead of past horrors, she told the man of her future plans as they drove through the nighttime countryside, the car's lights tearing a great hole out of the darkness.

"I was on my way to stay with some friends."

"Stay permanently?"

"Yes. They've got this great squat. It's a converted railway carriage in the middle of a huge orchard." Rosemary talked enthusiastically about the countryside there, the barbecues they'd enjoy on summer evenings.

"Sounds nice. But don't the railway carriages get cold in winter?"

"No. You see, Kirk put in this huge stove last year. It could heat a warehouse. That's Kirk Bane; he's brilliant with his hands; he can fix anything."

"What's he like?" asked the man suddenly as if he might know him.

"He's seventeen, blue eyes, blond hair, tall, slim, but really muscular. He does a lot of hard physical work—chopping wood, working on the squat, and he's—"

"The others. How many are there?"

"Five."

"What do they call themselves?"

"It's silly, really. The Apple Clan. You know, living in an orchard they—"

14

"Everyone gets on well together?"

"Yes. Like one big family, really. They've been together so—"

"Names?"

"Kirk Bane, Vince Peel, Jamie Laing, Sarah Greaves and Trish Twinkle. Trish won't tell us her real surname. But if you saw the way her eyes twinkle you'd . . . what's wrong?"

Suddenly, he braked, his eyes fixed on the rearview mirror as if he expected to see something come rolling across the horizon after them.

Then his eyes widened suddenly. He *had* seen something. Startled, she looked back along the moonlit road. She saw nothing. Not even another car.

But she sensed the man's anxiety as he pressed hard down on the pedal. The BMW roared away into the night. Where to—God alone knew.

Thursday afternoon. A mountain road. 8 hours left.

The man drove slowly, as if looking for something in the hillside fields. As he did so, Rosemary talked about the Apple Clan. He told her about his family. He had a wife. Two teenage sons. "They're motorbike mad. When they take off on their bikes I pace the garden, worried sick, until I see them come tearing back into the driveway." Also, he had a daughter. At weekends she did voluntary work at a refuge for abandoned dogs. "I'm always telling her she won't get rich working for nothing."

Smiling, he looked at Rosemary. "There's one thing I've never told anyone about my family."

"And what's that?"

"They don't exist. I invented them." He held eye contact with her. "Like you invented Kirk Bane, Jamie and the rest of the Apple Clan."

She sat in stunned silence.

He laughed softly. "Believe me, Rosemary, neither of us are mad. If people were more honest most would admit to daydreams and private fantasies. But it's the *depth* of your daydreams that shows you're really quite a special person, Rosemary Snow. Your powers of imagination are extraordinary." He fixed her with those downturned eyes again. "That's why you're perfect for what we're going to do next."

15

Thursday evening. The Sheffield road. 6 hours left.

The man glanced at the girl in the passenger seat.

Rosemary Snow. Pretty, with long black hair, but very quiet, very serious. She'd had a tough life. And if he failed tonight it would be a short one.

He hoped sincerely that if she did die it would be quick and painless.

Deep down he doubted it. He'd seen it happen too many times before.

Thursday night. A deserted country road. 90 minutes left.

The car hit ninety. Moths exploded against the windscreen. Headlights ripped open the night. They drove along the road between acre upon acre of oilseed rape crops. Rosemary, nervously gripping the seat belt across her chest, watched the hazy yellow sea of oil plants flow by.

Crack! Another moth splashed across the glass. Her tongue, as dry as paper, stuck to the roof of her mouth.

She looked at the man. His mouth must be as dry as mine, she thought, seeing his Adam's apple working up and down in his throat like he was trying to swallow a stone. He was troubled by some huge problem that he did not share with her.

She possessed enormous powers of imagination, he'd told her. Maybe right now *he* was imagining *her* naked.

Thursday night. 67 minutes left.

"You want power?" He spoke with the intensity of a man about to slide the barrel of a gun between his lips. "Well, this is the place you get it."

He braked hard, sliding the car to a halt.

"Get out of the car, Rosemary."

She obeyed, shivering as the cool night air closed around her like a dead man's hand.

He talked to her through the open window, those gentle downturned eyes fixed on hers.

"Rosemary. In a moment, I'll ask you to climb the fence and walk into the middle of the field over there. First, I'm going to

16

give you some instructions. They'll sound strange but humor me, OK?"

She nodded. The light from the full moon showed everything with almost supernatural clarity. Beyond the fence lay a field recently cropped of hay. Two-thirds of the way across the field stood a lone tree. Disease had killed the top half of it. Although the lower branches were thick with leaves the higher branches were completely bare. Rosemary couldn't avoid the impression that those naked branches were like arms waving her away. If the tree could speak it would be crying, *Danger! Get away from here! Danger!*

Fifty yards beyond the tree another fence separated the field from a farmhouse. In the eerie glow of the moon she saw that the building had been abandoned. Around the boarded door climbed a mass of roses that nodded as pink as babies' heads. Upstairs, the two windows that faced her were intact and reflected moonlight like two wide, staring eyes.

Beyond the farmhouse, fields rose and fell in shadowy humps into the distance.

No people, no cars disturbed the stillness. The only sound was the man's low voice telling her what to do. And stressing the importance—the vital importance—of following his instructions to the letter.

"Imagine you're waiting for someone. He's had a long, tiring journey. Make him welcome. He's vitally important to you. Embrace him, love him like a long-lost brother. Keep thinking that and everything will be all right."

She saw him sitting there, looking like a ghost in the shadows of the car.

"I'll be right here if you need me, Rosemary."

Rosemary felt a stir of confusion. "But what do I do with him?"

"Keep him calm. He may seem a little strange to begin with, but that's because you'll never have met anyone quite like him before. Just hold onto him. And like you can direct Kirk's and the rest of the Clan's actions through your imagination you can direct his as well. OK?"

"I think so."

"Oh," the man said as if remembering some insignificant detail. "If he *does* behave badly and tries to climb on top of you, you tell him to sit down and not move one inch until you tell him to move again. He'll do it. Understand?"

"Yes."

"Okey-dokey. Go to the middle of the field and wait for him."

As she climbed the fence, the man called softly, "Good luck, Rosemary Snow."

Thursday night. 52 minutes left.

Silence. The kind of silence that hurts your ears.

Rosemary looked across at the grotesque tree frozen in mid-warning gesture and she felt suddenly cold, like someone had dumped a handful of snow inside her sweatshirt.

Rosemary gave a stuttering groan as if she'd woken from a deep sleep. Shivering, she thought: *He's hypnotized me.* She felt like someone who'd been mesmerized by a stage hypnotist into stripping in front of an audience, then abruptly woken in front of a crowd that was roaring with laughter and pointing at her little tits.

Other, more sinister images flickered like summer lightning in her head.

Don't go with strangers. Reports of girls taken to a lonely place, raped, half strangled, their pubic hair set alight, then stabbed through the eye with a screwdriver as they screamed for—

No. Keep a grip, Red Zed.

Despite the sweat rolling down her face, it felt so cold now. As if on this warm summer's night she had somehow been locked into her own personal winter. Above her, the moon blurred. Shadows deepened and slid like boa constrictors through the grass.

She tried to control her breathing. It had become rapid and shallow; it made her light-headed. She looked around constantly now and wiped her sweaty palms against her hips.

Now they came, like she knew they would.

Small shadows scuttled toward her. Suddenly she had visions of rats leaping at her face, biting her on the nose and lips, or running onto her feet to try and climb up inside the legs of her jeans, sharp claws hooking into her calves, the bristling snouts snuffling upward.

She threw a desperate look back at the white BMW. The stranger's face was hooded black by shadow.

Rats! She wanted to scream the word. *Rats! Rats! Get me out of here!*

18

They swarmed toward her like disgusting black scabs on the grass; soon they'd cover her thick as a fur coat, vicious little teeth crunching through her skin. She tensed, ready to run, but as they hopped close she let out an explosive lungful of pent-up air.

Rabbits!

Only rabbits, she thought, dizzy with relief. There must have been dozens, hopping fearlessly around her to nibble at clumps of dandelion.

Then, as she watched them, they abruptly sat upright on their haunches. As one, their heads swiveled to look in the direction of the farmhouse, their ears straight up as if snapped tight by invisible wires.

What had they seen?

Rosemary stared hard at the farmhouse.

Your new friend's coming, Rosemary. Welcome him like a long lost brother.

Then, as if there had been a gunshot she'd been unable to hear, the rabbits bolted up the field away from the farmhouse. She stared toward the building with its two upper windows like dead, staring eyes.

Nothing.

Something in the tree? An owl, perhaps?

She could see nothing. The tree stood with its branches clutched skyward in a deep-frozen gesture of warning.

Then what in God's name had frightened the rabbits?

Others ran by, little more than gray flashes in the moonlight.

Here comes your new friend, Rosemary.

Here he comes.

Fee-fi-fo-fum . . .

Whatever happens, the man had said, don't let him climb on top of you.

Fee-fi . . .

She looked about her wildly now, half-expecting to see the devil himself come stamping across the fields, spitting fire and farting sulfur.

Fee-fi-fo-fum . . .

More animals streamed by, all moving in the same direction: foxes, rabbits, stoats, badgers. No animal, whether potential hunter or prey, noticed the other. They were terrified. This wasn't a few animals scampering away from a tabby cat: this was the entire animal population of the whole fucking countryside. And they were running for their lives.

Chapter Three

And Yet Darker

Thursday night. 20 minutes left.

It came gradually. So gradually that Rosemary couldn't say with any certainty when she first noticed it.

The moon had almost gone, as if some wicked spirit had drowned it in a bath of milk, leaving a diffused smudge of white in the night sky. Shadows rose from the ground like the freshly risen dead.

Without trying, the image of Kirk Bane came to her with a clarity that was shocking; she could even see the blond stubble on his jaw. His eyes were wide; his mouth moved but not a sound came out. He was desperately trying to communicate a warning of danger that was here! *Now!*

When it came, the groan startled her.

It sounded human. Yet impossibly loud.

Her eyes jerked back to the farmhouse. The sound had come from there. Those staring window eyes seemed to shine more brightly.

The groan came again. So full of pain, so deep, the vibration rumbled through the earth to vibrate the soles of her feet.

I'm staying, she told herself savagely. *I'm staying. The man promised me the power to make my dreams come true. Anything's worth that.*

Isn't it?

The groan came again. It reminded her of an old man suffering an ache beyond endurance.

And something strange was happening to the farmhouse.

The roof had lost its straight line. Slowly . . . slowly, with the speed of the minute hand of a watch, its roof began to dip in the center.

The groaning grew louder; then Rosemary realized what it was. It was the sound of the ancient roof timbers bending under a massive weight.

Then came sharper sounds. Roof tiles shattered with the abruptness of corn popping in a pan.

What happened then happened incredibly fast.

The timber's resistance collapsed.

Rosemary watched, eyes achingly, stingingly wide as some force thrust the roof down into the body of the house with a crash, blowing out the two windows in a gust of shattered glass.

Below, the roses nodded frantically now, the pink babies' heads tossing in panic. Then—

Bang!

They exploded into a mist of petals.

To her astonishment she knew that something she could not see—something enormous—was rolling across the landscape toward her. She sensed its colossal weight.

Imagine it's a new friend, the man had said. *Welcome him.*

No. You could no more embrace *that* than you could embrace a tornado.

It hit the tree.

Branches shook as if waving for help; a series of gunshot-sharp cracks.

And the tree split from top to root.

Leaves from the lower branches gushed skyward in a plume.

Rosemary realized she was no longer breathing; shock had locked tight every muscle of her body.

The world had gone crazy.

Green snow fell; no, it was leaves. Followed by gobs of white spittle. *Angels are spitting on me*, she thought, dazed, and rolled a gob of white in the palm of her hand. No. It was the wood of the tree itself crushed to frothy blobs of fiber.

A word circled in the depths of her mind. She tried to bring it out. It seemed important, this word. If she could only catch hold of it, recognize it, she'd know what to do. Dizzily, she fished into her mind, trying to catch this slippery word, as something invisible bore down on her.

Fish for that sneaky word, Rosemary.

That *something* came closer. Rolling the grass flat in a band as wide as a truck.

Closer.

Word, Rosemary? What's the word that will tell you what to do?

Suddenly she hooked it:

RUN!

Thursday night. 17 minutes left.

She thought: *For Godsakes, move! You're next!*

She turned and ran toward the car as this thing rolled after her, like a lion pursuing a gazelle.

A hundred yards away the white BMW with its shadowy occupant waited on the road.

That bastard got you into this, he can get you out!

She ran, shouting, waving her arms. In the car the man shook his head, his face glowing eerily.

Then she knew why she could see his face in the dark. It reflected the lights of the instrument panel. He'd started the engine.

He was leaving.

"No! Don't you dare . . . *don't you fucking well dare!*"

Tires screeched against the road, propelling the car forward like a rocket. For one insane moment she tried to outrun the car but soon it accelerated into the distance, headlights blazing across the fields.

"Bastard!"

Though her legs felt suddenly weak, she kept running. Because she sensed the approach of some dark, pounding force.

Her Destroyer.

Her running feet clipped dandelion clocks into sprays of white. Stitch skewered deep into her groin; her throat burned.

Fence! Her blurred eyes never saw it; she only felt the jolting concussion as she ran into it.

Her lungs burned like two clumps of molten plastic in her chest as she put one foot clumsily on the bottom rail.

When she had her feet on the second rail she rolled forward, allowing gravity to pull her over to the ground. Then, on her hands and knees, she shuffled through a clump of tree saplings to the road.

Crack!

22

The fence smashed flat, posts snapping at ground level.

Panting, she rolled onto her back to see what had so violently destroyed the fence. Above the fence she saw only night sky.

She sensed movement in the air above her. Something descending.

And she sensed its strength.

Her own strength had all but gone as she heaved herself onto all fours. She tried to get to her feet. She couldn't. All she could manage was to shuffle forward on her hands and knees, the road grit pricking the palms of her hands.

Gonna die, Rosemary.

She wanted desperately to live, but she couldn't manage to move any faster than this tortoise shuffle.

She sensed it approach.

It reached the saplings. One after another, they were whipped down flat to the earth with a crisp snapping sound. The last sapling whipped down to slap her foot so hard she cried out.

This broke the spell. A massive kick of adrenaline jerked her to her feet. In seconds her feet powered her along the road, faster than she'd ever run in her life before.

Unable to resist glancing back, she saw the fence that divided field from road being hammered flat to the ground as if some monstrous yet invisible lawn roller was running along it, shattering post after post into bursts of splinters.

A car, she thought, dazed. *A car comes . . . Flag it down . . . We drive out fast . . . We'll be safe . . .*

If only a car would come trundling down this bit of road. Everything'd be fine. Damn, DAMN fine. But a car? Here? In the middle of nowhere? At this time of night?

You might as well wish that the Apple Clan would sprout butterfly wings and carry you away to the moon.

Because she knew: *Here comes my Destroyer.*

The fence behind her shivered into splinters.

Then a concrete gate post. It exploded with the force of a hand grenade, and she knew her Destroyer was gaining on her. She sensed her ending.

A wail came across fields of darkness. Long, low and full of sorrow, wailing her epitaph. Death was calling her.

It came again.

No! she thought. *It's a horn. A bloody train's horn!*

Two hundred yards away, across a field of yellow oilseed rape,

23

ran a railway track. Even in this dim light she could see that the line began its run down into a cutting at the end of the field. And heading toward the cutting came the train, slowly hauling coal trucks.

She knew the only way she'd outrun this thing was to get herself into one of those trucks. Basically all she needed to do was step from the top of the cutting onto the top of the truck, as if stepping onto a train from a station platform. If she landed on loose coal it'd break her fall. If she didn't she'd break her neck.

Run faster. The train'll soon reach the downhill stretch. If it picks up too much speed you'll never catch it.

Behind her came a female-sounding shriek as a metal road sign crumpled flat to the ground.

She ran across the grass verge and jumped the fence like an Olympic hurdler. She landed awkwardly, her feet skidding forward from under her. She sat down heavily on her backside.

But when the pain hit her, it was in the back of her head. Sickened and dazed by its intensity she clawed at her scalp.

Something held her by the hair.

Unable to turn her head, she fumbled awkwardly where she sat, her back to the fence post. At first she scratched wildly at fresh air, convinced something had grabbed her. Then her fingers hit the fence post itself. That was it! A handful of her long hair had become knotted as she ran; now the knotted strands had looped over the top of the post like a lasso.

Free yourself, she thought frantically, *then you can run. You must reach the train if you're going to have any chance!*

Then the fence began to shiver like it was alive.

She looked to her right.

Fence post after fence post snapped; the fence rails slammed earthward beneath the crushing weight.

She counted the fence posts away from her. She'd reached ten when she saw it shatter. Again she thought of an invisible lawn roller of monstrous dimensions; it rolled relentlessly along the length of the fence toward her, snapping post after post.

Post nine.

Same again. Crushed.

Dazed, she thought, *Eight more posts between me and my Destroyer.*

Crack!

Post eight.

24

It burst into a spray of splinters. *Here it comes: what will I feel?*

Brilliant images squeezed into her head, showing her her final seconds of life. The weight settling on her; the stab of agony as it forced her—*CRACK*—flat on her back.

Then, like having an invisible rock descend on her from the sky, she'd feel the agony of her skin splitting, then muscle stripping from bone, ribs going: crack! crack! crack!

Down, down, down . . .

Until it broke her open to expose her beating heart. She saw herself struggling to scream through a mangled mouth, choking as teeth splinters slid down her throat . . . Down, down, down . . .

Bones squelched to the marrow. Then, finally, her heart bursting as easily as you could pop a tomato beneath your heel.

Vividly, she saw herself lying there in the dirt, like one of those rabbits flattened to the thickness of cardboard by the tires of a truck.

This is how it ends for Rosemary Snow.

"No!"

Crack!

Post seven. Gone.

"Red Zed! You've got to get that train!"

Crack!

Post six.

"My hair! I can't!"

The train's horn wailed. The sound of its wheels quickened. In a moment it would be gone.

Scrambling into a squatting position, she lunged forward, simply trying to rip herself free. Hairs parted from her scalp with a crackling sound, but still a fistful of it held.

Post five.

She pictured the stranger's face, those downturned eyes. *Now I know why you drove so fast. This thing's following you. You know what it is. Are you laughing at me like all those other torturing sadists that've made my life hell? Are you enjoying the thought of my death?*

"You bastard!" she screamed. "I'll kill you."

Snap!

Post four.

She tried to reach the lasso of hair caught on the fence post. And all the time she screamed her hatred for the stranger.

25

Post three.

Timber crumpled into fragments smaller than matchsticks.

Come on! You can still make it to the train. But this is your last chance. You've got to move now!

Crack!

Post two.

She raged at the stranger.

Post one.

The post nearest to her exploded. The rails she leaned against snapped downward, a clump of thistles an arm's length away slapped flat.

Suddenly she stopped twisting. Cold, she jerked her face upward.

Above her, the still summer's night air was suddenly stirred. Displaced air gusted into her face, then she sensed something rush down at her. Like the hammer of God.

Rosemary Snow screamed.

Part Two

There is something strange about the city in Turkey known as Istanbul.

In the year AD 330 the Romans made it the new capital of their Empire. Then it was known as Byzantium. The Romans renamed it Constantinople. They didn't change the place so much as the place changed them. They became Byzantine. And when they did things they did them in a strange, convoluted, you might even say Byzantine way.

When a new Emperor ousted the old one it was customary to mutilate the outgoing Emperor by gouging out his eyes with a sharpened iron bar.

In 1453 the Turks conquered Constantinople. They renamed it Istanbul and set out to change the city. The city changed them. They became Byzantine. The things they did and how they did them became strange, again you might even say Byzantine.

When a new Sultan ousted the old one it was customary to execute the outgoing Sultan by crushing his testicles.

Chapter Four

Whatever Happened to Amy Young?

Do you want power?

More precisely, do you want power over people?

Do you want the power to command someone to die for you?

And for that power to be so absolute, so complete, that they not only die for you willingly, they go to their deaths so full of joy, so full of pride that they cry out your name with their final breath.

Do you want that kind of power?

Do you?

If you'd asked Richard Young that question he'd have been in too much of a hurry to give you a proper answer.

For the third time that afternoon Richard Young had growled to himself, "Well, Dicky Boy . . . it's going to be one of those days."

He pulled open the bureau drawer in the dining room and began tugging out fistfuls of old gas bills, insurance policies for cars he no longer owned, all liberally mixed with loose photographs of his family.

"Christine. How much time have I left?"

"Temper, temper," sang back his wife from the kitchen. "Less than an hour."

Swearing under his breath, he thrust both hands into the drawer and resumed the search. Where was that damned passport? He had an appointment with his doctor at 5:30. This damned wild goose chase was the last thing he needed.

Today was the first day of a week's leave from work where he scripted video promos. Just last night he'd stayed thumping the keys of the computer until one in the morning to finish scripting a sales video for a tennis ball manufacturer. He enjoyed his job and constantly surprised himself at the satisfaction he derived from turning in a good tight script that gave clients bloody good value for money. And would create a video (he referred to them as his "five-minute blockbusters") that would entertain as well as inform. Nevertheless, after working ten months straight with no holiday, it would be good to give himself a break.

Now he planned nine days' relaxation with his family: pottering around the garden, a couple of day trips and basically doing a lot of nothing in particular.

But, inevitably, the shit had already started to fly fanward.

He'd had a phone call from his wife's brother who, over the years, had managed to become the consummate running sore. The reason for brother-in-law Joey's phone call? Yet another frigging stupid scheme that would put them all on the fast track to bankruptcy.

All he needed, now was for lightning to smite the TV aerial and everything would be flaming well tickety-boo.

"Jesus Christ!"

"What's wrong?" called his wife, sounding startled.

"I've only gone and found our marriage certificate."

"Good grief, Richard, I thought you'd severed an artery or something."

"I thought this'd disappeared years ago via the Family Young black hole."

With a clash of pans Christine called, "Has it expired?"

He could imagine her mischievous grin as she spoke and he couldn't stop himself smiling as he replied, "No such luck. You're stuck with me for life."

He pulled out more ancient guarantees for clock radios, irons, lawn mowers, electric tin openers, some of which had been trashed years ago. "Do you think everyone's cursed with something like this?" he said, half to himself. "Tins packed with old bank statements, expired insurance policies, telephone bills that are . . . six years old. My God, there's even ticket stubs for a U2 concert we saw before we were married."

Richard Young guessed that just about everyone was. Even though three quarters of this was basically waste paper that could be safely bagged and burned there was something about even a dead insurance policy with its grave black print that made you afraid to dump it—just in case.

"Richard?"

"Yeah?"

"Will you tell Amy her tea's ready?"

"Okay. Where is she?"

"How the heck should I know? I've been slaving in the kitchen for the last hour, *darling husband* . . ."

Richard knew that when Christine used the endearment "darling husband" it was time to get his backside in gear.

Suppressing the craving to put a match to the documents and dance howling with glee around the blazing pile, he headed for the living room.

"Amy? Grub up."

The television dutifully showed a Tom and Jerry cartoon to an audience of empty armchairs.

"Amy, come and get it before we feed it to the beasties at the bottom of the garden."

Richard dropped to his hands and knees and prowled the carpet like a dog. "Wuff, wuff. I'm going to chase you. Then I'm going to bite you on the bum!"

His four-year-old daughter had a devilish passion for hiding whenever she was needed.

Favorite hiding place: behind the sofa. And despite an afternoon's worth of irritations at not being able to crash out in the sun with an ice-cold tinny and the latest issue of *Q*, he began to grin, anticipating Amy's eardrum-busting squeal when she realized she'd been found. A squeal that managed to fuse terror with delight. Shrieking and laughing she would run from the room, looking back at her pursuer—not where she was going, which tended to leave her with no shortage of bruises. Not that she minded. Bruises were something she prized beyond gold.

"Gotcha."

Amy wasn't in her usual den. *Buggeration*, he thought, mildly surprised. *She's found a new hideaway*. Then she did have a trick of folding herself up into a football-sized lump of arms and legs from which beamed a huge grinning face, complete with a pair of eyes that twinkled like diamonds.

He checked the video clock. Time had donned its trainers and was rapidly running out. He decided to speed up the search on two legs.

Behind the door?

No. Only her rag doll with a red smear down its white T-shirt where she'd tried force-feeding it baked beans.

31

Behind the curtains?

No.

Beneath the sideboard?

Nope.

Under the coffee table?

Zilch.

"Give me strength," he muttered. "One of those days, all right."

But Richard Young, thirty-three, didn't know the half of it.

Because on that blistering day in June his life would change forever.

First: his daughter, Amy, managed to make herself vanish from the surface of the Earth.

Second: although Richard Young didn't know a damn thing about it, the stranger moved into their house.

Richard quickly checked all the downstairs rooms then headed upstairs.

"Amy? Tea's ready. Come and get it."

No reply.

Bathroom? Empty. But toilet clearly not flushed. He flushed it then cut across the landing in the direction of his daughter's bedroom. He was intercepted by his ten-year-old son, Mark, who looked troubled.

"Dad. It's happened again."

"Have you seen Amy?"

Richard looked into Amy's bedroom. Nope, it was Amy-free.

"Dad, it's gone and done it again."

"What? You've not gone and dropped the TV remote down the back of the radiator again?"

His son nodded, those widely-spaced blue eyes of his looking massive as he expected an irritable outburst from his father.

"Sorry, Mark. I haven't got time to fish it out again. Have you seen Amy?"

He shook his head. "But the wrestling's on in ten minutes and I can't change channels."

Richard suppressed the rising tide of bad temper. "Look, Mark, I haven't got time for this. Amy's slung her hook somewhere, I've still to find my passport and I've got to be at the doctor's soon."

"It's just that it's the title match. I want—"

"Mark," he said, gently pushing the boy back in the direction

32

of his bedroom. "If you want to watch it that badly go ask your mother to fish it out for you."

"It's not that important," he said quickly. "I'll leave it till later." Then he smiled, suddenly resolving the problem. "If Amy isn't watching cartoons I'll watch it downstairs."

"On second thoughts, Mark, you can help me track Amy down. Your mother'll go nuts if Amy's not sat to that table in two minutes flat."

"Someone's left the landing window open. Maybe she's climbed out."

"From an upstairs window? I very much doubt it."

Mark grinned. "I've not heard a wet thud, anyway."

"Not funny, Mark. And don't let your mother hear you say things like that. Now, start hunting."

"I'll look in the garden."

"Good lad," Richard said gratefully. "Don't worry about the remote. When I get back from the doctor's I'll hook it out with the coat hanger again."

As his son thumped heavily downstairs Richard checked their bedroom. It wasn't unknown for Amy to hide in the built-in wardrobe. He opened the door and slid aside the clothes on the rail. He did this carefully. Nothing was guaranteed to raise Christine's fury more than finding creased clothes on hangers.

The first thing he saw brought an explosive sigh to his lips.

"Great . . . You find your passport but you lose your daughter."

Above his head a biscuit tin sat on a shelf. Wedged right in the front in plain view was his passport along with the airline ticket for Egypt. Just the sight of it made him prickle with anger. Now he remembered why he had stuck the thing in the wardrobe: because every time he clapped eyes on the ticket he felt a surge of bitterness. They couldn't afford it. Worse, deep down, he knew the Egyptian trip would be yet another case of chasing the wild goose that would get them damn-all in return.

As he closed the door he was gripped by the urge to throw the ticket onto the pile of papers on the table downstairs and burn the bloody lot.

"Richard?" Christine called from downstairs. "Any sign of Amy?"

"Not yet. I've sent out search parties."

"Make it snappy, love. Her tea'll be cold."

33

"Shouldn't be long now," he called as he hurried downstairs and through the front door into the garden.

Although the house itself wasn't at all large, it stood alone in a huge plot of land. Because it fronted a busy main road they'd had it fenced when Mark was a baby, so Amy couldn't have wandered far.

He found his son pointlessly poking a stick into a gap between the shed and fence that was so narrow it wouldn't have admitted a mouse never mind a four-year-old.

Richard asked, "No sign?"

"Nope."

"Best check the garage; she might be playing in the car."

"She's not allowed."

"I know she's not allowed but she still does it. I'll check the back."

Damn, what time is it now? He didn't know how long he'd got before he had to leave for his doctor's appointment. When his brother-in-law railroaded him into this stupid Egyptian trip he'd not realized he'd need a whole series of needles shoved into his butt to inoculate him against typhoid and polio, not to mention the gamma globulin shots. *Chuffing marvelous, Joey, thanks a bloody lot.*

"AMY!"

The girl had vanished. The late-afternoon sun was still sufficiently hot to raise his own internal temperature enough to tempt him to dish out a couple of stinging slaps when he got his hands on the little hooligan. At the bottom of the garden was the privet hedge. Conceivably she might have been able to crawl through the twiggy gaps at the bottom, although she'd never done so before. But where kids are concerned there's a first time for everything.

He jogged to the bottom of the garden where he'd built a brick barbecue. He rarely put together anything actually visible with his hands and the barbecue was something that gave him a solid wedge of satisfaction every time he looked at it, or used it to barbecue the occasional beefburger-and-burnt-sausage feast. Now he used it as a look-out post.

He climbed onto it and looked over the hedge into the tract of open land beyond. Officially it was known as Sunnyfields, but he had dubbed the two hundred acres of grassland and clumps of woodland Misery Meadows or, when in a melodramatic mood,

The Pastures Of Pain. Gold is found everywhere; you will even find gold in your own back garden—albeit in piddling quantities of one part per million. But Richard Young was in no doubt at all that there was bugger-all gold in Sunnyfields.

They say that when you marry, you also marry your lover's family. Try telling that to a love-struck teenager and see if they believe you, but come Christmas or some domestic crisis and they'll suddenly realize it's the truth and nothing but the whole damn truth.

Only Richard managed to go one better. He married the girl, the family—and something unexpected. Something that had the power to give him more than one or two sleepless nights in twelve years of marriage. And that something was Sunnyfields. Owned jointly by his wife and brother-in-law that two hundred acres was a towering, monumental, epic pain in the ass.

"Dad, I can't find her."

Richard looked down at the boy from the top of the barbecue. Something in Mark's widely spaced eyes signaled alarm as clearly as a hundred-decibel siren.

A sudden jab of guilt ran through him. He'd been so busy grousing about Joey, Egypt and Sunnyfields he'd been short-tempered with his son; worse, he'd been treating the hunt for Amy like a hunt for a lost sock.

Alarms began to buzz in the back of his own head.

"Do you think she's got out of the garden, Dad?"

"She'll not be far, kidda. Probably in the shed tormenting spiders."

"She isn't. I've looked."

Jumping down from the barbecue he put his arm around the little lad's shoulders and playfully gave him a wrestler's bear hug.

"Come on, we'll find her together."

They searched the garden. Richard's anxiety increased. This wasn't like Amy. Normally she wouldn't miss *Tom & Jerry*. She'd sit in front of the TV frozen, every shred of concentration locked onto the screen.

"Amy!" Mark shouted her name constantly now, his expression showing concern. "Amy . . . Amy? Amy!" He moved faster, his head twisting from left to right looking for her, or ducking to peer under a bush.

"We'll try Sunnyfields," Richard said. Both father and son unconsciously transmitted to one another the urge to run.

They ran through the bushes to a gate that led into the field.

"Amy!"

Adopting an instinctive hunting formation, they spread out as they called her name.

Richard was unnerved to see his son's frightened eyes, scanning the field for a sister who sometimes tormented the living daylights out of him. Now all Mark wanted was to be walking hand-in-hand with his sister back to the house saying in that scolding way he'd picked up from Christine, "Now, Amy, you must never run away like that again. It's dangerous."

Dangerous.

The word loosened up the flow of fear through Richard. He willed himself to see his daughter peering through the long grass, eyes twinkling, impish grin across her face.

But suddenly, despite the hot sun, he felt cold.

Mark stopped, struck by a shocking idea. "Dad. What about the pond?"

"She wouldn't go there alone." Even as Richard said the words he started to run. No. She wouldn't go there alone. *Would she?* Fear gushed through him freely now, swirling terrible images into his head.

The pond was deep, with steep dirt sides. Easy to fall into. Hard to climb out. Particularly if you're only four years old.

Leaving his son behind, he raced to where the pond lay hidden within a ring of trees and bushes.

An image came hard into his mind. Bob, the cameraman, at the office; he was saying, "I'm sorry to hear about Amy, Richard. She was such a beautiful little girl."

Shut up, he told his imagination that was starting to run rogue inside his head. *Just damn well shut up.*

He bounded through the trees.

There was the pond.

At the side nearest him something floated in the water. He saw a soggy white T-shirt; a mass of dark hair floated around it.

Amy lay face down in the water.

He'd already gauged how far he had to jump to grab his drowned daughter when he actually identified what his imagination had so sadistically distorted.

"Hell fire, Richard. Don't do that to yourself."

He breathed deeply and shook his head at the sheet of newspaper that his jittery mind had morphed into Amy.

On the way back to the house he met Mark running toward the pond.

"Not there, son. Come on. We'll try the garden again."

"Find Amy, Dad. I'm worried about her. I'll catch you up."

Again he felt a rush of affection for his son. "OK. We'll have her found by the time you get back."

As he ran back through the gate into the garden his rogue imagination supplied suggestions of what might have happened to her:

A stranger leans over the driveway gates. Calls Amy closer. Then leans over, snatches her and runs to a waiting car.

The old well in the garden. She's managed to lift the iron grating and fallen down.

Shit, Richard. Even you and Joey together couldn't shift that grating when you tried last summer.

Nevertheless, pure fear for his child now powered him across the lawn. Still at a run he decided to follow the inside perimeter of the fence around to the front garden.

*Come on, Richard, it's a process of elimination now. If she's not in the house, not in the garden, not in Sunnyfields then she must be—*hell, no—*she must be out on the road.*

The main Sheffield road ran straight as a laser through the countryside. The kind of road that murmurs to drivers, "Come on, put your foot down. No cops here. I'm nice and straight; why not ride me hard. You know you've always wanted to see that speedo needle kiss one hundred. So what if a little kid should wander out? She'll never know what hit her, and no one'll ever know who did it. Keep on driving. Keep on . . ."

Shit!

The main gates were closed. She couldn't climb them. She couldn't climb the six-foot fence. The only other exit was a gate they never used tucked away behind the shrubbery.

Panting, he ran hard through the bushes.

He saw the gate. It lay open.

He blinked. Maybe like the newspaper in the pond it was just his imagination running rogue again.

It wasn't.

The bastard gate yawned wide open.

He ran at it. The cars sounded overloud now, roaring along the road like dragsters.

He ran along the grass verge, now searching with a terrible

fatalism for a lump of bloody clothes in the road.

But she couldn't be here. She'd have more sense than to walk dumbly out into the traffic. Wouldn't she?

Trucks roared by buffeting him with gusts of air.

"Amy?"

Cars howled by, overtaking the trucks. A nightmare torrent of steel and rubber moving at insane speeds.

A horn sounded, a pumping, bleating noise, sounded by a driver desperately trying to warn someone.

He looked in the direction of the sound.

Then he froze. A sight met his eyes that locked the breath up inside his lungs; even his heart seemed to stop in mid-beat; the sound of the traffic dropped to a muffled rumble; it all happened in a second, but it could have been hours as he stared in horror, unable to believe that what he was seeing was actually stone cold-hearted reality.

"Amy!"

Richard Young had found his daughter.

Chapter Five

Darker and Darker

Moonlight. An open meadow. A tree, its upper branches starkly naked. An abandoned house with two windows shining like wide, sightless eyes. The night air closes around her body like the ice hand of a dead man. And then comes the groan that rolls across the nighttime countryside. It sounds like the dying song of some lost and long-forgotten god.

Deeply unconscious in the hospital bed, Rosemary Snow lay dreaming. She was oblivious to the stitches that had rejoined her left cheek to the rest of her face, or the dark bruises that mottled her skin as plentifully as the black spots on a Dalmatian dog.

Rosemary dreamed of the moon shining on a meadow and cold air against her skin. And the groan.

Now she stood in the field, staring at the farmhouse with its two upper windows shining in the moonlight; the pink roses around the door.

And always the groaning.

The dream repeated itself endlessly like a tape loop running around and around inside her head.

The weight settling onto the house, driving the roof down with a crash, blowing out the two windows in a gust of shattered glass.

Then came her Destroyer. She ran. It followed remorselessly, crushing plants, bushes, fences, road signs.

She ran and ran. But she knew it gained on her. Her legs ached, her stomach hurt, lungs burned. She couldn't outrun it. It would crush her.

She jumped the fence. Her feet slipped from under her and she was caught by her lasso of hair by the fence post. To her right fence post after fence post snapped; the fence rails slammed earthward beneath the crushing weight. A clump of dandelion clocks exploded in a spray of misty white.

Here comes my Destroyer, she thought in a way that was eerily detached; the nearest fence post to her shattered into splinters. *This is how it ends for Rosemary Snow.*

Above her, the still summer's night air was suddenly stirred; displaced air gusted into her face, then she sensed something rush down at her like the hammer of God.

She screamed.

Instinctively she crouched into a ball to protect herself. But a concrete bunker couldn't save her now.

Then she realized something that astonished her: *I can move. I can bloody move!* The very destruction of the fence beside her had freed her hair.

She rolled sideways just as the grass she'd been sitting on was crushed to green paste.

In one second flat she was on her feet again and running and running, and chewing down massive lungfuls of air. Behind her the ground shook beneath the weight of something she could not see.

She glanced back as she ran through the oilseed crop. The thing followed like a speedboat cutting across a lake of yellow paint, throwing up yellow petals in a plume shaped like a gigantic V.

Somewhere in the darkness ahead the train gathered speed downhill; its horn cried across the nightscape like a soul damned to hell.

Run, Rosemary Snow! Run! Run!

Figures ran at her side. Kirk Bane and the rest. They willed her to outrun this thing—her Destroyer.

If you die, we die, they seemed to be shouting at her. *Live, Rosemary Snow, live! You've work to do, Rosemary Snow.*

The sound of wheels turning on track quickened.

Behind, the V-shaped yellow plume drew ever closer to her.

Where was the rail track? She couldn't see it in the darkness. Only the rumble of steel wheels and cry of the horn.

Yellow flowers rained down onto her. *Confetti at a funeral*, she thought, dazed—*your funeral, Rosemary Snow. Your funeral. That thing crushes you? Wow! Only gonna need a flat coffin, Rosemary. Flat as a paperback book. Don't need a hole in the ground, just a slot as thin as a mailbox opening. Hell, you'd never be as thin as this even if you didn't eat for a year, Rosemary Snow.*

Red Zed, Red Zed, Red—

"No! I'm . . . not . . . going . . . to . . . DIE." She screamed defiance at the sky. "*He* is! *He* is!" And she pictured the face of the stranger who'd brought her here.

To her astonishment she found herself running alongside the cutting. Ten feet below rumbled the steel trucks piled high with coal. They moved faster than she herself was running. The train was too fast; the distance too great.

Behind her a telephone pole was snapped in half as easily as a boy breaking a pencil; cables cracked across her back like whips.

Rosemary Snow leaped from the banking like she was leaping into a swimming pool.

What followed the bolt of blue light searing through her brain was darkness. A darkness that grew darker, impossibly darker . . .

. . . and *darker* . . .

In the hospital bed, saline drip tube running from her arm like a transparent worm, she never stopped dreaming the same dream. And each time she dreamed it, the thing that followed her grew a little more distinct. As if the dream itself was enhancing some enormously attenuated image. Tantalizingly something was emerging from the darkness. Something that she knew she would one day see. And recognize.

Moonlight. An open meadow. A tree, its upper branches starkly naked. An abandoned house with two windows shining like wide, sightless eyes. The night air closes around her body like the ice hand of a dead man. And then the groan that rolls across the nighttime countryside. It sounds like the dying song of some lost and long-forgotten god.

And here comes my Destroyer.

The dream had begun again.

Chapter Six

Car Wreck

When Richard Young saw his daughter on the far side of the road he froze. He saw; but he did not believe. And what he'd do next he, for the life of him, did not know.

Dressed in a white T-shirt, jeans and sandals she stood statue-still. Something fascinated her in the field at the side of the road; her eyes fixed on it, she stood apparently oblivious to the juggernauts roaring by, their slipstream blowing her shoulder-length hair this way and that as if she stood in a gale.

Richard asked himself: *How the hell did she manage to cross the road without getting hit?* He felt the strength run out of him, leaving him so absurdly weak he didn't know if he could actually put one foot in front of another.

An appalling thought suddenly struck him. What if Amy turned and saw him? He could imagine a big smile lighting up her face, then putting her head down to run toward him, just as she did when he walked toward the house on returning from work.

He found himself staring at her, willing her to keep watching the bird or rabbit or whatever it was that fascinated her. He waited for a gap in the traffic.

Trucks, tankers, mail vans, cars, motorbikes roared by, until Richard told himself the bloody things must be welded together nose to tail in an unbroken line. *For Christsakes, you bastards, I need to get across the road to my little girl so you morons don't put your tires across her back!* Close to screaming at them, he inched forward onto the road itself.

Then Amy turned, saw her dad and smiled delightedly. In the next second she'd charge toward him oblivious to the traffic.

"—king idiot!" was all he heard shouted from some trucker's window; but he paid no attention as he hit the far side of the road. Scooping Amy up into his arms, he held her so tight that later he

42

was surprised he hadn't cracked a couple of her ribs.

"Dad. I want to show you something."

"Amy," he panted. "What the . . . what on earth are you doing here . . . you know you're not allowed out of the garden by yourself."

"Dad, I want—"

Earlier he'd wanted to slap her. Now he gave her a heartfelt kiss on her forehead. "Jesus, Amy. Don't ever do that to me again . . . OK?"

"OK."

He kissed her again and this time he felt his heart begin to subside to a more normal beat. Even so, his legs shook. *Jesus, you don't come much closer to losing your child than this.*

"Amy. You don't know how close you came to giving your old dad heart failure. Come on, tea time. If we can get across this f . . . flipping road."

"Daa—aad, I want you to see something."

"Show me later. Come on, home time. What your mother's going to say I don't know."

As he hunted for another gap in the traffic so he could carry Amy home she screamed in his ear and her body went so rigid it shook.

"Jesus Christ, Amy. What's wrong?"

At first he thought she was having some kind of fit; her face turned bright red and her eyes glittered in a way that was nothing short of disturbing.

It was then he noticed she was pointing with her arm outstretched at something in the field.

"OK, Amy. OK. We'll see what it is, then home." Now he was over the shock, once more he was tempted to smack her for wandering away like this. And her behaving like a spoiled brat didn't help matters. Even so, she'd not been like this before; it had felt as if her whole body had been electrocuted, leaving her rigid and quivering. He decided to humor her, let her show him a big daisy or beetle or whatever it was that had caught her attention, then get the hell home, and maybe let off some steam by giving her a good yelling-at.

"What is it, Amy? What're we supposed to be looking at?"

"There! There! No. Not in the field. Down there."

Between the broad roadside verge and the field ran a ditch a good six feet deep, maybe ten feet wide and with enough water

43

to reach perhaps as far as a man's knees. He looked into it. That was when he saw the white BMW.

"Car!" she shouted triumphantly. "It's a car! Why's it down there, Dad?"

"Jesus," he breathed, his eyes taking in the scene. It didn't take a genius to see what had happened. Although the road here was straight as a ruler, the car had left it a good hundred yards to the south, leaving two parallel marks in the short turf before crashing down into the ditch maybe fifty yards upstream. Richard saw the car must have been moving at a hell of a pace because it had continued along the ditch, channeled by the near-vertical banks. It had gouged up a mound of silt as black as old engine oil that all but covered the front half of the car.

Amy protested at being carried and he set her down on her feet. After first making sure he'd got a good tight grip of her hand, he crouched down to get a better look at the car itself. Its roof was perhaps a couple of feet below the top of the banking.

The white BMW looked new. In fact, he could even see that plastic sheets still covered the backseat. He look closer, his eyes widening in surprise. Through the rear window he could see that the backseat appeared to be covered by a layer of bank notes.

Amy chuckled. "Can we put *our* car down there, Dad? Dad, stop pulling me. What you pulling me back for?"

Richard didn't want Amy to see anymore, because he'd just noticed a reddish-brown handprint on the car's roof. Blood. He'd no doubt about it. The doors were held shut by the mud banks of the ditch pressing at either side. The driver or a passenger had climbed through a door window and pressed down on the roof, and they'd been bleeding badly enough to leave a perfect handprint.

Richard looked along the ditch and then scanned the field beyond. It was possible whoever had escaped from the car lay injured, even dead nearby. Equally possibly there might be more injured or dead passengers in the car. He didn't want Amy to see something that sure as hell wouldn't be a pretty sight.

"Can we climb down and look inside, Dad?"

"No," he snapped, shocked by her ravenous curiosity; then added gently, "No, love. Mum and Mark are worried about you." This would cut no ice with Amy and he automatically tacked on a bribe. "And your tea's ready. Mum's baked a cake."

Amy gazed down at the car, fascinated. "Can we come back and play here later?"

"Not tonight, love." As he spoke he looked up and down the ditch again, expecting to see a figure lying facedown in the water. He knew he should check inside the car but he couldn't leave Amy up here beside the busy road. And he couldn't take her down with him. He just didn't know what he'd find in the car.

All he could do, he reasoned, was get Amy home, then telephone the rescue services. Quicker the better. If no one had seen the car plunge into the ditch chances were that it had happened last night when the road was quiet.

Heart pounding, he picked Amy up and waited for a gap in the traffic. Almost straight away he saw it approaching.

This time he stepped into the road and held up his hand, palm outward. The police car pulled over to the side of the road. Heaving a sigh of relief, Richard, with Amy still in his arms, walked up to the car and told the policeman what he had found.

Chapter Seven

Blood

"Dad, there's blood all over the path," Mark shouted as he climbed the stairs.

"Blood? Where?"

"On the path near the shrubbery. There's splotches as big as this." Excited, Mark held up his palm to indicate the size. "And then there's a big puddle of it by the lilac."

"Yuk, sounds gross."

"Do you think someone's been shot?" the boy asked hopefully.

"Doubt it. I think we'd have heard the gunfire. Were there any feathers near it?"

"No. It looks really cool; it's all starting to go dark red and lumpy. Will you come and have a look at it with me?"

"Sorry, no can do at the moment, Mark. Amy's in the bath so I'm going to have to stay here and keep an eye on her."

"Mum could do that."

"Mum's been working hard. She's spent all day baking for your Uncle Joey's garden party. So I reckon she's entitled to put her feet up for a minute, don't you?"

"Aw, Dad. Come and see the blood. Amy's four now, she'll be all right for two . . . no, one minute."

Richard looked down at his son's expectant expression. The blood would no doubt belong to some poor bird that'd fallen victim to a cat or hawk but he had to admit he got a kick out of his son's enthusiasm.

"OK, then," Richard said, smiling. "Amy can look after herself for a few seconds."

"Da-ad!" came Amy's shout from the bathroom right on cue. "Dad! Got soap in my eyes. It stings. IT STINGS!"

Richard smiled and shrugged at his son. "That'll teach me to open my big mouth."

"Dad," Amy shrieked.

"OK, Amy. I'm here." As he went in the bathroom he called back to Mark, "I'll have a look at it with you later."

Grumbling something about Amy stealing all the attention, Mark stomped off downstairs.

Richard soon managed to rinse the soap out of Amy's eyes and it developed into a game with Amy squeezing the sponge onto her face, then blowing her cheeks out as she explosively released lungfuls of air and laughing so much she ended up with a mouthful of bathwater. After that Richard made bathfoam beards for both of them which they took turns at admiring in Amy's Fisher Price play mirror.

"Dad?" said Amy through a huge white beard that would have done Santa Claus proud. "Do you think that mister got died in his car in the ditch?"

Richard smiled as he crouched beside the bath molding a white bubble wig on his own head. "No, I don't think the mister got died. I suppose he's home now eating his supper."

"What about his nice white car?"

"Mark watched the police tow truck pull it out this afternoon. I expect it'll be all right after a wash."

"No one got died in it then?"

Richard looked at his daughter's serious blue eyes above the foam beard. She'd obviously been thinking about the car and the fate of its occupants since she'd found it that afternoon. He told her that everyone in the car was fine, then shaped a couple of white devil's horns on her head to take her mind off the car wreck. More than once he'd shuddered at the thought of what could have happened to Amy on the road that afternoon. And what if she had found a mutilated body lying torn and bloody on the bonnet of the car? Something like that could screw a child up for life. From what little the police had told him the whereabouts of the car's driver was something of a mystery. They'd said that the driver hadn't turned up to claim the car. Richard imagined the most likely explanation was that last night someone had had half a dozen beers too many and simply driven the thing off the road. Then probably tottered home to sleep it off to avoid ending up on a drunk driving charge. No doubt they'd read all about it in the *Advertiser* this week.

"Dad, your beard's dropped off."

They laughed as he scooped up the bubbles from the bath mat.

"Don't tell your mum about the mess, she'll stick my head down the toilet."

"And flush it?" Amy's eyes were wide with wonder.

"Yes, flush it." Richard said pretending to be terrified.

"Mum! Mum!" Amy shouted in glee. "Mum. Dad's messing up your bathroom. Come and flush his head down the toilet."

"Oh, Amy! You've told on me."

"Gonna get you done, gonna get you done," she sang with a delighted grin showing through the beard.

Smiling broadly, Richard stood up. "Now you behave yourself while I get the towels from the airing cupboard. Promise."

"Promise."

As Richard left the bathroom he happened to look up and noticed the hatchway lid to the attic had been moved. The lid was simply a white painted square of hardboard that rested on the timber frame of the hatchway. The board was so light it only needed a gust of wind or someone to slam a bedroom door to pop the thing off at an angle, leaving an unsightly gap. It really needed weighting with a chunk of timber but he'd got into the habit of simply standing on tiptoe and straightening the board with his fingertips.

"Are you going in the attic, Dad?" asked Mark from the bottom of the stairs.

"No, I'm just straightening the board."

"It's just that I need my rucksack from up there for when I go camping on Monday."

"It's not in the attic, laddie. It's where you left it last time. Wedged under your bed, no doubt with your dirty socks and underpants still festering away inside."

Any hints that Mark was habitually untidy slipped as cleanly off him as a fried egg off a Teflon-coated pan.

"Will you come and look at the blood, please, Dad?" he asked hopefully.

"Just give me a minute, kidda, I'm just getting your sister out of the bath."

"It's all going black now and there's this big meat fly crawling all over it."

"Scrumptious. Can't wait to see it."

Mark bounded eagerly downstairs again, no doubt on his way to stare in rapture at the blood once more and probably even give it a hefty stir with a stick. Smiling, Richard shook his head and went to find the towels. When he reached the bathroom the bath-water was already gurgling away down the plughole while Amy, holding onto the bath sides, slipped backward and forward on her knees.

"Right, just stand up, Amy, and I'll lift you out. There . . . Oh, just a minute, I forgot to wipe the jam off your mouth. There, all done."

"Who's making the noise?"

"What noise?"

"The banging noise upstairs."

"We are upstairs already."

"I heard someone going bump, bump, bump up there." She pointed up at the ceiling.

Richard, toweling her hair, said, "That's the attic. There's no one in there."

"I heard it."

"Probably mice with big boots on."

"It'll be The Boys."

"Those naughty Boys get everywhere, don't they, Amy? Now let me do your arms."

"Boys!" she shouted painfully into his left ear. "Boys! Stop making a noise and come down out of the attic."

He grinned. "Tell them we'll stick their heads down the toilet."

"And flush it." She beamed. "Boys! Come down from that attic meed-meditly-meed—"

"Immediately?"

"Come down him-meedittly or we'll flush your heads down the toilet!"

"Trouble with The Boys again?"

Richard looked back over his shoulder. "Christine? I'll get Amy sorted if you want to finish your magazine."

Smiling, she ruffled his hair. "Thank you, darling hubby, but I best see to Amy's hair. You like it blow drying, don't you, swee-tie?"

"And can I have my new slide in?"

"OK, we can take it out before bedtime." Christine took over from Richard to towel the back of Amy's neck gently. "Now let's see to you. Stone me, you're growing into a big girl, aren't you?"

As Christine dried Amy she talked to her in that low husky voice that Richard found so appealing. Hearing it would often transport him back to before they were married, when he'd phone her. She lived then with her brother and father in a huge town house. Invariably brother Joey would answer. "Oh, it's you, Dicky. You'll be wanting Chrissie." Joey would laugh a sleazy laugh. "I'd go get her for you but she's gone up to her bedroom with a man." Another sleazy laugh. "God knows what they're doing up there but it sounds like a wrestling match." Joey would continue with what he obviously believed to be a hilarious routine (while Richard forced himself to remain polite while hungering ferociously to give the idiot a slap the next time he met him). Eventually Joey would call Christine and for what seemed an unbelievable length of time Richard would hear doors opening and shutting in some distant part of the house, then footsteps echoing on bare boards along corridors that in his imagination stretched away into infinity. The footsteps would echoingly approach the phone, Joey would chuckle and say to Christine something that Richard could never catch but which sounded pretty seedy. Then a pause. Then he'd hear Christine's husky voice, coming low over the line. That, to Richard, was one of the most thrilling sounds in the world.

Now, twelve years later, it still sounded pretty good. Just as he was convinced the sky is blue and the sun always rises tomorrow, he was convinced he'd done the right thing marrying this husky-voiced girl with soft dark hair down to her shoulders and dark, nut-brown eyes.

As Christine helped Amy with her pajamas she chatted light-heartedly. "What were those rascally Boys up to this time?"

"They're jumping about in the attic. Dad's going to flush their heads down the toilet."

"If anyone's going to get their head flushed it's Dad for giving you ideas about such things." She turned and raised her eyebrow at him. "I remember when Mark was five your Dad put ideas into his head; that there really were people inside the television set. I walked into the living room one day to find him pushing a biscuit into the ventilation slots in the back of the television because he thought Laurel and Hardy might be hungry."

Richard grinned. "Guilty, your honor. But I was young and foolish then."

"And I don't believe you've changed for a minute," she said, smiling. "Like putting pies, *still* in foil containers, into the micro-wave and nearly blowing us all up."

"Just an oversight."

"And the time we had the barbecue and you set fire to the hedge?"

"Could happen to anyone."

"How come I fell in love with a one-man disaster area?"

"That's because I've got the body of a Greek god."

"Yes, the fat one with the trident."

He laughed. "Now don't go mocking my body. It's suffered enough today."

"The inoculations? Did you have to wait long at the surgery?"

"Not long. Anyway, it was the nurse who did the injections. With a hypodermic that I swear was as long as my arm."

"Did you feel a prick?"

"With my pants around my ankles? Yes. Actually I did."

"Idiot." She threw a towel over his head as she followed Amy out of the bathroom. "My God, I wish I'd been there to see your expression as she rammed it in."

"Sadist." Richard smiled, happy that his wife was in such good spirits.

"Where does it hurt, Dad?" asked Amy sympathetically.

He pointed to his left buttock. "Just there, sweetheart."

Amy punched him on the bottom as hard as she could.

"Ow! You little monkey, I'll get you for—"

"Ssh." Christine held her finger to her lips. "Did you hear it?"

"Hear what?"

"The Boys," sang Amy.

"There." Christine's dark eyes regarded the bedroom ceiling. "Can you hear it?"

Richard listened. This time he *had* heard something. A sort of muffled clunking. Like something knocking against timber.

"We haven't got birds in the attic, have we?"

"The Boys," added Amy her eyes bright. "We'll flush their naughty heads."

Richard cocked his head to one side. "Well, I can't hear anything now. It might be a seagull on the roof. They're heavy brutes."

"Perhaps you should have a quick look," Christine suggested. "The last thing we want is bird poop all over the Christmas decorations."

"I can't see that a bird'd get in there. There's a window in the attic in the gable end wall but I know it's shut."

"Shh. Listen." All three listened hard.

Then it came. A loud rumble that vibrated the windows.

"Well, that's your answer," Richard said. "We're in for a thunderstorm. I'll just check the bikes are inside."

"Make it snappy, love, it's looking as black as a gorilla's whatsits out there."

"What a lovely turn of phrase you have, dear."

He hurried downstairs. In the living room Mark was watching a video where one robot was struggling to pull the head off a second robot.

"Mark, do you want to show me the blood?"

"Too late, Dad." He nodded at the window. Outside, rain had begun to fall with the force of a jet wash. Then came a crash of thunder that, Richard would have sworn, sounded like a gigantic hammer had fallen upon the house.

Chapter Eight

Living Pains

Moonlight. Meadows. Thistle leaf pricks her shin. Tree. Branches starkly naked; the abandoned house where two windows shine like the eyes of a ghost. And then comes the groan. Rolling across the night. It sounds like the dying song of some lost and long, long forgotten god.

Here comes my Destroyer.

Unconscious in the hospital bed Rosemary Snow dreamed the same dream. She had no way of knowing if she'd dreamed it a hundred times, a thousand times or a hundred thousand times. Always the same:

The destruction of the farmhouse.

The crushing of the tree.

And then the agonizing hunt, with her pursuer destroying all that lay in its path. The chase only ending as she leapt from the cutting into the coal truck. Then nothing.

But although the events' sequence was always identical, the fabric of the dream had begun to alter. As if each time the image of what pursued her grew a little clearer. As if she watched something solid and identifiable emerging from a fog. Perhaps something she had known once, only forgotten.

Now she began to see tantalizing details of the thing that had pursued her so mercilessly across the field.

She saw—

Christ!

Pain. A ball of flame shot like a meteor through her body. It came again: something hot and stinging being forced between her legs. She sensed it moving up higher inside her stomach.

A tiny part of her mind remained conscious but hid deep inside her brain like someone hiding inside a concrete bunker during a nuclear war. They feel the shock waves of exploding hydrogen

53

bombs and scramble from corner to corner trying to find the safest place.

Someone's raping me, she thought. *Some fat-bellied hospital porter sees me alone in the room late at night. He chuckles. "Oh, look what we got here, all warm and soft in the dark. As long as it's got a pulse and don't tell mamma I don't mind."*

The bolt of fire came again, ripping a burning path up between her legs, up through her stomach to crush her lungs. The conscious fragment of Rosemary Snow ran frantically inside her skull looking for somewhere to hide; somewhere where the pain wouldn't find her and—

—and bear down onto her like some fat bull of a man stuffing a whiskey bottle inside her.

Fucked by Jack Daniels and he never asked your name, Rosemary Snow.

Now the sadist pushed a needle through her cheek as far as her teeth. He forced harder. The needle passed through her cheek and grated between her teeth to spear her tongue. She tried to scream but nothing above a murmur reached her lips.

Fat Belly, the hospital porter, forces in the whiskey bottle. This time it went all the way up, a burning lump of sheer pain that went up beneath the pubic bone, splitting her fallopian tubes like pasta, bursting her womb like a balloon; this time it didn't stop: the ball of fire scraped its way through her blood vessels down through her arms, down to her fingertips; more needles penetrated her face; a hacksaw started to grate away across her left knee cap.

". . . hear me . . . Can you hear me? I'm a nurse. You're in hospital. Can you hear . . ."

So she wasn't being tortured, realized the conscious fragment of her, balled away in the corner of her mind. What the pain meant was that she was slowly waking. Christ, she must have been mutilated by the fall into the coal truck. Now she lay like a broken doll in some nameless hospital: stitched, sutured, bandaged, kept alive on baby food and saline.

She tried to open her eyes. With an effort they peeled open. She'd expected a brightly lit hospital ward and the nurse's face.

Instead it was gloomy. The ceilings were low and sloped down at either side of her. She saw a small window at the far end of the room. The impression was of dust, cobwebs and objects stacked carelessly here and there. On a table a pile of Christmas lights, beside those a box of Christmas decorations, plastic sacks: one had split; magazines poured out.

She didn't tell herself to turn her head, but constantly the image panned from left to right as if she was watching a film. Suddenly the image would go into a close-up of bare floorboards on which sat a green rucksack; then there was a dressing table; then an exercise bike, lying on its side.

At last Rosemary realized she wasn't actually looking through her own eyes. Maybe the old dream of the chase across the countryside had been replaced by a new one. Of her, or someone, sitting in what seemed to be an attic full of junk.

In the distance she heard a muffled female voice calling, "Mark? Mark . . . Switch off the computer now. It's time for bed."

Rosemary Snow dreamed she saw a hand glide like a gray fish from out of the gloom in front of her, just as if she was watching her own. She saw it open the rucksack. She saw it reach inside and pull out a handgun; a dull metallic gleam twinkled along the length of its barrel; another hand moved into view, pulled out a magazine of gleaming bullets from the butt of the gun, then snapped it back home.

The image shifted again. This time she saw a dusty mirror fixed onto the dressing table. And this time she saw a face reflected back.

It was the stranger's face. That same stranger who had pulled up alongside her in the white BMW and told her to climb inside.

Chapter Nine

Firing Rockets at the Sky

"Dad, can we stick woodlice in the end?"

Richard grinned. "It's not referred to as the end, it's the nose cone."

"Well, can we stick woodlice into the nose cone?"

"Best not. Your mother'll be along in a moment and she's not keen on you torturing defenseless creatures."

"Woodlice can't feel anything." Mark beamed his widest smile. "I've stood on tons and not heard a single one scream."

"Dad. Da-ad! Can I press the button?"

"Good grief, not yet, Amy. If you press the button that rocket'll fly up my left nostril at three hundred miles per hour."

Amy chuckled delightedly and pressed the button anyway.

"Amy's trying to fire it, Dad."

Richard grinned. "Don't worry, son. I removed the battery from the control pad. Now, if you just stand back I'll pop the rocket onto its launchpad and we're ready for countdown."

"Ten-nine-eight-six-three-two—"

"No. Not yet, Amy, sweetheart," Mark said in a near mimicry of his mother's voice. "Dad's not ready."

"Hurry up, hurry up! I want to fly it." Amy, dressed in a pink cotton dress and engine driver's cap, jumped up and down excitedly with a grin so impossibly wide Richard would swear that one day the ends of her lips would meet up somewhere at the back of her head.

Richard had brought them out here onto Sunnyfields first thing after breakfast. After the thunderstorm of the night before they'd woken to blue skies and a sun already hot enough to sizzle bare arms and necks.

The rocket had been his idea. When he'd seen them in a local model shop a couple of months ago he'd been unable to resist buying the thing. Immediately it'd brought back childhood memories of him playing for hours and hours with those little balsa wood gliders. As a glider soared on the air currents he'd imagine himself into its cockpit so vividly that his stomach responded to the glider's swoops and dives as if he was actually flying. He'd naturally thought his ten-year-old son would be equally captivated. Yes, OK, Mark did enjoy flying the rocket but it hadn't captured the boy's imagination as much as the pocket-money gliders had captivated a ten-year-old Richard Young.

"Woodlice in the nose cone'd make it more interesting, Dad?"

"Not today, my laddo, your mother'll be here any minute." Richard concentrated on readying the rocket for its voyage into the hot summer sky above Sunnyfields. Smiling as he worked, he experienced once more a buzz of that old boyish enthusiasm.

The rocket, standing waist-high with yellow nose cone and fins, resembled an elongated version of the cardboard tube you find in the middle of toilet rolls. At first, it had struck Richard that the rocket appeared too flimsy; pessimistically, he'd reckoned it would last a couple of flights before becoming terminally busted. He'd been surprised to find it ruggedly survived flight after flight.

"I'm ready, Dad," Amy called.

"Me, too," replied Richard as he finished slotting the rocket onto the dowelling tripod that constituted the launchpad. "Right, I'll just pop the battery into the launch controller, like so, and *Free Bird 2* is now ready for lift off."

"Stand back, everyone," yelled Mark, sprinting to a safe distance. Amy tried to follow him but as the launch controller was connected by a limited length of flex to the launch pad she ended up dragging the pad and rocket after her across the grass.

"Whoa." Richard ran forward to straighten the rocket. "Right, ready to go again?"

"Yep!" she squealed with excitement.

"Pity we haven't got any woodlice astronauts," commented Mark.

"Just think, Mark. Seven hundred years ago when we had bows and arrows, the Chinese were using rockets. They'd fix an iron spike on the end, point it at the enemy and—"

Amy pressed the button. With a powerful *whoosh* the rocket blasted skyward in a blur of yellow, covering the thousand-foot-high journey in barely more than two seconds. A trail of white smoke streamed from its tail. As it almost disappeared from sight into the dazzling blue Richard heard the faint pop that told him the ejection charge had detonated; there was a puff of white smoke high above their heads and seconds later the rocket came swinging down to the earth a hundred yards away beneath its parachute.

He watched Amy and Richard running hand in hand through the knee-deep grass toward the rocket's landing site. Often the pair could argue like cat and dog but today they were enjoying one another's company, with Amy every so often dashing up to Mark to make him kneel down so she could plant a wet kiss on the back of his neck.

On an easygoing take-us-as-you-find-us kind of day like this with everyone in a good mood Richard could almost enjoy looking out across Sunnyfields. Outwardly it was a pleasant stretch of countryside richly covered by plants with exotic names such as Venus's Looking Glass, Scarlet Pimpernel, Red Dead Nettle, Groundsel, Fool's Parsley and Shepherd's Purse; sometimes you could even find Giant Puffballs which, although looking like bare skulls against the ground, tasted surprisingly good when roasted like a joint of beef.

But in the house a filing cabinet contained reports labeled *Sunnyfields—Topographic Surveys*. Automatically he could reel off the findings of what lay beneath the rye grass and Cock's Foot: detailed concerning the soil mechanics. The equivalent for a human being would amount to a detailed medical examination. And the diagnosis would be terminal.

He knew those bloody reports by heart. All because of the good intentions of one "Biscuit" Bobby Barrass, Christine's and Joey's father. He'd bought the land thirty years ago as an investment for his two children. Only for the first time in his life the shrewd old man had been duped. Sunnyfields had been a Victorian municipal dump. Beneath a skin of top soil and turf the place was a two-hundred-acre lagoon of Victorian potato peelings, apple cores and even human excrement rotting beneath their feet. You could no more build a house on this land than you could build a house on quicksand.

"Dad?" Mark called. "Can *I* launch it this time?"

He and Amy came bounding through the grass toward him, their faces still beaming excited smiles.

Oh sod it, thought Richard, the smile returning. At least Sunnyfields made a decent playground and a terrific site for launching rockets. Their nearest neighbors were half a mile down the road so it was unlikely they'd find *Free Bird 2* crashing through greenhouse roofs.

"Can I refuel, Dad?" asked Mark.

"And me," added Amy.

"Let Mark do it, sweetie. These rockets can be dangerous if you're not careful."

"OK," she agreed, surprisingly. Often she'd kick up a fuss if she couldn't do exactly as her brother.

"Unclip the old motor first. That's it." Richard handed Mark a fresh rocket motor.

Amy had been watching Mark poke the rocket motor up into the hollow tube of the rocket. When she spoke Richard assumed it'd be some comment about the rocket but it was one of the odd, off-the-wall ideas she'd sometimes trot out.

"Dad. We're not real, are we? I mean . . . we're not real people. We're like toys or statues, and someone else moves us around. Like we're over here and someone says move there."

Richard saw that the four-year-old was no longer watching Mark prodding the rocket motor; her eyes had slipped dreamily out of focus. Richard frowned. Of course it was just one of those peculiar ideas that children sometimes have. Didn't he believe that God used to parachute babies to earth when they were born? But there was something almost eerily wise about what she had said. Wasn't the question of determinism one of the philosophers' evergreen questions? Weren't they always asking whether human beings could plot their own futures or whether fate had decided it all already? And that we were just following Fate's carefully prepared timetable?

"What do you mean, we're not real people, sweetheart? Of course we're real. At least I feel real. And I can still tickle you."

He tickled her neck; she hunched her shoulders and came out of the dreamy gaze with a grin.

"We're *not* real, though, are we?" she insisted, reluctant to let the idea go. "Someone else moves us. Like we're toys or statues, they move us about, and sometimes they make us do what we don't want to do."

Richard shook his head, puzzled but intrigued. "Who is it that makes us move, then?"

Amy looked up at him, then turned abruptly and ran toward a bush. "Boys!" she shouted. "Boys! Boys! How many times have

I told you, get out of that tree. Come here. Walk in a line. Eat those buttercups. Stand still. Not there! Stand under that big leaf."

Richard smiled. The Boys had moved in with the Youngs about six months ago. Amy took great delight in ordering them around mercilessly like she was a sergeant major with a band of raw recruits. Richard had once asked what they looked like. She'd given him a look that said pretty clearly, "Are you blind or stupid?" then, sighing as if taking the time to talk to a retard, she'd told him the Boys were blue with no eyes and no ears. Now Richard, hand shielding his eyes against the sun, watched her bully them into obeying her, as usual, precise set of commands. "Now sit there. Boys! Eat three pieces of grass. Hands on head. Sing 'Ba Ba Black Sheep.' Louder! Boys! Now, jump in the pond. Now swim. Now come back here."

"Ready, Dad!" Mark connected the crocodile clips to the rocket motor's detonator then ran back to where the controller rested on the turf.

"Amy. Come and watch the launch."

"Boys!" she ordered. "Quick: climb into the rocket. You're going to the moon."

"Are they on board?" asked Mark.

"Yep!"

Mark's thumb hit the button. With a roar the rocket hurtled skyward again, leaving another thick trail of white smoke.

Mark asked, "Dad, why aren't you watching the rocket?"

"Your mother's looking out of the bedroom window. I think she wants me."

"You're nuts."

"Thank you, son, I love you, too."

"Well, you *are* nuts."

"I only said I can see your mother looking out of the bedroom window."

"You *must* be nuts because Mum's over there by the pond."

Startled, Richard looked in the direction of the pond. Christine was walking toward them, a chillbox in one hand. Richard looked back at the window. Strange. He was positive he'd seen Christine watching them from the window. Or at least someone watching from the bedroom window. He searched each window in turn, squinting against the glare of the sun. There was no face now.

He shook his head. Of course there never had been a face, he told himself. It was a good fifty yards back to the house. Reflected in the windows were the trees in the garden. He'd merely seen some rogue reflection that looked like a face. Just as he'd imagined seeing Amy lying drowned in the pond. *Well, I am a writer, after all*, he thought. *I'm paid good money to have an imagination*. He smiled to himself. Even if it was only to imagine how to make an industrial process that sticks labels on shampoo bottles look fascinating.

Christine had brought bottles of coke for the children and a can of ice-cold lager for him.

"I know it's only the middle of the morning," she told him with an easy smile, "but what the hell, you're on holiday, you've earned it."

He kissed her. "My God. A sunny day, a well-fueled rocket, happy kids, a generous wife, ice cold tinnies. What more could any man ask for?"

"Keep asking," she said with a more than slightly wicked smile, "you might get some more surprises before the day's out."

"Wow," he raised his eyebrows. "Keep talking like that and you just might turn me on."

"Well, listen to this then." Huskily she whispered in his ear.

Enjoying the feel of her warm breath tickling his ear as much as the sensual words, he looked back in the direction of the house.

Again he found himself searching the windows for that white, staring face.

No, Richard, there never was a face there. Just your slippery imagination, always off and running at the drop of a hat. Nevertheless, he'd almost talked himself into checking that the house really was empty when Christine playfully grappled him to the ground, demanding that she be allowed to launch the rocket. He tickled her, sending her into a choking fit of giggles. Seconds later Amy was happily kicking him in the back. Grabbing his daughter he tickled her, too.

And he wished happy days like this would never end.

Chapter Ten

Hotter

"Joey phoned earlier," Christine said as she and Richard sat at the patio table drinking white wine. "He asked if you'd still be going to his garden party."

"I haven't really decided yet. If the weather's going to be like this on Saturday I thought of taking Amy to have a ride on the steam engine at Keighly."

"You could do that any time."

"Saturday's a special Thomas the Tank Engine day. They'll have staff dressed up as the story characters, sticking big faces on the locos, that kind of thing." He chatted lightly as he sipped his wine.

But there was no way on God's Earth he'd go willingly to Joey's garden party. In the main, the people there would be the sort that'd go anywhere for free booze and food. They liked to call themselves businessmen, but this bunch leeched along on the periphery of the town's genuine businessmen. As far as Richard could tell they lived off family trust funds, money that granny had left them, or simply sponged off hardworking wives. They were all full of grandiose business plans that they were always on the verge of launching, but somehow never quite did.

Joey fitted in well. He'd never done a day's genuine work in his life. In theory, he headed Barrass & Son Properties, the company Christine's father had created and run shrewdly and extremely profitably until his death ten years ago. Its only valuable asset was an average-looking office block in town. The rent paid by its tenants covered Joey's salary and, sure, Richard was forced to admit there was an annual dividend that was split between Joey and Christine.

Christine's share of the profits paid for the Young family's day out at a local theme park every summer. And every time they returned from the theme park Richard would drop what remained of the dividend into the penny jar and wonder if Biscuit Bobby Barrass would turn furiously in his grave if he knew about the slipshod way son and heir Joey mishandled the family business. The only other asset, the so-called asset, was Sunnyfields which was worth zip all.

"Stop it, Richard. Didn't you hear me?"

"Sorry?"

"You were squeezing that glass so tightly I thought you were going to break it."

"Was I?"

"Are you all right?"

He laughed it off. "It's probably all this relaxation. I don't know how to handle it."

She smiled but he glimpsed concern still lingering in her brown eyes. "Well, we'll have to work just that bit harder to make you relax that bit more. You're not worried about the Egyptian trip?"

"No," he lied and realized that Sunnyfields and Joey's exploits were tending to preoccupy him more and more. "Want a refill?"

"Go on, then, we'll be devils."

He refilled the glasses and stretched, feeling himself begin to unwind again. The sun had set and the last traces of blue were leaving the sky. Richard had to admit that pretty much all was well with the world. They'd sat for an hour or more around the patio table drinking wine, chatting about nothing much in particular, but feeling contented in one another's company. A candle in a lantern cast a peachy glow over the clematis blooms, moths fluttered in and out of the light; above their heads, bats whispered to and fro, and above the bats the stars burned brilliantly.

Occasionally he'd glance in the direction of the house, standing in silhouette against the starry sky. The kids were sound asleep in bed and it was rare for them to wake once they were settled beneath their Bart Simpson quilts.

Christine moved her chair nearer to his so she could stroke his neck.

She was wearing a plain white T-shirt that seemed almost luminous in the candlelight, her eyes twinkled and her teeth were a vivid white between her full lips.

She smiled. "Is that relaxation starting to kick in yet?"

"I'm getting there," he said, smiling back. Her soft fingers felt good, lightly working the muscles of his neck.

Her eyes looked larger and larger in the gloom.

"Well. My objective for tonight is that you become totally relaxed. And totally happy."

"And how do you propose to do that?"

"By doing this."

Without any hesitation she went down onto her knees in front of him, pulled up his T-shirt and began kissing his bare stomach.

He closed his eyes and allowed the sensation to carry him away: the delicious feel of her cool lips, the light tickling sensation of her hair stroking him down from his chest to the top of his jeans.

"Christine. I think we'd best continue this inside."

"Who's going to see?" She alternated each word with a kiss on his stomach. "Bats . . . moths . . . fox . . . rabbit . . . angels . . ."

She unbuttoned his jeans and he breathed out with pleasure. The erotic sensation of her lips stroking across his skin quickened his heart; he breathed faster. With barely a pause she slipped her T-shirt over her head. He stroked her smooth back, feeling her stretch and arch her spine; he sensed her own excitement. Somehow managing to pull his own jeans down over his legs, awkwardly kicking off his trainers, he let her lead him, not by the hand—*Oh God, not by the hand*—he allowed her to lead him to the lawn. His lips worked against hers as they tumbled onto the grass, feeling its springiness against their bare skins as they rolled over and over, each trying gently to be the one on top.

His tongue worked its way along her body from head to heel, licking, kissing, gently biting.

"Oh, Richard," she moaned, hungry for his touch. The candlelight barely reached them there and it was by starlight alone that he saw her body beneath him: the jiggle of her breasts as she pushed herself up to him, rotating her hips to buff his stomach with her pubic hair.

It seemed as though a salvo of rockets was launched through his bloodstream, filling him with a burning power as he scooped her up into his arms and held her with a force that mated violence and tenderness.

"I want to feel you inside of me," she panted over and over. "I want to feel you inside of me. I want to—ah! Yes . . . I like it like that. Yes. I like it like that. Don't stop, don't stop. Harder. Oh, harder . . . please."

All self-control left him. Everything excited him; making love

64

in the night air; the hot intimacy of this woman's body pressed to him; her passionate need to give herself to him; to pant huskily into his ear. "I'm here, I'm yours, do what you want. I'm yours, *I'm yours*." She wanted him to take and to take; like a sweet sacrifice. As if she wanted him to devour her very life and fuse it with his own.

He had no sense of time, or even sense of himself: he was a natural force like thunder or a waterfall or a hurricane that roared forever without stopping or thinking why. Taking his weight on his fists like a buck gorilla he thrust his hips forward to stab deep. She gasped. With each thrust she dug her fingers into his buttocks, cried his name, rolled her head from side to side on the turf, mouth parted, teeth glinting white as her lips tightened. As he moved faster, as if trying to pile-drive her body into the earth beneath her, her eyes opened wider and wider, her brown eyes glinted up into his; her breathing came in hard, ragged gasps: the air from her lungs jetted into his sweating face.

"Oh, oh," she panted gently at first, then louder and louder. *"Oh. Oh. Oh."*

He couldn't stop now, hammering his body down onto hers in a bruising collision.

She looked up into his face as if not believing what was happening.

"Oh. Oh. Oh. Oh."

Her ecstasy overloaded her senses.

"Oh. Oh. Oh. Oh."

She tore up handfuls of grass.

"Oh. Oh!"

Ripped from its roots, it covered them.

"Oh! Oh!"

She began to thrash from side to side like an animal being pinned alive to a board.

"Oh! Oh! Oh!"

Now! Now! Now! He stabbed furiously into her. A million detonations exploded in every cell of his body.

"Yes. YES!"

Her convulsions lifted him up with her like he was a doll.

Then she was crying and laughing at the same time; she kissed his face, her lips scorching hot, her cheeks hotter, bled sweat, grass stuck to their bodies like they'd grown a fuzz of beast hair.

They panted and giggled and lay on their backs. Caressing each other, they said whatever came into their heads that was tender, loving.

Richard's heart still beat with the solid rhythm of an engine as he lay there looking at the stars.

They lay like that ten minutes or more, feeling their bodies cooling. Richard watched a meteor flash in a streak of light across the sky, fancying he heard a faint crackle as the piece of interplanetary stone burnt itself into nothing but dust eighty miles above their naked bodies. For a time, probably no more than a second—but it felt so palpably real that he stopped breathing—he felt he was a component of the cosmos's infinite engine. Some small but vital part of it. Like the meteor had been. For millions of years it had floated between the planets. For most of that time it would have drifted in a cold darkness. A moment ago it had met its destiny to become a fiery and vivid flash of heat and light and noise that might have been seen by millions of people.

Richard wondered if human life was like that. For the most part led in some dark, almost aimless obscurity. Then, just for a brief moment, you become the center of attention. You become important because something beyond your control demands you to become important. Briefly, Fate's spotlight falls on you. Perhaps whatever it is you say or do then, whatever words and actions, become suddenly so important that they affect the lives of others, maybe forever.

"What are you thinking about?" Above him, Christine was a dark female shape cut from the night sky.

He smiled. "It's you. You've turned me all mystical. All I can do is think cosmic thoughts."

"Mystical? You're not thinking of taking a vow of celibacy, are you?" She chuckled. "That would never do."

He gave a low groan of pleasure as he felt her cool hand caress him.

He could only see her in outline as she knelt over him, then her breasts jiggling softly as she sat astride him. She straightened and a single erect nipple covered Venus.

Then she slid down onto him, impaling herself, taking him inside into the very core of her body. She gasped with pleasure; her fingers gripped his shoulders. Stretching her torso, her breasts obliterating whole constellations. She breathed in deeply, arched her back and the woman annihilated a whole universe.

This time, their lovemaking was slow and gentle. This time

he was conscious of his own existence. This time he was aware of his surroundings.

And this time he had a powerful sense they were not alone. That someone was watching them.

Chapter Eleven

Burning Snow

Curled in some back alley of Rosemary Snow's brain the conscious part of her felt the needle puncture the crook of her elbow. The voices of nurses seemed to come through a wall of cotton wool. A cold object slid through her lips into her mouth.

The pain came back so fiercely she would have screamed if she could, but all she heard was a gurgle in the back of her throat. Now it felt as if some mad stoker had dumped a shovel full of smouldering coal on her chest.

At last Rosemary Snow realized what was happening to her. She was slowly waking.

The dreams were different, too. Now, instead of being pursued across the dark countryside by something that shattered houses and trees like they were made out of polystyrene, she dreamed she lived in the attic of a strange house. An attic full of the kind of junk that clutters anyone's attic—old furniture, boxes of books, old toys, suitcases, Christmas decorations. And then there was the mirror. When she looked into it she saw the reflection of the stranger who drove the white BMW.

She had no control over her movements; sometimes she would feel as if she were carried like a child to look out of the attic window.

She saw brilliant sunshine. A large garden. Patio. Plastic table and chairs. A blue and white striped parasol; a child's bike; a toy buggy containing two dolls. Beyond a hedge stretched a meadow. There was a pond. And then she saw a man with two children. They were looking intently at something on the ground. A moment later white smoke spurted from the object; they tilted their heads upward watching something fly straight up into the sky, leaving behind a long tail of smoke.

As she watched it hit her. The first powerful emotion since

she'd arrived in the hospital. Her flesh tingled at the force of it. Dread. She looked down at the family in the meadow and she felt dread for them. It came in powerful waves; the same feeling a parent must have when they see their young child standing on the edge of a sheer cliff. Imagination intensifies that feeling of dread. Hundred-foot cliff. The child takes one step forward and—

But, no. She felt a swirl of confusion. Why did she feel dread? What danger did that man and the two young children face? She watched them running through long grass carrying their toy. They were laughing happily. And she wanted to shout . . .

She wanted to shout *what*, for Christ sakes? What was it she wanted to warn them about? What did it matter to her? A stupid dream, dreamed by a stupid girl lying mangled in a stupid hospital bed.

Why did she want to shout . . . the words were there, somewhere trapped deep inside her head. But why was it so important to cry out, "For . . . For?"

"FOR GODSAKES! THERE'S A MADMAN INSIDE YOUR HOUSE."

A second hypodermic needle jabbed into the back of her hand, but the jerk in her respiration had nothing to do with that. In that back alley way of her brain the conscious fragment of Rosemary Snow knew the truth. Somehow she was looking through the stranger's eyes. The madman who had left her to die in the field. He was inside the family's house, hiding in the loft and they didn't know a thing about it.

Oh, whistle, and I'll come to you, my lad.

She remembered the old ghost story. A man finds a whistle in a ruined church. He blows it like you whistle to bring a dog to you, only that whistle summons a ghost. A vicious ghost that will eat your heart.

She looked out of the window. Now it was dark. She saw the white table and chairs gleaming almost brightly against the dark lawn. For a moment she thought the garden was deserted. But then on the grass she saw a man and a woman. They were naked. At first she thought they were fighting. Then she realized they were making love with such passion that they rolled over and over on the grass.

Oh, whistle, and I'll come to you, my lad.

The title came to her again. And she remembered what happened when the man left her in the field. How something invisible approached, crushing the house and tree and fences and very nearly her.

Was the man with neatly brushed hair and smiling face even now whistling that thing, her destroyer? Would it come rolling across that meadow, splintering trees, churning through the pond, flattening grass and hedges and fences until it bore down on the naked man as he made love to the naked woman? Would the woman feel her lover press down onto her—and into her—harder than he'd ever done before? Impossibly hard, until she screamed as their skin and bone were literally pressed together and they became a mash of blood and bone and semen.

Oh, whistle, and I'll come to you, my lad.

She could almost hear the madman whistling his pet as it circled the house somewhere out in the night sky, like some terrible bird of prey.

She saw the two naked people caress one another, too wrapped up in each other to notice anything beyond the sweated heat of their bodies.

Oh, whistle, and I'll come to you, my lad.

Desperately she wanted to shout a warning to the two lovers down there on the grass. She strained her throat muscles and willed herself to beat the glass. *Look out! Look out! There's a madman in your house. Get your children. Run! Run! Run!*

But no sound came from her throat. She couldn't move so much as a finger of the body she looked out of.

She had to warn them, she told herself. She had to find a way.

Chapter Twelve

Dead of Night

Amy Young sat up in bed. For a while she wasn't sure whether she was asleep or awake. She could see nothing. She moved her hands around in little circles in front of her face. Then she understood what the problem was.

"Dark," she murmured. That meant it was still nighttime. Everyone would be asleep in bed. Sometimes if she awoke this late she could do what she wanted. Mum and Dad lay with their eyes shut and didn't know she was tiptoeing around their bedroom. Once she'd even gone into Mark's bedroom and eaten his chocolate that he'd left by his computer. He'd been right there. In bed. With his face pointing at her. But it was like magic. She could stand in front of him and eat his chocolate and he couldn't say or do a thing.

She clapped her hands. Even this small soft sound seemed loud at night.

She pulled up her quilt. The Boys must have pulled it off her. Normally the Boys did what she told them to do, but sometimes they could misbehave. Then she would have to shout at them. Sometimes when she was tired she couldn't make them do a single thing and they'd do naughty things like pull her hair or threaten to wee in her toy box. Then she'd have to go and ask Mum or Dad to help get them under control. She never asked Mark, though, because he'd say, all grumpy, "What boys? I can't see any boys. Go away, Amy, I'm watching television."

Now she could see dim outlines of furniture around her and the pale oblong of the curtained window. The Boys were running along her shelves, jumping from piles of boxes to the top of dolls' heads then down onto her fairy-story cassettes.

"Stop that, Boys."

She saw that they stopped and watched her, their blue faces all expectant as if they thought this was the start of a game.

Amy yawned, tired. "Go away, Boys."

The Boys vanished. Sometimes the Boys vanished for days until she forgot all about them. Deep down she suspected that as she grew older they would one day vanish for good. Just now, though, the Boys seemed real enough, and they made convenient playmates when other flesh and blood four-year-olds weren't around.

Amy lay down to try and sleep again. But that huge cup of milk Mark had poured her at suppertime had worked its way through.

She wriggled from under the quilt, tiptoed quickly across the landing to the bathroom. After she'd finished she returned to her bedroom tucking in her pyjama top as she did so.

But halfway across the landing something made her stop and look up.

The hatchway cover to the attic had been moved aside. Looking down out of the darkness were two glittering eyes. Then she saw the eyes belonged to a face with a wide smiling mouth. The man smiled down at Amy and said, "What's the matter, Amy? Monkey nicked your tongue?"

Chapter Thirteen

Eyescape

In the dream it happened again. Rosemary Snow ran across the field. Behind her the house lay in ruins, its window glass eyes torn out. Then her Destroyer crushed the tree. It followed her, closing the gap.

Panting, she ran on, saliva crackling in her throat.

Above Rosemary shone the bright eye of the moon; the eyes of scurrying animals glinted; her own eyes watered.

Eyes. Why eyes? That word buffeted persistently against her skull like a moth trying to reach a light.

EYE. EYE. EYE.

Why had she become obsessed with eyes? The invisible thing that pursued her, why did she associate that with eyes?

Her feet rustled through the ankle-high grass, and ahead of her stretched a carpet of dandelions glowing like yellow stars across the turf. Her toe caps clicked against the yellow dandelion heads as she ran. Something about those flowers, she thought feeling a confusion well up inside of her. Something about flowers . . . and eyes . . . the man in the BMW . . . and the family in the meadow . . . and the little girl.

What's she called, Rosemary? Is she called EYE? No, don't be ridiculous. Annie? Haley? No . . . Amy! Yes, that's the name. AMY.

But why should she think of that?

Dreams are funny things, Rosemary Snow.

Just look at what's become of this field.

Look how strange it's become.

As she ran she looked down. An eye lay there, unblinking, in the grass. It looked like a ball of glass the size of an apple, but she saw the pupil and blue iris, and the network of fine red blood vessels, and the optic nerve that rooted into the soil.

73

She ran faster. Behind her the thing grew closer, crunching grass and thistles.

Now she saw that, instead of yellow dandelion flowers, living eyes budded on the end of the fleshy stalks. All around her was a field full of eyes. They grew from the ground on plant stalks; from the branches of a bush eyes hung like heavy fruit. Rosemary shuddered. The eyes were wet, and juicy, and they all watched her running by.

Her running feet no longer clipped the heads of dandelions; eyes cracked against the toes of her boots, bursting in a crystal spray of jelly and tears.

The dream turned cancerous inside her mind. This was her universe now, a world of fruiting eyes. Red eyes, blue eyes, green eyes, brown eyes, wet eyes, dry eyes; they popped like sweet grapes beneath her feet; if she slipped, she'd slither facedown through a sea of cold staring eyes.

But as she ran a conviction took shape inside of her. This world of eyes couldn't hurt her; they were the fruit of her dreams. What was real was that she knew there was a family in danger. In real danger from the madman who had destroyed her own life. She knew, too, that she was the only person who could warn them.

And she couldn't do that lying dreaming mad dreams in a hospital bed.

She stopped dead in the field of eyes, clenched her fists, turned to the invisible thing that cut through the thousands of eyes like a speedboat through water and she shouted: "I'm not taking this anymore! I'm waking up! I'm waking up!"

Chapter Fourteen

Sunday

"Dad. There's a man in our attic. What's he doing up there?"

Amy, dressed in a lime-green T-shirt and matching shorts, rode her three-wheeler bike around and around the barbecue on the patio.

"Amy, don't ride too near the barbecue," Richard warned. "I'll be lighting it soon."

"But what about the man in the attic?"

"What man in the attic?"

"The one I was talking to last night."

"You were up in the attic talking to the man?" Richard was speaking on autopilot as he piled the charcoal onto the metal barbecue tray. He'd developed the autopilot talking trick when Mark had been Amy's age. Both his children seemed to have inherited a gene that allowed them to talk nonstop from the moment they woke to the moment they went to bed.

"I wasn't up in the attic," Amy said thoughtfully. "I went to the toilet in the middle of the night. He was looking down at me through the door in the roof."

"Oh, the attic hatchway?"

"Yes. He smiled at me and talked a lot."

"What about?"

"The Boys. He wanted to know all about the Boys. What they did, and he asked me if I told them to do stuff."

"Well, you do tell them to do stuff. You boss the Boys about all the time, don't you?"

"Have to," she agreed. "They're naughty."

Richard squirted barbecue lighter onto the charcoal. "Stand back, Amy, I'm going to light it now. Do you want me to cook you a sausage or a burger first?"

She looked at the barbecue and wrinkled her nose. "I want a cheese sandwich."

"What, no faith in my cooking? I bet the man in our attic'd like my burgers."

"I'll go ask him," Amy said and turned her bike down the pathway.

"Only joking, Amy. He's probably asleep by now, anyway."

"Who is he, then?"

Richard smiled. "Uhm . . ." He put his finger on his lips pretending to think hard. "I know. Maybe it's Santa Claus. Maybe he got stuck up there in our attic last Christmas Eve."

"Nah. Didn't look like him. No white hair and no white beard."

"Search me, then."

"He said his name was Michael," Amy said with a suddenness that made Richard pause. "And that he lived in a place called Chickens."

"Chickens? Funny-sounding place." Richard smiled and shrugged. For a moment he'd almost believed in Amy's mysterious man in the attic story. He guessed now that Michael from Chicken land was some second cousin to the Boys. As he held the match to the fuel dripping down between the lumps of charcoal he watched Amy as she circled around telling him about Michael from the land of Chickens, where there was a wall around the city and a big cathedral that wasn't a cathedral anymore and it was called after a girl she knew at school.

"Bugger!"

He blew on his hand where the barbecue lighter had flared and scorched his skin.

Amy stopped and looked at him quenching the sting with beer from his can. She said eagerly, "Is it burnt? Can I see?"

Smiling, he licked the beer from his hand. "No. Fortunately. It just shows, though, you have to be very careful with fires."

"Richard, can you move the table into the shade for me?" Christine walked down the path toward them. She carried a tray with plates covered with foil and kitchen tissue.

Richard slid the table into the shade of the tree.

"I hate it when the sun gets on the cheese and it starts to sweat."

Richard pulled a face. "Sweaty cheese? I think I just lost my appetite."

"Knowing you it'll come back . . . although as far as the cheese goes no one's going to be porking out on that."

76

"What do you mean?"

"I mean, sweet hubby, that someone's had their mitts on it."

"Not guilty."

"I bought a pound of Cheshire on Friday and it's nearly all gone."

"That'll be Mark. He's the one with the cheese fetish."

"Well, he seems to have lost his own appetite and found an elephant's. Food's been disappearing from the kitchen like it's sprouted wings. Half the tomatoes have gone, biscuit tin's nearly empty again and I could swear that we had some ham left from supper on Friday. Oh well, if he's eating he's not sickening for anything." Christine took the beer can from Richard and had a hefty swig. "Mmm, I needed that."

"Where *is* the son and heir, then?"

"Packing for his camping trip. Do you think the Abrahams know what they're letting themselves in for?"

Richard grinned. "With four sons of their own? They'll cope."

Christine straightened Amy's cap. "Do you want to get yourself a drink?"

"Right-oh." She pedaled off down the path like lightning and shouted at the top of her voice, "Super power!"

As Christine handed Richard back the can she kissed him on the nose. "How's lover boy bearing up, then."

"Surviving." He smiled. "Although if you keep me going as hard as last night you're going to wear me out."

"No worries. I'll trade you in for a younger model."

"That *has* put my mind at rest," he laughed. "Right, I think I'll risk a couple of sausages." He began laying a line of pale sausages out on the grill. "Is the steak still in the kitchen?"

Smiling, she said, "It's where you left it, in the fridge. Do you think steak soaked in red wine and coated in Parmesan will actually be edible?"

"Well, if you're going to ride life's highway with me, sweetheart," he said, impersonating Humphrey Bogart very badly, "you have to be ready for excitement and danger."

"If your barbecuing's anything to go by we're in for one hell of a white-knuckle ride."

Amy bounced through the kitchen door. "Super power!"

"Amy! You scared me to death!" Mark began mopping the fruit

juice he'd just spilt on the worktop. "Don't go shocking people like that."

"Will you open me a carton?" she asked sweetly.

"Open your own, I'm busy packing."

"Please." Then she added shrewdly. "I'll tell Mum you spilt."

"Oh, all right then. Orange or strawberry?"

"Strawberry, please. Mark, did you know there's a man living in our attic?"

"Is there, now?" He spoke without so much as a shred of interest. "I'm going up to finish getting my stuff together. I'm going camping."

"He said his name's Michael. And he says he comes from a place called Chickens."

"Can't do. There's no such place as Chickens."

Amy frowned, then her face brightened. "No. Stupid me! He didn't say Chickens, he said Turkey!"

Tomatoes, lettuce, olives, feta cheese tossed in olive oil sat gleaming in bowls on the table. Alongside them, more bowls full of crisps, coleslaw, potato salad and Waldorf salad. Richard was on his second beer, turning sausages that were singing like mad as the fat bubbled out of them and he felt . . . he searched for a word. Good? Fine? OK? Chipper? Funky as a monkey? The professional writer in him rooted through this vocabulary, looking for something distinctive to describe the pleased, warm feelings oozing syrup sweet from the top of his curly head to his toenails.

Ebullient. Yes, he felt ebullient. He checked it with his mental dictionary. Ebullient: overflowing, enthusiastic, exuberant. Yes indeedy. That fitted the slot all right. Singing to himself, he flipped over the sausages. Fat dripping onto the charcoal ignited in puffballs of yellow fire. He drained the can of beer. "Just one more. Or you'll be horizontal by two—and that would never do." He chuckled.

"What's so funny, dear heart?" asked Christine.

He whistled appreciatively. She'd changed into shorts and a loose white blouse that was almost transparent at the back, yet heavily lacy enough at the front to be decent enough for daywear.

"I just feel good to be alive," he said, grinning.

"Pleased to hear it," she smiled back. "How are the sausages coming along?"

"Nearly done. You could give Mark and Amy a call for their hot dogs."

Amy was running out down the path toward them. "Mum. Dad. Mum. That pop made me wee out of my eyes," she called excitedly.

Christine dabbed her eyes with a tissue. "If you don't drink it so fast it won't make your eyes water."

"FOOD!" When Richard heard the voice from behind, it startled him. "GIVE ME FOOD!"

Chapter Fifteen

The Man in the Attic

"FOOD! GIVE ME FOOD!"

Richard forced a smile as he turned round. "Joey. What brings you to this neck of the woods?"

"Got to see my favorite Sis, Dicky."

"Hallo, Joey!" Christine called, genuinely pleased to see him. "Have a beer; they're in the bucket."

"Cold beer, too. God's teeth! The pair of you know how to live!"

"I didn't hear the car," Richard said.

"Oh, I left it outside. Can't stop."

Yipeeeeee! Richard thought with gusto.

Christine smiled. "You can stay for a hot dog or something can't you?"

"Go on, then."

"Gonna sit with me, Uncle Joey?" asked Amy. "That place is Mark's, but he's messing about upstairs. Boys! Boys, move out of the way so Uncle Joey can sit down."

While Christine and Amy made a fuss of Old Rubber Lip, Richard dropped more sausages onto the barbecue with a sigh.

The buttons of Joey's white shirt (the kind of shirt you'd wear with a business suit) took the pressure of his inflated gut. One day one of those buttons is going to ping off, thought Richard morbidly; and some poor wretch will lose an eye. Joey sat, talking like he was taking part in a contest to see who could squeeze the most words into twenty minutes. Constantly he used a stubby-fingered hand to push back an oily-looking fringe; when he did pause from speaking for the odd millisecond his bottom lip, which always seemed too large for his mouth, would poke outward. Richard noticed Joey looking greedily at the food spread out on the table; Joey Barrass's eyes were as dark as his younger sister's but they always appeared to be covered by a thin film that left them glazed and dull-looking whereas Christine's were bright as gemstones.

"Heavy on the mustard, Dicky Boy," Joey called before draining his can and crushing it.

"Have another one," Christine pulled a can from the bucket.

"Careful," Richard stabbed a fat sausage. "He's driving."

"Won't do any harm." Joey's thick finger found the ring pull. "Like gnat's pee, anyway."

Amy laughed.

"Dear God," Richard murmured under his breath.

"Got those proposals with me for you to look at."

"From the Egyptian developer?"

"Yep. Also he faxed through the directions, so you can find his office without getting lost in the bloody Casbah."

"It's going to be an expensive visit," Richard said, transferring sausages to bread buns. "If he's so interested in Sunnyfields he should have come across here."

"That's Egyptians for you." Joey's fat face grinned. "Perhaps his Mummy wouldn't let him."

Joey and Christine laughed loudly while Richard squirted on enough mustard to burn tungsten. "Here you are, Joey. Let me know if you need more mustard."

Joey munched through it. "Bloody gorgeous, Dicky Boy. You know, Christine, he's going to make someone a decent housewife one day."

Richard called in the direction of the house. "Mark! Hot-dogs ready in five minutes! Come and get it or it's bird food."

Joey hauled his lard butt over to where Richard stood at the barbecue. Joey looked pleased with himself; he pushed his oily fringe out of his eyes and said, "Who's a lucky boy, then? You, in Egypt. Alone."

Richard's smile didn't quite come off. Christine sat with Amy in the shade of a tree, luckily too far away to hear.

"Well, I don't consider myself lucky, Joey. What I *do* consider is that I've drawn the short straw. I need this Egyptian trip like I need a hole in my head."

Joey chuckled wetly. "What, a young virile lad like you, all on your oni-owe in the land of belly dancers who'd do anything for the price of a Mars bar?"

"You've got mustard on your chin, Joey."

81

"I've heard Egyptian girls like it pretty brutal and they're not fussy where you stick your—"

"Joey . . . look, if you think it's such a hot place to visit why don't *you* go?"

His lip came out in an expression of a boy punished for doing nothing wrong. "Dicky. You know I'd have gone. But it clashes with the golfing weekend."

"Golfing? At least you got your priorities right."

"I'm not going for my own selfish pleasure, y' know?" He pushed back the fringe. "It's business; you know, contacts; networking?"

"It's another of your piss-ups and you know it," Richard said with a broad artificial smile and Joey gave a hesitant laugh not knowing if Richard was joking or not.

"Anyway," Joey sucked the mustard off his thumbs. "Forget the birds; when you get to Alexandria you can visit the pyramids or something."

"Alexandria?" Richard looked at Joey's rubber face in disbelief. "You told me the office was in Cairo. Joey, I'm booked on a bloody flight to Cairo, not bloody Alexandria."

"Cairo. Alexandria. It's all Egypt, isn't it?"

"Jesus Christ, Joey. Alexandria and Cairo are hundreds of miles apart. Across an African country that I know as well as the dark side of the fucking moon." Richard cast a glance at Christine. She'd not heard that he was within a hair breadth of an argument with her brother. It'd be one way to shit up the day completely, but this tub of a man, who looked as if he was going to explode from that white shirt at any moment, could pitch Richard into a furious rage in sixty seconds flat.

"There's trains, aren't there?" Joey's bottom lip came out. "Get a train. Stop an extra night if you have to." He smiled. "If you *want* to. Dusky-eyed maidens, Dicky Boy."

"I don't want to stop another night," Richard said in a low voice. "I don't want to go there at all. I'm flying out there on the Friday and I'll be back on the Sunday once I've seen Mr. Siyadd. And I'm only doing that because I'm clutching at straws. I've persuaded myself into half-believing, just half-believing you'll notice, that this development plan might work and I can get that load of shit laughingly known as Sunnyfields out of my life forever."

"Listen, Richard. That's a valuable plot of land out there. You

didn't just marry my sister, you know, you married a pot of fucking gold."

"Pot of gold? It's a pot of shit. Yes, you could dig out all the
crap, pay for its decontamination, import fill for the foundations
of a nice industrial estate of factories and warehouses and offices,
but you know as well as I do, Joey, that even . . . even if you sold
every shed at its market value you'd still walk away with a loss
of around half a million."

"Okay, Richard. Tell Christine that. Tell her you're saying that
my father, Christine's father, has left us in the shit?"

Joey's filmy eyes had taken on a stony hardness now. He'd
found the weak spot. Christine worshiped her late father. She
believed everything he'd ever done had been shrewd to the point
of being supernaturally clever. If Richard rubbished Sunnyfields
he rubbished Biscuit Bobby Barrass, the backstreet orphan who'd
made his fortune selling biscuits door-to-door then moved up into
the property business.

"Okay, Richard." Joey nodded heavily. "You win. We've been
wasting our time. Sunnyfields is a big load of crap. Let's go break
the news to Christine."

"Joey. Look, don't be hasty."

"No. You obviously thought it through. I'm going to tell Christine our father was a cretin to leave us saddled with a piece of
land that's worth bugger-all."

"Joey, there's no point in—"

"Christine? Christine," Joey called. "Can you come across here,
I've got something to tell you."

Richard let out a lungful of air and stood with his hands on his
hips. *Let Joey blab*, he thought, *then I don't have to keep pretending to Christine that everything's all right and Sunnyfields is
actually valuable. Then when Joey's finished speaking I'm going
to give him such a hell of a slap he won't know what's hit him.*
Actually, the mental image was surprisingly thrilling; he found
himself relishing the idea of dishing out a stinging slap and Joey
clutching his red cheek, those brown eyes round with shock and
surprise.

I'm gonna do it, I'm gonna do it, thought Richard, surprised
at his own eagerness. *I'm going to give him a slap he'll remember
until doomsday.*

"What is it?" Christine asked, walking up.

Joey began, "Richard has—"

"Dad! Dad!" Mark came running along the garden path. He was clutching his eye, his face bright red.

"Dad! My eye!"

"What's wrong?" Christine reached him first. "For Godsakes, Mark, what have you done?"

After Richard had managed to calm Mark down, the story came out. Mark had decided his haversack was in the attic after all. Ingeniously he worked out that if he stood on a chair and poked off the hatchway lid with the sweeping brush handle he could somehow hook the bag out by the handles. Part way through this inventive operation the plywood board had slipped down from the frame it rested on and whacked the boy in the face. After some dabbing with a piece of tissue Christine convinced him it hadn't ruptured his left eyeball. That the injury consisted of a graze so slight it was barely visible to the naked eye.

Richard and Mark left Joey to beer and burgers and went back into the house.

"You know, I reckon I can reach into the attic and get your bag without bothering with hauling the ladders up out of the shed," Richard told his son.

"Do you want the brush?"

"No, thanks. No more accidents today if I can help it, thank you."

Richard positioned the dining room chair beneath the attic hatchway. When he stood on it, the top of his head was just an inch or so below the level of the hatchway. He was still too low to see anything but a gloomy void of the attic above him, but he reached in. He might be able to find the bag by touch alone. He was surprised to find that the first thing he touched moved quickly away from his fingers.

Still unconscious in the hospital bed, Rosemary Snow felt the pains return to skewer her jaw and knee. The images that flowed through her head were now of the attic in the strange house. She'd seen the wooden board that covered the opening to the attic being lifted up; then it suddenly slipped down. The images had blurred. When they cleared again, she was looking down through the hatchway to a brown carpet covering a landing and stairs that were brilliantly sunlit. Running down the stairs was a boy; he clutched his forehead or his eye, she wasn't sure which.

Then there was a sensation of moving backward.

Then she was at the attic window. In the garden the family were having a barbecue. A fat man sat with them.

There was movement forward with an unlit light bulb passing her shoulder, then moving beneath wooden beams that rose diagonally to meet above. Then crouching.

She looked down. She saw a hand holding an automatic pistol. The madman's hand.

She sensed the madman creeping forward to the lip of the hatchway, the reflected light from below shining on particles of dust suspended in the air.

She watched, feeling frustrated and helpless. Events in that family's house moved to a climax. And she'd been able to do nothing to warn them.

Stupid Rosemary Snow. Stupid, stupid. You should have dragged yourself out of bed and phoned the police. Now you're going to watch that innocent family, the little girl, the little boy, suffer like you suffered.

A hand, followed by a wrist, then a forearm, came up through the hatchway. It stayed there for a moment, swaying slightly from side to side like a strange, stumpy snake. Then it moved decisively. It touched the madman's foot. The foot moved sharply back.

The hand paused as if its owner was surprised by what it had just touched.

"What's wrong, Dad?" It was the boy's voice.

"I don't know. But for the life of me I think I just touched something that moved."

"A rat?"

"No. Let's see if I can feel it again."

The madman was crouching, the gun muzzle positioned to point in the man's face as soon as he put his head above the hatchway.

"Dad, lift me up to have a look."

"You're joking, aren't you? I'd break my back if I tried lifting you up here."

"I need my haversack, Dad, I'm going across to Tim Abraham's tonight."

"I know, I'm trying to reach it for you. It's no good. It must be farther inside. Look, Mark, if you hold the chair still I'll just lift myself up and have a proper look inside."

85

The hand with the gun moved nearer to the hatchway, the finger easing around the trigger.

Any second now, Rosemary Snow. You're to blame. Should have warned them. Now you'll see what a plug of metal traveling at a thousand feet per second does to a man's face. Bullet holes aren't neat holes, they're bloody holes, bloody enormous holes. Holes the size of eye sockets.

Two hands gripped the timber lip of the hatchway. Rosemary saw the fingers grip tightly; she saw each finger, each fingernail, the hairs on the backs of the hands, the wedding ring.

"Mark? Richard? Is this what you're looking for?" The woman's voice.

"Dad, it's the haversack," shouted the boy, delighted.

The man asked, "Where was it?"

"In the cupboard under the stairs. Hurry up, Richard, I've put the steaks on the barbecue."

The hands disappeared. A second later the wooden board came up to be dropped back into place.

The attic grew suddenly darker.

Richard returned to the barbecue to find Joey chewing on great mouthfuls of steak.

As Christine dished out more hotdogs for Amy and Mark who sat on a blanket in the shade of the tree she looked up at Joey.

"Weren't you going to tell me something?"

Richard watched Old Rubber Lip smile a victorious smile. "Just that I've realized I've no reason to rush off. I'll stick around for a while." He flashed Richard a greasy grin. "If you'll have me, that is, Dicky Boy?"

The smile didn't come easy but Richard forced it. "Be my guest, Joey."

"Oh, sorry I ate your steak, sunshine. I thought you'd got more."

Richard's laugh sounded more like a machine gun executing dissidents than an expression of amusement. "I'll be all right with this, Joey." He viciously stabbed the sole surviving sausage and threw it onto the barbecue.

That evening the Youngs, Richard, Christine, Amy and Mark, stood by the driveway gates. At this time the Sheffield road was quiet. The hot summer's day had turned pleasantly cool. Overhead the sky darkened and swifts were replaced by the bat shift as they took their turn to feed on moths and Daddy Longlegs.

A car pulled up.

"Have a good time," Richard said and ruffled Mark's hair.

"Behave yourself." Christine kissed him, which made him flush red. Richard grinned. When you're that age, to be kissed by your mother in front of your friends is excruciating torture.

They waved good-bye as Mark climbed into the back of the car. He was talking nonstop, excited by the prospect of his week-long camping trip.

As the car pulled away the remaining Youngs waved until it had vanished into the distance. And for some reason Richard could not explain, he wished—he wished desperately—that he was going, too.

Chapter Sixteen

Burnt in Blood

It was when the man let himself down from the Youngs' attic to find food in the middle of the night that he saw the two men walk into the garden. It was 2 a.m. The men didn't walk so much as scurry like a pair of rats along the hedge.

With the lights out he slipped into the dining room and through the sliding doors into the garden. Although the moon was on the wane, he could find his way easily enough along the path into the shrubbery. There he could watch without being seen.

As he crouched behind a rhododendron his left foot gave a protesting ache from the sprain it had sustained when his car left the road three nights ago. He had no clear memories of those few hours immediately after the accident. Like a wounded animal he'd instinctively found somewhere to hide. He'd woken the next morning in the attic, his forehead throbbing where it had hit the steering wheel, his face caked with dried blood.

He'd intended lying low a couple of days to recuperate before moving on. An automatic loaded with Glazier Safety Slugs that could drop a wild boar stone dead with a single shot would have disposed of any difficulties if the family had discovered they had a squatter up in their attic. But by accident he'd ended up talking to the little girl. She had told him surprising things.

The runaway, Rosemary Snow, had seemed promising, too. Of course, he knew she lay dead in the long grass now, in a field fifty miles from here. But this little four-year-old, Amy, interested him. She had potential.

Now the two men poking their heads over the rose bushes as they looked at the house were going to foul things up.

If he let them.

He could see that both of them were in their twenties. Both wore jeans and black sweatshirts. One, although carrying too much fat, looked physically strong: his bull neck was the same width as his shaved head. The man had left the gun in the attic, and without it, these new intruders would be tough nuts to crack.

The other, thinner, wearing a dark baseball cap, looked the meaner of the two. Even as the two moved up to the kitchen window to look inside, he surmised the man in the cap probably verged on the psychotic with his peculiar fixed and disdainful mouth. The tattoos on his face and hands backed that up. A loner who spent his life either on bail or in prison.

The man moved silently through the bushes to get a little closer. The two were whispering on how best to break in. They were heading for an argument. Fat Man wanted to forget the house and go for the car in the garage. Cap Boy wanted the house. Cap Boy lifted something in his hand. It was a hammer; the kind used for smashing in doors, or maybe even a pensioner's face.

Cap Boy liked to do that kind of thing. He got a kick out of it. Probably even more than from the crack cocaine he'd suck into his lungs.

The man's lips and neck tingled. It was coming on without warning. Jesus, Jesus, this's Christmas come early. The tingling flashed through him. Cap Boy—yes, he could do it to Cap Boy.

The man looked at the back of Cap Boy's head. The tufts of hair poking beneath the cap, the tattoos on the neck. Carefully, he focused on the back of Cap Boy's neck, the bleeding-heart tattoo, a mole the size of a chocolate button that bled every time his neck was shaved by the prison barber.

Yes, the man knew what Cap Boy was like. What he loved to do when they switched out the cell lights or when he broke into a house. Ha! Ha! Fun to shit on the beds; fun to stick the budgie in the microwave . . . flutter, squawk, thud.

Something clicked into the man's head as his imagination went onto auto.

Without trying now he stared at the back of Cap Boy's head and thought:

I know you: you were always the funny one at school. You did crazy things that made the other kids laugh. You were always in a gang because they got a kick out of you taking all the risks when you kicked in a shop door. You were always the one who got so drunk you'd piss in through the police car window. You were the one that always got arrested. But what did you care: you got the laughs and the respect, only—

—only things changed. Your buddies all got steady girlfriends. But girls think there's something creepy about you. You thought you'd always be part of the gang, but other gang members started acting straight, getting jobs, buying houses and carpets and talking about wallpapering the baby's bedroom. Boring twats. Soon you were the only one left to piss into police cars and kick in shop doors. But you'd shit your hole. The courts got nasty and started sending you down for six months at a time.

But nothing hurts you, right? Not when your mother's boyfriends beat you. Or hearing that cell door bang shut.

You live in a bedsit. You've got a girl now. OK, she's only probably with you because you give her crack. And boy, oh boy, do you need a lot of crack; so you rob houses and cars and maybe knock over an old lady in the street for her purse. Getting good at it, too. Move onto bigger and better.

Like this house. Take what you want. So what if Mr. And Mrs. Family Normal don't like it, give them a smack with the hammer; then they'll be sweet and generous. Maybe Mrs. Family Normal likes a bit of rough, yeah, then she'll have a bit of rough, and it'll be so rough she'll not sit down for a fortnight.

But Fat Boy here's not got the stomach for it. He wants to nick a car stereo that ain't worth the price of a fix. Just look at him, fat face, fat backside, but he ain't got no guts.

So why's he hanging around with me, then?

Because he's giving your girl what you can't, pin prick. Every time you're out busting a house to get money to buy her sugar and spice and all stuff nice, Fat Boy here's walking into your bedroom and walking straight into your bitch.

She doesn't give a toss about you, Cap Boy. Fat Man's all she cares about. You can see them, can't you? She's laying naked on your bed, high on your crack and she's begging Fat Boy to pump her. You can see them, now, can't you? All bare arses and tits, all flappity-flap. She's bouncing up and down on him, those long ear rings you bought her jingling away like little tinker bells, and she's saying, "Christ, Fat Man you know what I like . . . not like that stupid cretin . . . with his baseball cap . . . and his poxy tattoos. He can't get it up: pin prick—that's what he is. If you ask me he'd be better with a boy."

You're not going to take it, are you? You're not going to let them bleed you dry? Then laugh at you the moment your back's turned.

Teach them a lesson. Next time Fat Boy's there with his bare backside heaving up and down on top of her take that bloody hammer and hammer him, right on top of that fat head. Then show that bitch that you're the one with power. Take back what she owes you. Hold her down by her hands; you'll see her head twisting from side to side, because she knows what you're going to do next.

But you're too strong for her.

You bend over her; grip those ear rings in your teeth, pull them out one after another, then all the studs that cover her ears and nose; pull them out with your teeth one after another—pop, pop, pop, pop.

Blood all over the place. Show her you've fucked Fat Man lover boy with the hammer; his skull's split in two like a cabbage. Pow! You can do it.

Wait . . .

You can do it now.

Look at Fat Boy, peeping through the kitchen window. Nice big head he's got, ain't he? Nice big hammer you've got. The two sort of go together, don't they? Yeah, do it now. You've got the guts, you've got the power; all that sexy power; you've got it: Now, do it; do it; do it; do it . . .

Yeah, that feels good, doesn't it. The way the hammer head came down with a nice popping smack. Did you see how he went straight down into the flower bed? Look, his mouth is full of dirt; he's looking up at you; his mouth's going like he's saying his prayers or something but you can't hear because his mouth's full of Mr. & Mrs. Family Ordinary's garden dirt. Plant a hammer in it, that's it, wonder if it'll sprout a hammer tree in the spring; and yeah, yeah, little hammer fruit in the autumn. Teeth all broken up now; but his eyes are staring at you as if you're a little piece of shit. Pop those, too. Down comes the hammer. Pop! Down comes the hammer again! Pop!

Fat Man's got no eyes, do dah, Fat Man's got no eyes, do dah, do dah, day.

Fat Man's not moving now. Not even his lungs or his iddy biddy heart.

Get rid of the sucker. That's it, pick him up, you can do it.

You carry him to the truck. Easy peasy.

You dump him in the back. You climb into the cab whistling, a job well done. Lights on, engine revving, and away you go, with the lucky dice swinging on the end of the chain from the rearview mirror.

You've driven a good ten miles. This should do it. A nice quiet forest, pull off the road and drive through the trees.

Right, you stop the truck here. Fat Man's still sleeping the sleep of the eternal in the back of the truck.

Still whistling, feeling as big as a tree and as strong as a lion, you take the can of petrol from the back and start sluicing down the cab and Fat Man, laying there in the back of the truck, flat on his back, hands across his fat gut; the red holes where his eyes were watching the stars.

Now this is real power. You sit on the cab roof of the truck and pour what's left of the petrol over you. It runs as cool and as refreshing as mountain spring water over your face and down your chest; it soaks your jeans; you laugh happily and pour petrol into your mouth; gargle with it then squirt it out in a thin jet. Now, where did you put those matches . . .

He woke. Hell, that was some shit-weird dream. Killing his best buddy with a hammer? Driving into a forest; dousing the truck with petrol, then sitting on top of the cab roof and dousing himself?

He opened his eyes expecting to see the pair of striped curtains and Shaz sleeping off a headful of crack.

It was dark. But not dark enough. His eyes widened. Shock made him breathe in sharply; petrol fumes felt like needles stabbing up into his nostrils. He sat on the cab roof, his legs dangling down into the back of the truck. Bomber lay on his back, his face smashed to a bloody mess. It was night. But why could he see so much? With a feeling of dread, his eyes swept up to see the burning match between his finger and thumb.

The flame kissed his petrol-wet finger. He screamed. Instantly a sleeve of purple flame rolled up his arm; then down his body like he was one big fuse. The flame hit the pool of petrol in the back of the truck.

With a roar, a ball of flame as big as a house rolled up through the branches to the tree tops.

His eyes were wide open. It seemed he'd been locked in the heart of the sun. Everywhere was an eye-blistering light, and heat that felt like a million sharp teeth biting his skin.

He jumped from the truck roof to run through the trees, a human fireball screaming and lighting up the green ceiling of leaves.

He ran screaming, knowing he was dying, yet hoping if he ran faster than he'd ever run before he might leave this second skin of fire behind. Through bubbling eyelids he saw tree trunks zip out of the darkness to rush by him, patches of grass, frightened rabbits running frantically out of the way of this earthbound comet that blazed and crackled across the forest floor.

Then miraculously a lake appeared in front of him.

A deep cool lake. Hope surged up inside of him. If he could make the lake. Put out the fire. He'd be all right. *He'd be all right!*

He pounded across the dirt, leaving shreds of burning sweatshirt behind him; incredibly the only thing untouched by the fire, his baseball cap, was still pulled tightly onto his head.

The lake reflected the golden wash of flame. He ran toward it, a blazing comet. Nearly, nearly there . . .

The tree root caught his burning trainers. He fell forward, screamed; the next time he breathed in, the fire melted his lungs. Gurgling, he rolled onto his back and lay there. The fatty tissue in his body ignited.

The lake was as good as a thousand miles away. Skin and blood boiled together. The flames illuminated the branches above. And the ceiling of green leaves seemed to dance lightly with the stars themselves, beyond his burning eyes.

Chapter Seventeen

Monday

By the time the man's unwitting host came down to make breakfast there was no sign of what had happened the night before. The man had thrown the hammer in the pond and carefully covered Fat Man's blood in the flower bed with a layer of top soil.

The early-morning sun was hot enough to shrink the wound on the man's face. It stung painfully. The activity of the night before made his injured leg ache so that he now limped back to the house.

Still, he felt good. Things were going his way. The little girl, Amy, appeared a promising subject for his purposes.

Now he crept nearer to the kitchen window so he could see inside. His unwitting host was cheerfully singing along to a song on the radio. He knew the man's name was Richard Young and from overhearing conversations he knew a fair smattering of the man's background too.

Now it was vital that he gain some kind of control over the man and his family.

He watched Richard Young pour cornflakes into bowls, fill the kettle and light the gas hob.

The man stared at the back of Richard Young's neck.

I know what you're like, Richard Young, he thought. *You're a happy family man. Everything would be all right in your world if you weren't burdened by the useless bit of wasteland at the back of your house. You know the land's not even worth the price of that box of cornflakes in your hand. But you don't say anything because you don't want destroy the dream your father-in-law planted in your wife's mind.*

Stop.

Don't go on with this. It's not your problem. Just because your

*father-in-law loused his business up you don't have to carry the
can for it all your life.*

Break free from it.

Start right know.

*Do something, some big gesture, that shows people you've got
a mind of your own.*

*Do you see that gas flame in front of you? Turn it up. Hear it
begin to roar now? See how blue the flame is. See how high it
leaps.*

*You can use that, you know. You can use it to get rid of this
thing you've got around your neck.*

*Imagine if you put your hand into the flame and held it there.
You'd feel no pain, I promise you. It would feel as cool as
holding your hand under the cold water tap.*

No pain, Richard Young.

*All you would be doing is releasing yourself from that shitty
piece of land that threatens to screw up your life.*

Put your hand in the flame and wait.

*Now imagine your fingers are five fat sausages. You put them
on your barbecue and you watch them fry. Until the skin splits,
until the meat inside oozes out in a thick, sizzling paste . . .*

Do it, Richard Young. Put your hand in the flame.

Rosemary Snow opened her eyes.

They were crusted with matter. Her whole face felt so tight it
felt as if she wore a rubber mask that had shrunk hard against
her skin.

She tried opening her mouth. At the third attempt her lips
parted with a faint tearing sound.

Every movement hurt. Her teeth ached. Her head tingled. And
it felt as if half her stomach was missing.

Anyone else would have lain there, feeling three parts dead.

But Rosemary Snow had a mission. She knew she must find
the man who did this to her. It was the only thing that mattered
now.

She would find him. And she would kill him. Everything was
subordinate to that—the pain, the stiffness in her arms, the ache
in her knees.

She pulled the IV needle from her arm. Distantly she realized
blood trickled down to her fingers. She ignored it.

She pulled the feeding tube from out of her nose. It felt like

95

she was pulling a snake down her nostril; the pipe seemed to go on forever. At last it came out with a spurt of milky fluid.

Rosemary looked around the hospital room. Any second someone might walk in. She couldn't allow that.

Her mission was the one thing that kept her alive. Hatred had become her body's fuel.

As she dragged herself out of the bed, she saw the mirror above the sink.

She paused. The idea of looking at her reflection appalled her. But curiosity was stronger. She had to see what had happened to her face in the fall. Pushing one foot in front of the other, she shuffled across the floor.

For perhaps twenty seconds she stood, her hands resting on each side of the sink to support her shivering body. She stood with her head down, not daring to look into the mirror.

"Do it, Red Zed." She gritted her teeth. *"Do it."* Taking a deep breath, she gripped the sides of the sink. Then she lifted her head and looked directly into mirror.

And screamed.

The gas jet flared bright blue. The heat from it tingled Richard's face. He looked at his hand. At the fingernails, at the creases in the skin, at the bluey hue his wedding ring had taken from the flame.

Just for a second the absurd impulse to stick his hand into the flame had flitted across his mind. Grinning, he shook his head and slapped the kettle down onto the hob.

"Morning, sleepy head," he said cheerfully as Amy walked into the kitchen, yawning a mighty yawn.

"Boys kept me awake," she said. "They're making a boat in the loft."

"By gum, the bad Boys. We'll round them up and throw them in the pond. Hey, what do you say? Hey . . ."

He tickled her neck and she squidged her shoulders up to her ears, giggling.

"Fun and frivolity so early in the morning?" Christine came in wearing jeans and a white T-shirt. She kissed Amy, then sat down at the table, smiling broadly. "Right, then. I'll have the fresh orange juice, croissants, followed by bacon, mushrooms and scrambled eggs."

Richard laughed. "It's cornflakes. Like 'em or lump 'em."

Through the window the man could see the family eating breakfast. He'd tried to get into Young's head. It hadn't worked, but then, he never expected it would. Last night was an unusual case. The psychopathic kid had been peculiarly receptive.

The man watched the Youngs closely. They laughed as they talked. Their happiness lit up the house like some kind of interior sunlight.

Just for a second, the man felt an aching sense of loss. But it vanished as quickly as it had come.

He'd come too far to be distracted by sentimentality. He had a job to do. And nothing—but NOTHING—would stand in his way.

The handgun was in the rucksack hidden in the shrubbery. He'd retrieved it from the attic after disposing of Fat Man and Cap Boy. In a minute he'd collect the gun and—

Jesus!

It hit him.

Hard.

It was coming. He knew it must only be a matter of time, but he thought he'd have had more warning.

Drawing in a sharp lungful of air, he turned round, his heart pounding. It was out there. Somewhere beyond the land they called Sunnyfields. He sensed its approach.

A dark pounding force. Colossal. Invisible. Powerful enough to shake the earth.

He moved back into the bushes, thinking fast. His plans had just gone belly-up. No doubt about that.

The thing that followed him could be here any minute.

He needed to do something. He needed to do it fast.

Then he did the only thing he could think of. Deliberately he forced his thumbnail beneath the scab that ran down the side of his nose.

It ripped away from his face with the sound of a stick of celery being broken in two. Then he gouged at the wound. Again and again until blood poured freely down his nose, across his lips and chin, soaking the front of his white shirt in a dirty red stain.

Chapter Eighteen

Appearance

"Please! I need to use your phone. I—I'm sorry to bother you, but I'm in trouble."

The man stood on the doorstep. Richard was shocked to see the stranger's face and chest were soaked red with blood.

"Your phone . . . please. I don't want to be here ten seconds longer than I have to be."

"There's been an accident? Sit down. I'll call an ambulance. Is there—"

"No. It's got to be the police. And quickly."

The man panted with urgency. Richard stepped back to allow him into the hall. He limped inside, carrying a rucksack which he dropped into a chair.

"Where's the phone?"

"The kitchen. But if—"

"Just let me phone the police. There isn't much time."

"You're in no state to telephone anyone. If you tell me what's—"

"What's wrong?" The man shook his head so vigorously, blood flicked from the end of his nose to speckle the wall. "Believe me, you don't want to know. I don't want to put you into anymore danger than—"

"Danger? What danger?"

"Don't ask. Please don't ask." With the back of his hand he wiped his face. "In here?"

"Yes. Do you want—"

Christine appeared "What's wrong?"

"There's been an accident," Richard told her. "This gentleman needs to make a phone call."

At the kitchen door the man turned to Richard and hissed something that not only puzzled Richard but turned him cold. "Once

98

I've made the call, I'll wait at the bottom of the drive for them to collect me—"

"But you need—"

"I need you to promise me one thing. Lock all the doors until the police arrive. OK?"

Stunned, Richard watched the man walk into the kitchen and shut the door behind him.

"Richard," Christine whispered, her eyes frightened, "who is he?"

"Search me."

"Has there been a car crash?"

"I don't know. But I don't like it. There's something wrong. He wants us to lock all the doors after he's gone."

She shivered and rubbed her arm. "He's not on the run, is he?"

"No . . . I don't know. I don't think so. He said—"

"God Almighty!"

Something solid crashed against the front door, knocking it open.

Richard spun around to see what was coming into the house.

"Joey?"

"Can't stop. Should've been on the golf course ten minutes ago. I'm just dropping in those development proposals from . . . Jesus Christ."

The sight of the bloody man coming out of the kitchen stopped Joey dead in his tracks.

"The phone . . ." the man said in near panic. "What's wrong with your phone?"

"Nothing," Richard said, bewildered. Everything was happening too fast. "It was OK when—"

"It's dead," the man said.

"I'll check the lines," Christine said quickly. She left the house at a run.

"What's happening, Dad?" asked Amy from the lounge doorway.

"Nothing, sweetheart. You just watch the cartoon for a minute and we'll—"

"You," the man said to Joey "bring the lady back into the house. She's not safe out there."

Joey didn't move. He stood there openmouthed.

"I'll get her," Richard said. But he'd only crossed halfway to the door when Christine appeared, holding up garden shears.

"Someone's used these to cut the cable. Where it runs down the outside wall."

"Damn," the man said. Anxiously he looked out of the window. Richard shivered. "What's all this about?"

"I'll tell you. I didn't want to. But it's only fair you know something." He'd torn off a bundle of kitchen roll which he used to mop the blood from his face. "There are some men who want to give me a hard time.

"Who—" Christine began.

"No . . . believe me, you don't want to know." He looked from Richard to Christine. "I wouldn't blame you if you said no. But I really do need a lift to the nearest police station."

"I can run you there," Richard said quickly. "I'll bring the car to the front."

"No." the man held up the blood-soaked kitchen roll. "Just a moment. It's not as easy as that now—"

"What do you mean?" Joey spoke for the first time, panic sounding loud and clear in his voice. "What do you mean? Not as easy as that?"

"What I mean is, we all have to go. Including the mother and child . . . and you."

"Me?" Joey looked stunned.

Richard was astonished how quickly the stranger had regained control of himself, talking in a brisk, businesslike way: "These men are bad—very bad, believe me. If they've seen me come in here . . ."

"Oh, Jesus," Richard said under his breath, realizing the implications.

". . . if they've seen me come in here and leave with one of you, then they're going to walk in here. And anyone they find they will make tell them where I've gone. Do you understand?"

Richard nodded. "I'll get the car keys. Everyone get into the car." He felt strangely breathless. "You." He looked at the man who'd blundered into their peaceful world and torn it apart. "You sit in the front."

The man picked up his rucksack.

Joey blurted out. "My car's on the road. I'll leave in that."

The man shook his head. "You've got to come to the police station with us. They might follow you."

Joey looked as if he'd faint.

"Follow me? *Follow me?*"

"Look," the man said, "don't worry. Within ten minutes of notifying the police they'll have picked this gang up and got them behind bars. Now . . . get in the car. Please. They might be here any minute." Joey looked as if he was going to protest. The man looked at him. "In fact they might already be in the garden."

Joey was first to the car.

Chapter Nineteen

Closer

"Don't drive too fast." The stranger sat sideways in the front passenger seat so that he could look back the way they came. "We don't want to attract attention to ourselves. But nor do I want you to stop for anything."

The drive into town was surreal. When the stranger first appeared at the house Richard had felt as if he'd been pitched onto a runaway train; events moved at a dizzying speed.

Now everything seemed to move in slow motion. The Monday-morning traffic was light. The sun shone. A tractor harvested hay in a field. A huge orange sign at the filling station he visited twice a week announced a competition to win free petrol for a year.

In a detached way he found himself wondering what the competition would be. A raffle? A lottery? Collect ten vouchers then enter your vehicle registration number?

He licked his dry lips. After thirty bizarre minutes his mind was hunting for signs of what was normal and safe.

He glanced in the rearview mirror. In the backseat sat Joey and Christine with Amy in the middle. No one was talking but the tension was clear enough. Joey nervously nipped his heavy bottom lip between finger and thumb. Christine ran one hand up and down her forearm as if trying to erase a dirty mark. Only Amy watched the passing houses as if they were merely driving to the supermarket.

By Richard's side the man seemed quite calm now. He'd managed to clean off most of the blood, leaving just a few reddish-brown stains on his cheek and jaw.

Perhaps he'd been beaten up by the gang. But Richard saw that apart from bloodstains on his shirt his clothes looked reasonably tidy. His expensive-looking shoes were clean. His thick brown hair looked as if it had been recently brushed.

The man continued to look back. His eyes told Richard that here was a man of energy and intelligence. No doubt women found him handsome and charismatic. A businessman, perhaps? Who'd fallen foul of some underworld gang? But he seemed too much in control of the situation. As if this kind of thing had happened to him more than once. Maybe he was an undercover cop? Perhaps he'd infiltrated a gang of crooks only to—

"Careful. Red light," the man warned.

"What do you want me to do?" Richard asked.

"Stop for it, of course."

"But you said—"

"I don't think there's a need to risk life and limb anymore."

"You mean we're not being followed?"

"I can't see anything out of the ordinary. Best not count our chickens though."

"These people," Richard asked, "they're not likely to bother any of my family?"

"How much farther to the police station?" The man's keen eyes searched the road ahead.

"Two minutes. You've not answered by question, Mr.—"

"Michael."

"Will we be safe from those people who are following you?"

"Get me to the police station, Mr. Young." The man gave a ghost of a smile. "Then everything will be fine."

When Rosemary Snow screamed it didn't bring nurses running. A fortnight of coma had wasted her vocal chords.

The scream, though full of pain and horror at what she saw in the mirror, sounded more like a dry hiss.

The mirror showed her what she had become.

Her hair had become matted; a clump of dead fibers. Bruises mottled her face. Her left eye was nearly closed and a dozen stitches like black spiders followed a miniature mountain range of scabs down her left cheek.

She looked at the thing that had been Rosemary Snow. Now it had the face of a monster.

Her stomach muscles heaved. But there was nothing in her stomach to vomit.

For a full five minutes she stood there her legs shaking so hard that she thought any second she'd simply fold.

But she pictured the stranger's face. And the shaking stopped.

He's done this to you, she told herself. *And now he's going to do the same to someone else*.

She took a deep breath and forced herself to stand straight and look the monster in the mirror right in the eye.

"Rosemary Snow," she whispered. "Don't go to pieces now. You've got lives to save. And one to destroy."

She began to look for her clothes.

At the same time Rosemary Snow had begun to search through the hospital locker Richard Young drove Christine, Amy, Joey and the stranger, Michael, into Pontefract.

He turned off the Knottingley road and cut up by All Saints Church which had been blitzed to a shell in the Civil War and on uphill by the castle ruins in the direction of the police station.

Everything appeared so banally normal. Even down to the smell of fresh licorice from the sweet factories that permanently filled the air over Pontefract.

Richard wanted rid of this stranger as quickly as possible. He was still astonished and bewildered by the speed his life had been turned upside down. Richard had decided to insist on a police escort home. After all, there was the question of who had cut the telephone cable? The idea of the ease with which someone could just stroll into your garden on a summer's morning turned him cold. What if Amy had been playing out? What would this gang of thugs have done to silence her?

As Richard pulled off into the car park across the road from the police station, he felt increasingly uneasy. He saw this situation wouldn't end with the man walking into the police station. Had the gang seen the man go into the Youngs' house? Good God, they might even think they were all in this together. He began to sweat.

And right now the thing he wanted most was to be pushing open the doors of Pontefract police station. Then he would see the around welcoming face of the desk sergeant, while in the offices behind him would be a building full of solid, no-nonsense Yorkshire coppers.

It was so early that the car park was virtually empty. They drove by the concrete bollards and pay-and-display ticket dispensers waiting for the day's shoppers. They passed a lone yellow Fiat sitting in the middle of the car park.

"Mum! Look!" It was the first time Amy had spoken since

104

leaving the house. "Look! There's Bart Simpson!"

Richard noticed Michael shoot a relaxed glance in the direction of the yellow Fiat. There, suction cups held a Bart Simpson doll to a rear side window. The doll's eyes bulged out of the yellow face and a pink tongue jutted impudently out of its mouth.

Ahead were a line of a dozen or so civilian cars mixed with police cars. Richard pulled up into the row of parking bays behind them.

"Come on," Michael said in a soft voice. "Let's get this over with, then you people can get back to your lives."

Without another word they all got out of the car. Richard glanced anxiously at Amy, concerned that she might be frightened. She seemed happy enough and was more interested in the Bart Simpson doll in the car. Christine looked calm and businesslike. She just wanted to get this over and done with as efficiently as possible.

Joey, Richard noticed, looked his usual spoiled self because his plans had gone to cock. He was running his fingers through his straggly hair; the bottom lip pushed out in a way that Richard had come to detest over the years.

As Richard locked the car he found himself wondering whether he should buy a ticket. Even trying to guess how long they would be. He shook his head. There's a gang of thugs pursuing your passenger and you stand there wondering whether to buy a ticket?

The main thing is: Get rid of this stranger. Then get the police back to your house. Make sure it's safe. Then put this whole damn episode behind you.

With Christine leading the small group by the line of parked cars, Michael, looking relaxed, occasionally turned to look back across the car park. Richard followed his line of sight. But all he could see was his red Volvo, a hundred-yard gap full of nothing but concrete bollards and the occasional ticket dispenser, then the yellow Fiat. Beyond that was only an expanse of deserted car park, then the town cemetery.

As he caught up with the group Michael said, "Thanks for the lift, Richard. Once I've told the cops everything you'll be able to take your family home."

That's when he stopped. Richard? The stranger had used his name twice now. Only now the penny had dropped. The man had not been told his name. And, as far as he could remember, no one else had used his name in his presence. This was getting weird. Nothing was adding up as it should. And although the man looked as if he'd been given a damn good thrashing why did his hair look so perfectly brushed? Why was he so relaxed when—

The sound was the first indication that it had begun.

Richard stopped. The same kind of creak a hinge that's in need of oiling makes. Only it was too loud. Much too loud.

"Oh, God." Michael's eyes went wide. He looked as if he'd just seen his own coffin. *"Oh, God. We're too late."*

Chapter Twenty

The Day Hell Came to Town

That's when it happened.

And that's when Richard Young knew his vision of the world, and the notion of reality he'd been taught from childhood to manhood was wrong. Completely, totally, incontrovertibly wrong, wrong, *wrong*.

The creaking sound had stopped him and the stranger as they made their way to the police station just thirty yards away.

The expression on the stranger's face was one of shock and disbelief.

Richard looked across the car park, shielding his eyes against the brilliant sun. It seemed normal. Birds sang. The smell of licorice turned the air sweet. But Richard sensed some kind of change stealing over that Pontefract car park.

It was almost like before a thunderstorm when you sense a charge of energy building; the quality of the air seemed different.

Richard glanced at Joey, Christine and Amy. They'd stopped. They sensed it, too.

He tilted his head to one side, listening hard.

Nothing. No sounds.

The birds had stopped singing.

His arms prickled as the hairs on his skin stood upright. Birds flew overhead, wings frantically beating the sky. It wasn't a single-species flock. It was just all the birds flying away from some unseen danger.

The creak came again. A stuttering metallic sound. Louder than before.

"What's happening?" demanded Richard.

The stranger's face drained. "We're too late," he hissed. "We've got to go back to the car. Now!"

"No." Richard took a step back from him. "We're going into the police station."

The man shook his head. "You do, and you've killed your family."

"Are you threatening us?"

Before the man spoke the creaking sound turned into a groan. Loud enough to make Amy clamp her hands over her ears, it echoed from the police station and rolled away across the town.

Now Richard saw . . .

He saw something. Only he didn't damn well know what it was . . .

"It's the car," blurted Joey. "The yellow car."

Richard knew what he'd seen. Transfixed, they watched the car. It was moving. From side to side as if invisible hands rocked it.

"Jesus . . ."

Richard turned on the stranger. "What's happening? Who's doing that?"

Even at this distance they could see the Bart Simpson doll stuck to the inside of the window by suction cups. The doll's head whipped from side to side, the tongue flashing pink. For all the world it looked as if it was clamoring to be let out of the car. As it rocked like a boat on a stormy sea.

Then—

BANG!

"My God!" Joey held his forehead. "Did you see that!"

Richard stared at the car. Glass shot from it like spray from a fountain.

Even as they watched the yellow Fiat made a series of loud popping sounds as it settled lower and lower into the tarmac as if some tremendous weight bore down. A tire exploded with a sharp crack. The ground ran wet around it as the car's body fluids—water from the radiator, brake fluid, fuel—squeezed from ruptured pipes, reservoirs and sump.

Michael shouted, "Now! Get back into the car. Everyone get into the car!"

Richard looked at the police station. It seemed indestructibly safe. Inside, down-to-earth coppers were brewing tea.

"Don't even think about it," Michael hissed. "You'd be dead in less than a minute. The car! Get everyone into your car!"

108

With a judder the yellow Fiat gave a final squeal and lay still, like a slaughtered animal.

Three seconds later a ticket dispenser *shri-iked* as the metal post it was bolted to was hammered flat to the ground.

Someone's firing at us, thought Richard in near panic as something rattled on the tarmac all around them. No . . . money. *Hell's bells, it's money!*

Coins from the burst machine rained down, tinkling on the car park and rolling in circles.

"It's your last chance!" the man shouted. "The car!"

Richard picked up Amy who'd rooted to the tarmac and ran. Even though instinct told him to run to the police station, even though a line of concrete bollards exploded one after another, he found himself trusting the stranger.

"Get in the back," he shouted to Joey and Christine.

The keys were in his hands but his fingers felt like frozen sausages; he fumbled at them uselessly.

At last he found the door key, stabbed it into the lock.

It wouldn't turn.

It had jammed.

Thirty yards away. A *Welcome To Pontefract* sign slapped down to the ground with a crack. Blue sparks flew from the impact.

Joey squealed. "Richard, for Godsakes hurry, man!"

"The key's jammed; I can't—"

Hell, he suddenly realized. *Wrong way, you idiot. You're forcing the key the wrong bloody way!*

Michael said simply, "Richard. You've got ten seconds to save our lives."

"Inside!"

The car doors swung open as one, then slammed as one.

This time Richard slammed the key into the ignition square on. Started the engine. Engaged gear. And powered the car across the car park.

Within seconds Richard was screaming the car out of Pontefract. Out past the racecourse. Beneath the railway bridge. Then he fired the car up the slip road to join the motorway.

In the back his family were statues. Not speaking. Not moving. No expression. Only their eyes expressed the shock they felt.

The stranger looked back through the rear window. Then he turned to Richard and said in a low voice. "Faster. I think it's gaining on us."

Chapter Twenty-one

Dead Beat

. . . a few hours later he would be dead.

Beside Richard, sat the stranger in the bloodstained shirt. He sat still; his expression revealed nothing of what he felt or might be thinking.

From the backseat Joey shouted the same question over and over: "What happened? Who did that? What happened? Listen to me, you bastard! Who did that? I said—"

Amy was crying.

". . . police," Christine insisted. "Richard. You've got to find a phone. Call the police."

"I don't know who you are, or what you've done," Joey screamed. "But you can't involve us. For Christsakes what happened back there? That car exploded. The whole fucking car park was exploding. Why did—"

No, the car didn't explode, Richard told himself. *It imploded. It squashed flat beneath an enormous weight.*

An invisible weight.

"I'm sorry," Michael said in a low voice. "I didn't mean—"

"I bet you're fucking sorry." Spit flew from Joey's lips. "Yes, I bet you're fucking sorry. Dropping us in the shit. Are we going to die for this? Are we?"

"I didn't want this to happen, I—"

. . . his life could have been saved. If the true nature of his condition had been known . . .

Richard drove the car along the motorway at over a hundred. Joey's savage shouting, Amy's crying, Christine persistently asking to telephone the police, the occasional softly-spoken word from the stranger in his bloodstained shirt; they all managed to seem distant and painfully close at the same time.

Richard passed a petrol tanker on the inside lane of the mo-

110

torway. He was driving suicidally fast but what he'd experienced just sixteen minutes ago had scared him; brutally scared him. In a detached way that was bizarre he found himself thinking *When was the last time I was so frightened?*

. . . in minutes he was dead. Why he died, a mystery . . .

Who was it that died? Richard asked himself. It was as if his mind had split itself into a number of distinct compartments. One handled the driving. *Thruuppp.* Now he used the hard shoulder of the motorway to overtake (or was that undertake?) a phalanx of bastardly slow vehicles hogging the other lanes. Breathing came hard. He felt incredibly breathless and had to inhale hard.

And another compartment of his mind listened to the radio that had somehow been left on amid all this bastard mayhem. Someone had died, said the girl on the radio. *Who was it?* To Richard it seemed absurdly important. So much so, he wanted to turn up the radio and scream to the others to keep quiet. The feeling that he would suffocate intensified.

. . . he was just twenty-eight years old, said the girl on the radio. *But the world of rock music would never be the same again . . .*

Twenty-eight years old? Male? Jim Morrison, perhaps. No, wasn't Morrison older than that when his heart stopped in that too-hot bathwater in his Paris apartment? Maybe Brian Jones . . .

"Look," screamed Joey; his spit tingled on the back of Richard's bare neck. "You fucking know who did this to you! What did they use? A fucking cannon or something—"

The stranger replied, "If I can explain. What happened was—"

"Mum . . . Mum . . ." sobbed Amy, burying her face in Christine's lap. "I want to go home. I don't like this. I don't—"

"Richard! Look out!"

Christine's voice cut through the wall of sound. Richard's head snapped forward. They were heading straight for the back wheels of a truck parked on the hard shoulder.

Richard's jaws clamped together. At this speed the car would ram beneath the truck. While the truck's tailgate would slice the top off the car, their upper bodies and heads with it.

Tires screeched. Horns sounded. Richard hauled the steering wheel right, flicking the car so far across its tires scythed the grass of the central reservation.

"Stop the car, Richard," begged Christine.

111

"You can't stop," the stranger insisted in a low voice. "Keep driving."

"Mum. I-I-I want to go-oh home . . ."

. . . while the man has died, his music lives on . . .

"Who's fucking chasing you? Who's fucking doing it?"

The car straightened and independent chunks of his mind still worked on their own problems. Who was the musician who died? Elvis Presley? Buddy Holly?

And what had frightened him as much as this in the past?

Suddenly Richard remembered the night he stood in the garden. It was dark. Snow lay thick on the lawn. But he was dripping wet. Why?

For the life of him he couldn't remember. He only knew he was so wet his clothes dripped. He must have been ten years old. He was shaking. Not with cold. With fear.

Something terrible had happened. The answer lay in the house he stood watching. The curtains were open. Lights blazed inside. A Christmas tree stood in the window with clusters of green and red lights that winked on and off. And he desperately wanted to walk up to the door. And when someone opened it, ask a question. The question was enormously important. He couldn't leave the garden until he asked it. But he was too terrified to do it. So he stood there ankle-deep in snow, with water dripping from his nose; his clothes felt as wet as mashed potato against his skin.

Horns sounded. The needle rested on one hundred and twenty.

Any second now the car would somersault away over the fields. Then smash to bastard scrap.

He could see it coming. Another compartment of his mind clicked in, feeding images of bloody lumps scattered in the dirt. Bloody lumps of meat that had once been his wife, his four-year-old daughter . . .

. . . we leave you with the music of the man who died on that fateful day in 1970.

1970. Richard hunted his memory. Which rock star died in 1970?

Jimi Hendrix . . .

As soon as the name flashed across his brain, the sound of feedback wailed into the car as "Foxy Lady" tore from the speakers.

It was enough to blow through the accumulation of crap that shock had blocked the channels of his head with.

"All I want to know is," Joey screamed, "Who are these people? What are they going to do to us? Can't you—"

"Joey." Richard spoke in a calm but forceful way. "*Shut up*."

"But for fuck's sake, I'm—"

"Shut it, Joey. You're frightening Amy."

Joey shut it, looking stunned.

Then Richard said to the stranger. "At the first opportunity, I'm going to stop the car and telephone the police."

The stranger looked straight at Richard. "It might be too late for that."

"Believe me. That's what I'm doing. Next telephone box I see, I'm phoning the police." As he spoke Richard took his foot off the pedal and slowed the car as it ran down the slip road from the motorway.

The stranger spoke almost gently, "Please. I know you've just had what must be the shock of your life—"

"Now that's an understatement."

"But please just give me ten minutes to tell you what's happening."

Richard shook his head. "We're not interested in what's happening. We just want to go home."

"Believe me when I tell you this: I don't want to merely satisfy your curiosity. I want to tell you something that might stop you—and your family—from getting hurt."

113

Chapter Twenty-two

Huntress

How will I find him?

For Rosemary Snow this seemed the biggest problem, bigger
even than *how shall I kill him?*

Her eyes weren't used to the bright sun. And as she limped
away from the hospital her eyes were nearly screwed shut. The
light reflected from the windscreens of passing cars so brilliantly
they each seemed to contain a chunk of the sun itself. So every
few yards she would have to stop and wipe her streaming eyes.

She managed to walk better than she thought possible after
being unconscious for so long. Maybe this pure hatred for the
stranger powered her legs. Certainly it screened out most of the
pain.

Purposefully she pushed on. The town, unfamiliar to her, bustled busily by, not noticing the girl with the long dark hair, gray
track suit and sandals.

Rosemary had been unable to find her own clothes, so she'd
walked along the hospital corridors in a hospital dressing gown
until she came across the physio department. There she'd found
a locker full of the same gray track suits which she guessed were
the uniforms of the hospital physios. There, she'd also come
across rows of cubicles. Beyond those she'd heard the splash of
water and voices that echoed from tiled walls. That must have
been the physio pool where patients were exercising seized joints
and ligaments.

On impulse she had walked along the line of cubicles. Then,
with no one in sight, she'd opened a door. Inside was a tweedy
skirt, blouse and flat shoes. The kind an elderly woman might
wear. Rosemary saw a handbag hanging from the peg. She'd
opened it. Inside was a face-powder compact, handkerchiefs and
a purse.

114

She needed money. She realized that.

Her hand went to take the purse out of the handbag.

Then, shaking her head, she left the cubicle, the purse untouched.

Sounds came louder from the pool room, as if a door had been opened.

Rosemary limped back the way she had come.

As she passed the last cubicle she paused, then pushed open the door. Hanging from the peg was a man's business suit. Heart beating fast she went through the pockets. Nothing.

Then she saw a pair of black brogues beneath the bench. She lifted a shoe and shook it. It chinked. Inside were car keys and loose change. Quickly she scooped a handful of coins and pocketed them. Then she tried the next shoe. Inside that one, a wallet. Bank notes had been stuffed in so tightly the press-stud catch popped open as she held it in her hand.

Oh, God, please, let that be a sign from you, she thought guiltily as she opened it. She pulled all the cash from the wallet, a great, thick wad that felt absurdly heavy in her trembling hand.

She found she couldn't take all of it, so divided it roughly in half.

Outside voices sounded suddenly loud. Male laughter; a comment about a girl in a swimsuit.

She'd frozen expecting the door of the cubicle to bang open.

Instead the voices passed by. Quickly she stuffed half the money back into the wallet and replaced it in the shoe. Then, gripping the other half of the banknotes in her fist, she walked as calmly as she could out of the cubicle and followed the exit signs.

As she headed into the town center she still felt guilty about taking the money. She'd never stolen before in her life. As she walked she reasoned with herself that she had no choice. That she could never return home. That with this ruined face her life was as good as over. That the only thing that mattered was the death of the man that had done this to her. She knew, also, that an innocent family was in danger and that only she could warn them.

She had thought of going to the police but they'd only send her back to the hospital or back home. In any event they'd get word to her mother and stepfather. The idea of her stepsister grinning at her ruined face filled her with fury.

By the time she'd reached the town center she had a raging

thirst. She bought three cans of Lilt and drank them one after another.

That helped. Her mind sharpened. She knew she had to find the stranger and now her mind turned to how actually to accomplish that.

First she needed to make the necessary preparations. She counted the money. Two hundred and fifteen pounds in notes and another eight pounds in change.

She bought sunglasses, a dark green sweatshirt with a hood, a change of underwear, a pair of cheap trainers, a hand towel, soap, shampoo, a comb, a holdall. Then she bought the biggest carving knife she could find.

Chapter Twenty-three

Fire and Ice

The stranger said: "Here should do fine. Stop the car."

"Are you sure it's safe?" asked Richard.

"It's safe. For the time being."

Richard pulled off a country road into a lay-by and stopped. Thirty yards ahead stood a roadside fast-food caravan. Painted in red letters on the end of the caravan: HANK'S YANKEE DINER. Chalked on a blackboard below that: *Full English Breakfast Our Speciality*.

For a moment they sat without talking. Amy had stopped crying. Richard swung open the door. It only let more hot air in but he breathed it deeply. It had the dusty smell of the sunbaked wheat field over the road. Stiffly, he hauled himself out and rubbed his neck.

The sun pressed down on him like hot metal. Cars ambled by. In the field behind Hank's Yankee Diner cows stood motionless apart from their swinging tails.

Michael, who had been cleaning what remained of the blood from his face with a tissue, climbed out the car. "We might as well grab a drink. We've got time."

Richard glared at the man who was responsible for this hell. Why did he seem so calm again? Richard felt he'd never be able to get his breath back again. He breathed in deeply. The shakes started in his legs.

Michael opened the back door. "We're stopping here for a few minutes." Joey and Christine climbed out blinking into the sunlight. Richard saw they were still dazed by what had happened. Amy, her eyes red and sore-looking, clung tightly to her mother's hand.

Like refugees from a war zone they walked in the direction of the diner. There was no one else about. Only a bored girl chewing

117

gum and reading a magazine in the doorway of the caravan.

A warm breeze briefly stirred two Stars and Stripes flags hanging from twenty-foot poles at each end of the caravan. Beyond the caravan itself was a free-standing canopy about twenty by twenty. Again the canopy itself was a huge Stars and Stripes flag supported by scaffolding poles. Beneath that the red and blue shade looked welcome relief from the sun.

As they sat at a plastic table Amy spotted a play area with swings and a slide. "Mum! Look! Can I go and play?"

Richard looked at her, surprised by her rapid recovery.

"Go on, then," Christine said. "Not too long, though, you might get sunburn."

Richard slumped into the chair. Above him the Stars and Stripes canopy rippled slightly in the waft of air.

As he sat there, shell-shocked, he gazed without seeing at a bowl of sugar lumps. Then he remembered why he'd been standing in the snow, dripping wet, all those years ago.

He blinked and shook his head. For some reason his mind had hidden the memory from him since the day it happened.

Ten years old. He and his friend Daniel Masson had been playing on the frozen lake near Barking Dog Farm. That wasn't its real name, of course. They didn't know the real name. Only that whenever they passed it a dog would run along the farmyard wall barking loud enough to wake the dead.

Richard remembered as clearly as if it had been yesterday.

There had been Danny Masson on the frozen lake, laughing and lobbing snowballs. He couldn't run fast because polio had left him with a wonky foot.

There had been a cracking sound.

And Danny had disappeared.

Richard ran across the ice as near as he dared to the hole.

He saw nothing but black water with big blades of ice stuck at angles this way and that.

He'd called Danny's name and sheer brutal terror had run through him from head to toe like lightning bolts. Tears had rolled down his face.

His friend was dead.

Then he felt a concussion through the soles of his boots. He looked down. Incredibly, a face, as indistinct as a ghost's, filtered through the ice beneath his feet. He could even see wide, staring eyes through that thick skin of ice.

"Danny!"

He didn't think about it. He jumped up and down on the ice. Until, with a crunch, he felt it sag beneath his feet.

Then, suddenly, he was in the freezing water; it flooded chokingly down his throat.

Somehow, and he didn't know how he did it, he hauled his best friend out onto the ice. His friend lay there, his eyes shut; not moving. He was dead. Richard knew it. There was no heartbeat he could feel. No sign of breathing. Just a wet lump of dead skin and clothes lying on that ice.

Sobbing, Richard rolled the body onto the sledge and dragged it across the deserted fields to Danny Masson's house on the edge of town.

Not knowing what to do, at last he simply hauled the sledge up to the front door. Knocked as hard as he could on the door, then ran away.

But he found he couldn't go home. For twenty minutes he walked the streets, sopping wet. It was an evening not long before Christmas. There were carol singers. Children having snowball fights. Dads walking home, whistling, with Christmas trees under their arms. It seemed the whole world was happy. Also the whole world was ignorant of a ten-year-old's terror knowing he'd killed his friend.

At last he couldn't stand it anymore: he'd gone back to Danny Masson's house.

It was dark by then. And that's when he'd stood in the snow watching the lights on the Christmas tree blinking red and green and he'd wondered what terrible events were happening in the house.

He imagined the boy's parents kneeling weeping at Danny's side as he lay in a pool of lake water on the kitchen floor. Upstairs would be Danny's Christmas presents that would never be opened.

More than anything in the world Richard had wanted to go home. But he knew he couldn't. It was his fault that Danny lay cold on the kitchen lino. He had to go and face the boy's parents. Admit everything. Say he was sorry . . .

He'd walked up to the door, knocked hard. Then waited.

It was the longest wait of his life.

And that's when he felt most afraid. Waiting for Danny's

mother to appear, tears streaming down her face. Then he'd have to say the words that frightened him so much:

"I'm sorry, Mrs. Masson. I'm sorry I killed Danny."

He heard shuffling behind the door. A key turned. Then a long, a horribly long pause. Then the door opened.

Richard blinked.

There stood Danny in a black and white Kung Fu dressing gown. His hair still damp. He held a mug of steaming milk in his hand.

"Richard?" He sounded subdued. "I got my new shoes wet. Mum's really pissed off."

Richard hadn't known what he felt. Stunned, he'd turned and walked away.

By some unspoken agreement that bordered on the mystic, they'd never discussed what happened. Richard had seen Daniel Masson five years ago; now a plump little man, he'd launched his own business selling agricultural machinery.

Richard blinked again. In front of him on the table was the bowl full of sugar lumps. His mind on something else, Joey sat eating one sugar lump after another. His heavy bottom lip slid from side to side, then drooped open as another sugar lump reached his mouth.

Now Richard knew why he'd remembered the Danny Masson incident. A: until today it had been the most frightening episode of his life. And B: for twenty years he'd forgotten it had ever happened. And right now he wished he could forget this. But he knew he'd remember it all his life.

"Richard. You'd like a cold drink?" asked Michael.

Richard shook his head. "Coffee. Black."

When the girl came to take the order Michael sat the rucksack on his knee and rested his forearms casually on top of that, covering the bloodstains on his white shirt. He switched on the charming smile as he talked to the girl who, Richard saw, was clearly attracted to the man. She blushed and smiled as she wrote the order on the pad.

Richard glanced at the rucksack. Packed so full of something the material was stretched tight, Michael was keeping a tight grip on it. What was so important in there? Clothes? A sleeping bag? For Christsakes, it might be stuffed tight with Ecstasy tabs for all they knew.

Across at the play area Amy had made an amazing recovery.

She sat on a horse set into the ground on a spring and rocked violently backward and forward shouting, "Boys! Follow me, Boys!"

Perhaps she's forgotten what happened already, thought Richard. *Like I forgot what happened when Danny Masson fell through the ice*. Perhaps she'd recall what happened in Pontefract under hypnosis when she was forty-something; when a fondness for the gin had got the better of her.

The coffee arrived and he took a scalding mouthful. He watched Christine sipping hers. She studied the stranger's face as if she was trying to read his mind. Joey looked at his surroundings with a bewildered cast to his brown eyes which made Richard think of a cow stuck in a hole and not knowing what the hell had happened to it; or how the hell it could climb out. Joey took a mouthful of coffee that burnt his mouth. He grunted and looked around as if not knowing what had hurt him. "Shit . . . I'm getting something to eat." He heaved himself to his feet, then headed unsteadily for the fast-food trailer.

"He'll come around soon enough," Michael said. "It's been quite a shock for all of us."

"*Quite a shock*," echoed Christine. "Christ, that wins first prize for understatement."

Richard was still thinking of terms of gangsters with a grudge. "What did they use? Grenade launchers? I mean that car just . . ." Descriptions failing him, he finished the sentence with a gesture of bewilderment.

Michael smiled compassionately, his gentle downturned eyes constantly flicking from Richard to Christine. "No. Nothing like that."

"But what, then . . . there must have been a bomb . . . the car exploded like—"

"No," the man interrupted. "*Im*ploded. Think what happened. The car did not *ex*plode. It *im*ploded. It was crushed by an external force."

Richard remembered. The man was right. He'd realized that himself. "But what did—"

"Wait until Joey returns. It'll save me having to explain twice."

As Richard worked his way steadily through the coffee the world began to look more normal. His mind didn't feel as if it had been yanked somewhere half through his skull anymore. He looked round, seeing the fast-food trailer with Joey standing at

121

the counter; Amy now climbed the slide steps; someone had defaced a menu with a ballpoint pen: instead of *Hank's Yankee Diner* it read *Hank's Wankee Diner*. Sparrows, their eyes as bright as glass beads, hopped around the tables, pecking crumbs.

Joey returned with a plate stacked with four hotdogs. He squirted a thick stream of mustard over them. Then he began to eat like he'd not touched food in three days.

Michael placed the rucksack carefully at the side of his chair. Then he leaned forward, forearms resting on the table, hands clasped together. "I wouldn't blame you if you ditched me here and ran to the police."

Richard looked up. "That's exactly what I've got in mind." He drained his coffee and stood up. "And that's exactly what I'm going to do. Christine, Joey. Come on, back to the car."

Michael leaned forward. "Listen. If you did that there's a distinct chance you'd all be dead within the next thirty minutes."

Richard shook his head. "Come on, Christine, we're leaving. And you, whoever you are—you're staying."

"Richard. You saw what happened to the car?" Michael looked him straight in the eye. "That could happen to you."

Chapter Twenty-four

Michael's Story

Richard sat down. Amy was shouting: "Boys! Not up the green steps. Follow me up the blue steps." He needed another coffee.

"Listen," said Michael. "I want to get to a police station as much as you do. But it's only fair to warn you that it might not be as easy as you think."

Christine's shrewd eyes watched the man's face. "What do you mean? Do you think whoever's chasing you is somehow keeping watch on local police stations?"

"No. Not exactly, Mrs. Young. There is the chance you—"

"Well, what the fuck *do* you mean, then?" Joey spoke through a mouthful of hotdog. "What's going to stop us?"

Michael looked at his watch. "Look, give me ten minutes to explain. Then you make up your minds. You can leave me here and go to the nearest police station. Or you can decide to take me with you."

"Leave you damn-well here," Joey grunted. "Sooner the bloody better."

"Ssh, Joey," Christine leaned forward. "If he's saying we might be in danger it's best we hear what he has to say first. Agreed?"

Richard nodded. Joey snorted and leaned back in his chair, wanting no part of it.

"This won't take long, I promise. Then—"

"You've been promising a lot," Joey snapped. "You've delivered bugger-all."

"I'll tell you what I know. Then you decide. Leave me. Or take me with you to the police."

"Go on, then," Christine said. "You've got ten minutes."

"I was born in Cambridge. My father was a hospital administrator and I grew up in a—"

Joey snorted. "I don't bloody believe it!"

123

"Please—"

"He's telling us his life story. The next thing you know he'll—"

"If I can ask you to just give me ten minutes. Without any interruptions or questions. It's important I tell you what I know."

"But—"

"Please, Joey. I don't know how much longer we can stay here."

That shut Joey up. He looked around uncomfortably as if expecting to see snipers stalking among the cows in the field.

"As I was saying. I was brought up in a safe, middle-class family. When I was eighteen I rebelled. With two of my friends I left for Greece. We were going to set up a scuba diving school. Of course, we were as green as that grass over there . . ."

The man continued in that softly-spoken way. He moved his hands as he talked, in slow gestures that were graceful, even calming. Richard suddenly found the man familiar. Then he made the connection. The realization surprised him. No, it wasn't so much his looks. It was his manner; the slow, calming gestures as if he were an artist making long, slow sweeps across an invisible canvas; the compassionate eyes. The man sitting across the table from him reminded him of movie portrayals of Christ. The softly-spoken words; the slow gestures; the permanent expression of compassion as if he cared deeply for those around him.

And, as the man spoke in a softer and softer voice, Richard, Christine and Joey found themselves leaning farther and farther forward as if afraid to miss a single word.

"The diving school ended in disaster. Our equipment was stolen; insurers wouldn't pay; my friends became, to put it mildly, dispirited. They returned home. I felt I couldn't. I'd lose face. Eventually I left Greece and headed for Turkey. There I lived little better than a beggar. I became thin, shabby and depressed. I couldn't speak more than a few words of the language. To the locals I was the strange Englishman who looked like a drug addict.

"My life went from bad to worse. One night as I walked to a nearby town I was jumped by some thugs. They beat me, then dumped me into a ditch. Half dead, I dragged myself out, aching all over, blood running from a gash in my head like it was on tap.

"I made it as far as this old shell of a building that stood on a hillside. It must have been used as a stable. The floor was a

124

mixture of dirt and I guess six hundred years' worth of goat dung. The building itself was an old Byzantine church, complete with domed roof. When the Muslims conquered the place in 1453 a lot of the old Christian churches were recycled as warehouses, grain stores or even somewhere dry to keep your goats. Anyway, by this time I could no more make it home then fly to Mars. I was throwing up, and my temperature shot up like a rocket. Some bug, I think, had worked its way into my bloodstream through the cuts.

"Soon I was completely out of it. My body felt hot enough to fry eggs. I was crying and laughing. The whole delirious bit. I was holding conversations with the Archangel Gabriel about Divinity, Moses in a basket, chicken in a basket, Charlie Chaplin, you name it. Then I'd hallucinate about Hitler or Donald Duck or ghosts. Then I'd believe the floor had turned into chocolate and I'd crawl along eating this goat dung like it was the sweetest thing in the world.

"It must have been then." Michael fixed each in turn with his brown eyes. "It must have been then that it happened . . . Now, looking back, I can only think of it as the miracle. It transformed me. Later it transformed the lives of others. One day, God willing, it will transform the lives of everyone." He gave a faint smile. "I'm getting ahead of myself. Anyway, for day after day I crawled about that derelict chapel, shouting, screaming, laughing. Sometimes I'd stand at the door and look down through the almond grove, at the blossom looking like white snow on the branches in the moonlight, and I'd think I saw an army of men in gold armor looking up at me. With my brain hot enough to cook from the fever I believed they'd come for their orders. So I told them, go forth, conquer cities, bring back gold." He smiled and shook his head. "Believe me, I was out of my skull."

Then his face became serious. "But soon after that I was lying in the corner of the church, balled up tight on some old gravestones; shivering and groaning because I hurt all over. Then I looked up. This time I saw something, but I didn't feel as if I was hallucinating. Even though I suppose I must've been. I remember seeing this man. It seemed as vivid as I see you now. He walked across the church to me. And I remember seeing every detail. He was dressed in a purple robe. I even remember his boots. They were purple, too. And each bore the motif of a double-headed eagle. He had a long beard and mustache with the

125

ends so long they drooped down to his chest. He walked up closer, then looked down at me. It was shocking. I even stopped breathing. Because he had the fiercest eyes you've ever seen in your life. So sharp they seemed to stab right through into the back of your head. Then he asked me this:

"Do you want power?

More precisely, do you want power over people?

Do you want the power to command someone to die for you?

And for that power to be so absolute, so complete, that they not only die for you willingly, they go to their deaths so full of joy, so full of pride that they cry out your name with their final breath.

Do you want that power?

Do you?"

" 'Yes! Yes!' I remember shouting. 'Yes! Yes! That's what I want!'

"I shouted so loud that my voice echoed off the walls like thunder; the bats started flying until it seemed like a black cloud had filled the church.

"I remember the stone floor became soft as rubber. Then it curved up at me. For a moment I thought someone was inflating it like a balloon. Then I fainted and slammed down cold onto it.

"The hallucinations continued. Men and women walked into the church. I gave them orders. To bring me food and drink mainly; then they went away again."

His brown eyes met theirs, each in turn. Then he looked far away to the horizon shimmering in heat haze. "Bizarre story, mmm? Now I want to tell you I don't believe in ghosts. I don't believe in fairies, or astrology, or the prophecies of Nostradamus, he was a flake and a fake. I don't believe Spiritualists who claim they can see your late Uncle Abraham, and that he's here to warn you not to buy anymore ice cream because he knows your freezer's going to go kaput next Friday. I don't believe the spirits of the dead come back in any shape or form. However . . ." He looked back at them again, his face serious. "But I do believe there are far more things in our universe that we do not recognize yet. Phenomena that are perfectly natural but, equally, perfectly astonishing. And I believe that as I lay half dead in that broken-down old church something entered into me. I actually felt it. I felt it move from outside of me, in through my skull, and move into the back of my head. And it stayed there. No . . ." He smiled gently. "I'm not completely mad. Although I will admit to being a little bit mad." The smile became a grin. "We're all a little mad. After all, it would be a living hell to be totally sane."

Again, he gave that disarming smile. "One fine Turkish morning I woke up. God, I felt this change inside of me. I knew, also, the virus had gone. Although I was a bit shaky on my feet, I felt rational, healthy. I sat there where the altar must have been and I remembered all the weird hallucinations, my giving ghostly figures orders. But then I noticed all around me were plates and bowls, plastic cups, mugs; they'd clearly had food and drink in them. There were blankets. Set around me in a big circle were old Coca Cola bottles with candles stuck in the top. A few still burning.

"For a minute I just sat and stared, then I noticed movement in the doorway. Outside it was brilliant sunshine. And I could see what looked like a farmer and his family, old folk with wrinkled faces, some children, and a pretty girl with her hair beneath a headscarf. They were peering around the doorway like they'd come across a werewolf in their stable. They looked scared to death. But, this is the odd bit. They were fascinated, too. I looked down at myself and I realized they couldn't take their eyes off me because I was caked head to foot with goat dung. It stuck my hair down like glue.

"Then before I could stop myself I said: 'Clothes. I need clothes.'

"That did it. They just ran like hell. Nice one, Michael, I told myself. You've just gone and scared your Good Samaritans away. Now they'll bring the police and you'll end up on a trespass charge.

"Well, I was wrong. In a couple of hours they were back with brand new clothes, still in plastic wrappers. They looked a poor lot and they must have spent their last few lira on them.

"I thanked them but said I needed to wash first.

"And in this odd way, almost bowing and walking backward, they asked me to follow them. We went out through the doorway and around the side of the church. There, the hill fell away almost like a cliff. I followed them down the steps, then this old guy says, 'I'm very sorry. We thought how we could make the water warm for you, but we couldn't think how.'

"By this time I was completely bemused. At the bottom of the cliff, directly under the church in a cave, was what looked to be a stone coffin. Water ran in at one end from a spring and trickled out the other. They'd spread out rushes to make a big mat around the thing, and there were towels so I thought what the hell. I felt good . . . no, I felt better than that. I felt like someone who'd just found a pot of gold in their back garden. The water in the stone coffin looked pure enough to drink. So in I went. My God, it was cold. Not that I minded. After I'd bathed I dressed in the white shirt, trousers and shoes they'd bought me." Michael shrugged. "Then I moved in with them. And I knew . . . I knew as I know this table here is real that something had entered into me in that church. Something that gave me the power to enthuse people. To inspire them. But I also knew this: although I had that power I also realized I had a responsibility toward them. They'd do anything for me. So I knew I had to improve their lives.

"They owned some poor arable land near a crossroads. I saw that it would make valuable building land. They told me that the government wouldn't allow building there. But from that day on I felt this supreme self-confidence. So I walked into the government offices with a roll of building plans under my arm and told them I was going to sell part of the land to raise capital, on the rest I'd build a factory. They said yes so quickly I thought it was a joke before they threw me out.

"But it wasn't a joke. They gave me government grants to improve the access roads. We built the factory. Then, on land on the coast, we built one hotel after another. Within one year, whenever I went to the bank the manager himself would run out and open the door. Our income came in so fast we couldn't even count it. I built new houses for my Good Samaritan family, with a pool, and rooms for domestic staff. I even had the church on the hill restored and the dome covered in gold leaf."

"Yeah," Joey grunted, "so you learned you could boss some piss-poor peasants about."

Christine said quickly, "And you expect us to believe that you've been possessed by some kind of spirit that allows you to have total control over people?"

"Not control. That makes me sound like a tyrant. I like to think of it as the power to inspire. To be able to outline a proposal or plan to someone and make them enthusiastic about it."

"OK, let's not split hairs, but you're telling us that some kind of . . . entity moved into your head?"

Michael nodded. "It's not easy. But think for a moment about theories relating to animal development. More than two thousand years ago Plato and Aristotle developed ideas of how life on Earth was created. Then the Western civilized world believed they were true. Later came the Christians with their own beliefs on the creation of life. For centuries Christendom believed that was the truth and nothing but the truth. Then came the beginnings of modern science. In seventeenth-century France, Lamarck suggested animals gradually evolved into higher forms over thousands of years. Some believed his ideas were true. Then came Darwin with a far more powerful theory of evolution. Today Darwin's theory is accepted as fact by most." The man smiled. "But don't you bet your bottom dollar that in a few years along will come a new evolution theory and we'll all say, my God, how can we have believed that primitive Darwinist stuff?"

Joey snorted. "But what's this got to do with—"

"Got to do with what flattened the car in Pontefract this morning?" Michael raised his eyebrows. "It's got everything to do with it. With the example of various theories of evolution all I'm trying to illustrate is that what one generation will believe as fact the next generation might dismiss as claptrap. And what this generation might consider impossible, the next might find perfectly natural." The man scooped some crumbs from the table and threw them to the sparrows which fluttered around his feet. "What many people might find hard to believe in today is that whatever entered my head in that ruined church in Turkey is the same thing that destroyed the car. And is following us now."

Joey and Christine looked sharply at the man. Richard glanced uneasily in the direction of Amy, now sitting on a tire swing.

He remembered when Mark was six. The boy wasn't well and for an agonizing three weeks doctors speculated he might have leukemia. Richard, not normally credulous, had become painfully superstitious overnight. Desperately worried Mark might have the disease, Richard began to behave in a completely irrational way; he'd find himself standing watching a kettle boil, thinking, 'If I stand and watch it from the moment I put it on the hob until it actually boils, everything will be all right and Mark's tests will come back negative.' He even came across his dead father-in-law's watch in the attic and carefully wound it up. As if, deep down, he hoped it possessed magic powers. That if he could keep the old man's watch going it would supernaturally keep the leukemia cells out of his son's body.

129

The tests did prove negative. The doctors assured Richard and Christine that Mark suffered from no more than anemia. Richard later found himself chuckling over his idiotic superstitious practices. But, deep down, he had believed that, however absurd they might appear, they were somehow true. And now he couldn't shake off that same feeling. That what Michael had said was the stone cold, incontrovertible truth.

Christine frowned. "But how can this thing—"

The birds pecking at their feet took off as one, their wings beating the air.

Michael looked up. Above their heads the Stars and Stripes canopy moved sluggishly in the breeze. A truck droned by on the road.

Richard's eyes met Christine's and he knew she was alarmed.

"Did anyone feel that?" Michael asked.

"Feel what?"

"That someone-just-walked-over-my-grave feeling." Michael looked at the horizon, eyes narrowing against the sun's glare.

Christine asked "What's happening?"

"It's OK," Michael said soothingly. "I don't want to worry anyone, but I think we should be making a move."

Joey was first out of his seat.

"Leave him here," spat Joey. "He knows all about this thing. Leave him to it."

"We've plenty of time," Michael said. "Nothing will happen for twenty minutes or more yet."

Richard shot him a look. "Happen?"

"Once we're back in the car we can talk to our heart's content."

"I'll get Amy," said Christine.

As they walked back to the car Richard saw Joey anxiously looking this way and that. Richard scanned the horizon. The heat-haze distorted everything, until he could imagine that even the trees were massive figures stalking hungrily toward them.

And in the fast-food trailer the girl had begun to sing softly to herself the hymn "Jerusalem" as she wiped down the counter:

"And did those feet in ancient times, walk upon England's pastures green . . ."

Chapter Twenty-five

Vision

The swings and slide looked as if they were made for the children of giants. But Rosemary Snow saw everything clear as day in the brilliant sunlight. A fast-food trailer beside a country road. Cows in a field. A canopy in a Stars and Stripes design, supported by steel poles to provide shade for diners. Occasionally it would undulate slowly in the slight breeze. White tables and chairs. Then she saw a pair of little suntanned hands in front of her face. They gripped the rail that ran either side of the slide steps. As she climbed she heard a voice shouting:

"Boys! Amy says come up here! Amy says, down the slide. Boys! This way. Don't push or I'll tell that cow to bite you!"

Beneath the awning sat the family she'd seen before. They looked unhappy. Then she saw the stranger. That same phoney smile as he talked. She—

She awoke with a start, lifting her head as she did so. The right-hand side of her face pulled painfully tight. She felt the crust of scabs and thread that stitched her cheek back to her face.

"Here." The voice was kind. "You dropped this."

She opened her eyes. She must have fallen asleep on the shopping precinct bench. Shielding her eyes, she saw a good-looking boy of about seventeen. He held out her holdall.

"Oh, thank you. I must have . . ." Her voice faded as she saw the expression on his face that said it all. "Hey," he'd been thinking as he roller-booted along the precinct, "Great-looking girl on the bench. She's dropped her holdall. Chance to get acquainted there." Then she'd seen him recoil.

From beneath all that sexy hair appeared a mask of scabs set with two bloodshot eyes. *Gross!*

Forcing a smile, he muttered, "Don't mention it," and roller-booted away.

Rosemary shouldered the bag, slipped on the sunglasses and walked away, head down. *Forget it*, she told herself. *Forget what you look like, you've got a job to do.*

She'd seen through the little girl's eyes. Somehow the stranger had got his hooks into the family just as he'd hooked her. He had plans for them, she knew that. And she knew it wouldn't be pleasant.

As she walked in the hot sun, a shiver ran through her. And the title of a book she'd once read came vividly to her. *Something Wicked This Way Comes.*

She stopped dead, shivering again from head to toe. The thing that had chased her across that field now followed the family. Her Destroyer.

Ahead, a sign pointed in the direction of the railway station. She followed it, shivering again and again. And all she could think of was the title of that book:

Something Wicked This Way Comes . . .

Chapter Twenty-six

Police

As Christine buckled Amy into the backseat Richard happened to look into the rearview mirror.

Then a wonderful thing happened.

Quickly he glanced away from the mirror. He didn't want Michael, sitting beside him, to notice he'd seen something that sent his mind racing. This whole shitty situation would end here and now.

Because Richard had seen a police car pull off the road into the lay-by. It parked between the fast-food trailer and the Stars and Stripes canopy. And from this position the fast-food trailer now blocked Michael's line of sight. He couldn't see the police car.

Richard said, "I forgot to get Amy a drink."

"Buy her one later," Michael said as he buckled the seat belt. "We need to be moving on."

Damn, thought Richard. He saw his plan go up in smoke.

"She'll need a drink," Christine insisted. "She'll flake out if she gets too warm."

Michael rubbed his jaw, thinking, then looked back at the horizon, as if expecting to see something come striding above the treetops. "All right," he said quickly. "Don't dawdle. We need to be leaving here in the next couple of minutes."

As Richard opened the door Joey grabbed his shoulder from the backseat. "Hey, if that thing's coming this way, forget it. She can have a drink later. I don't—"

"Joey," Richard spoke in a low voice. "I thought you didn't believe in it. If it's not real, it can't hurt you."

"Hey, I didn't say that, Richard." Fear jittered his voice. "I only said—"

"Take it easy," Michael soothed. "We've plenty of time. I just don't want to go breaking any speed limits."

"So, I've got time to buy Amy a drink?"

"Sure . . . just don't hang around, that's all."

"I'm thirsty, Dad," Amy called.

"It's OK, honey. I'll be right back. Fruit juice OK?"

"Yes, please."

Richard walked back to the fast-food trailer. The girl had started to fry beefburgers on the hotplates in front of her. For a moment he thought the cops had walked off somewhere, then he saw them in the shade of the canopy. They were both eating ice creams while they waited for their burgers. One wiped his bald head with a handkerchief that looked big enough to swaddle a baby in.

My God, he thought, *you two are in for a surprise when I tell you what happened this morning.* As he bought Amy a carton of black currant juice he felt a trickle of something that felt almost like elation. He'd solved the problem of how to get out of this mess—and get rid of the stranger. Sooner or later questions would be asked. And already the implications were beginning to hit him. Why, the police would ask, just why did you run from the explosion in Pontefract this morning? No, he put that line of thought into the back of his mind. They were home and dry. In a couple of hours he could be slapping a couple of steaks onto the barbecue while drenching his throat with an ice-cold beer.

Pocketing the change and holding the carton in one hand he walked by the police car. The two cops were laughing over some joke as they spooned the ice cream.

At the edge of the canopy Richard cleared his throat to attract their attentions.

They looked up.

But they didn't look up at Richard.

They looked directly up at the canopy above their head.

It rippled like a sheet on a washing line.

Then the fabric snapped tight as if something had fallen on top of it.

Richard looked back at the two policeman, sitting there with their tubs of ice cream in their hands. Both stared up in surprise, their mouths open.

Then, with a crack, the Stars and Stripes snapped from its mountings. The poles crumpled like coat-hanger wire.

134

Richard instinctively leaped back so far his backside slammed against the police car.

He couldn't take his eyes off what was happening in front of him.

The still summer morning had become a maelstrom of rushing air, dust blasted up from the ground, stinging his face as the air was displaced by some massive object as it crashed down upon the canopy. Metal poles shrieked.

The canopy had dropped squarely down. Richard could see the shapes of tables, chairs and the two policemen below the fabric. They struggled to pull it off them.

Then, as Richard watched, the fabric became tight almost as if a huge steel sheet was pressing it flat. Tables and chairs shattered beneath the weight. The two men were pressed down hard. Richard saw the two squirming human shapes beneath.

Weight increased . . .

. . . pressing down . . .

. . . down . . .

Then the lumps beneath the canvas flattened.

Richard slid along the car sideways, then backed along the path toward the fast-food trailer. Still he couldn't take his eyes off the flag. Without a crease in it, it looked as if the damn thing had just been ironed. Red stripes. The blue oblong, containing the white stars. Then he noticed that, one by one, the stars were turning red.

A wet red that spread, soaking the white stars. It kept on seeping outward like a red dye across litmus paper filling in the white stripes with a deep, wet crimson.

Richard would have stayed there. But a plastic waste bin gave a tremendous *pop* and flattened.

He kept moving backward.

One second later, the police car rocked once, then it collapsed in on itself, suspension groaning, tires rupturing with ear-battering explosions. The car mashed flat. Steam from the hot engine whistled out in a thin jet high into the blue sky.

He froze. Because he realized he had perhaps half-a-dozen seconds before whatever crushed the car crushed him, too.

The moment she saw the pictures on the TV sets in the shop window she knew what had happened.

She limped in through the door, the holdall on her shoulder, and turned up the sound of one of the sets.

"... mysterious explosion rocked a quiet Pontefract car park this morning. The incident has left police baffled. No terrorist group has claimed responsibility for the bombing at the moment; however, police suspect ..."

Rosemary studied the close-ups of the wrecked car cordoned off behind tape. Then came more shots of flattened car park signs and a crushed ticket machine.

She didn't need to see any more. Now she had a destination: Pontefract.

Richard saw death.

Just ten paces from him it was coming his way.

The Stars and Stripes canopy lay crushed on the ground. Then the police car—now no part of it even reached knee height.

Crack!

A Walls ice cream sign flattened eight paces from him.

Something rolled the parched grass to dust. It came nearer.

He turned. And he ran.

First he reached the fast-food trailer. He had to get the girl out of there. Or she'd be ground to paste beneath whatever followed him.

But she'd got a strong fix of self-preservation of her own. She'd seen what had happened and slithered butt-first toward the service counter. First she slid across the hot plates, bare palms sizzling alongside the burgers, kicking bread rolls, canned drink stacks in front of her.

Then she slid out over the counter, dropped to the ground. And she ran like hell; faster than Richard. Instead of heading to the car she cut off behind the trailer, vaulted the fence and belted across the field, scattering cows in front of her, her Stars and Stripes apron flapping.

Richard ran hard at the car, shouting ... God knows what he was shouting, just a sheer bloody howl that was terror and warning and shock all mixed into one.

He glanced back. Like the hammer of God something he could not see plunged out of a clear blue sky.

To hit the fast-food trailer. It vanished in a blur of white shards. Gas bottles ruptured, ignited, and a ball of flame the size of a house mushroomed into the sky.

Christ . . .

Then he saw the grass flatten behind the wrecked fast-food trailer; the swings and slide *screeeeee-ched* flat to the ground.

It's not following me anymore. It doesn't want me, he thought, panting. *It's chasing the girl.*

She's dead.

Although he could not see it, he could see the trail it left, crushing plants, smashing fences, pulping trees.

Cows blundered wildly away.

Too slow.

He saw one cow, then another, pop like ripe tomatoes.

Then he saw the path it crushed through the grass curve back toward the lay-by. It had sensed the human it pursued wasn't Richard Young.

Christ. A pang hit him in the stomach. *Oh Christ. It wants* me.

The red Volvo nearly hit him.

Joey's red face appeared in the side window. He screamed, "Get in!"

He slammed himself into the passenger seat. The car jerked, pushing him back into the seat, tires ripped at Tarmac, they were bouncing in an arc over a strip of grass between lay-by and road, then they were powering away from it all. Richard looked back, almost paralyzed with shock. The trailer, a jumble of plywood, plastic and cooking oil, burned, smearing an otherwise perfect blue sky with filthy-looking smoke.

For the first time he realized Michael was driving.

Richard looked down at his clenched fists. One was running with red. After the third attempt he managed to unclench his fist. And he saw he still held the carton of blackcurrant. Only at some point he'd crushed it until it ruptured.

Michael glanced sideways at Richard. This time there was no smile, only a deeply troubled look.

Richard groaned. "What the hell was that?"

"It's what I was afraid of." He looked at Richard. "You've become infected, too."

Chapter Twenty-seven

Cat and Mouse

"Infected?" said Richard. "Exactly what to you mean by *infected?*"

Michael accelerated into the motorway's fast lane. "I mean you're infected. You're all infected like me."

Richard turned to look at Christine in the backseat. With one arm around Amy she leaned forward to hear what Michael was saying. Joey looked as if what he'd seen and heard had been too much to get his head round. Face as white as paper, he leaned back staring at the car's ceiling with eyes so deepset they looked like a pair of bullet holes.

Christine said, "So this thing will follow us? It'll—"

"It'll do to us . . ." When Richard spoke the words didn't come easily. "It'll do to us what it did to those two cops back there?"

Michael nodded, his eyes on the road ahead.

"Jesus . . ." Richard whispered. "I was responsible for that. If I hadn't gone back to buy that drink they'd still be alive."

"If anyone's to blame," Michael said, "It's me. I should have seen it coming. Well, to be precise, *sensed* it coming. But I didn't." Troubled, he rubbed his jaw with the back of his hand. "I should have realized. But it's changing . . . evolving . . . it's become unpredictable."

"Look," said Christine, eager for the truth. "You've told us we're infected. By that I take it we've got to keep moving or it will catch up with us."

"Correct."

"But how do we get rid of it?"

The man looked at her in the rearview mirror. "We don't."

Richard clenched his fist. "But what the hell *is* it?"

"To explain fully," Michael said, "I'd need to sit you down at a desk and talk to you for six months. But, in a nutshell, it is

POWER. It is the power that emperors and kings have used for thousands of years; it was probably used by prehistoric war lords before the last Ice Age when men lived in caves and wrapped themselves in animal skins." He looked sideways at Richard. "This power is a separate entity. A lifeform as individual as an elephant or a fish. In that church in Turkey it passed into me. From that day on I found I had this power to inspire anyone I met. It was when I attempted to bring that power to Britain that it all went wrong."

"How?"

"Its natural habitat is the Eastern end of the Mediterranean. Now it's separated itself from me. And I'm guessing here, but I think it wants to go back?"

"So, do what it wants. Take it back."

"I only wish to God I could." Michael gave a tired smile. "That's why it's pursuing me. But there's no way I can communicate with it. The thing's like a raging bull."

"What are we going to do? We can't drive around the country forever."

"I know. Don't worry, I've got some people working on it. They'll come up with an answer soon."

"An answer? You mean you can—"

"Please, Richard. We need to sit down and talk this through when our minds are clear. Then I'll explain whatever I can. At the moment, though, this is a bloody dangerous situation."

Christine said, "But we're safe if we can keep driving?"

"Yes."

"But what about stopping to sleep? Buy petrol?"

"And what if we end up stuck in a traffic jam?" asked Richard.

Michael shrugged. "Pray that we don't."

"Look," Richard said. "We can solve this easy. Drive to the nearest police station."

Michael shook his head. "You're not thinking this through, Richard. You saw what happened in Pontefract and at the lay-by. If we go to the police they're going to put us through some pretty rigorous questioning. So we're going to be confined to one location. What happens when that thing comes? Do you say, "Sorry, can't answer anymore questions, I've got to run like hell now?" No. They'll keep us there; under lock and key if necessary. And that's where we'll die. With everyone else in the police station, too."

"Christ, this is a nightmare."

"Yes, it *is* a nightmare." Michael spoke calmly. "But we'll get through this if you do exactly as I say."

Christine sighed. "I don't suppose we have a choice."

"You don't," Michael agreed. "These are the facts: one, you're infected. If anyone tries to go their own way, it'll find you and kill you. Simple as that. Therefore, two: we must stick close together at all times. Three: it's likely the police have linked this red Volvo with the two incidents this morning. We have to assume that they will be looking for us now. If only, as they so reassuringly put it, to eliminate us from their enquiries." He glanced back at Christine through the mirror. "So, again, we must assume that basically we are now on the run from the police as well. We mustn't allow ourselves to be stopped by the police. If we fail, the thing that follows us will kill us and it will kill them."

"This thing . . . this . . . power. Does it have a name?"

Michael smiled. "No. Not as such. But I think of it as "the Beast."

"The Beast? Christ, that's reassuring as hell."

In the passenger seat, Richard turned to look back at Amy. She stared forward, statue-still, her eyes glassy and tired-looking. Four years old. Already she was on the run from the police. And running from something they could not see, but that might stamp the life from them in the next ten seconds.

"Don't worry," Michael said soothingly. "I've been outrunning this thing for the last five weeks. As I said, I have a team of people working on a solution. As soon as we have that you can go home."

Richard licked his dry lips. "Well, you better come up with something in the next five minutes."

The man shot him a puzzled look.

Richard nodded at the petrol gauge. "Because any minute now we're going to run out of petrol."

Chapter Twenty-eight

Shadow Thoughts

The train clunked over a level crossing. Even this slight jolt rocked Rosemary's head enough to raise pain, flaring from the stitched wound on the side of her face.

Drowsily she opened her eyes. Sunlight burst in brilliant flashes from greenhouses in gardens.

Although Pontefract lay just twenty minutes away, she found it hard to stay awake. Her wasted muscles were exhausted from the walk from the hospital to the station.

Now as she drifted in and out of sleep on the train she found herself looking through the little girl's eyes again. The images made little sense. A roadside diner. A tire swing. Climbing frame. The roadside diner bursting like a balloon, spraying bread rolls and broken glass onto the road. A wrecked car. Brilliant sunshine. A child's climbing frame. A police car. Her father running. Her father? No, not Rosemary's father. But she knew it was the girl's father. The girl called . . . Amy. That was it. Amy Young, age four, with a brother, and a taste for toffee ice cream and Tom and Jerry cartoons.

Now, in the back of a car, she sat between her mother and a man. Amy's mother leaned forward talking urgently to someone in the front seat. Her hair blew back in the breeze from the open window.

The other man by her side looked ill. He rested his head back and stared up at the car's ceiling. He had a face that was so heavy with flesh it wobbled as the car rode over bumps.

Rosemary sensed the little girl's fear.

The train jolted again. Rosemary winced at the pull of the stitches in her face. She opened her eyes. Just in front of her the carriage ended in a wall of plastic laminate, on which had been printed a mural showing paintings of local scenes. There were the cooling towers of a power station, Wakefield Cathedral, a shopping mall, a castle ruin.

As she stared drowsily at it her eyes slipped out of focus. She heard the stranger's voice saying over and over: "I was afraid this would happen. You're infected, too . . . you're infected, too . . . you're infected, too . . ."

In front of her, the mural seemed to grow transparent. As if the ruined castle and church were painted on dark glass. She imagined she could see a shape moving beyond it.

Her Destroyer.

The rhythm of steel wheels on the track and her own weariness lulled her into a state that was hypnotic.

Beyond the laminate panel the shadow moved. Now, and without any sense of surprise, she knew it had always been like this. The world she'd known: the world of cars, houses, streets, schools, factories, supermarkets, parks, tables, kitchens . . . the world was like that thin laminate panel with its painted castle and church and power station. Behind those familiar images was another world, a world that was at the same time weirdly unfamiliar, and yet familiar in a way that was disturbing—even frightening. A world where some shadowy form prowled restlessly backward and forward.

As she dozed she found herself pitched back a dozen years or more to a springtime morning when her father had taken her out to sea in his boat. They must have been a mile off shore when he called her in a hushed voice, "Rosie . . . Rosie. Quick! Look what's down there."

He pointed down into the water. She looked but could see nothing but bubbles and a stalk of seaweed floating by.

"No, Rosemary. Don't look at the surface of the water. You have to look beyond it. Like you're looking through a window. Quick! Or you'll miss it."

She'd looked down through the water. Then she'd caught her breath.

A shape, as big as a car but dark as a shadow, slipped smoothly beneath the surface and under the boat. Then, still no more than a shadow beneath the glassy surface of the sea, it slowly circled them.

"What is it?"

"It's big," her father had said. "It might be a dolphin. Or a shark."

"A shark?"

"Could be." Then he'd smiled and put his arm around her. "Don't worry. You're safe up here in the boat."

She had felt safe with his arm around her as they watched the circling shadow.

But as she gazed at the mural in front of her, and imagined another darker, more menacing shadow, swimming through a world beyond this one, she felt anything but safe.

Chapter Twenty-nine

Running on Empty

"Believe me," Richard said in a low voice. "I've run this car three years. If that gauge says the tank's empty, then you can take my word for it—*it's empty*."

Michael dropped the car's speed to sixty and cruised along the slow lane.

Michael said, "Even with the gauge registering empty a car's usually good for a gallon or so."

"Not this one. It caught me out the first week I bought it. I had to walk home from town."

"Damn," Michael whispered, his eyes scanning ahead. "We'll have to risk pulling in at the next services."

"You'll be lucky." Joey spoke in a fear-dried voice. "We've just passed a sign. The next motorway services aren't for another fifteen miles."

Richard said, "It'll be a miracle to get another five miles out of it."

Christine leaned forward. "Michael. How do you know this thing is near? We might have left it behind at that lay-by."

"No such luck. It'll follow us like a hunting dog."

"You can see it now?"

"No. I can't see it. I can sense it. It feels like a dozen electric shocks running across my skin. You see, it sucks up a lot of static as it moves."

Joey sounded bewildered. "And you've never seen this thing?"

"No, but if you like, you can hear it." Michael switched on the radio. An old Beach Boys song rolled from the speakers. Michael turned the tuning control to take it off station, then he turned the volume up full. The sound of static hissed loudly then faded . . . louder again . . . then faded.

Michael's hands tightened on the wheel. "Hear it? I told you it carried a static charge. When it gets close you can switch on a radio or television and you can hear it. Sounds like a heartbeat, doesn't it?"

"Then why," asked Christine, "why didn't you sense it approaching back at the lay-by?"

"I did. I only misjudged how close it was."

"But if what you say is true, you've lived with this thing, the Beast, you called it, for the last twenty years?"

"In Turkey, yes. Not here in Britain. It's becoming unstable . . . unpredictable. I think it's changing."

"Can we go home now, Mum?"

Richard glanced back at Amy. Her eyes were big and tired-looking as if she was coming down with a cold. Christ, what was this doing to her?

"Soon, sweetheart," she said.

The girl closed her eyes and nestled under her mother's protective arm.

Richard clenched his fists and stared forward.

"What happens," asked Joey, "if the car runs out of petrol?"

"That's obvious," Richard snapped. "The car stops. Then . . ." For Amy's sake he didn't complete the sentence.

"We'd have to flag down a car," Joey continued. "We'd have to make one stop."

"On a motorway?" Richard shook his head. "You've got to be joking."

"Where are you going?"

Michael had pulled the car off the motorway at the next exit. "We'll probably find a service station faster off the motorway." He drove carefully now, never taking it above forty as if trying to conserve what precious little remained of the fuel.

Joey gnawed his thumb. "If we run out of petrol we could get out and run?"

Michael slowly shook his head. "You can't outrun it on foot."

"We split up; run in different directions."

Michael shook his head again.

"Shit." Joey sagged back into the seat, his face gray.

Richard's eyes strained into the distance, willing himself to see a service station. There were only fields.

"When we reach a service station we'll have to move fast," Michael told them. "I can't guarantee we'll have more than about sixty seconds before this thing starts stamping down on our heads."

"What do you suggest?"

"I'll stay in the driving seat. You, Richard, pump a couple of gallons into the tank, that'll be enough. Joey pays the cashier."

"Pay?" Joey sounded incredulous. "We won't have time to pay. Get in there; slap in the petrol, then we're off. Like a bat out of bleeding hell."

Michael shook his head. "We can't afford to draw attention to ourselves. The police are probably already looking for a red Volvo. With luck that girl at the diner was in too much of a hurry saving her skin; she won't remember much more than a few details—color, maybe make of car, four adults, one child, that kind of thing. But if we hare off without paying you can bet the cashier'll take our plate number as well as the color and make of car. That's when the police put two and two together."

"Maybe it's best we try our luck with the police after all."

"And sit in a police station interview room waiting for the ceiling to come slamming down?" Michael shook his head. "Think it through, Richard."

"That's what I'm trying to do. Maybe there's a way we can keep moving but still talk to the police."

"What, from call boxes, or maybe drive by the side of a police car talking through the window as we go?" He gave a humorless laugh.

Christine spoke quickly. "Or a mobile phone. If we could only get hold of—"

The car gave a cough and everyone sensed the engine miss a beat. Richard held his breath as the engine faded.

Then it picked up again. He breathed deeply with relief. "Don't worry. Just some dirt been sucked in through the fuel pipe."

Joey rubbed his face. "Just dirt? That means it's sucking on what's left from the bottom of the tank. It could run out any minute."

"Take it easy." Michael spoke softly. "There's a service station right there at the bottom of the hill."

Joey let out an explosive sigh. "Thank Christ for that."

"Remember what I told you." Michael licked dry lips. "Richard, have you enough cash for a couple of gallons?"

"A fiver."

"That's enough. Put in five pounds' worth, then Joey won't

have to waste time waiting for change. Joey. Don't run, or scream or anything like that. Look relaxed."

"Relaxed? Jesus, you've got to be kidding."

"Try." Michael slowed the car to thirty. "When I say GO, get out quickly and do what you have to do. OK?"

They nodded.

It was a self-service garage. Fortunately all the pumps were vacant. Richard could see the female cashier sitting behind the counter. With luck they could be in and out of there within forty seconds or so.

Come to think of it, they would *have* to be long gone within forty seconds. A thought struck him as Michael shifted down the gears as he pulled in. "Wait a minute, won't that thing trash this place?"

"Not if we're quick. As soon as we put some distance between us and it, it'll merely switch to following us."

"But—"

"Later, Christine. Here we are. Pump three . . . *Go*."

Richard and Joey climbed quickly out of the car.

Richard handed Joey the cash, then took the nozzle from its holder. Joey tried hard to walk casually toward the cashier's window.

Richard's eyes were drawn back the way they came. Hammerhead storm clouds bubbled up from the horizon. Somewhere close, that thing the man described as the Beast was coming their way. Dark, pounding, with the destructive force of a nightmare god that was old before Moses.

The display on the pump flicked to a row of zeros.

Here comes my Destroyer. Despite the heat he shivered. *Here it comes . . .*

. . . that dark and pounding and irresistible force . . .

BANG!

"Richard! Joey!"

Richard had almost reached the car, the nozzle in his hand. His head snapped up. Michael was out of the car; his fist had hit the car's roof to attract their attention.

"Get back into the car," Michael shouted. "We're too late. It's here!"

Richard rammed the nozzle back into the pump. A hundred yards away in a cornfield a swathe ten feet wide appeared. Something invisible crushed it flat. It ran across the cornfield toward

147

the filling station, scything corn, destroying fences.

Joey swung himself into the backseat and slammed the door. Richard hit the passenger seat as Michael revved the engine. The car swung out of the station and onto the road. A horn sounded from an irate trucker.

"Just in time," panted Michael. "It came in fast that time."

Richard took a deep breath and looked back. The swathe running across the cornfield had ended in a flurry of movement as through a cyclone had hit it. Then the force seemed to evaporate into nothing leaving the corn swinging this way and that as if the surrounding air had been displaced by its disappearance.

Michael wiped his forehead. "We were lucky that time."

"Lucky?" Richard echoed. "We're going to run out of petrol any second now. You call that lucky?"

Michael's eyes anxiously scanned ahead. "All we can do is pray it holds out."

"If it does? And we fill the tank, what then?"

"We drive fast and put some space between us and it. Then we can lose it for a few hours."

There was hardly any traffic on the road. Michael took the car up to seventy, eyes flicking anxiously from gauge to road. An insect hit the windscreen with a crack; a blood spot trickled up the glass before the push of air.

Two trucks lumbered up the hill toward them, a police car following. Richard watched it pass. Its driver didn't notice them. Again he felt something that blended relief with disappointment. He still held out a fragment of hope that if they went to the police they might be safe. Christine had mentioned getting hold of a mobile telephone. Maybe there was something in that. Maybe if—

The engine died.

As simply as that. It faded. Then died. Still coasting under the momentum, Michael slipped the car into neutral, and tried starting the engine. Above the rush of air the starter motor cranked away uselessly.

"It's no good." Richard clenched his fists. "The tank's empty."

"Jesus, oh, Jesus." Joey bleated. "What now? What the hell do we do now?"

Rosemary made it as far as Pontefract's town center. It was a market day and the precincts bustled with people buying fruit and vegetables. She knew her strength was at an all-time low. Leg and face hurting, she forced herself to eat a bar of chocolate. After that she swallowed salted peanuts one by one as if they were pills. They felt like pieces of concrete grazing down the inside of her throat. But she knew she needed the protein and the salt.

The town was strange to her. She wandered around the streets looking for the car park she'd seen on the news.

After a great deal of trial and error she found it. Instantly she saw where it had happened. Most of the car park was full of cars but a good chunk of it had been taped off. The wrecked car had gone, but there was still an oily slick on the Tarmac where it had been. Elsewhere she saw the traces of where that *thing* had destroyed signs and concrete bollards.

Without a shred of doubt she knew it had been here. The smiling stranger with downturned eyes had been here, too. When she pictured his face her skin prickled and she felt the handle of the knife through the fabric of the rucksack.

Maybe she would be too late to save that family and the little girl called Amy. They might be already dead. But she would find him. And then she'd slice great crimson rents in his face. She would have her revenge. She would bathe her wounded Frankenstein face with his blood.

Richard looked back at Amy and Christine as the car free wheeled down the slight incline. Christine's face was tight and expressionless. But he knew what she was thinking: HOW DO WE SAVE OUR LITTLE GIRL?

Christ. How *do* we save her?

The car sounded absurdly silent as it coasted along, engine dead, the tires making a soft rippling sound against the road-tar.

"You." Joey sweated. "You. Michael. You've got us into this. You get us out."

"Believe me, that's what I'm trying to do."

"But for crying out loud, what *can* you do?"

"Keep the car rolling, for one."

Richard glanced at the speedo. Steadily it was dropping. Sixty-five . . . Sixty . . . The rippling sound slowed.

He found himself trying to push the car on by willpower alone.

"Big problem is . . ." Michael licked his lips. "The road's running uphill. Only a slight incline . . ."

"We'll not make it," Joey said heavily.

Fifty-five. Richard's jaw clenched.

Michael whispered, half to himself, "Wait and see, wait and see."

Fifty.

In the back Christine's eyes looked huge. Richard found himself thinking about all the things he wished he'd told her.

Forty.

Christ. It's as if something more than gravity was slowing the car; big scaly hands wrapped around the back bumper hauling the bastard car to a stop. Richard twisted to look back, expecting to see something there, cruelly slowing them. *So that bastard wretch of a thing that this smug bastard Michael what's-his-fuck-name had inflicted on them could catch them.*

Here comes my Destroyer . . .

Here it comes to kill me, my wife, my four-year-old girl, who gets so excited at birthdays and Christmas she can't sit still and bounces around the room like . . . like . . .

Richard bit his lip, his eyes watered

This couldn't be it . . . this couldn't be the end of everything he'd poured his heart and soul and life into . . .

It was coming.

Thirty-five miles per hour . . .

. . . his Destroyer . . .

That dark and pounding and terrible force . . .

Those two policemen . . . *Please God, tell me they died quick.* But they had died bloodily beneath that tarpaulin, crushed like woodlice under your heel . . .

"Come on, come *on* . . ." Michael rocked backward and forward in the car as it slowed.

Twenty-five.

"Come on."

Twenty.

Michael yelled: "Nearly there, nearly there. It's the brow of the hill. If we get past that we've got a run down the other side . . . It'll be fast enough . . . we'll find a filling station . . . We'll be safe . . ."

Fifteen.

"Come on!"

Ten miles an hour. Richard's eyes were nailed to the speedo.

The rippling of the tires had turned into a sticky sound. As the wheels turned slower, slower . . . slower . . .

Five miles per hour. The brow of the hill thirty yards away.

150

Richard thought bitterly, *IT MIGHT AS WELL BE FUCKING THIRTY MILES AWAY.*

He thought of Mark safe on his camping trip. *Take care, son. You'll have to grow up without us now. Maybe, some time years from now, Mark would fire that old rocket at the sky. And recall the time long, long ago when his parents were there, and little Amy, whose lives were cut so brutally short in that bizarre car wreck. Were his mother's eyes blue or brown? Brown, he was sure they were brown. Then maybe he'd watch the video of Amy's birthday. When she ended up with cream from the trifle on her nose and Joey's dog had licked it off, sending her into a giggling fit that—*

"Richard," Michael yelled. *"Get out and push!"*

Dazed, Richard almost fell from the car. It still free wheeled at walking pace but it was slowing all the time. Joey also tumbled out, slammed himself at the back of the car and pushed, his cheeks blowing out frantically.

"Push! Push!" Joey screamed, his face as red as blood. "Push, you fucking stupid twat!"

Richard ran to the back of the car and pushed alongside Joey. Christine on the other side appeared. She pushed until the muscles in her neck stood out like taut wires beneath her skin.

Michael pushed the car with one hand still on the steering wheel. Incongruously, Amy kneeled up in the seat and stared back at them, her eyes saucer-big, thumb in mouth.

The Volvo was a heavy lump of steel. Richard would swear they were pushing with the handbrake on.

Move! Move! MOVE!

"Come on, you . . ." gasped Joey, sweat streaming. "Push!"

They pushed together until they felt their muscles would strip from their thigh bones. Pains flashed like lightning up Richard's spine.

"It's moving!" Michael yelled. "Keep going!"

The car's pace quickened up the slight incline; soon Richard found he was having to run to keep up with it; that great chunk of steel and rubber and plastic powered by pure adrenaline.

Richard felt a snap of static electricity across his palms where they pressed against metal.

It was coming closer.

Their Destroyer . . .

Pounding darkly toward them.

Something screeched and bellowed behind them.

A truck. It was a bloody truck. It weaved by, the trucker shouting something about mad bastards pushing cars . . .

"Christ," Joey squealed in amazement. "No . . . Michael can't do that!"

Michael had jumped back into the car. *For crying out loud, what's he doing?* thought Richard in disbelief. *He should be pushing the car, not riding like Lord Shithead in the front seat.*

Then Richard heard the starter motor whining as Michael turned the key.

"My God . . . what's he playing at?"

A clunk. The car juddered. And suddenly pushing became easier. Now they had to run hard to keep up with it.

Then Richard realized what Michael had done. He'd put the car in gear, turned the ignition and used the car's powerful starter motor to pull it the last few yards.

They reached the brow of the hill. It ran steeply away in front of them. A good two miles of straight, empty downhill road-tar.

Jesus, that looked sweet . . .

Michael shouted. "I'm not stopping. You'll have to jump for it."

Joey ran, his head pumping up and down, lank hair flicking from side to side. He reached the passenger door behind Michael, opened it, dragged himself in.

Richard reached the front passenger door, opened it.

"Richard!" Christine screamed. She was losing her balance, tumbling forward.

Forty paces behind the car roadside bushes, signs, fences shattered.

The Beast had found them.

Jumping onto the framework of the car, door open under his arm, Richard caught his wife's arm and hauled her through the doorway, both somehow falling onto the front passenger seat in a tangle of arms and legs.

At the third attempt Richard shut the door, his wife crammed between him and Michael.

Michael didn't seem to notice. "Come on! Come on, baby! That's it!"

The speedo needle pointed to thirty . . . thirty-five . . . forty . . .

With an agonizing slowness the speed increased down the hill.

Then the speedo kissed sixty.

"Done it!" Michael flashed an exhilarated grin. "It won't catch us now."

"Until we reach the next uphill section of road."

Michael looked along the road. "About a mile away. There's another filling station."

He glanced at Richard then at Joey. "Right, Gentlemen. Get your breath back. We're going to try again."

Chapter Thirty

Faith

She walked through town with no particular place to go. Heavy clouds reared ugly thunderheads over the town center church; the heat felt sticky, oppressive, and Rosemary Snow ached from head to toe.

She weaved her way through the market stalls; shoppers crowded the precincts.

Outside the town's redbrick museum, she stopped. Standing outside the entrance was a totem pole. She stared at it as if she'd seen it before and for a reason she couldn't explain she disliked the look of it. She shook her head, puzzled. There was nothing unusual about the thing. It stood about ten feet tall. And like any other totem pole it was simply a stack of carved heads one on top of the other.

She shivered. It fascinated her. Yet it repelled her. Really she wanted to turn her back on it and walk away. But she felt compelled to let her eyes take in every detail. There were seven gargoyle heads carved from a dark worm-eaten wood. Some of the heads had a nose that curved outward and downward like a hook, others had eagle beaks. All had hooked ears.

She shivered.

What fascinated her, and disturbed her most, were the eyes—the staring, staring eyes.

"Sweet as a bloody nut." Joey sounded pleased with himself as Richard drove away from the filling station.

Michael smiled. "You didn't think we were going to make it, did you? And we had time to buy sandwiches and milk. Would you like a carton, Amy?"

"I'll decide when she has a drink," Christine said shortly.

Richard glanced back at her in the rearview; her eyes glittered

154

angrily. He realized she wasn't being pointlessly possessive of Amy by refusing the drink. She felt that Michael was beginning to take over. Already he decided when they drove, how fast they drove, where they drove, making suggestions in that gentle un-assuming voice that now sounded more like orders. "Best take a right here, Richard . . . Might be better to speed it up a little. Sixty should be about right . . . If you follow the signs to the motorway, that might be for the best . . ."

Now Christine had rebelled at him slipping into the role of food and drink provider.

"Cold milk gives her stomachache."

The man smiled and nodded, still maintaining the friendly, al-most apologetic, image.

Joey was grinning, pleased with himself. Richard, too, felt on a high. They'd beaten the Beast, slapped into the tank enough petrol for the next sixty miles, and the road ahead was clear. As Richard drove, Michael managed to swap his bloodstained shirt for a brand new one from the rucksack. White, pristine, short sleeves, he could have been a dentist or a doctor enjoying a day's ride out into the countryside.

Christine stroked Amy's hair as she spoke. "I don't see what everyone's so pleased about. That thing's still following, isn't it?"

Michael nodded.

"And the police might be looking for us now?"

"True."

Richard's buzz fizzled. He remembered the two cops crushed beneath the canopy. Guiltily he realized he'd no right to feel good about anything. A shadow pulled darkly over his spirits.

"You are right, Christine. All I can say again is that I apologize for getting you mixed up in this. I was desperate. If it's any consolation, you saved my life this morning," Michael went on.

Richard said, "It goes without saying that this morning you weren't being followed by a gang of thugs?"

"Spot on. I knew you wouldn't have believed me, so I told you the first thing that came into my head that would get us away from the house."

"But nothing did happen to our house. Did it?"

"No, it's untouched. We managed to get away before the thing managed to condense itself into a state where it could cause phys-ical damage."

"So while we keep moving we're safe?"

He nodded seriously. "Completely safe."

"But we can't drive forever."

"Agreed. But if we can put some space between us and it, then it will take it quite a while for it to . . . to home in on us, if you like."

"Just how long is *quite a while?*"

"Ten hours. Twelve if we're very lucky."

Richard shot him a look. "That's if the police don't stop us."

Michael nodded. "That might be the main problem. We mustn't allow the police to interfere. Not under any circumstances."

"Great," Joey said, the smile leaving his face. "How do we do that? Fire a bazooka out of the back window at them?"

Michael gave a tired smile. "We'll think of something."

He'd no sooner spoken the words when the police car appeared behind them. Richard looked back into the rearview mirror, then down at the speedo. They were doing perhaps fifty-five on a road with a fifty speed limit.

Richard looked back at the police car again just as the blue lights started flashing and the siren began to howl.

Rosemary Snow stood watching the televisions in the shop window. If she saw more news of the destruction in Pontefract that morning it might offer another clue. Instead, two dozen TV screens showed a woman with white permed hair making fruit pies.

Rosemary needed to sit down. Her legs shook so much she was in danger of falling flat on her face. From the date on today's newspaper, she knew she'd lain unconscious in that hospital bed for twelve days. Twelve nights ago she had run from that thing as it shattered the farmhouse and, very nearly, her too. And twelve nights ago that leap into the coal truck had left her with the Frankenstein face.

She sat on the market hall steps and rested her arms on her upraised knees, then closed her eyes. Sometimes she saw through the eyes of the little girl. Perhaps that was the way to find the family? Perhaps the girl would see something that Rosemary would recognize, or a place name on a sign.

Against the lids of her eyes she only saw that blend of black and red. The blood in the lids backlit by light filtering through the skin.

She tried harder.

156

She found herself seeing images of the totem pole outside the museum, with its hook noses, eagles' beaks and staring gargoyle eyes.

She forced out the totem images and willed herself to see through Amy's eyes. Darkness. Just darkness. A blood-red darkness that made her think of the billion miles of nothingness that lies between the stars.

"Damn," hissed Richard. "What happens now?"

Joey gripped the back of Richard's seat. "Floor it, you stupid twat. You've got to outrun them."

"Outrun them? They're driving a Cosworth. They could outrun this in third gear."

The siren wailed, the blue lights beat back from the mirror into Richard's eyes.

"Mum, what's the police car doing that for?" Amy twisted around to get a better view.

"Put your foot down, man," Joey snarled. "You can do it."

"No. Can we hell," Richard snapped.

"Richard's right," Michael said. "Richard. Indicate, then pull over. Nice and easy does it."

Richard did as he was told. Indicated. Braked lightly and pulled over to the side of the road.

Rosemary could see nothing. But she realized the truth. She'd thought the man had been running from the thing that had very nearly crushed her as flat as rolled pastry. In a way he was. But now she realized he could call it to him. Like you might call a dog. That's what he'd done twelve nights ago. But it must have been for something more than the sadistic pleasure of seeing her crushed to a strawberry pulp. He'd planned something. Only it had gone wrong. Now, perhaps, no, shit to *perhaps* . . . now he was planning something again. A definite plan as firm as concrete. A plan that would involve that thing she called her Destroyer. And the little girl called Amy.

He'd leave the little girl alone in a field. Then: he would whistle that thing to him. Only between him and it would be a four-year-old girl.

"Excuse me."

She opened her eyes. Standing over her was a middle-aged man. He carried a white stick and wore dark glasses.

157

"Yes?" Her voice came in a croak.

"You don't happen to be looking for someone, do you?"

"Well . . ." she began, surprised. "Yes. I am."

The blind man smiled. "I had a feeling you were."

"But how—"

"But how did I know?" He smiled. "Call it sixth sense. Come on." He held out a huge paw of a hand to help her stand.

"But I don't understand how you knew I was looking for someone."

"Oh, I knew you were looking for someone. And I know exactly who it is you are looking for. Follow me." With the stick tapping, the blind man led her through the crowds.

The police car's blue lights filled the car; the siren gave an exultant whooping sound; it had caught its prey.

Richard felt a black ache press down on him. It was over. God only knew what would happen to them now. Locked in the station interview room he'd glance out of the barred windows waiting for it to come. Like a giant stalking across the roof tops—fee, fi, fo, fum. Then the crash of the roof as it hammered down onto their heads.

He'd slowed the car to twenty before the police car roared by, siren whooping. Richard stared glassily in front, expecting the police car to brake.

Incredibly, it accelerated away.

"Jesus," Joey whispered. "They're not stopping us. Jesus Christ! They're not even looking for us!"

"Don't count your chickens," Michael said. "What they haven't got yet is the license number. It's a good guess that they are looking for a red car with four adults and a child. Obviously, that cop was in too much of a hurry to notice us."

"So next time we might not be so lucky," said Christine.

"Got it in one."

Joey sniffed. "We can't change the color of the car."

"But we *can* change the car," Michael replied calmly. "I know where we can do that."

Richard licked his dry lips. His arms and shoulders ached with tension. When they passed a truck that lay on its side on a roundabout with its load of beer kegs scattered across the road he barely looked at it. Paramedics were working on the trucker who lay flat out in the dirt. Stuff like that was no longer important. Foreign

158

wars weren't important. Bank robberies weren't important. Drug dealers slicing each others' throats weren't important. Richard's mind had snapped into hard focus. *They* were the important ones now. And his sole ambition now was to bring his wife and daughter through it in one piece. The keyword: *Survive*.

The same cop who had overtaken him waved their car through. The paramedics covered the trucker's face with a blanket. Richard put his foot down and powered the car away toward the distant horizon.

"You'll find who you're looking for in here." The blind man held open the door and Rosemary entered the church.

"Where?" she asked looking around at the deserted pews.

"Don't you see him?"

"I think there's been a mistake." Rosemary hugged the holdall to her breast nervously. "I'm sorry, good—"

"Don't you see him? There in the window, all bright and golden."

"There's been a mistake. I have to go."

"There's no mistake. I know who you're looking for." The blind man's hand clamped around her elbow. "You're looking for Jesus Christ. Aren't you? *Aren't you!*"

The fierce grip hurt. She tried to pull away.

"I've got to go. Please . . . let go of me."

"You're looking for Jesus Christ. And he's looking for you."

"No, please, I'm—"

"Kneel here. We'll pray together."

Roughly he pushed her to her knees. Splitting pains ran up her side from her bruised ribs. He kneeled beside her, one arm around her shoulders to hold her down, using the other great paw of a hand to clamp her hands together in a posture of prayer.

"That's right," he hissed, panting heavily. "We'll pray together. Thank the Lord that He has found you today."

Frightened, Rosemary looked around the church. It was deserted. The blind man was too strong for her to break away.

His grip tightened. "Now. Say the words with me." When he began the prayer, his voice became hoarse, almost guttural, and instead of his breathing easing he began to pant. "Our Father. Which art in Heaven . . . hallowed be Thy . . . name."

In front of her, Jesus Christ stood smiling down from the stained glass window. A burst of sunlight pierced His eyes. White doves shone pure as milk, the blue of His robe glowed as blue as the sky. Christ's eyes, a deep soulful brown, looked huge. They seemed to say that he cared deeply for people in trouble. People just like Rosemary Snow.

As she prayed with the blind man he moved his arm. From above her shoulder to under her armpit. The big fingers groped across the material of the sweatshirt. Found her breast. Then squeezed hard.

"Thy will be done, Thy kingdom come"

Fingers locked around her right breast, he squeezed harder, cruelly pinching already bruised skin as he recited the prayer.

". . . For ever and ever, world without end. Amen."

With those brown compassionate eyes of Christ gazing down, Rosemary wept.

"Outrun The Beast?"

"Yes, why can't you outrun it for good?" Christine pumped Michael for answers. Richard listened as the car devoured miles of motorway.

"I can't simply run until I lose it. I . . . I don't know the mechanics of it. But I can put enough space between myself and it to give me a few hours respite. But it always finds me again."

"As if there's some kind of link between you?"

"I imagine it like this: we're connected by an invisible length of elastic. It'll stretch five hundred miles, but inevitably it snaps this thing back to me."

"So what do we do now?"

"I propose we keep driving. That'll put some space between us and Beastie." He gave a tired smile. "Then we get some rest."

"Well, that's all right in the short term. In the long term, what happens then?"

"My plan's very simple. We keep at least a couple of steps ahead of the thing. Meanwhile my people are working on the solution to the problem."

"Then you can destroy it?"

"Destroy it?" The man looked back at her; those downturned eyes showing surprise. "Destroy it? Good heavens, no. Whatever gave you that idea?"

By now the blind man was using both hands to knead Rosemary's breasts. There was no love in this act. He squeezed them with the

160

same brutal strength a sadist would use to crush a puppy.

Oh, please, Jesus, please . . . She looked up at the painted Christ in the window. *Make him stop, make him stop. He's hurting, oh* . . . *not down there. Don't let him put his hand down there* . . .

With one arm still around her, the hand clamping her right breast, his other hand was tugging at the drawstring of her tracksuit trousers. The movements were hurried, clumsy. More like those of a starving man tearing open a bag of biscuits.

Please, Jesus . . . *make someone come into the church. Make someone stop him* . . . *please Jesus. He's going to hurt me* . . . *oh, he's going to hurt me so much, I know it.*

The brown Christ eyes gazed down.

Then she knew the only way the blind man would stop this was if she did the stopping. By now he'd let go of her hands so he could tug at the drawstring.

She snatched up the holdall from by her side and swung it at his face.

"Uckkk." The grunt was surprise as much as pain. The blow was no worse than being hit in the face with a pillow. He scrabbled for her throat but she swung the bag again; this time it knocked off his dark glasses.

"Oh, God," she whispered.

He looked at her with a single bloodshot eye. There wasn't a second eye. Only an empty socket. The sheer size of the socket was shocking. It looked like an open toothless mouth where the eye should have been. As red as the inside of a mouth, it was big enough to accommodate a hen's egg.

"Damn . . . ungrateful . . . bitch." he hissed. "Damn . . . bitch. Come here."

She was quicker to her feet than him. This time she gave the holdall a full-blooded swing. For some reason—Rosemary couldn't understand why—the bag stuck to his face. He wasn't holding it with his hands but something was holding it there. She yanked hard.

As the bag pulled free he screeched.

Then she knew. The holdall buckle had lodged in that huge, empty eye socket.

As he screeched he fell back against the stone slabs. "Bastard bitch!"

Rosemary backed away, looking down at the man as she did

so. He managed to sit up. He swore and pressed the palm of his hand to the eye socket. A thin yellow liquid trickled over his thumb. The other eye glared at her fiercely. "Come here. I'm going to sod you till ya split. Bastard bitch!"

She had decided to turn and run. But then she stopped. Something made her change her mind.

With a burst of rage she kicked as hard as she could. Her trainer smacked solidly between the man's legs.

Roaring, he jumped to his feet.

She put her hands up in front of her face expecting a beating. The man made two paces toward her before the pain in his testicles registered.

"Oh-ck . . . Oh . . . bast . . . oh . . ." With both hands clutching between his legs he slumped down onto the floor. He drew his knees up to his chest into a fetal position, coughing and groaning.

Then Rosemary surprised herself again. She marched up the aisle to the altar. There she glared up at the Christ who gazed benignly down. *"Thanks for nothing."* Savagely she stuck her middle finger into the air. Then she turned and swept down the aisle. The man had managed to make it to his knees. Coughing a silver trail of spit from his mouth.

She aimed another kick at his belly. He squealed shrilly, then fell puking to the floor.

Rosemary stormed from the church. She was looking for a car. She had no idea how to steal one. But she'd learn fast.

Nothing on this Earth could stop her now.

Chapter Thirty-one

Symbiosis

Richard drove north at Michael's suggestion. Richard noticed that Michael still kept the haversack between his feet on the car's floor. He almost gripped it with his knees as if it contained something precious and he was afraid someone would try and snatch it from him. *What's in there?* wondered Richard. When it seemed as if the police car would pull them over Richard had noticed Michael slip his hand surreptitiously inside the flap and down into the rucksack as if he was trying to feel for something at the bottom of the bag. At the first opportunity, Richard decided, he'd take a look in there. And see what it contained that was so important.

Meanwhile, Christine still asked Michael questions. And he still answered in a polite, even friendly way that suggested he was eager to tell them everything he knew about what followed him . . . well, followed them all now, Richard told himself, seeing as they were all infected. They were all connected to the Beast by something that Michael had likened to a piece of invisible elastic.

We can get away from it for a while; then it comes twanging back . . .

"But why don't you destroy it?" Christine persisted, leaning forward, hands gripping her knees. "It's dangerous. It will kill you."

"It's as dangerous as a knife, Christine. With a knife you can cut someone's throat. Or if you're a surgeon you can cut out a cancer."

"You're saying it depends on who controls it?"

"Yes."

"And you want to be the one to have that control? Why?"

"To improve the world we live in. The emperors and kings who entered into this symbiotic relationship with the Beast in the

163

past built huge empires; their subjects were happy and prosperous."

"Symbiotic?" Joey sounded out of his depth. "What the hell's that when it's at home?"

"Symbiosis," Michael said, looking back at Joey. "It's a term used in biology. It means any mutually beneficial association between two or more dissimilar organisms."

"Huh?"

"It's where creatures of different species help one another to survive. You'll have seen examples before, you know, like sharks and pilot fish. They swim so closely together that it looks as if they're glued together. The pilot fish eats parasites that stick to the shark's skin. The shark protects the pilot fish from other predators."

Christine asked shrewdly, "And what does the Beast get in return?"

"I think it experiences life through us."

"Experiences life? Do you mean—"

"Sorry, Christine. Pull into this service station. I imagine we can safely fill the tank now. And anyone who wants to go to the toilet grab your chance. Only don't hang around. OK?"

Within ten minutes they were on their way again. Richard felt happier seeing the petrol gauge hard on full.

Christine still wanted to know more. "So you're saying that for thousands of years this Beast thing has been prowling around the eastern end of the Mediterranean seeking out suitable partners for a symbiotic relationship?"

"In a nutshell, yes."

"If this Beast thing has played such a large part in history why isn't its existence better documented?"

"People who used the Beast kept it a closely guarded secret. After all, you don't want your enemies getting their hands on something that gives you the edge over your competitor."

"Surely they had to share it with someone," Richard said.

"You can speculate they did share it with some close confidantes. But only rarely. Remember, we're talking about people who, although rulers of empires, often were so insecure about their leadership that they'd have their closest friends murdered in case they challenged their leadership."

"So," Christine said thoughtfully. "These rulers either told their successor about the Beast on their deathbed, and instructed them how to enter into that relationship with it or . . ."

"Or the secret died with them. As it must have done time and time again. Again, you can look at a list of Byzantine Emperors and you realize that there'd be a whole run of leaders who didn't enter that relationship and as a consequence the Empire crumbled, whole armies deserted, the treasure houses became empty."

"You still haven't answered the question, though," said Christine. "When you manage to regain this power, what do you intend to do with it?"

There was a pause as Michael thought of an answer. Then, from the backseat, Amy asked suddenly, "Who's Rosemary Snow?"

Chapter Thirty-two

Power over Men

Mayor's Walk. The name of the residential road made Rosemary think of something extremely respectable, extremely prestigious. It was. And Rosemary thought it was the ideal place for her to steal the car.

The walk from the town had exhausted her; her leg ached mercilessly. But she wanted to be well away from those paddle hands of the bastard who had groped her in the church. *I hope the twat chokes on his own vomit*, she thought savagely as she limped along the road looking for a suitable car.

Her anger had become an energy now. Powering her on so she could nail the bastard who'd given her a Frankenstein face.

As she had guessed, on a millionaire's road like this there were plenty of cars in the long sweeping drives—BMWs, Mercedes, Jaguars. But they were in clear view of the houses. The moment she walked into a garden there was a danger she'd be seen from a house window.

Come on, come on, she thought. *Time's running out.* She still didn't know how to find the stranger and the family he'd somehow gotten under his power. She only knew she had to be out on the road, searching, searching, searching—until she found the bastard—then she'd slice holes in his face so big you could put your hand inside his head.

Ahead lay a house with a garden full of trees as high as the rooftops. Great clumps of bushes blossomed from the sides of the drive.

Without hesitating, she walked onto the drive. Everything had an overgrown, neglected look to it. She guessed whoever owned the house would be elderly: they were letting things go now. Lawn ankle-deep, ivy starting to grow over window panes.

Halfway along the drive she came upon an elderly-looking

166

Ford Granada. She carefully eased up the handle.

Thank Christ for that.

It was unlocked. The car was hidden from the house by banks of bushes. Quickly Rosemary slipped into the driver's seat. She pumped the pedals and checked that the gear lever was in neutral. Those drives along the lane to and from her friend's house came back to her. I can do this, she thought, I can do it.

She looked for the key in the ignition. There wasn't one.

Shit. This wasn't going to be as easy as she thought.

"Rosemary Snow?" Michael's smile widened as he sat looking back from the passenger seat. "Never heard of her. Is she a cartoon character?"

Amy bit her sandwich and gave an emphatic shake of her head. "You know Rosemary Snow."

"I'm afraid I don't, Amy." Michael grinned and looked at Christine. "She's got a heck of an imagination, hasn't she?"

Christine nodded. "And you haven't even met the Boys yet."

"The Boys?"

Christine told Michael about Amy's Boys. The imaginary friends she could summon at will. Richard saw that Christine was finding comfort in talking about what was familiar to them.

As he drove, he glanced at Michael who listened attentively as if fascinated. No doubt the man was just being polite, thought Richard wearily, but at least he did a good job of being interested. Even asking questions and nodding thoughtfully at the answers.

"And The Boys come to play whenever you call them?"

"Yep."

"Where are they now?"

"Riding on top of the car."

"Bet it's windy up there for them."

"They like it. They're singing." Amy sang: "Three blind mice, three blind mice, three blind mice . . ."

"What're their names?"

"Not telling, nosy parker."

"Amy," Christine scolded.

Michael laughed softly. "What do they look like?"

"Big and blue. No ears and no hair."

"Oooh, scary."

"They're not."

"Bet you have fun with them."

167

"Yes."

"Are they still singing?"

"No."

"Do you tell them what to do?"

"Yes, she does," said Christine. "You're a right little sergeant-major, aren't you?"

Amy folded her arms. "I give them orders."

Michael nodded. "You give them orders." He repeated as if it was important.

Amy grinned brightly. "Boys! Stop picking your noses. Boys! Go to the toilet. Boys! Boys! Jump off the car and go and find Rosemary Snow!"

Rosemary Snow was in trouble.

She hunted through the glove compartment and felt under the dash for a spare key.

Nothing.

Bloody nothing.

She swore under her breath. Weren't cars supposed to be the easiest things in the world to steal?

She felt beneath the dash again, her fingers finding clumps of cable. She'd heard you could hotwire cars by cutting certain cables and connecting one to another. But how the hell did she do that? And how could she break the steering lock with her bare hands?

Shit.

She looked out through the windscreen.

Damn.

He must have been watching her for the last five minutes. Standing in the bushes, an old guy in a straw hat. He was watching her with a look that was more amused than outraged.

She felt a thorough pedigree idiot.

Blushing, she grabbed the holdall and ran from the car.

Later, she found a service station and hung around near the forecourt. When a driver had filled his tank and then gone to pay the cashier, maybe she could simply jump in and drive away. They left the doors unlocked.

But they take the bloody key with them, stupid. She swore again. If she messed up, she'd be handed over to the police. She could do nothing to help that family then. She'd only have all

168

her life ahead of her to imagine the little girl's screams as that thing trod her into the ground.

Come on, Rosemary Snow. Think, think—THINK!

You haven't the technical know-how to hotwire a car. You don't know how to break the steering lock.

So. What have you got?

You must have something that's of use.

Yeah, right, Rosemary Snow, you've got two bruised tits and a Frankenstein face.

Why not go across there and scare that guy right out of his Mini Metro . . .

But you have *got something.* The realization surprised her, and in a strange way uplifted her. *You've got something that one-eyed twat in the church wanted. Shame about the face, but you've got the slim girlish body that men would love to get their hands on, given half the chance.*

As she walked away from the garage she was thinking hard.

"Have the Boys found Rosemary Snow?" Michael asked. He yawned in a deliberate way.

Amy sat, her eyes becoming stary, the way they did when she was tired.

"What's wrong, Amy?" Michael grinned. "Monkey nicked your tongue?"

Still staring straight ahead she said in a small voice. "They've seen the big thing."

"What big thing?"

"The big thing. The big thing that's following us."

"Oh," Michael whispered. "*That* big thing."

Richard shivered and looked in the rearview mirror. He could only see cars on the motorway and storm clouds bubbling up over the horizon; nevertheless, he shivered again.

Christine looked at Michael. "Can Amy sense it, too?"

"Children are sensitive to things like this. She knows, all right."

Amy blinked as she came out of the stary phase. "Mum, where are we going?"

"That's what I'd like to know."

Michael smiled. "How about a trip to the seaside?"

It was early evening by the time the plan looked as if it might actually work.

The fish took the bait.

Rosemary had been standing in the car park of a motorway service station. Deliberately, she'd adopted a lost look; even tried to make herself look more than a little simple, too. She'd brushed her long hair back to life again and had stood toying with a strand. She hoped it had broadcast a "Hi there, big boy, look what you been missing" kind of message; also, pulling her hair across the side of her face hid the mess of scabs and stitches that looked like a line of dead spiders stuck to her skin.

It didn't seem to be working. And time was rolling away like a driverless juggernaut. She needed to be moving. Now, now, *NOW!*

Then the VW van had pulled up.

Winding down the window the driver, a man wearing Deidre Barlow glasses said, "You look lost."

"I'm waiting for a lift."

"Oh." The man sounded disappointed. "You're expecting a friend?"

"No. But I need a lift." She tried to sound casually sexy.

"A lift?" The man looked around nervously as if afraid someone might be watching him, the big window lenses of his glasses flashing red in the setting sun. "Why don't you hitch down by the roundabout?"

"If I hitched anyone might stop and pick me up. I wanted a lift with someone nice."

"Where are you going?"

"Where are *you* going?"

"Sheffield."

"That'll do." She waited, twirling her long hair. "Well?"

"Uh? Oh, yeah, yeah. Here, get in. I'll, eh, get the door . . . I . . ."

Flustered, he opened the passenger door of the van. As she shut the door she smiled at this nervous man in his Deidre Barlow glasses and thought, "For Christsakes, Rosemary. What have you done? More to the point, how are you going to actually pull this off?"

Stammering something about it looking like rain, he pulled out of the car park.

You need this van, she told herself. *Find that anger inside you. You can save that family; you can get your revenge on the*

170

stranger. Remember. It's because of him you're now cursed with this Frankenstein face.

"You know, I—I think we might be in for a thunderstorm," he said, pushing the Diedre Barlow glasses up the bridge of his nose. "It'll be a relief, won't it?" He beamed at her. "It's been so bloody hot."

He was younger than she had first thought. She imagined he'd be the kind to be tormented with taunts about being an Anorak. His clothes were unfashionable, the hair laughably curly, the Deidre Barlow glasses absurd. And he was as nervous as a kid on a diving board who couldn't swim to save his life. What she did feel for him was a wave of sympathy. She'd had enough of the jeering and Red Zed taunts because of the birthmark to know keenly the kind of teenage years he must have endured.

"If you want something to read . . ." He pushed the glasses up the bridge of his nose. "There's some magazines under the dashboard." He looked away as he spoke. "Haven't looked at them myself . . . . I've, eh . . . I've a girlfriend who—who likes looking at them."

The magazines were hard porn. Her first instinct was to push them back onto the shelf. But she sat and forced herself to thumb through them calmly as if they were a pile of knitting magazines.

He bit his lip and looked out of the window. She could sense his trembling excitement. Suddenly she thought: *Once he's had sex with me, will he kill me?*

171

Chapter Thirty-three

Desperate Measures

Amy closed her eyes. The seaside. She liked the sea, and the sands. And they always had fairs and cafés. She liked Burger King best. They might go there.

She was tired and the rhythmic sound of the tires on the road made her too sleepy to be frightened now. Sometimes when you're four years old things happen that make no sense. And today nothing made any sense. There had been a lot of shouting. Joey usually laughed and talked a lot. Now he hardly spoke at all. Mum and Dad seemed very serious. Michael smiled a lot; he seemed nice. But what he said puzzled her, too. He said he didn't know Rosemary Snow. But somehow she knew, and she knew it as well as she was called Amy Young who was four years old, nearly five, that he *did* know Rosemary Snow.

And then there was something she could see in her head. Just like she could imagine the Boys; but somehow this was darker. And it was something she didn't like. She snuggled closer to her mother. This dark thing followed them. She didn't know what it looked like. But for some reason she thought of her shelf on her bedroom wall. That's where all her teddy bears sat. In the morning she'd sit up yawning, and inside the bedroom it would be so gloomy she could see nothing but their button eyes. Loads and loads of dark button eyes gleaming at her.

She yawned and thought of the seaside again. She remembered the last time she had been to the seaside. She couldn't recall the name of the place but she remembered the big roller coaster rides, the pier, and there was a big metal tower made up of criss-cross bits of metal, and it went right, right up into the sky . . .

The images came to Rosemary with a brilliance that was blinding. The man, Robbie, drove the van south and talked about the exhibition of model aircraft he was going to visit.

172

In her mind's eye the brilliant images paraded past. She was seeing what Amy was seeing. Roller coaster rides, piers, sand, sea. And the distinctive tower built out of iron girders that was a replica of the Eiffel tower in Paris.

Blackpool, she thought triumphantly. *Michael's taken the family to the west coast resort*. At last she had a definite destination.

Now she had to get her backside in gear. She had to get there fast.

She thought of asking Robbie to drive her there; perhaps if she hinted about passionate nights in a backstreet hotel? No. She didn't think he'd bite on that. From the look of the model airplane parts—wings, engines, airscrews—covering the floor in the back of the van, that was his abiding passion in life. What he obviously wanted now was what he saw as a quick and very dirty fumble; then, when he'd got all those annoying and intrusive sexual tensions out of his system, he'd be back with his beloved Focke Wulf fighter again.

Maybe she should have picked up some trucker. He'd have been married, no doubt. He'd have copulated with her without any fuss, or even much excitement. He'd just be notching up another mark on an already impressive score. But she guessed a middle-aged trucker would be too worldly-wise; he'd probably suss she planned something more than ten minutes of thrusting and a cigarette.

Robbie was naive, but he was also scary.

Rosemary watched his hands tremble as he gripped the steering wheel. His sexual tension was mixed up with darker passions.

"Do you think girls enjoy that?" she asked in a deadpan way as she pointed at the magazine centerfold.

"I . . . I don't know . . ."

"She's smiling, so she must be enjoying it, I suppose."

"Do you . . . do you think *you*'d enjoy doing it like that?"

She shrugged. "I've never done it like that before."

"Have you *ever* done it before?" Robbie sweated hard.

"Loads."

"Oh . . ."

She glanced quickly at him. He'd recoiled as if he'd been too close to something that disgusted him.

"It was a while ago now. And I've only had one boyfriend."

She'd have to tread carefully. Robbie looked a neurotic mess of sexual tensions. Women probably frightened him as much as they fascinated him. If she came across too worldly it'd probably scare him off.

"It's the first time I've seen magazines like this," she said, trying to sound as naive as possible. "That page there. Do you think it would hurt to do it like that?"

"I'm not sure."

"Me neither."

"It might be nice for the girl?" he suggested, sweating.

"It might," she agreed. Then, in a matter-of-fact way, she said, "Why don't we try it?"

The tremors down his arms jerked the steering wheel enough to make the whole van twitch.

"Why not?" he said as nonchalantly as he could, but he was trembling and sweating, and repeatedly whispered something under his breath she couldn't catch.

"Find somewhere quiet," she told him.

As soon as Robbie was clear of the town he drove slowly along a country road, his eyes behind the Deidre Barlow glasses eagerly scanning left and right for somewhere quiet to pull over. Rosemary watched a ball of sweat roll down his nose.

She thought: *I hope for your sake this works, Red Zed. Otherwise you could end up in serious trouble.*

He found an opening in the hedge and drove onto a cart track. It led the van bumping uphill between two lines of trees. In the back of the van the model airplane fuselages, wings and tail units rolled from side to side.

Eagerly he asked "Quiet enough, you think?

"Quiet enough," she agreed. And she wished she were anywhere else on Earth but here.

As the trees thinned higher up the hill he pulled off the track and U-turned the van across the grass, braked, switched off the engine, then turned to face her.

He was trembling hard now, teeth chattering. "Ah . . . well, then . . ."

"Well, then?"

The smile he tried to give should have been a charming one. But his lips slid from side to side. "Do you think . . . page fifteen . . . shall we try that?"

Rosemary pulled out a smile. "Fifteen. My lucky number."

"*Jesus*. What happened to your face?"

174

"Oh . . . I had an accident. I—"

"Did . . . did he do that to you?"

For a moment she was stunned, thinking that somehow he knew that Michael had—

"Your . . . your boyfriend. He did that, didn't he?"

Robbie had supplied his own answer. She nodded.

"Oh, what a mess . . . what a fucking mess." There was no sympathy. Her injury excited him. Tremors ran up his neck to shake his face, making the glasses slip down his nose.

"Does it hurt?"

"Yes."

"Oh . . ." That really excited him. He breathed deeply. "Does it hurt a lot?"

She nodded, solemn.

"How did he do it? With his fist? Were you naked when . . . I mean were you doing it . . . you know . . . Jesus, he ripped your face in two!"

She nodded, her mouth dry. *Go on, Red Zed, get it over and done with. Time's running out. You've got to get to Blackpool and find the bastard who dropped you into this hell.*

"You don't have to kiss me," she said.

"All right." He sounded relieved. "But it's OK if I . . . I?"

She nodded.

He squealed with excitement. She clenched her jaw. *Christ, he actually squealed like a piglet. Oh, get me through this one, God . . . please get me through it in one piece.*

A thought struck her. "It's a bit cramped here. Can we go in the back?"

"Sure. Sure. I'll just make some space. You know—you know I've got some valuable models back there. There—there's a Messerschmitt, that was a jet-powered World War Two fighter. Probably the only effective jet fighter of the war."

She heard the exhilaration in his voice. He was sharing his special love of the model planes with her.

"I—I'll move it to one side. I'm strong when I get going you know, really strong." He sweated faster. "Things get broken when I get going, you know." He swung open the door and climbed out. "I've broken things before. I—I'm stronger than I look . . ."

As he went around the back of the van Rosemary slid across to the driving seat, locked the door, then twisted the key in the ignition. The VW motor started with its characteristic metallic clicking sound.

"Hey!" shouted Robbie through the window. "What you playing at? I thought—"

There seemed a heck of a difference between a car and a van. She stamped at the clutch and tried to force the gear into first.

Metallic grinding.

"Get out of my van! I'm warning you!"

Robbie's face was bright red. He thumped the window.

She released the handbrake. The van stood facing down a slight grass incline to the cart track. Very slowly, it rolled forward.

"Stop it! Stop it!" he shrieked. "This's my van!"

He ran around the front of the van and tried the passenger door. But she'd already locked it.

Damn, where's that gear? She revved the van. Still in neutral.

Thud.

She looked back. He'd opened the door at the back.

Christ, she'd assumed it would have been locked. He was climbing in.

Clunk. She found the gear. It was the wrong one, maybe even third, but she took her foot from the clutch pedal and floored the accelerator.

On the level it would have stalled.

But facing downhill gravity helped. It rumbled forward across the turf, bumping over tree roots.

"Stop it now, and I won't hurt you," screamed Robbie.

She looked back in time to see him crouching in the back of the van, his eyes blazing furiously through the huge spectacle lenses.

Then the van lurched over a deep rut. A stack of fuselages, wings, and cockpits slid back across the metal floor, hit Robbie, and pushed him back out of the van.

In the rearview mirror, she saw him sitting on the grass amid the wreckage of the model planes. She accelerated downhill. Behind her, the rear door flapped and banged.

But even after she reached the road she drove a full mile before stopping to close it. As she ran back to the driver's seat she felt the first heavy drops of rain smack against her face. The storm was breaking.

Chapter Thirty-four

Wales

Michael told Richard to park at the back of the hotel.

"Is this Blackpool?" Amy asked expectantly.

Michael smiled. "No, I'm sorry, Amy, it's not Blackpool, but, look, you can just see the sea down there."

"Oh . . . I like Blackpool."

"This is a very nice hotel, though. There's satellite television in all the rooms."

Christine let her out of the car and Amy stood looking at the mountains in something close to awe.

"This is Wales," Michael explained. "See that big mountain over there? That's Snowdon. One of the biggest mountains in Britain. And do you know something?"

"What?"

"A railway goes all the way to the top of it."

"Very nice," Joey grunted, hauling his bulk out of the car. "Christ, I need a drink. I need a drink *now*."

Richard climbed out, stretching his tensed arm muscles. He felt lousy. As if he'd been dragged down to hell and back. Twisting his head from side to side, he tried to dislodge the ache from his neck.

He looked at Michael. "Will we be safe here?"

"For the next ten hours or so. We've put a good few miles between us and Beastie boy. You did a good job, Richard."

Richard glared at him. "I did nothing of the sort. All I did was kill two policemen back there."

"You weren't to know—"

"Weren't to know what? I'd seen what that thing could do. I as good as called it down on them."

"Richard, I'm sorry, I—"

"*You're* sorry. I think it's their widows and their children

177

who're going to be the sorry ones. We should have . . . we should have . . ."

The truth was he didn't know what they should have done. Richard turned his back on the whole lot of them and glared along the valley. But he didn't see the green mountains or the lake in the valley. He only saw two men being crushed beneath that damn tarpaulin. Crushed to crimson paste. He ground his teeth so hard he bit his tongue but he didn't feel a sodding thing.

"Richard . . . Richard." Christine spoke gently. "It's starting to rain. Come inside."

He tried to speak but his mouth stayed clamped. No words would come. He shook his head.

"Richard. We're going to get this sorted out. We'll be home soon . . . come on, Amy's frightened to see you like this."

He glared at the great wall of cloud sliding across the mountaintops.

"We've all been through it, you know. I think Joey's on the verge of cracking up. He's hardly said anything for hours."

Richard breathed deeply. "I'm OK. But you know something, Christine? All I wanted to do then was just run down that hillside and keep running and running until I'd lost myself somewhere out there."

Rubbing his face, he turned. Christ, what a pathetic sight they all made. Joey stood, shoulders slumped, lank hair falling over his eyes. He looked twenty years older. Amy was ready to fall asleep on her feet. Michael looked as if a cancer was eating him up—thin looking, exhausted, but his eyes uncannily bright and alert. Christine, tired but still finding love to give to her husband and daughter.

He gave a faint smile. "Christine?"

"Yes?"

"You've got oil on your cheek. Come on, let's get you cleaned up." They walked back toward the hotel. It sat out on the hillside in the middle of nowhere. A dark granite fortress of a building complete with a circular stone tower.

Behind them thunder rumbled. To Richard it sounded like the footsteps of stalking giants.

Rosemary surprised herself: she could actually drive the van. If she'd had time to think about it she probably wouldn't have had a clue. But it had all happened so quickly. With the sex-starved

Robbie trying to climb into the van she'd acted on autopilot. Now he was back in that field gathering bits of his beloved airplanes up into his arms in the rain, while cursing womankind for all eternity.

She made it to the motorway and headed west. Before long, she saw the signs for Blackpool. Another hour or so would find her there. Hopefully before it got too dark. She didn't relish the idea of driving at night yet. For one, she hadn't a clue how to switch on the lights. There had been a fumbling forty seconds of trial and error before she found out how to switch on the wipers.

The rain came down in a steady stream; some even leaked onto the floor of the old van.

"Don't break down on me," she whispered. "Keep going. We've got lives to save."

But the old VW engine ticked sturdily on. And for the first time she felt confident about her own abilities to get things done.

Back there with Robbie she'd made a significant discovery about herself. She had a power of her own. Not the kind of power Michael had talked about. What she had was a sexual power. It had been strong enough to get what she wanted from poor old sweaty Robbie. She still couldn't help but feel sorry for him but she had discovered that along with power came ruthlessness. She couldn't allow anything to get between her and her goal. *Yes, you WILL stop Michael hurting that little girl. You WILL destroy Michael. Your ambition . . . Yes, Red Zed, even your passion to carry that plan out has attained the power and the glory of a holy quest.*

Chapter Thirty-five

Monday Night

". . . and when the wolf tried to climb down the third little piggy's chimney, he fell down into the big pot of boiling water and that was the end of him."

"Did he die?" asked Amy her eyes round.

Michael smiled. "Afraid so. Go get yourself another biscuit and I'll read you 'Jack and the Beanstalk.' "

At the other side of the hotel room Christine said under her breath as she brushed her hair, "I hate it when he does that."

Richard looked at her and nodded.

Christine said, "He's taking charge of us again."

"He's the only one who knows how to get us out of this."

"Let's hope so. But does that mean we now have to obey his orders?"

Richard pulled his trainers off. He felt emotionally battered. He needed a bath. But there were too many unanswered questions for him to relax in a hot tub just yet. He looked across to where Amy sat beside Michael on a window seat. The hotel room was vast. You could have parked a truck in the place, and still had room to park a car in the medieval fireplace.

He guessed the place was a converted manor house. The walls were paneled with oak. Heavy black beams ran from one side of the ceiling to the other. The expanse of red carpet looked as big as most people's back lawns. Earlier, room service had efficiently and discreetly supplied cooked meals along with a couple of bottles of fine French brandy that Richard had only seen in glossy magazines before. When he'd asked Michael how they were going to pay for it all, he'd given a shy smile and told him not to worry, that he had a financial interest in the place. Which, Richard guessed, meant he owned it.

Joey came into the room and walked across the vast spread of carpet, looking uncomfortable. "Do you mind if I join you for a few minutes?" He ran his thick fingers through his hair. "I feel a bit stupid sitting in my room all by myself." He gave a watery smile. "It's big enough to keep an elephant in there."

"Brandy, Joey?" asked Richard.

"Oh, God, yes. Thanks."

Richard had always seen Joey Barrass as conceited, a stuck-up sod who couldn't name anyone more important than himself on the face of God's earth. Now, he looked small and bruised. The muddy brown eyes were just plain scared.

"What's he doing?" Joey whispered so Michael wouldn't hear.

"Reading Amy fairy stories."

"Jesus. He should have his butt in gear getting us out of this shit."

Christine said, "Joey, have you been able to call Sonia and let her know you're OK?"

"Sonia?" Joey repeated as if hearing the name for the first time.

"Yes. Sonia. Your wife." Christine didn't sound impatient with Joey, she was being the caring sister.

"Uh, no, not yet." Joey spoke painfully. "You see, things haven't been going that well between us lately. Well, for a couple of years now. Sometimes I don't go home at night."

"So she might not even miss you?"

"No."

Richard said, "I know we haven't had a chance to talk properly together, seeing as Michael's been with us, but . . ." He changed the subject as Michael walked across the room toward them. "Want another brandy, Joey?"

Stonefaced, Joey nodded and held out his glass. Michael smiled. "Room OK, Joey?"

"Yeah . . . Look, do you mind if I use your bath? I keep thinking, what if that thing comes for us? I know you wouldn't leave me . . . but what if you couldn't warn me?" He sucked down a mouthful of brandy. "And that thing came. I keep thinking—it's absurd, it's fucking absurd—but if I'm sitting there stark bollock naked in the bath and the fucking roof comes down on me." He laughed but anyone could tell it was the laugh of someone on the edge of cracking up. His hands shook; he rubbed his eyes repeatedly with the heel of his hand.

Christine put her arm around him. "Course it's all right," she said gently, pouring him another brandy. "Now just try and unwind."

He nodded and stumbled away to the bathroom. He didn't close the door, only pushed it to. Then Richard heard the sound of him running the bath.

Collapse of stout party. No sooner had Richard thought the words than he had to bite his lip to stop himself braying out with a manic laughter. Christ, this tension was hitting him. He poured himself a brandy. When he offered Michael one the man shook his head.

Michael spoke in that gentle voice. "Don't worry. Everything's going to be fine. I'm going to my room to make some calls now. When I come back I should have some good news for you."

"What kind of good news?" asked Richard. "Do you mean—"

"Don't worry, Richard. Enjoy the brandy. I'll be right back. See ya, honey bunch," he waved to Amy.

"See ya, honey bunch," Amy echoed, grinning.

When Michael had gone Christine said to Amy, "An early night for you, I think."

"Aw, Mum."

"Let her stay up a few more minutes," Richard said.

"Oh, all right. Ten minutes—maximum."

"Maxi Mum." Amy chuckled.

Richard switched on the television.

Amy gave a happy squeal. "It's *The Simpsons*! Look, there's Homer riding Lisa's bike . . ." Immediately Amy was in a world of her own, watching the TV.

Richard glanced at Christine who watched Amy with a pure motherly affection. He wished he had his own world to retreat to, too. Here he was sitting in a five-hundred-year-old hotel on a Welsh mountainside. Outside it thundered. And God knew what was walking toward them through those thunder-clouds. Like a malignant old God that wanted more than its pound of flesh.

So this is it. The life you knew just fifteen hours ago is in ruins. Who knows what the future holds. For Godsakes, you might be dead this time tomorrow. Caught in a traffic jam when that thing decides to attack. Or maybe you'll have just called into a filling station to visit the toilet. As you sit and crap that thing roars down on you like the hammer of God and crushes you flat.

Christ, thought Richard bleakly. There was something about the idea of dying on the toilet that filled him with a feeling that was

182

a half-breed born of horror and embarrassment. *Didn't medical statistics show that you're as likely to die sitting on your toilet seat with your pants around your ankles as in your own bed?*

Not everyone did, though. And again he was struck by the absurdity of sitting here with a glass of brandy in his twitchy fingers, watching a cartoon, while in a mortuary somewhere what was left of two men coagulated in half a dozen or so plastic tubs.

"Christine!" screamed Joey from the bathroom. "Are you there?"

"Joey . . . Joey, it's okay," called Christine. "We're still here."

Joey sounded shaken. "I—I couldn't hear voices. I thought you'd left me. I—is everything all right?"

"Yes, Joey," Richard said, surprised by how relaxed his own voice sounded. "Take it easy. We'd tell you if anything was wrong."

Joey called twice more in that panicky way as they watched television. Amy didn't seem to notice, still locked safely away in the familiar world of the cartoon.

When it was finished she turned to any empty area of carpet and said, "Right, Boys. Outside. You can sleep in the car park."

"Ready for bed?" asked Christine.

Amy nodded and yawned. "Can we go home tomorrow, Mum?"

"We'll see, honey. Kiss Dad good night."

Richard kissed his daughter and hugged her tight, as if she was all that stopped him from falling down into a pit full of darkness. "Good night, love."

Christine led Amy to the bedroom that opened directly off theirs.

Later, after she'd returned, Joey came out of the bathroom, rubbing his hair with a towel. When he spoke it sounded sheepish. "I'm sorry about that. Nerves. I just kept imagining that Beast thing was directly over the room, and . . ." With a visible shudder he helped himself to more brandy.

Michael tapped on their door and walked quickly in.

"Any luck?" asked Richard expectantly.

"In a minute. But first . . ." He changed channels. "I think you'd want to see this."

Twenty miles outside Blackpool, Rosemary's plans began to run less smoothly. She was low on petrol and looking at the gauge when she heard the horn.

She swerved across the road, pumping the clutch instead of the brake. The van crunched up onto the pavement and ran twenty yards across a strip of grass, crunching bushes before stopping a foot from a garden fence.

By this time it was all but dark. In the house in front of her the occupant whipped back the curtain in obvious surprise at the sight of a van almost plunging into their garden. "Christ, Rosemary," she hissed. "Don't get yourself caught now!"

She switched the headlamps onto full beam. All the occupants of the house would see were the dazzling lights. And that's all the description they'd be able to give to the police.

Then she slammed the van into reverse. The tires buzzed like chainsaws across the rain-soaked grass. Juddering, the vehicle moved backward, crushing more bushes, tires throwing up a spray of mud.

Without looking, she bounced the van back out onto the road. Another horn sounded. Spitting fury, she yelled at them to *Shut it!* as she crashed the gears into first and pushed the van toward Blackpool.

No sooner was she out of that when more images, crystal bright, began to flash through her head.

Amy was transmitting images of what she saw again.

Rosemary saw what looked like a bedroom in a very old building, with beamed ceiling and leaded windows. Beyond the windows were mountains dotted here and there with sheep and every so often a farmhouse. Amy was being led by the hand to bed in a small room off the large one. Through the window there she could see the red Volvo Amy had traveled in, standing in a car park. Beyond that, the ground sloped down toward a fast-flowing stream. Raindrops began to slap the window panes.

The woman tucked the girl into bed. She said, "Sleep tight, Amy."

"Don't let the bed bugs bite." Big yawn. "Mum. Why does Michael say he doesn't know Rosemary Snow when he does?"

Again horns sounded, lights flashed. Something crunched along the side of the van. Rosemary didn't think it was another car. Perhaps a road sign or lamp post.

The van still ran soundly enough so she pushed on. Plenty of time to look at the damage later.

But she knew two things for sure. She knew Michael hadn't taken the family to Blackpool. That mountain scenery could be either Scotland or Wales—or even the Lake District, come to that. Secondly, Amy knew the name Rosemary Snow. Maybe this telepathic link was two-way. Maybe if she thought hard enough she could get some message through to Amy.

On the outskirts of Blackpool, she parked the van in a side street, then, climbing into the back, she kicked aside balsa wood spars, rolls of masking tape, the Messerschmitt wings and Stuka fuselage. Once there was a big enough space she lay down, covering herself with a coat that had been draped over the driver's seat. It smelled of poor hapless Robbie's sweat. It would have to do. There'd be time for comfort and clean bedding when this was over.

Rosemary closed her eyes. For the next ten minutes she pictured Michael's face. And she said over and over:

"AMY. TELL MUMMY MICHAEL IS BAD. TELL HER HE WILL HURT YOU. TELL MUMMY TO TAKE YOU AWAY FROM HIM. MICHAEL'S A BAD MAN. MICHAEL'S A VERY BAD MAN . . ."

Chapter Thirty-six

Nature of the Beast

In the hotel room in Wales, Richard sat with Christine, Joey and Michael and watched the television news in a silence that was as solid as stone.

Outside, columns of rain stalked the valley like shadowy giants. The thunder was a muted grumble, the lightning a silver-blue flickering around the mountain tops. Richard took another swallow of brandy as the TV replayed his nightmare in a series of brutal close-ups. There was the yellow Fiat in Pontefract, mashed flat in a tangle of steel and ruptured tires. Then the fast-food diner. Not that there was anything recognizable. Scorched debris and shattered ketchup bottles that left splodges of red on the Tarmac.

He felt numb. The news reader's commentary never sank in beyond that the police were baffled by two mystery explosions; one of which left two policeman dead.

"The dead policeman were," ran the news reader's voice, "Terry Glass, 42, and John Clifford, 37. Both officers were married with children. John Clifford was in the news last year for his part in freeing two young children held hostage in a Bradford house siege . . ."

Richard swallowed more brandy. Not that it helped much. He'd screwed up trying to tell the police. Now they were dead. And here he was, watching the result of his screw-up. Body bags stretchered to ambulances. Moving tributes by the men's colleagues, photographs of the two men with their families.

The news reader added that the only witness to either bombing had worked at Hank's Yankee Diner. She was still in a state of shock and unable to help the police at this time.

"Thank heaven for small mercies," breathed Michael with relief. Both Richard and Christine shot him dagger looks.

"Sorry," he said, "that sounded callous. But it means that for the time being we're off the hook. They haven't linked the damage to us."

Richard grunted. "Watch me jump for joy."

"I know this is rough," Michael said, leaning forward, his fingers knitted together. "But the truth of the matter is, we need to look after number one. Us. We must accept that people died today. But we can't let that prey on our minds. We need to stay alert. And be ready for whatever might come at us."

Joey said, "You said today we were infected, too. That might hunt any of us now?"

Michael nodded. "Imagine it's a hungry shark. That's got a scent of our blood."

"You've got a vivid way of putting things," said Christine, tartly.

"I only wish I could make it even more vivid. The plain truth of the matter is this: it is hunting you all now. If anyone was stupid, no, suicidal enough to decide to go it alone in the middle of the night, I'd give them twenty-four hours, if they're lucky, *miraculously lucky*. Then . . ." He slapped his hand down on his knee as if crushing a butterfly.

"But I take it that it can't split itself into pieces and hunt us all at once?"

"No, it'll simply hunt down the slowest first."

"What if we caught a plane?" Joey sounded suddenly hopeful. "Put ten thousand miles between us and the thing."

"That's not as easy as it sounds. You've got to buy tickets. Do you have your passports? Are you prepared to sit for two hours in a departure lounge where you're effectively a prisoner? When the plane taxis down the runway will it be going to meet the Beast head on with you sitting strapped into your seat unable to do a dickens thing about it?"

Joey's shoulders drooped. "You've got a point."

"Yes, and the point I'm making," said Michael firmly, "is *Stay with me*. I know how this thing ticks. I can get you through this and safely out the other side."

Christine leaned forward. "And how *does* this thing tick? Where does it come from? What are you going to do with it in the future?"

"You've every right to ask questions and, believe me, I'm going to answer as fully and as honestly as I can."

"Damn right you are."

187

Michael smiled. "Richard, you've got yourself one hell of a wife there."

Richard didn't return the smile. "She's got a way of putting into words how I feel, too. We all want answers. You said you've been in touch with your research people. What have they had to say?"

"OK, OK," Michael held up his hand. "Let me take this in some kind of order. Right, what *is* the nature of the Beast? What makes it tick? What does it look like? The answer is, I don't know what it looks like because it doesn't exist in a physical sense. It is composed of energy. You know, like sound or electricity. Where's it come from? Again I can only guess. Maybe it's something that evolved independently on Earth. Yes, it is new to us. An unknown life form. But until a couple of hundred years ago we didn't know of the existence of micro-organisms such as bacteria or protozoans or viruses." Michael looked at each of them in turn. "Sometimes I lay awake at night and I wonder if this thing may have drifted in from somewhere, out of the depths of the universe, a million years ago in search of a host body."

"Then it's a parasite."

"No. Parasites offer nothing in return to their host; parasites like hookworm or tapeworm damage the host animal. I call it the Beast but it is actually beneficial. We exist—or at least we existed—in this symbiotic relationship. We each give something that the other wants."

"You said that in return for giving you power you gave it experience of life."

"Yes, I'm not one hundred percent sure but I *think* that's what it needs. If you imagine this thing as a cloud of energy then, it has no eyes, ears, sense of smell or touch. So it finds a host with these senses so it—"

"What?" Christine frowned. "So it can enjoy a sunny afternoon and share your sensations of eating ice cream and drinking lemonade?"

"Yes, basically. You could also speculate it's some kind of probe sent by an alien civilization to learn about other worlds. What better way to find out about other cultures than through the eyes of a native of that culture? Imagine what you could learn about a dolphin if you could somehow magic yourself into its brain, see through its eyes, share its thoughts. And not just speculate what it would be like to be a dolphin but feel EXACTLY what it's like to be a dolphin."

"So the beast might be a kind of research probe?" echoed Joey pouring more brandy. "So some ET up in Moo-moo land might be looking at us right now." Joey raised his glass at Michael. "Cheers, bug-eyes."

Christine took a deep breath. "So, if you follow this 'what-if' line of reasoning: what if alien life-forms are seeing the world through your eyes? What if they are learning about us? What if they do give you power over people as some kind of good-boy treat? But have you thought about *this*?" Her hands shook as she sipped the brandy. "If *you* have power over people, do these things have power over *you*?"

"No," Michael shook his head emphatically. "What good would they derive from—"

"Christine's got a point," Richard said quickly. "It's a hell of a way to conquer a world, isn't it? Forget death rays and fighting machines. You just find someone who you can turn into a puppet president and rule through him."

Michael still smiled. Only now Richard detected a harder edge to his voice. "No. It's not like that. After all, I'm only speculating myself. Now, we all want answers. Sometimes I find myself answering my own questions with 'What if it is some kind of alien probe composed of pure energy? Or what if it is some unknown life form that evolved alongside life on Earth? Or what if this thing is really the spirit force known by the early Christians as the Holy Ghost?' "

Richard stood up and went to the window. Outside clouds boiled around the mountaintops, rain came down in drenching sheets. The brandy hadn't made him drunk. He felt calm now. His shattered nerves were healing.

"So," Richard said softly. "There are records of this happening before. You mentioned Greek and Byzantine Emperors entering into a relationship with this thing you call the Beast?"

"Sounds more like a pact with the devil," slurred Joey, pouring himself a tumbler of brandy.

Michael nodded. "Most historical records don't say so as plainly but there are indications, if you read between the lines, that such a symbiotic relationship existed."

"Symbiotic re . . . rela-shun-ship . . ." Joey drained the glass in one. "Still sounds . . . like a pact . . . with the damn devil . . ."

"That's Christian prejudice," Michael said. "Maybe even Christian jealousy. You see, when the Roman Empire was on the verge of collapse around the fourth century AD it split into two halves. Both halves became Christian. The western half, headed by the Pope, became what we now term Roman Catholic. The eastern half, based in Constantinople, in what is now Turkey, was the rival Orthodox Christian Church. The early Popes in the western church wanted this power—"

"But the eastern Church had got hold of it first," finished Christine.

"Got it in one, Christine. It was wielded by the Byzantine Emperors. Not all of them, sometimes the secret of how to acquire and control the Beast was lost for decades at a time. During these bad times the Byzantine Empire dwindled. They lost much of it to the Muslims who invaded from the South. Every so often an Emperor would regain control of the Beast; he would inspire his people; his battered armies would rediscover their vigor; inspired by their new charismatic Emperor they would put down rebellions and reconquer the old Byzantine colonies that had been lost."

"But it was still a downhill slide?"

"True, Christine. Around the twelfth century AD the Byzantine emperors lost the Beast for good. In 1453, Muslim forces conquered Constantinople itself. The last Emperor died fighting. But," Michael smiled, "the Sultans discovered the Beast and it started all over again. Constantinople was renamed Istanbul and it became the center of another great Empire and another great faith."

Michael leaned across to the food trolley and picked a grape from a bunch on the table. "And now, I imagine, you'd like to hear what my research team have come up with?"

Chapter Thirty-seven

Codex Alexander

Richard, Christine and Joey leaned forward to hear what Michael had to say. They knew that what he had to tell them would be important. Lives would depend on it.

Michael swallowed the grape. "You have a clear enough idea of what's happening now? When I took the Beast out of its natural environment at the eastern end of the Mediterranean it could no longer remain inside me. And once on the outside, it changed and became destructive. My research team are trying to rectify that problem."

Joey sniffed. "Why don't you just somehow get the thing back to Turkey, stay there living all cozy together and have done with it?"

"Because," Michael said, "the benefits this creature can bring to humankind are enormous. If we can utilize it fully we can create a new world order. A united, peaceful world."

"So you want to start this new world order in Britain?"

"Only I learned to my cost that the Beast won't travel more than a thousand miles from Istanbul without detaching itself from its host. Exactly why it does that I don't know."

"But you believe you can solve the problem?"

"I think so. And that's what my team have been working on."

"Can it be done?"

Michael nodded. "We know it can. Alexander the Great was in partnership with the Beast. He knew he couldn't take it much farther than the northern coastline of Egypt. But then something miraculous happened. After that he was successful in taking it all the way to India. And with it, he conquered the known world."

"But how?"

Michael smiled. "That's what we're trying to find out. You see, the secret died with Alexander but we believe the method of how to take The Beast out of its home territory was written down in a document known as the *Codex Alexander*."

"And you've got hold of a copy?"

"Hold your horses, Christine. No, not exactly."

"What do you mean, 'not exactly'? Either you have it you haven't."

"The *Codex Alexander* is basically an instruction manual on how to control the Beast. It was given to Alexander by the Egyptians when he liberated them from the Persians in 331 BC. Unfortunately it became lost shortly after Alexander's death. Then last month, in Cairo, my archaeological team discovered the tomb of a certain Egyptian priest buried in 200 BC."

"And this Codex was in the tomb?"

"Supposed to be, according to an ancient inventory found in the tomb listing its contents."

"But they found no documents?"

"On the contrary, we found plenty of documents. Over six hundred of the things. The problem has been to find which one is the *Codex Alexander*. That isn't as easy as it might seem. Some of the documents are in poor shape. Thousands of papyrus fragments have to be fitted together like jigsaw pieces before we can even identify which document is which."

"Christ," Richard breathed out heavily. "Which is going to take time."

"Correct," said Michael. He smiled. "But we can take a short cut. My people have tracked down a collector in Yorkshire who owns a later Byzantine manuscript which is a history of the Emperor Constantine. And the good news is that it contains lengthy excerpts from the *Codex Alexander*."

"That'll be enough?"

"It should be. So, tomorrow morning we'll drive across to Yorkshire, collect the document, and a few hours after that all this will be over."

The words worked a magic spell. Despite what had happened, Richard saw Christine's and Joey's faces break into relieved smiles. They continued talking to Michael in an animated way. But there was something more relaxed about it. Michael rang room service for more brandy and sandwiches.

Christine still asked Michael questions, mainly about his future plans now. Michael answered, his hands moving with graceful slowness to emphasize points.

"Most people don't realize," he said softly, "that we have the technical know-how to turn the deserts green once more. All we lack is the willpower. I am lucky enough, through that freakish accident, to be able to give people all across the world that will-power to turn deserts into lush pastures; to end starvation. I plan—"

. . . *to become Emperor of Planet Earth*, were the words Richard used to complete Michael's sentence mentally. For a split second the idea made him uneasy. Then it might have been the brandy, exhaustion or the way Michael moved his hands in gestures that were almost hypnotic that allowed the notion of this gentle-eyed man as world tyrant to slip away from him. Richard relaxed, feeling the aching tensions flow out of him while a warm easy feeling flowed in.

Outside it was dark. Lightning still flickered around the mountaintops but he could hear no thunder. And he could almost believe there was nothing out there that could hurt them. He listened with half an ear as Christine and Michael talked. He thought of Mark and wondered if it was raining where he was camping. The sound of rain on canvas would probably keep the boy awake. He could imagine seeing Mark on Saturday and his son grumbling about never going camping again because the tents had flooded out.

Richard's eyes opened. He was looking straight up at the ceiling. He rolled his head to the left. Christine's soft outline stood out against the plain white walls. For a moment he thought he was at home. Then he looked up and saw the dark wood beams running like pairs of rail tracks across the ceiling.

For the life of him he couldn't remember going to bed. He guessed he must have dozed off from one brandy too many.

Suddenly he sat up, his mind alert. There were no sounds but he found himself convinced that at any moment the ceiling would come crashing down upon them.

What were they doing asleep? That thing, Michael's Beast, could creep up on them as they slept. Sweat pricked his forehead. Richard imagined it swimming like some great shark up through the valleys: smoothly cutting through the mist, its snout hungrily pushing forward, searching for the five sweet morsels of flesh that lay sleeping here beneath the beamed ceilings.

Anxiously now, he swung out of bed and ran across to the window. The cloud had broken. The moon lit the mountains with

193

a silver light. There were the trees, the distant farmhouses, the river in the valley bottom looking like a snail's silver trail.

Richard was looking for the tell-tale disturbance of the grass or listening for the sudden snap of a tree trunk. Any moment he might see his car detonate in the carpark, the bushes flatten, then down would come the Beast, like the hammer of God, down upon the hotel roof, bursting their bodies as easily as you can splat an egg.

Something caught his eye just beyond his car. He looked hard, trying to make out what it was in the moonlight.

It moved nearer to the car.

Jesus . . .

It was Michael. The man was standing guard outside. If that thing approached he could warn them. Within seconds they would be in the car and driving out of . . .

Richard cocked his head slightly to one side. If it had been important to stand guard outside, surely they could have taken it in turns, to allow Michael to get some sleep. And, surely, he *did* need to sleep, didn't he?

And is he actually standing sentry for us? Richard wondered. *Or is he guarding the car? In case we should decide to run away and leave him here in the middle of the night?*

Chapter Thirty-eight

Tuesday Morning

Rosemary Snow woke in the back of the van. 7 a.m. Already cars were moving along the side street. She yawned, stretched. The pain cut from her head to her left knee as smoothly as if she'd been run through a bacon slicer. Her bruised body still ached from the leap into the coal truck two weeks before. *For Godsakes,* she thought, *you can't put yourself through this. You need time to heal.*

She curled up under Robbie's coat and closed her eyes. Images streamed seamlessly through her head. The hooked noses and staring eyes of the totem pole in Pontefract. A motorway. Michael at the wheel. "Sorry about the early start," he was saying. "We need to be in York by eleven."

Through Amy's eyes she saw cars and trucks, fields, cows, a canal with a ship plowing steadily along it. She noticed the car was different now. Higher from the ground, and bigger. Rosemary heard Michael's voice saying, "And don't worry about your car, Richard. It'll be safe in the hotel garage. But I thought it safer if we switched it for—"

"Oh, go away," muttered Rosemary. Her body ached. She only wanted to sleep. She couldn't keep running across the country in a stolen van, with stolen cash in her pocket. She'd had enough. Why didn't she just walk away from the van, catch a train to London and start a new life there?

The idea appealed. Yes, she could do that. Maybe she could salvage something from this wreck of a life.

She shut out the flow of images that Amy saw and closed her eyes. She needed sleep.

But a nagging thirst wouldn't allow it. She remembered the bottle of mineral water in the passenger seat. She'd have a drink, a couple of hours' more sleep, then find the railway station. She could be in London by nightfall. The idea pleased her. A new life. With no one to tell her what to do.

She had to stand to reach into the front seat for the bottle. As she did so she looked into the rearview mirror.

Christ, she'd forgotten about that.

The Frankenstein face stared back at her. Bile rose up through her throat as she looked into eyes that were ringed black, and saw the crispy ridge of scabs that ran down one side of the face.

Who are you kidding, Frankenstein? she asked herself grimly. *You're not running away from this one.* Anger gripped her again, fuelling her tired arms and legs, suppressing the ache in her bones. She wanted—no, not wanted—she NEEDED revenge. She lusted after revenge. Beautiful, beautiful sweet cleansing revenge. The idea of it shone like that star that shone brilliantly over Bethlehem two thousand years ago.

Her need for revenge was the power that would drive her all the way to Michael. Then she would open up his face.

She slipped into the driving seat and started the motor.

Chapter Thirty-nine

Cruising for a Bruising

"Damn," Michael said under his breath.

From the passenger seat Richard looked across at him. "What's wrong?"

"Sign for roadworks up ahead."

"Can we make a detour?"

"We could, but it'll take longer. If we stick to the motorway we can be in York for eleven."

"But if we get stuck in a traffic jam?"

"Well, as the saying goes, the brown stuff could really hit the fan."

"Great," said Joey from the backseat. "Why risk meeting the guy in person? Can't he just stick this Roman book in an envelope and send it first class?"

"He won't do that," Michael accelerated to overtake a lorry. "He knows this thing is too valuable to me."

Joey ran his fingers through his hair. "Why don't you use your heebeejeebee powers to make him drive down to your place in Norfolk and deliver it in person?"

"As I told you, Joey, when the Beast left me at that airport hotel I lost my ability to . . . inspire people."

"You mean *control* people," Christine said pointedly.

Michael shook his head. "I think of it as inspiring people."

"But these people under your and this Beast thing's influence don't have the choice to disagree with you, do they?"

"The Beast gives me the ability to make people enthusiastic about what I believe in. If I try to inspire them to act completely against their natures, they can refuse. They still have free will."

Joey pushed his bottom lip out. "So you're not sure that this bloke with the Roman book will even turn up?"

"When I spoke to him last night we agreed a price that made him extremely keen to sell."

Joey asked bluntly, "How much?"

Michael smiled. "Two million."

"Phew," Joey whistled. "You've got some money to throw at this thing."

"It might sound arrogant but I just see money as fuel to drive my plans from conception to execution. So, if it takes bucketfuls of the stuff to get from A to B, so be it."

"I'd like to see your bank statements." Joey spoke as if he was joking but Richard knew he meant it.

"What price would you put on a child's life, Joey?"

Joey shrugged. "I don't know."

"The truth of the matter is," Michael said, "that politicians and hospital administrators do just that. Sometimes for the want of a few thousand pounds a child's life is lost."

Amy woke up in the backseat. Yawning, she scratched her chin and said, "Michael, Rosemary Snow's following us."

"Rosemary Snow?" Michael shot Richard a grin. "By heaven, that imagination works overtime." He smiled back at Amy. "Amy, is she sitting on the roof with the Boys?"

"No, *stupid*."

"Amy," Christine said. "Don't call people stupid."

Then, as if stating the obvious Amy said, "Rosemary's driving a big, big van. She's following us."

Richard noticed that beneath the smile something troubled Michael. "Is she far away?" He spoke in a way that adults use to humor imaginative children.

"Not too far away. It's a big van and . . . and it's got some airplanes in the back."

"Some airplanes?" Michael's smile was almost one of relief. "Bet there's a swimming pool in there, too."

"No. It's real. I saw it when I was asleep; only it—"

"Christ," whispered Joey, appalled. "We're in for it now. Just take a look at that."

Richard looked forward through the windscreen and his heart slipped a beat.

Rosemary Snow floored the accelerator. The VW engine clattered. Blackpool was a good thirty miles behind her now.

She'd seen enough through Amy's eyes to know that Michael's

destination was York. She could be there in a couple of hours. She swung around a roundabout, almost putting the van on two wheels. Behind her Robbie's model airplanes slid across the van's metal floor.

Richard's hand tightened around the seatbelt and he clenched his jaw. Because ahead the motorway was a solid mass of unmoving traffic.

"Christ," breathed Joey. "The mother of all traffic jams and we have to be slap in the middle of it."

"Mum, what's wrong?"

"Nothing, honey, just a bit of a traffic jam, that's all."

"Why's Uncle Joey so worried, then?"

"He doesn't want to be late," supplied Richard lamely. But the last thing he wanted was to put Amy through the same trauma she had been through yesterday.

They joined the queue of traffic. Michael eased the Range Rover behind a car in the slow lane and pulled on the handbrake. Here, the motorway was raised up above the surrounding fields with grassy banks running sharply down. The next exit from the motorway was still several miles away.

"There's a sign up ahead," Richard said, "Damn. Three lanes are being condensed into one. It might take some time to get through."

Joey leaned forward until he'd squeezed himself between the two front seats. "Michael. Can you tell how far away that thing is?"

"It won't be that far. We put a lot of miles between us and the Beast yesterday but we've been stationary at the hotel for more than twelve hours."

"Hell fire," Richard breathed. "Well, we're not going anywhere fast here; the traffic's choked to a standstill."

"If I see anything, I'm getting out and hoofing it," Joey announced.

Michael glanced back. "If you want to look like a doormat, be my guest."

Richard looked out at the hundreds of cars and trucks choking the M62. Nothing moved. The car in front, an ancient cream-colored Morris Minor, puffed balls of oily smoke from its exhaust. Inside sat an old guy in a corduroy cap, placidly smoking a pipe. Richard felt a burst of irritation that was as savage as it was irrational. Here they were, trapped in their own personal hell, with God knows what bearing down on them, and all the rest of the smiling, smug, don't-give-two-hoots population of the whole damn planet were doing their own sweet thing. They just didn't know what he was going through. His daughter sat in the back. Just four years old. And he didn't even know if she'd still be alive by suppertime.

Richard began to sweat. He felt it dribble down his chest beneath his shirt. He wound down the window. The air smelled of exhaust fumes. No cars moved. They were just sat there waiting for—

Christine said, in a low voice, "Michael, we can't just sit here."

"Any suggestions?" He spoke calmly, too, but Richard noticed him begin to tap the steering wheel with his finger.

"Can you sense it, Michael?"

Michael nodded. "But I don't know how far away it is. It still might take another half an hour to get here."

Quickly Richard switched on the car's radio. He tuned it to the dead zones between stations and upped the volume.

Static sizzled through the speakers. Beneath the steady hiss came a regular burst of static that pulsed in a rhythmic squelching beat. Richard let out a breath. "Well . . . there she is."

They listened to the heartbeat of static coming through the car's speakers.

"Turn it down," Christine whispered. "Please turn it down."

"I have turned it down. It's getting louder by the second." He turned to Michael. "You heard it, Michael. Now what?"

"It . . . it's so unpredictable. I just don't understand it anymore."

Joey clutched Michael's shoulder. "Understand this. That thing'll be here any second. Don't dress it up in silly names—the Beast does this, the Beast does that—you know as well as I do it's going to roll over about two hundred cars, flatten every poor sod into the road, then us, too."

Richard had noticed that Michael had been looking forward in a detached way at the old man smoking his pipe in the cream-colored Morris Minor.

Michael rubbed his face with both hands and took a deep breath. "Everyone hold on tight. Christine. Put your arms around Amy . . . dear God, here goes."

Shifting the Range Rover into four-wheel drive, Richard slowly

200

but deliberately drove the car forward into the rear end of the Morris Minor. There was a crunch. Richard had a clear view of the pipe popping out of the old man's mouth. The old man looked around angrily, his lips screwing into a shout around the yellow dentures.

The big Range Rover easily pushed the Morris forward until it crunched into a milk tanker in front. Michael flicked the car into reverse. Richard saw the old man climbing out of the car shouting in fury and waving his knobbly hands.

"Sorry about that, sir," said Michael under his breath, "but I really didn't have enough space to pull out."

Richard heard the static heartbeat of the Beast getting nearer and nearer. He looked back, expecting to see the cars behind them beginning to implode under its crushing weight.

Not yet. But, God knew, it must be here any moment.

The static heartbeat cracked at the speakers like a hammer.

THUD-THUD . . . THUD-THUD.

Richard gasped. Joey cried out. They were falling.

"Damn," hissed Rosemary Snow. She'd reached the tail end of the same traffic jam on the motorway. All she could do was sit it out. Unless she could glue sweaty Robbie's balsa wood wings onto the van's side and glide above the traffic like something out of a Spielberg movie.

She looked at the fuel gauge. It was running pretty low. She'd have to try and get some petrol into the thing at the next service station.

The traffic didn't seem to be moving anywhere fast. She switched on the van's radio. *Christ, hear that crappy reception.* Almost drowning out the song were great fat bursts of static. For all the world they sounded like a giant's heartbeat.

At first Richard thought Michael would drive along the hard shoulder and exit the motorway at the first opportunity.

Instead he felt his stomach strain for his mouth as Michael drove off the motorway altogether.

Hell . . . the slope down from the motorway was so steep he hung forward against the seatbelt. In fact, if it hadn't been for the belt he'd have fallen slap into the windscreen.

"Christ, what're you doing?" Joey panted. "You'll turn the friggin' car over."

Michael didn't answer: he let the car run faster as gravity took control. And with the car almost standing on its nose there was a real danger if he did brake they would end up rolling forward nose first to cartwheel down to the bottom.

"Just pray there's not a deep ditch at the end of this slope," Michael grunted, hanging onto the steering wheel as it tried to wrench itself from his fingers.

With an almighty crash the car hit the level. Still Michael didn't brake.

Richard held his breath. Because now Michael raced the motor, powering the big car straight at a hedge. It bust through it in a spray of leaves.

"They say," shouted Michael. "These are off-road vehicles." He gave a grim smile. "Let's put the sod to the test."

He put his foot down, driving hard through a field of waist-high corn. Richard hung onto the grab handles. For all the world it looked as if they were speeding across a straw-colored sea, sending out a rippling wake behind them, the corn stalks swishing noisily across the paintwork.

Behind Richard the three on the backseat were bounced around like peas in a tin. Incredibly, Amy had a huge grin on her face. Christine looked stoic. Joey looked as if he was going to up-chuck.

Michael didn't hesitate. Driving the car hard, he crossed corn-field after cornfield which, fortunately, had been raked pretty flat. When he reached a fence he simply crashed through it. In the distance a man on a tractor stopped it and stood up to watch them pass.

Michael shot Richard a grim smile. "Next stop York."

Chapter Forty

Blood on Road

Michael cut through the last fence and bounced the Range Rover onto a country road. He drove purposefully, but kept the speed down so as not to draw attention to the vehicle.

When Joey managed to speak, he grunted, "Nice driving, but you've guaranteed to get the police onto us."

"What for?" asked Michael.

"For shunting that old guy on the motorway and doing a rally cross over Farmer Whatsit's field, that's what for."

"You really think the police are going to be that interested?" Michael carefully overtook a bus. "Believe me, Joey, the old Plod are overworked as it is. What'll happen is that that old guy will file a complaint: maybe he took our number, maybe he didn't. In a few hours one overworked, footsore bobby will be given the complaint to work on. Our number will be fed into the constabulary computer. Out will come an address. What then? Will our bobby dash out to his car, slap on the blue lights and go screaming off looking for us? Will he hellfire. He'll amble up to the canteen for his egg and chips and mug of tea. Then he'll waddle back to his desk and stick our piece of paper with another fifty pieces of paper like it. Then gradually plod through them."

"You have to admit," Richard said, "playing dodgems on motorways is one way to get noticed."

Michael smiled. "Schoolteachers and your parents have done a good job. You've been brainwashed into being nice law-abiding citizens."

"There's nothing wrong with that."

"There's nothing wrong with being a sheep but I wouldn't chose to be one." Michael shook his head. "Forget it. An old guy got his bumper dented, Mr. Farmer's got a few bent stalks of corn and maybe five quid's worth of damage to his fences. Hardly crime of the century, is it?"

"OK," Christine sounded businesslike. "What now?"

"Number one objective is reach York and get our hands on the document that should solve all our problems. Also, we need to keep moving quickly. Beastie Boy ain't too far behind."

"What will have happened to those people on the motorway?"

"They're OK. It didn't have time to begin condensing itself enough to do any damage before we started moving. Amy?"

"Yes, Michael?"

"Monkey nicked your tongue?"

She chuckled. "No."

"You haven't had much to say for yourself, sweetheart."

"You drove over so many bumps it bumped my breath out of my body."

"Sorry about that, Amy. We had to get away from that stinky traffic jam. Would you like some Rolos?"

"Oh, yes, please."

Richard glanced back at Christine, expecting to see in her expression her irritation at Michael taking control of their daughter again. But Christine looked out of the window, her face expressionless. He guessed this cascade of events, the destruction, the total rupture of their everyday life had left her numb. He was feeling that way, too. Even when he recalled what had happened to the two policemen at the diner he didn't feel the horror anymore. It had happened—that was all. Perhaps nature had a way of anesthetizing the mind when the body was plunged into a dangerous situation. He remembered what his great-grandfather had told him when he was a boy. His great-grandfather had been a corporal in the Army in the First World War. He'd stood in a trench that was waist-deep in rainwater for three days while the enemy had bombarded him and his comrades with artillery shells, night and day. The men were cold, hungry, disorientated by the constant noise of exploding shells. After a couple of days men would simply fall asleep and sink down into the water where they drowned. At first Richard's great-grandfather had tried to haul his pals out of the water. But, after a while, a kind of cold trance set in. At the end of three days he'd stood there and watched with a strange detachment as his best friend sagged down into the water just an arm's length away. He remembered watching the bubbles popping to the surface. Then his friend's cigarettes floated out of his pockets to lie on top of the water. At the time Richard's great-grandfather had just felt a distant kind of disappointment that the cigarettes had got wet. The realization that he'd watched his best friend drown in the ditch inches from him only hit him a month later when he was on leave.

Richard guessed that same detachment from reality was happening now. Probably part of the instinct for self-preservation. No matter what happened around you, no matter how bad, you kept going; you did what you had to so that *YOU* survived.

And Richard, in a blinding flash of insight, knew it was going to get worse—far worse—before it got better.

The first part of the journey, after rejoining the road, was uneventful. Michael looked as if he'd begun to relax as he skirted Manchester and powered the car uphill to the high roads that would carry them across the mountainous Pennines from Lancashire to Yorkshire. Sheep nibbled grass at the side of the road.

"What do all the sheep have bleed on them?" Amy asked.

"Bleed? Oh, you mean blood?" Michael asked.

"They've blood on their wool."

"No. It's just a red marker dye. So the farmer knows which sheep are his."

"Why?"

"Because they let them wander about where they want. They're not fenced in like cows."

Richard leaned back against the headrest listening to Amy talk to Michael. After the night's thunderstorm the air felt fresher up here; the sky was clearing and slabs of sunlight slanted spectacularly down into the valleys below.

A tractor lumbered uphill. A steady stream of oncoming traffic meant they couldn't overtake. Richard noticed Michael begin the impatient tap of his finger on the steering wheel.

"Is it close?" Richard asked.

"Closer than I'm comfortable with." Michael tried to pull around the tractor but a bus was coming in the opposite direction.

"We're doing twenty," said Richard, "is that fast enough?"

"No. And we've not put enough space between us and the Beast since the motorway. Come on, farmer boy, out of the way."

Joey twisted around to look anxiously behind them.

Christine said, "Can't you pass him on the inside? The grass verge looks wide enough."

"I might have to if . . . come on, come on. Gotcha."

An oncoming truck held back the stream of traffic behind it to give Michael the space he needed. He accelerated past the tractor and the Range Rover sped up the hillside road like a bullet.

Joey sighed with relief. "Thank God for that."

"Well, while you're thanking God, can you ask Him to shift *that* lot out of our way?"

Ahead the road was blocked by, Richard guessed, forty to fifty sheep.

"Damn." Michael sounded the horn. The flock walked a little faster, but the Range Rover was barely crawling.

"Look at all those sheep," cried Amy with delight. "Sheepies! Sheepies!"

"Christine," said Michael tersely, "make Amy sit down. And you best cover her eyes."

Richard looked at Michael. His tone expressed far more than the words. Richard switched on the radio.

. . . thud-thud . . . THUD-THUD . . . *THUD-THUD . . . THUD-THUD . . .*

"Jesus, it's right on top of us!"

Michael drove at the sheep: their heads sounded as hard as concrete bumping against the metalwork.

The sheep bleated.

One sheep jumped to land sprawling across the bonnet, its horns scraping the paintwork. Richard had a glimpse of its terrified rolling eyes. The pink tongue slapped out to leave a streak of sheep spit on the windscreen.

Amy screamed.

"Sorry," Michael hissed. "It's them or us."

Michael forced a path through the sheep at maybe fifteen miles an hour. Richard saw the sheep weren't being badly hurt, merely buffeted away from the car. The main problem was that the car and sheep were both hemmed in by the narrowness of the road which was bordered to their left by a wall and to the right by a crash barrier that separated the road from a fifty-foot drop.

"It's OK," Christine reassured Amy. "Michael's not hurting the sheep. But we've got to get through."

Richard saw another sheep leap; this time over the crash barrier. It bounced away down the steep slope like a big ball of wool, legs and head swinging wildly as it cartwheeled.

"Nearly through, nearly through . . ." Michael whispered.

"For Christsakes hurry it up," snapped Joey.

Christine whispered, "Oh, my God. *It's here.*"

Richard looked back through the rear window. A road sign crumpled flat to the ground. The wall disappeared into a blur of stone shrapnel, as if heavy machine gun fire traversed along it, rushing with blinding speed toward the car.

"We're through. Hold on."

Michael powered the car on.

Richard still looked back. The sheep were running after them. They'd sensed the thing's approach.

He watched as first one sheep exploded, then a second, then a third, then five, six . . . dozens.

It was like watching balloons filled with red paint explode.

They were crushed with such unimaginable force that blood sprayed into the air twenty feet above the ground to create a crimson cloud.

"Lucky there were no other cars nearby," said Michael as he accelerated safely away.

"Yeah," said Richard feeling that creep of icy detachment. "Lucky." Behind him the last sheep had erupted into a spray of blood and internal organs.

Chapter Forty-one

York

With forty miles of Tarmac between them and a carpet of sheep meat back in the Pennines, Michael pulled into the car park behind the Barbican Theater, York.

"It's almost eleven." Michael pulled on the handbrake. "Our man should be here any minute now. Anyone want to stretch their legs?"

"Is this wise?" Christine asked.

"Yeah," said Joey. "Maybe we should keep driving around until it's eleven, pay this book collector Johnnie his money, then scarper."

Michael opened the car door. "Don't worry. We've put some space between us and Beastie. We're OK for a good half an hour or so."

"Yeah, sure . . . it makes you think of the *Titanic*, doesn't it?" Joey pushed back his heavy fringe. "Richard, I said it made you think of the *Titanic*. Unsinkable and—"

"Yeah, yeah, Joey, I heard you," Richard said wearily and climbed out into the sunlight.

York's a tourist magnet. The car park was filling quickly and the roads were thick with cars and open-topped buses trundling around the places-of-interest routes.

Stretching, Richard looked around the car park for the man with the book that would get them out of this shit. There was no sign of anyone yet. *Just keep praying the guy turns up, Dicky Boy*.

He walked around the car, feeling the life come back into his legs after sitting for so long.

"Don't wander too far, Richard," Michael said. "Once we've made the transaction we're out of here."

"Right."

Richard saw Michael lean against the side of the car and pull

Join the Leisure Horror Book Club and

GET 2 FREE BOOKS NOW—
An $11.98 value!

Yes! I want to subscribe to the Leisure Horror Book Club.

Please send me my **2 FREE BOOKS**. I have enclosed $2.00 for shipping/handling. Each month I'll receive the two newest Leisure Horror selections to preview for 10 days. If I decide to keep them, I will pay the Special Members Only discounted price of just $4.25 each, a total of $8.50, plus $2.00 shipping/handling. This is a **SAVINGS OF AT LEAST $3.48** off the bookstore price. There is no minimum number of books I must buy and I may cancel the program at any time. In any case, the **2 FREE BOOKS** are mine to keep.

Not available in Canada.

NAME: _____

ADDRESS: _____

CITY: _____ STATE: _____

COUNTRY: _____ ZIP: _____

TELEPHONE: _____

E-MAIL: _____

SIGNATURE: _____

If under 18, Parent or Guardian must sign. Terms, prices, and conditions subject to change. Subscription subject to acceptance. Dorchester Publishing reserves the right to reject any order or cancel any subscription.

a white envelope from his pocket. He guessed it contained the two-million-pound check.

"Richard," Michael nodded. "Here he comes."

Richard watched the motorbike pull into the car park, approach and stop half a dozen feet from Michael who smiled and nodded.

The rider, in black leathers, pulled off his helmet, revealing a man of around twenty-five with dyed blond hair. He stood astride the idling machine and asked, "Are you Mr. Michael?"

"Just Michael. Where's Heath?"

"He's waiting across by the Minster."

"Have you got the book?"

"Not with me."

Michael's smile didn't falter. "I thought we had an agreement."

"It's been changed."

"By Heath?"

"By me. I'm his business partner."

"It's Heath's book. We agreed a price."

"He hadn't discussed it with me." The blond man stroked flat his hair where it had been ruffled by the helmet. "The book was undervalued; we're going to ask you for another million."

"Three million pounds for a book?" Michael raised his eyebrows. "Rather pricey, isn't it?"

"From what I can gather," said the blond man, "the book is worth considerably more than that to you."

"Can I speak to Heath?"

"No."

Michael put his finger to his lips as he thought about it. "You know you have a gun to my head?"

The man shrugged.

"Are you sure you speak for Heath?"

"Yes."

"You *do* have the book?"

"If you have the money."

"It's a deal, then. Three million. You'll still accept a check?"

The blond man's expression was hostile. "I wouldn't personally, but Heath trusts you."

"We've done business before."

The blond motorcyclist buckled on his helmet.

"Where are you going?" Michael frowned. "Hey, I said where . . ."

The bike roared to the exit where its rider waited, revving the engine impatiently.

"Damn," hissed Michael. "Back in the car, Richard."

As they climbed in Christine asked, "What's wrong?"

"Michael's just been shafted," Joey grunted. "I heard what he said. Three million quid for a bloody book."

"Not just any bloody book," said Michael in a low voice. "Hang on tight. We'll have to follow him."

"Are we still OK for time?"

"Hopefully. As long as the traffic doesn't get too heavy. Richard, keep an eye on the bike in case I lose sight of it."

Christine said, "But where are we going?"

"To meet Heath, I hope. He's the guy with the book."

"And you're going to pay an extra million just like that?" asked Richard in disbelief.

"Want to know a little secret, Richard? I'd have paid twenty million for it and not batted an eyelid."

"For a book?"

"Not just any old book. As I said earlier. What price do you put on a child's life? So what price do you put on the future of the human race?"

Michael had to drive hard to keep up with the motorbike as it drove along York's streets between rows of medieval timber-framed shops. Ahead, Richard could see York Minster, the twelfth-century church that dwarfed many a modern cathedral.

In a deserted side street, just behind the Minster, lying in its massive shadow, sat a vintage Jaguar. The motorbike stopped.

"There's Heath," Michael murmured. "Just hope he remembered to bring the book."

Richard climbed out of the car with Michael. Absurdly, he began to feel like Michael's sidekick. Not that anything should go wrong. Michael walked forward and shook hands with a small wisp of a man of about forty-five in a charcoal suit and silver-rimmed glasses.

"How are you keeping?" asked Michael warmly.

"Not bad, thank you, Michael. Although all this heat is rather fatiguing."

Michael, still smiling, dropped his voice. "Why all this cloak and dagger stuff with young men on motorbikes? I thought we had a perfectly simple business arrangement."

Heath shrugged. "No fool like an old fool, is there?" He smiled in the direction of the motorcyclist. "For the first time in my life I went and fell in love. All Tommy's trying to do is look after me."

"Tommy's doing a good job." Michael pulled out his checkbook and began to write a fresh check, resting on the roof of the Jaguar. "Three million. And you have the book?"

"Justinian's *The Divine Epitome*. Yes. You'll—"

"*The Divine Epitome*? You told my team you had the Constantine biography."

"You are interested specifically in the part that contains a copy of the *Codex Alexander*?"

"Yes." Michael's smile had vanished. He glared at the little wisp of a man in a way that Richard would have described as dangerous.

"Don't worry, Michael. *The Divine Epitome* contains a verbatim copy of the *Codex*. You'll find an elegant rendition of—"

"Richard," said Michael quickly. "Find out what's wrong with Joey. I'll finish off here."

Richard glanced across at Joey. Christine was walking with her arm around him, Amy was leading him by the hand.

"What's wrong?" asked Richard, running up.

"Joey's feeling faint. It must be with sitting in that hot car. There, Joey, sit down. Put your head between your legs."

"Don't worry, Uncle Joey." Amy said. "You'll be all right."

Joey sat down on a bench by the side entrance of the Minster. It was cool with plenty of shade.

Michael and Heath came up. "Is your friend all right?" Heath inquired, peering at Joey who was leaning back against the Minster wall, his belly sagging out through his shirt.

"He'll be fine," Richard said. "It's the heat."

Still wearing the motorcyclist's helmet, Tommy walked toward them, perhaps wondering if there was some kind of double cross being set in motion.

"Don't worry, Tommy." Heath smiled. "This gentleman's just taken poorly, that's all."

"You've got the check?"

"I've got the check, Tommy."

"And I've got the book," Michael said, holding up the brown paper parcel. "How're you feeling, Joey?"

"Not too bad, now. It's the heat."

"It's happened before," Christine said, rubbing the back of his neck. "Ever since he was a young boy, if he got too hot he'd just flake out."

Amy skipped forward to hold Michael by the hand and asked if the parcel in his other hand was a birthday present. Smiling, Michael pretended it was an early birthday present to himself.

Casually, Michael held out the car keys. "Christine. If you back the car down here we'll get Joey into the backseat."

"Can't we wait a few more minutes? I think—"

"Christine." Michael tried to communicate more with his eyes than with what he said. "I really do think we need to be moving on quite quickly."

"Oh." She understood and hurried to the car.

"We need to be getting home, too, Heath," said Tommy. "I'll follow on the bike."

Heath smiled apologetically. "That's youth for you. Always in a hurry. Cheerio, everybody. Look after yourself, Michael."

"I will." Michael smiled.

Richard remembered precisely where everyone was at 11:22 that Tuesday morning. Joey on the bench. Amy holding Michael's hand. Richard standing on the pavement beside them. Christine had reached the Range Rover and was opening the door. Tommy stood ten paces away beside his bike, waiting for Heath to reach the vintage Jag fifty paces away down the side street.

Richard remembered where people were at that moment so precisely because that was when, without warning, the Beast struck.

Chapter Forty-two

Carnage

--------/--/--

ENTRANCE TO MINSTER
M/BIKE   RANGE ROVER   HEATH'S CAR

Richard could have drawn a diagram of it. Every detail, every damned detail burned itself deep into his brain tissue.

There was the quiet side street. It finished in a dead end. On one side, rising like a cliff face, was York Minster, the medieval church that had towered over the city like the eighth Wonder Of the World for, as near as dammit, a thousand years.

In the street were cars, a van, but no people other than himself, Amy, Joey (still faint and sagging like a bag of potatoes) and Michael holding the damned book parcel. There was Tommy, dressed in leathers, wearing the helmet, and sitting astride his bike. Christine now sat in the driver's seat of the Range Rover, getting ready to pull it forward so they could tip Joey Barrass into the back. Heath, the wisp of a man, now three million richer, stood by his vintage Jag, smiling back at them.

Richard could see it all. He could see every bloody thing.

The way the sun shone on the cars. The picturesque redbrick houses lining the other side of the street. He heard distant traffic, he heard the birds singing in nearby trees; he felt the heat of the sun.

Then he felt the blast of wind. It came down from a clear blue sky like a hurricane, almost knocking them flat with its fury.

Richard saw Heath look up at the sky as if he sensed the coming of the Lord God Jehovah in all His righteous fury.

BANG

The Jag no longer existed. Heath no longer existed. He vanished like the sheep had, back on that hillside road. Richard saw him simply burst like a balloon filled with crimson paint. There was a lick of blood on the pavement and nothing more. The car shrieked into a layer of metal scrap no thicker than a living room carpet.

Michael started shouting.

Then, after the downward blast of air, there was a sensation of air rushing upward. The Beast actually created a vacuum as it reared up for another blow. Richard felt the air being sucked from his lungs, pain stabbed his ears. Amy was screaming, her hands over her ears.

Then stillness. Complete, total, absolute stillness.

Silence.

From the ruptured van, newspapers torn upward by the force of the suction floated slowly down like giant snowflakes from a mythical snow kingdom.

"Run!" Michael shouted. "It's going to hit again!"

"Christine!"

Richard began to run toward the Range Rover which lay between him and what was left of Heath. "Drive! Drive!"

He heard the starter motor turn. The engine wasn't firing.

"She's flooded it," Michael yelled. "Richard. It's too late!"

Richard looked at his wife. For a second their eyes met and a stream of meaning passed between them. He could do nothing to save her. She knew it, too. In her eyes he saw her love for him, her love for their children.

And her final good-bye.

It came again. Metal shrieked as a road sign quivered flat. Houses burst into a spray of rubble. A dog barked hysterically, then . . .

. . . then it gave a screeching yelp—and stopped.

"Richard! Come on! *Come on!*"

There was nothing but noise and fury. Dust from the houses obliterated the sight of Christine sitting frozen with shock in the car; dust blasted into Richard's eyes, blinding him.

Any second now—

Any second now it would all be over.

All the hurting and the running and the misery and the guilt and the pain.

Richard dropped to his knees. His wife. Christine. Why did—

"Richard! In here," Michael was shouting. He'd picked Amy up in his arms: she clung fiercely to his neck. Richard could just see through his stinging dust-filled eyes. Joey and Tommy lumbered through the side entrance into the Minster. Michael followed, carrying Amy.

What now?

What on Earth do you fucking do? thought Richard desperately. Follow Michael? Amy would need her father now. Or try and find Christine, buried somewhere in that boiling cloud of dust?

No. She's dead, Richard told himself. *Help Amy.*

So, scrambling on his hands and knees through that choking, blinding dust, Richard clawed his way in through the door into the Minster.

Chapter Forty-three

Terror

Inside the church the silence was as sudden as it was eerie. Richard, panting, covered in red dust from the pulverized brick, could only stand there, trying to stop panic from sending him crashing over the edge into madness.

Outside a street lay in ruins.

Inside, here, stillness. The sun shone through the stained-glass windows that were as big as house fronts. They depicted saints and angels. The walls of the Minster soared upward; above him timber beams held the roof high above his head. The space within the building was so vast you could have actually flown a microlite plane through the thing.

He blinked, looked round. There were tourists everywhere. They were looking at each other and up at the stained-glass windows. They'd heard something happen, but what? Two men in black cassocks and dog collars ran by him toward the side entrance to see what was happening.

A sound like thunder rumbled across the building.

"Come on, Richard." Michael called as he hurried along the aisle, carrying Amy. "We can't wait here any longer."

As if coming out of a dream Richard saw Joey half-walking, half-stumbling after Michael, his face gray; he clutched his chest as if his heart edged on bursting. Tommy was there, too. Helmet off, he looked around in bewilderment, his blond hair pink from the light coming through the Rose window.

"Heath. What happened to Heath?" he murmured, shocked.

"Stay here, and you're dead," snapped Michael. He wasn't waiting for them now but turned and ran for the main exit at the front of the building.

"Dad!"

216

Amy's head bobbed up and down as Michael ran with her in his arms.

Dazed, Richard followed. Tommy grabbed hold of Richard's arm and babbled, "What's happening? What happened to Heath? Heath needs a doctor. He needs an ambulance."

"Does he shit," hissed Richard at last. "The poor bastard doesn't even need a coffin; neither does my wife."

Frightened tourists pushed for the exit now. There were shouts. Names of wives and fathers were called as people were separated from their families in the narrow aisles.

The Beast struck.

Richard looked back over his shoulder.

With an almighty crash the wall they'd just come through bulged inward. As if that vast expanse of cream-colored stone had just become as soft as a curtain. It bulged . . . bulged . . . splitting cracks appeared. The noise began. A constant thundering like a mighty waterfall as blocks of stone heavier than a man could actually lift poured down, smashing wooden pews, statues, lecterns, tables.

Richard moved backward, unable to take his eyes from the terrible sight. Rubble cascaded onto the stone heads of statues, shattering them, then crashed down onto the human heads below, bursting them like raw eggs.

Screams pierced the thunderous rumble; people ran. In panic some ran into the destruction; falling timbers broke grown men like toys.

Crash.

Stained-glass windows punched inward, in clouds of streaming colored fragments. Richard looked up. They seemed to hang forever there, a hundred feet above his head, twinkling shards of glass in brilliant reds, blues, greens, yellows; then he realized they were falling. He threw himself, under the shelter of a lectern as ten thousand slivers of glass pelted down.

A wave of screams filled the building as the shards of glass buried themselves deep into necks and heads and faces.

Move, MOVE, *MOVE!*

The Beast's coming your way.

Any second, You'll be flat as shit beneath a road roller. Accept it, Christine's dead. Amy needs you now. You've got to live for the sake of your daughter.

"Amy!" he called. He couldn't see her now, or Michael, or

Joey. *Jesus, don't let Michael leave Amy in this hell. She's four years old, for Christsakes; she wouldn't stand a chance in this mad stampede of people.*

He ran along the aisle, looking for Amy. He barely noticed that Tommy still ran with him, screaming, "Who planted the bomb? Who planted the bomb?"

Crimson and rose-pink blades of stained glass studded the back of his leather jacket; a lick of fresh blood reddened his blond hair.

"Amy! Amy!" Richard shouted into the roaring mayhem.

Behind him a stone column buckled and exploded. Dust filled the church, blotting out the sun that streamed through the remaining stained-glass windows.

Richard clawed his way on. The dust turned day into night until he could hardly see a foot in front of him. Sometimes he tripped over people lying on the floor. Sometimes hands clutched at him; injured people begged for help.

The dust mist thinned. He could see that the tiny exits at either side of the Minster's huge locked main doors were clogged with people. For a second he thought he saw Joey being pushed forward by the surge of people. *Where was Michael? Did he still have Amy?*

Christ, let her be safe, let her be safe, the desperate prayer whirled through his head over and over. *Christ, let her be safe, please let her get out of here.*

Behind him, tons of stone blocks fell onto the church organ; it bellowed out a great fugue of notes as the air was crushed from the metal pipes. For all the world it sounded like a great beast, gored to its very guts, roaring its fury and its pain as the House of God came tumbling down.

Down, down in a splash of stone, glass, and blood.

Blood spattered the walls. And it hung in the air in a fine spray as dozens of men and women burst beneath the rocks, or beneath the invisible fist of the Beast itself.

He realized it couldn't have reached him yet, otherwise he would have been crushed, too. The carnage around him had been caused by the lethal shrapnel of glass and shattered masonry.

He scrambled over upturned pews. A Japanese woman lunged out of the dust cloud, vomit covering the front of her dress. She begged in Japanese. Shaking his head, dazed, ears bleeding from the sudden compression of air, he pushed on toward the exits.

Now Richard's insane world was by turns plunged into darkness and filled with dazzling sunlight as the dust screened the windows before blasts of air cleared them again.

Darkness. Light. The endless rumble thundered on. The church organ still bellowed a cacophony of discordant notes.

Darkness. He moved forward by touch alone. Then came a flashing light. He saw a severed hand. Still clutching a camera, the twitching fingers clicked the shutter button, sending out a strobing flash.

Light. Thirty feet away he saw a statue of St. George slaying the dragon crushed to a dust as fine as talcum powder.

Richard cleared the last of the pews and raced across the expanse of stone slabs to those oh-so-tiny exits blocked by people struggling to get out of the collapsing church. A fat priest swung his fists, trying to punch his way out through a party of schoolchildren.

"Richard!" screamed Tommy as he was enveloped in dust. Richard was just able to make out the leather jacket and blond hair as the man fell. Richard turned to help.

Darkness again. Richard thrust his hands out blindly. His hand closed over the blond hair. He pulled.

Again came the sensation of the air being sucked from his lungs as the Beast lifted itself upward ready for another strike.

The updraft of air sucked away the dust cloud. He could see again.

"Tommy, get to the—"

He stopped talking. Tommy's head hung by its hair from his hand. The body had vanished.

From the torn throat hung long strands, like a fistful of spaghetti the color of blood. For a split second Richard stared in ghastly fascination at the man's face. The tongue moved backward and forward between the blood-red lips. As if the severed head was actually trying to speak.

Richard dropped it and ran.

Sunlight blasted into the church in front of him. Someone had managed to open the huge twin doors. People flowed out through them like water pouring through a break in a dam wall.

Not knowing whether Amy was still inside the church, whether she was alive or dead, Richard was carried outside into the sunlight.

Chapter Forty-four

Wreckage

He couldn't stop.

That thing was right behind him. He had to keep running on through the city.

He glanced back as he ran across the paved area in front of the Minster. Now the massive doorway set in the face of the church between two towers looked like an almighty mouth.

An almighty mouth that vomited people and dust and masonry, as the Beast moved through the interior of the building like a piston through its cylinder, forcing everything before it.

Or crushing everything beneath it.

"Richard!"

He looked round, dazed.

"Richard!"

He looked again. Michael stood at the side of the road, covered in dust. He gripped the book parcel so tightly he looked like a drowning man clinging to a stick.

"Richard," Michael called. "Have you seen Amy?"

"Amy? You had her! *You were carrying her!*"

"We got separated in the crush."

Richard looked back. The huge church seemed to be folding in on itself as if it was made out of cardboard. A two-hundred-foot tower sank down with a surreal majesty. Dust clouds burst high into the sky.

Richard knew he had no alternative. He had to go back. He had to find Amy. Or die trying.

"Richard . . . Richard . . ." Joey lumbered out of a knot of people. "Don't go back there." Spit gobbed from his mouth. "They're all dead . . . don't go back . . . run . . ."

"I'm not leaving her," yelled Richard.

"And neither am I," Michael said. "The crowd in the road.

Look there," he told Richard. "Joey . . . Joey . . ."

But Joey had already gone. Clutching his chest, he ran in the direction of the bridge that spanned the River Ouse.

Michael shook his head, dust fell from his hair. "I'll check in the square."

"But—"

"Make it snappy, Richard. It's coming. I reckon we've got all of twenty seconds."

As he ran toward the road he saw an impossible sight.

He slowed down, his eyes straining forward in disbelief.

A gray car bumped onto the pavement and accelerated toward him.

"Christine?" He began to run forward. "Christine!"

At first he thought he was hallucinating. But he could see his wife in the car. Dust covered the windows and paintwork. A fist-sized-dent in the bonnet showed where a brick had slammed down onto it.

Christine used the wipers and screenwash to clear away the worst of the dust. He saw her expression. Grim. Determined.

The car screeched to a stop in front of him.

He threw himself into the passenger seat.

Christine's eyes locked onto the road in front of her. "Where's Amy?"

"I don't know. I was going to look—"

"Too late." Her voice was coldly matter-of-fact. "Joey?"

"He took off on foot. Michael's . . . wait. *Christine, wait!*" Richard beat the dashboard with his fist. "Michael's there on the other side of the road. Thank Christ for that! He's found Amy!"

Christine pulled over. Michael pushed Amy in the back, then scrambled in after her. Christine was accelerating away before he'd even closed the door.

At that moment Richard felt a great surge of gratitude toward Michael for saving Amy's life. At that moment he would have given him everything he owned.

"Quick," Michael panted, his arm protectively around Amy. Her eyes were glazed with shock; her hair was clotted with white dust. "You've got to get us away. It's right behind us."

He looked back. Feet away a tree shivered, branches sheered from the trunk, then the trunk itself slapped flat to the ground.

Christine floored the accelerator. The car rocketed forward, weaving around cars and dazed tourists. She drove in the direction of the bridge, concentrating on nothing but getting them clear.

"Joey." Richard pointed. "There's Joey."

Joey tanked it toward the bridge, his stride slow and heavy, still clutching his chest with one hand as if his heart would snap.

Christine slowed, ready to pull alongside him.

Michael said in a low voice. "Don't, Christine. It's too close."

"No."

"Keep driving."

"No." She'd made up her mind. "I'm stopping for my brother." Michael sighed and rubbed his face in frustration as much as exhaustion.

Richard looked back to see Joey collapse in through the back door, his head and torso falling across Michael's legs. Michael pushed him back into a sitting position. Joey couldn't speak, panting for breath. Drool slid from his mouth in strings. His brown eyes looked up sightlessly at the roof of the car.

Richard closed his eyes. But he knew he'd seen sights today that would stay with him until the day he died.

He heard Christine accelerate away from York's shattered heart. He would only open his eyes again when it was a long, long way behind them.

Chapter Forty-five

On the Road to York

Ten miles from York Rosemary Snow heard the news on the radio.

She pulled the van over to the side of the road. Her blood turned cold.

". . . unconfirmed reports say that more than thirty people are dead, with many more injured by falling masonry."

"Oh, my God," she whispered. She knew what was behind this.

"York Minster has stood for nine hundred years in the city of York, a magnet for tourists. It will be a long time before experts can tell us what actually did happen. But the people of York will remember forever the day their most famous landmark and place of worship came crashing to the ground. Now . . . we can go over to Stephanie Robson, live at the scene of the disaster."

In the background sirens, shouting. The voice of the reporter quavered. "I'm standing here in front of what should have been a magnificent Gothic building. All that remains . . . all that remains is a mountain of white stone, shattered gargoyles, fragments of once-beautiful stained-glass windows crunching like snow beneath my feet. Ian Garside was standing just here when it happened. Ian, what did you see exactly?"

The man sounded both shocked and excited. "I'd been to buy a newspaper. I was standing just where I am now. Heard an almighty bang, then . . . thunder. Just thundering on and on. I looked up and the whole building gave way in the middle. Towers crashed down. I thought of all those poor people; I saw—"

Rosemary switched off the radio. Her mouth was dry and the side of her head had begun to throb.

She had to stop Michael. If it was the last thing she did.

Closing her eyes, she breathed deeply. Images flashed chaotically across her mind like a madman hitting the controls of a TV remote. First there were images of people running through a vast building. A church organ thrashing out discordant notes. Lumps of rock falling from above. Amy . . . Yes, she was seeing through Amy's eyes. She was being carried. By her father. No . . . The man's anxious face swelled into close up. The downturned eyes, the brushed hair.

Michael.

Michael carried Amy through the collapsing building.

Obviously the little girl was important to him. Just as Rosemary had been. Until she had failed him. Then she had been left to the mercy of that thing.

Then more images leaping out of the darkness. The totem pole again. All hooked noses, beaks, hooky ears and the eyes. The staring, staring eyes that . . .

That for some inexplicable reason terrified her more than words could say.

Stay with it, Red Zed, stay with it. See what Amy sees now. You can do it. Amy, where are you? What do you see?

Images came. They were flattened and distorted. Rosemary guessed the little girl was confused, frightened.

One second she could see the girl's hands knitted together in her lap. They were white with dust. The car moved fast. Tree branches whipped overhead. Someone was talking. To Amy it was a rapid mumbling sound that made no sense whatsoever.

With cars droning by the VW van at the roadside, Rosemary rested her throbbing head against the side window. Soon an image would come, she told herself. A road sign or a place name. She was so close now. She could feel it. She would find Michael.

And she couldn't wait to see the look on his face when she could say to him, "Hallo. Remember me?"

Chapter Forty-six

After the Storm

Amy sat on the climbing frame in the garden. The sun had begun dropping toward the hill that climbed up at the back of the cottage, trees whispered gently in the evening breeze, a dove called. And Richard felt like shit.

He guessed Amy did, too. Although she'd never use that particular word.

"Tired," was all she'd admit to when asked.

"Do you like the doll Michael bought you?" Richard asked, leaning forward against the climbing-frame bars.

Amy nodded, curly hair falling forward across her face.

"Aren't you going to give Dad a smile?"

She looked down at the doll and ran her fingers slowly through its long black hair.

"I bet you're hungry, Amy. Would you like some soup?"

Tiny shake of the head.

"It was kind of Michael to ask us to stay in his cottage, wasn't it?" After what had happened in York today Richard found it hard to speak at all. But he kept going. He wanted to reach Amy and draw her out of this icy silence she'd locked herself into.

"Uncle Joey's all right now. He felt poorly earlier when . . . when the accident happened. It was noisy in that church, wasn't it? All that running about, dust and . . ." Words failed Richard as the images came back. The Japanese tourist with her face studded with shards of glass. In his hands . . . the head . . . the way the tongue wriggled between the lips . . .

Richard turned away to look across the valley.

The peace here in Devon was so thick you could almost reach out and bury your face in it. He breathed deeply, hanging onto the normality of it all. The little white painted farmhouses on the valley sides, the fields, hedgerows, a flock of white birds moving with long lazy flaps of their wings. In the distance a farm dog barked. From here it was a musical sound that seemed to shimmer on the evening air. Any other time Richard would have drunk it in. But clanking through his mind like a rusty anchor chain came the jarring images. The man Heath pulped where he stood. Houses shattered. Running through the falling church. People crushed by masonry or turned into a paste the color of strawberry jam by that thing Michael called the Beast.

He rubbed his eyes with his fists. Michael had brought this pile of shit on them. *The bastard. Then again he's saved Amy's life today.*

"Daddy."

Amy's voice sounded like a silver bell. Richard looked up, surprised she'd spoken at all.

"Daddy. Do you know what I'm going to call this doll?"

"What, hon?"

"Rosemary Snow."

"Why Rosemary Snow?"

"Rosemary Snow's a nice name."

He said gently, "Amy, you keep talking about Rosemary Snow."

"Rosemary Snow's coming here."

"Now?"

Amy nodded.

"Did Michael tell you about Rosemary Snow?"

She shook her head.

How do you know about Rosemary Snow?"

"I just do, that's all. She's coming here. And she's mad at Michael, because she says Michael is a bad man."

"But Michael bought you the doll."

"I know."

"That's a kind thing to do, then, isn't it?"

She nodded. "Mark gave me one of his comics."

"Well, that was kind as well."

"Only because he'd thumped me and didn't want me to tell on him."

"Oh."

Amy climbed to the top of the climbing frame where she sat combing the doll's long black hair with her fingers and singing softly to herself, "Rosemary Snow, Rosemary Snow . . ."

After talking to Amy, Richard made his way back to the cottage.

It was long and low, built out of stone beneath a red pantile roof. The cottage looked out over the valley below. At the front lay a graveled courtyard where they'd parked the Range Rover. Beyond that a dirt track ran up through woodland to join the main road.

Inside the cottage it had been modernized to the point of luxury. A bedroom had been fitted out as a study complete with computer terminals, a fax machine and half a dozen boxes containing disks. Michael told them he had rented a network of properties like this across the country when he realized he would have to keep moving ahead of the Beast. At first he simply planned to move from one to the other, keeping clear of the Beast until his research team had solved the problem. Lately it hadn't been so easy, due to the unpredictable nature of the creature.

Richard walked into the cottage to find Joey fortifying himself from the whiskey decanter. Christine and Michael studied a leather-bound book.

Christine looked up from the book. "Richard. Have you seen this? The pages are made out of pigskin."

"Does it tell us what we want to know?" Richard said in a flat voice.

Michael said, "It'll take time. But it does definitely contain extracts from the *Codex Alexander*."

"You do realize that was going to cost you three mill." Joey's face was red from the booze. "But after what happened in York today you got the fucker at a knockdown price."

At first Richard thought Joey had got himself steaming drunk, but there was a mixture of challenge as well as fear in his eyes. In a half-drunk way Joey was trying to goad Michael into some kind of justification for what he was doing.

Michael let it pass. "Lucky it's written in Greek and not Latin or I wouldn't have had a clue. I'd better begin work on this right away."

"You said it would take time," Richard said shortly. "How long?"

"I can have the bones of it deciphered in a couple of hours."

"We've got that long, have we?"

"I think so."

"Are you sure? Or are we going to find this shack of yours coming down around our ears?"

"I'm sure, Richard. Look, trust me on this one. I've lived with the Beast for—"

"The Beast? The Beast! Why not call it Fido, or Rover, or . . . or even Cuddles? The thing's a killer. When it comes down to it, you don't know what it wants, or how to control it."

"Richard, I—"

"You're like a monkey with a machine gun. Look at this little lever, I wonder what happens if I touch it. Pow! Ooops, just wiped out half my family. I wonder if it'll do the same again. Pow!"

"Richard, I didn't intend to kill those—"

"Didn't intend? Well, mate, you might not have been paying attention but that's what fucking well happened."

Michael's downturned eyes were gentle. "What can I say? There's nothing I can do to bring those people back."

"This Beast thing. You said you could get rid of it for good. Send it back. You've got all the money you want, you don't need it, so . . . oh, shit to this. Give me a drink." Hands shaking, he took the decanter from Joey and poured himself a hefty slug.

"Richard," Christine said in a low voice. "What happened today wasn't Michael's fault. If anything, it was Heath and his boyfriend, stringing us along, asking for more money."

Joey nodded. "All this . . . cloak-and-dagger shermozzle."

"If they hadn't delayed us getting us the book," Christine continued, "and delayed us getting away from York, everything would have been OK. The Beast wouldn't have had time to attack."

"Christine's right," Michael said softly. "Imagine the Beast's attached to us by a long piece of elastic. Once we're moving fast enough it can't stabilize itself in order to affect anything on our physical plane."

"We're not moving now." Richard took a deep swallow of whisky and sang out as if calling a dog, "So here, Beastie, Beastie. Come on, boy, we know you've got a pressing appointment."

"It's not funny, Richard," said Christine, eyeing the amount of whiskey he was drinking.

"You're telling me." There was a hell of a lot Richard wanted to say. But he found the words had hit a log-jam somewhere in the back of his throat. He refilled his glass from the decanter and walked out of the house and back into the garden. Overhead a pair of swans flapped slowly toward the setting sun. And he wished to God he could sprout wings and follow them to a faraway place.

Chapter Forty-seven

Saviour

"Oh, Christ. No . . . no . . ."

Christine Young wept silently; a fat river of tears rolled down her cheeks.

She was alone, sitting on the hearth rug in the cottage, one elbow on the coffee table, her forehead supported by her hand. She'd just sat through a news report about the destruction of York Minster. The death toll had risen to forty-eight. She'd watched that with a cold detachment as if it had happened a hundred years ago. Not that morning.

What had opened the emotional floodgates was a report tacked to the end of the news about Darren Wakes, a boy of roughly Amy's age. It showed him playing with a toy tractor. His face was as yellow as a banana skin. Doctors had given him three weeks to live. They said nothing could be done for him.

Christine watched, the image of the five-year-old's face blurred through the tears that stung her eyes. The reporter added that a surgeon at a private hospital was confident he could save the boy's life with a liver and lung transplant. But it would cost £60,000.

There followed scenes of Darren's parents and neighbors desperately making door-to-door collections and trying to organize a sponsored parachute jump. "A brave effort," the reporter said, "but in their heart of hearts they must be thinking: is this too little, too late, to save this five-year-old boy's life?"

"Here. Take this."

Christine looked up startled. "Michael? I didn't realize you were there."

"Sorry if I startled you." Smiling kindly, he held out a clean tissue.

She felt as if she had to explain. "I was watching the news . . .

about York. Then there was a story about a boy. He's about Amy's age . . . he's going to die." She sniffed. "Christ. It makes you so angry. Sometimes you think the only reason you're put on this Earth is to suffer and die."

Michael nodded, his eyes gentle. "But we still keep bringing more children into the world."

"It's a joke, isn't it? A sad, pathetic joke. Do you know something?" She looked up at Michael. "When my father was dying in hospital—he had cancer of the bowel—a priest walked up to him and asked him if he was ready to meet God. My father said, yes, and when I get there I'm going to kick his backside all over heaven for all the suffering he's caused down here on Earth." She gave a bitter laugh. "You see, he'd brought up Joey and myself single-handed. My mother had suffered from diabetes since she was ten years old. After I was born she went blind, a couple of years after that she died."

"But you're carrying on. You've got two fine healthy children."

She nodded. "But the knocks come hard. Look what happened today. Forty-eight people dead in minutes."

"I know, Christine. That's something I'll have to live with for the rest of my life. It was my fault. I was too blinkered about getting my hands on that book. Instead of going to meet Heath I should have just kept on driving to put some space between us and the thing."

"Michael," Christine's voice was low, husky. "This thing you call the Beast. Can't you just let it go? Do you really think all these deaths are worth trying to hold onto the thing?"

Michael placed his fingertips together and touched his lips as he thought about what she had said. "Christine. What would you say to this? Imagine that little boy you saw on the television. Now imagine that the Beast could save his life. Would you still insist that I get rid of it?"

"From what I've seen the thing's a killer."

Michael picked the cordless phone from the wall, then crouched down in front of Christine. He put the phone on the coffee table.

"But if you could save little Darren's life? Would you still want me to get rid of the Beast?"

"I . . ." Wiping her eyes, she shook her head. "No. No, I suppose not."

"Pick up the phone, Christine."

She looked at him puzzled.

"Pick up the phone. You're going to save that boy's life."

"How?"

"You're going to telephone the TV station and tell them you will pay for that life-saving operation."

"I haven't got that kind of money."

"I have. And I acquired that money only because I formed the relationship with the Beast."

He found the TV station's telephone number in the directory, then handed her a printed card on which was printed the words: THE M FOUNDATION. Beneath that were telephone numbers.

"Christine. Telephone the TV station. Tell them you represent a charitable foundation, and that they will pay for Darren's operation."

Her eyes shone, full of hope. "You're serious?"

He gave a faint smile. "Yes, I'm serious. Just give them that telephone number at the bottom of the card. The TV station will help the boy's parents get in touch with the foundation. After all, there's a good news story in it for them."

As Christine began to dial, Michael's smile broadened. "How does it feel to save a life?"

Outside, in the garden, Richard sat on a low stone wall that separated formal flower beds from the sweep of the lawn where Amy played with the doll she had named Rosemary Snow.

Amy sang, "Rosemary Snow's coming to stay, Rosemary Snow's coming to stay, Rosemary Snow's coming to stay . . . Dad?"

Richard looked up. "Yes?" His sore throat coarsened his voice.

"Dad. Rosemary wants to know where we are?"

Richard wiped the back of his hand across his mouth. All he could think about now was the decanter of whiskey in the cottage. He needed a drink . . . shit, no, he needed lots of drinks, buckets of the stuff. Something that would slaughter this scalding heap of pain and questions and guilt that was rotting him from the inside out. And there were the flashbacks searing through his mind. The severed hand twitching on the floor inside the church. Spasming fingers still hitting the camera button? If they developed the film . . . what holiday snaps would they see? Richard Young's face; his terrified eyes blazing from all that boiling dust; rubble

231

crashing down. A river of blood running from beneath the mountain of fallen stone, like grape juice running from a wine press . . . where was the Beast now? Coming to eat you up, laddie . . . coming to—

"Daddy."

"Yes, hon?"

"Rosemary Snow wants to know where we are now."

Richard's eyes focused on the doll with long black hair being waved in his face.

"Daddy's thinking," he said hoarsely. "Go and play."

"But Rosemary Snow needs to know where we are so she can come and visit us."

"Amy, I said go and play."

Christine smiled, her eyes shining with a sudden elation. "They said they're going to get in touch with the family straight away. And as far as the reporter knew the hospital could do the operation by the end of the week."

"And Darren will grow up healthy and strong, and marry and have children of his own one day." Michael smiled. "And he'll never know the name of his fairy godmother who made his family's wishes come true."

Christine blushed. "I've done nothing. It's your money."

"I'm just the middleman, Christine. If it wasn't for the Beast I wouldn't have the money. And if it wasn't for you seeing that story on the news Darren wouldn't be having his life-saving operation."

She shook her head, not sure whether to laugh or cry.

"Listen, Christine, I'm not suggesting this somehow cancels out what happened in York today. But you . . . Christine Young . . . have saved a life tonight." He rested his hand on hers and gently squeezed. It felt warm and reassuring. "You saved a life, Christine. Feel good about that."

She smiled through her tears. "Me and that thing of yours saved a life. That's the reality of it, isn't it?"

He nodded, his eyes so gentle that she felt something melt inside of her.

Amy was persistent. "Dad. Tell me where this is, so I can tell Rosemary Snow. She *really* wants to visit us, so she can tell us something *really* important."

"Come on, Amy. It's your bedtime."

"But Dad. Rosemary wants to know where we—"

"Amy!"

Shut up about Rosemary fucking Snow!

That's what he wanted to yell savagely. Then grab that stupid doll and rip its stupid head off like—

—like what happened today. When he held that blond head in his hands red strands of meat hung down; eyes rolled. The tongue and lips still twitching as if the severed head wanted to tell him something . . .

What would it tell him?

You're next, Richard Young. You're next. To be crushed into the dirt and . . .

Jesus . . . he took a deep breath; he was cracking up.

"Daddy. Do you feel all right?"

Amy stroked his back.

"Course I do, sweetheart." He swung his arm around her and held her tight, his face pressed into her hair. "I'm fine." He breathed deeply to settle the quiver in his voice, but he could do nothing to quell the trembling that ran through his body. "Now . . ." He cleared his throat. "What did your doll want to know?"

"Where are we?"

"This is Michael's house. Glebe Cottage. It's near a little village called Banwick, which is . . . uhm, let me see . . . about five miles from Dartmoor in Devon."

"I love you, Dad." She hugged him, the Rosemary Snow doll crushed between them.

"I love you too, hon."

Then Amy skipped across the lawn singing, "Rosemary Snow, we're in Banwick, we're in Banwick; we're in Devon beside the slippery sea . . ."

Chapter Forty-eight

The Road to Nowhere

"Come on, Red Zed," murmured Rosemary as she nursed the van along the slow lane of the motorway. "Are you on the road to nowhere or what?"

There had seemed no point in going to York. Although Amy, her family and Michael had obviously been there, they'd be long gone by now. She knew they were still alive because she'd seen disjointed mental images of motorway service stations: Michael driving; the car windows covered with dust. But there had been nothing definite she could identify.

The route Rosemary had taken was pot luck. But she needed to keep driving. She had a premonition that time was running out. She had to find the family.

Now she glanced down repeatedly at the engine's temperature gauge. The needle had been climbing steadily as she drove mile after mile through the hot afternoon sun.

When she glanced down again the needle had crept into the red zone. "Keep going, please keep going . . ."

Joey Barrass was comfort-eating. He'd started on his second microwaved chicken balti when Michael strolled into the kitchen.

Joey, spooning the spicy sauce into his mouth, didn't look up.

Michael yawned, then smiled. "Time for a beer break. Any left in the fridge?"

"Help yourself. You could get me one as well."

Michael opened the door of the refrigerator and reached for a bottle.

"Not that one. It's gnat's piss. There's some cans of Tennant's on the top shelf."

Michael passed him one of the cans. Joey tore open the ringpull and sucked at the can as if he'd just walked across a burning desert to get his hands on the thing.

Michael helped himself to one of the bottles of beer and sat at the kitchen table opposite Joey.

"Christ, that hits the spot." Joey held the iced can to his face. "Jesus, it's hot."

"There's a swimming pool on the terrace."

"I'll stick to this." He rolled the can against his forehead. "I don't care what anyone says, I'm having a night on the piss tonight."

"After what you've been through, who can blame you?"

"Christ." Joey looked at him, the muddy brown eyes clearing as he realized something. "We nearly died today, didn't we?"

"Don't dwell on it. We're safe now."

"For how long?"

"I think we've put enough miles between us and Beastie Boy to give us a good twenty-four hours."

"How far have you got with that old Roman book?"

"It's fairly slow going but I think I'll have learned what I need to know by around eleven."

"Where are the others?"

"Christine's putting Amy to bed. Richard's outside."

"You think this book will tell you what you need to know?"

"I think so."

"Thank God for that." Joey spooned in more balti.

"What are you going to do when this is over?"

Joey pushed back his fringe. "I haven't been able to think that far ahead. But I suppose it'll be back to the old routine."

Michael chatted casually, asking Joey what he did for a living. Joey told him about the property company he owned jointly with Christine and his plans for Sunnyfields.

Michael smiled. "It sounds as if you're going to have money coming out of your ears in a year or two."

"I would be if it wasn't for Dicky Boy out there. You know, every plan I've put forward for developing Sunnyfields he's blocked. 'Too ambitious,' he'll say. Or 'You'll never get planning permission for it.' "

"But it's a valuable plot of land. Why's Richard against you developing it?"

"The bastard's got no imagination. He keeps whining away that the land's contaminated."

"Is it?"

"There's an old refuse tip on the site. But it can be reclaimed. Look, my idea is . . . pass us that pencil." Joey tore open the card sleeves that contained the microwave meals and, taking the pencil, began sketching out a plan of the site, talking faster and faster as his old enthusiasm returned.

Michael listened attentively, nodding. "So Sunnyfields is, what? Two hundred acres?"

"Two hundred and thirty."

Michael pointed at the edge of the plan. "Didn't we go under a bridge when we were heading into town yesterday morning?"

"That's a railway."

"What lies between that and Sunnyfields?"

"About twenty acres of cornfields."

"You own them?"

"No."

"Buy them, then."

"Uh?" Joey looked puzzled.

"Get the farmer to sell you the fields."

"That'd give us another twenty acres but—"

"No. The important thing is to be able to link into the railway. With the new anti-pollution legislation there'll be an increase in rail freight at the expense of road freight. You could run a spur line from the main railway and anyone building a factory on Sunnyfields could bring in raw materials by rail and ship out finished goods the same way."

"Bloody expensive, though. We haven't that kind of capital."

"Trust me, buy those twenty acres; they'll quadruple the value of Sunnyfields."

Joey took the bait. Michael leaned back, nodding as he listened, lightly running his fingertips up and down the cold neck of the bottle. Joey talked quickly, sketching out development plans so energetically that the point of the pencil snapped.

When it looked as if he was running out of steam Michael pulled a few sheets of kitchen roll from the roller and began jotting down figures of his own.

"Joey, look, I'm looking to expand my business interests in the UK. I need approximately a hundred acres to build an electrical components factory. If I buy approximately half of Sunnyfields that will give you the capital to buy the twenty acres, put in the

236

rail spur and there might be enough left to build your industrial site on your half."

"Are you serious?"

"We're talking business here, Joey. Business is always serious."

"This is all a bit quick, though, isn't it?" Joey sniffed suspiciously. "You've not carried out any surveys, or even checked if the title of the land is—"

"Joey. I trust you. All I'm asking from you is that you trust me."

"In what way?"

"Just give me some support over the next couple of days. Nothing back-breaking. Basically, all I need to know is that you are on my side."

"And you'd buy Sunnyfields?"

"Yes. Part of it. Or all of it. You and your sister decide."

Joey's muddy brown eyes glazed as he made some mental calculations, then he said, "Don't worry about Christine, I can negotiate on her behalf."

"You trust me, Joey?"

"I do." He took a swallow of beer. "But how about an upfront payment, just to show how serious your intentions are? You know, Michael, just a nominal sum."

Michael smiled broadly. "Does one million pounds sound nominal enough to you?"

"Straight up?"

"Straight up. I'll make the telephone call now and have my bank transfer one million pounds into your account."

"Jesus," Joey whispered, his hands shaking. "Jesus, one million?"

Michael stood up. "I'll just need details of your bank account."

Dazed, Joey handed him his cash card.

Rosemary had stopped at a service station to buy sandwiches and give the engine time to cool. She was walking back to the van across the car park when the images came ripping through her mind with a brilliance that made her gasp.

She saw a cottage overlooking a valley. A doll with long black hair.

Then she was looking through Amy Young's eyes. The little girl was being tucked into bed by her mother.

Rosemary heard the voice. It was a little girl's voice but it was as loud as thunder. At first it was so loud she couldn't make out any individual words. Rosemary looked at people walking across the car park, wondering why they couldn't hear the voice, too, coming from the sky with an ear-splitting roar.

No one noticed. Then Rosemary realized the voice came from inside her head.

As she reached the van she began to make out the words.

ROSEMARY SNOW . . . ROSEMARY SNOW . . . BANWICK, DEVON . . . BANWICK, GLEBE COTTAGE IN DEVON . . . DEVON BY THE SLIPPERY SEA . . . ORANGES AND LEMONS, SAY THE BELLS OF ST. CLEMENTS . . .

The words became a song as the little girl somewhere in Devon began to sing herself to sleep.

Rosemary scrambled into the driving seat and turned the ignition key. As the VW's engine rattled into life the temperature gauge immediately climbed into the red.

Tough shit, she thought, savagely stamping the pedal to the floor. *You're going to take me to Devon if it's the last thing you do.*

Chapter Forty-nine

Night Talk

With Amy asleep upstairs, Christine, Joey and Richard sat in the lounge of the cottage in silence. The television showed a spy thriller. None of them would be able to remember its title or even a gist of the plot. They watched the images move across the screen, but a mixture of delayed shock and tiredness blunted their minds. Joey nursed a bottle of whiskey, automatically topping up his glass every few minutes.

Richard could smell the microwave meals that Joey had binged on. His stomach rolled but he couldn't decide whether he was hungry or nauseous.

As a brass clock on the mantelpiece chimed eleven Michael walked in. He was purposeful, businesslike: the thousand-year-old book was clasped under one arm, a wad of sheets covered in his handwriting was in the other.

Instantly the three sat up, alert and hoping for good news.

"Have you finished?" asked Richard, feeling a sudden low buzz of optimism.

"Just this minute. The relevant section about the Beast was shorter than I thought."

"And?" Christine prompted.

Michael sat down, putting the book on the coffee table and spreading out the sheets of paper. He said, *"The Divine Epitome"* is quite short and to the point, I'll give it that. The book was written by a monk in the tenth century. Because he was a devout Christian he decided to identify the entity I called the Beast as the Holy Spirit." He began to read. " 'If it is your desire that the Holy Spirit should dwell permanently in your heart, so that it imbues you with power over men in their tents and palaces and over beasts of the forest, fields and the air, then parcel a silver cross in pieces of burial shroud, then bind that to your forehead.'

It goes onto give specific instructions about how to make the silver crucifix, right down to its dimensions, weight and the purity of the silver."

Christine leaned forward. "Will it work?"

"Will it, hell." Michael dropped the sheets onto the table. "It's sheer mumbo-jumbo based on half-remembered folk tales and soldiers' tall stories."

"Great," Joey said thickly. "Bloody great."

"So all that happened today was a waste of time?" Christine said. "All those people dying?"

"All I can say is I regret it as much as you." He shook his head sadly. "But nothing I can say or do now will bring those people back."

"Ashes to ashes, dust to dust . . ." Joey slopped more whiskey into the glass.

"*The Divine Epitome* isn't completely useless," Michael said. "What does seem to be accurate is a reference to the *Codex Alexander*. You remember, that's an account of Alexander the Great's invasion of India and how he took the power out of the Purple Crescent, which is an area of the Eastern end of the Mediterranean?"

Christine nodded. "Your research team have that now?"

"Yes. *The Divine Epitome* tells us that," he began to read again, " 'Alexander's spell that binds the Holy Spirit to the heart is contained in the chapter that recounts his siege of the Indian City of Kush.' "

"Well, mercy me," chuckled Joey. "That sounds a big help."

Michael's smile was forgiving. "Believe me, it is, Joey. I've just been speaking to the head of my team by phone. The *Codex Alexander* is contained in one hundred and thirty-six separate documents. My research team would have needed to read them all to find what we need. Now they can home in on the relevant parchment and begin work right away on the translation."

"But how do you *control* the power?" Christine asked, her eyes sharply alert now.

Michael smiled. "It's quite easy, really. Once you have the knack."

"Or it *was* easy when you lived in Istanbul?"

"That's right. Once I moved outside the Purple Crescent I lost control of it and—"

"And it ran amok."

"Precisely. But the *Codex Alexander* will tell us how to regain control of it."

"Sounds like my bloody dog," Joey grunted. "It behaved itself, did what you told it. Bloody good dog. Then one day it wouldn't do a bloody thing you told it to do. We couldn't work out what'd happened. All we knew was that one day we had an obedient dog, then the next day you couldn't do a bloody thing with it. D'ya know what'd happened to it?"

Michael shook his head.

Joey topped up his glass. "It had gone bloody deaf, that's what." He laughed thickly. "There we were telling it to sit down or get my bloody slippers and the poor bloody mutt couldn't hear a bloody thing."

Michael nodded. "It makes a good analogy to what's happening here. When I arrived here in Britain it was as if the Beast could no longer hear me."

"But how did you control it before?" Christine asked. "I mean was it like a spell, or what?"

"I call it Active Imagination."

"Active Imagination?"

"Well." Michael put his fingertips together thoughtfully. "I can't see the Beast or hear it. So when I was first developing this partnership with it when I was living in Istanbul, I practiced the knack of imagining."

"And you had to imagine you controlled it."

"Yes. I knew I had to keep it close to me, so close it felt as if it actually shared my head with me."

"So how *did* you keep it close?"

"Well, I imagined it took the form of a dog that was well behaved as long as I kept giving it orders. So I developed the instructions in a phrase that I kept running through my head: *Walk with me, sit with me, stay with me. Walk with me, sit with me, stay with me*."

"And you had to keep repeating that."

"Yes. Not aloud, of course."

"How many times a day?"

"Well, that's the hard part. All day and every day."

"You had to keep that up *all the time*?" Christine said, astonished. "It's a wonder it didn't send you mad."

"At first I came close to it." He smiled. "But you get used to it."

"But what happened when you slept?" asked Richard.

"I learned it would lie dormant for at least an hour. So," he shrugged, "I learned to make do with one hour's sleep a night, with an hour's siesta in the afternoon."

"By rights sleep deprivation alone should have killed you."

"It's more common than you imagine. If you read about the Byzantine Emperors you'll see that those in symbiotic relationship with the Beast needed just one hour's sleep a night. Then they'd pace the city walls until dawn."

Joey snorted. "Doesn't sound bloody worth it to me."

Michael stood up, his eyes alight. "But you can't understand what the Beast does for you. The energy, the enthusiasm it gives you. Once you have it inside you, you feel your whole body comes alive; your senses—hearing, touch, sight, taste, smell—become more acute. You feel full of fire and you know in here," he thumped his chest, "you know in here that nothing is impossible anymore."

"So you think having to repeat that rhyme umpteen thousand times a day is a small price to pay for what you receive in return?" Richard said.

"I do. It *is* tough at first. However, you get used to it." Michael looked happier now than any other time they had seen him, walking up and down the room, his hands moving in slow graceful gestures as he spoke enthusiastically.

"Try an experiment," he told them. "Pick a nursery rhyme. Then repeat it over and over in your head. Do that for a couple of hours nonstop as you go about your everyday business. And you will see you do acclimatize eventually."

"I . . . I'll pass on that one, if . . . if you don't mind," Joey slurred.

"Once this energy is running through you," Michael said, "you feel wonderful, enthusiastic, strong. And the miraculous part of it all is that you can transfer that feeling to others. Whether it's a couple of people in a room like this. Or to a hundred people in a hall or a hundred thousand soldiers on a battlefield." His voice was low but fast. To Richard it sounded almost like a cat's purr. And there *was* something hypnotic about it.

"Imagine," Michael was saying, "that you are Emperor of Byzantium. Your Empire is under siege from a dozen different armies—the Russians, the Bulgarians, the Muslims. Because they know that you are Lord of Constantinople, the greatest city in the world that contains treasuries piled to the roof beams with gold bullion and diamonds by the sackful. Now, picture this: your army has just returned from fighting the Saracens. They are exhausted, their bodies are dripping with sweat and blood. They've come home to rest. But your Empire is being attacked again by another army. Your men can't fight anymore. But you have the Beast on your side. It fills you full of energy; it gives you the power to inspire your people. So you climb on your horse and you ride along the lines of exhausted men and you talk to them; you inspire them. They look like deflated balloons but as you speak you see that energy pumping into them. As if they are being inflated, they lift themselves up; they feel strong, and happy, and eager to fight again. They will die for you. And they will die shouting your name in ecstasy."

"There are records of this happening?"

"Dozens." Michael's eyes blazed with excitement. "In the eleventh century the Russians launched a seaborne invasion of Constantinople with a force of a hundred thousand men. Constantinople's fighting ships were elsewhere so the Emperor ordered that every old barge and merchant vessel that could float be armed with Greek Fire, their secret weapon which was an early form of flame thrower. Unwittingly, the Russian fleet sailed into range of the Greek Fire throwers and within a couple of hours most of the enemy fleet was on fire. With the ships on fire the Russian sailors and troops had to swim to the beaches where they were slaughtered by the Byzantine army. Eyewitness accounts say that the sea was reddened with the blood of the Russians as if a great river of blood ran from the land into the water."

Christine's shrewd eyes watched Michael closely. "But these old Byzantine Emperors didn't hold onto power forever?"

"No, they didn't. Where I used to live the young men had a rather cruel trick. If they saw a beggar in the street they'd heat a coin over a flame and drop it into the beggar's hand. The coin would burn the beggar's hand. But the beggar wouldn't drop the hot coin because another beggar would steal it. So they'd stand there clutching the hot coin until their hand blistered."

"So what you're saying is, that to hold onto the Beast, and so hold onto power, is like holding onto the red-hot coins? It hurts to hold on, but if you drop it you lose it?"

"Broadly, yes. It's not like that at first, but age takes its toll. As the Emperors who had this symbiotic relationship found. They

243

had no problem with it in their thirties and forties but by the time they were into their fifties it became exhausting and painful to maintain the relationship."

"And one day they'd simply wake up and find it had gone?"

"I imagine so. The effort of holding on was just too great for them. Of course, once the power had gone there'd be any number of rivals to seize the power for themselves. Then it was customary to burn out the old Emperor's eyes and retire him to a monastery."

"And that won't happen to you?"

"I sincerely hope not." Michael smiled. "After all, this is the twentieth century."

Chapter Fifty

Tuesday Night

At the same time that Michael was talking to the three in the cottage the old VW van died noisily and steamily.

"Shit," Rosemary hissed. "Shit, shit, shit."

She coasted the van onto the hard shoulder, the cloud of steam rolling out from under the van showing a brilliant white in the headlights of passing cars.

She must be so close now, she could almost reach out and touch them. *Damn.*

The night air felt cool when she stepped out of the van. Apart from the motorway she could make out nothing but fields and woodland. The engine made sizzling sounds, steam still gushed from beneath the van.

Christ! She kicked the van in frustration. What the hell could she do now?

Richard lay in bed beside Christine. 2 a.m. The dark was total. A tingling sensation ran from his head to his feet covering every inch of skin. As he lay there, skin crawling, he heard the sound. A huge muffled crash.

He held his breath, hoping it was a door somewhere banging in the breeze.

Crash.

It came again. *Crash.*

The sound grew louder. As if a giant approached.

Sweat prickled across his skin. He dragged in a lungful of air so he could shout a warning.

No sound came out. The prickling rashed across his skin like a thousand tiny electric shocks. He tried to cry out again. He couldn't. He tried to move his arms. He couldn't.

245

And the pounding beat of something immense grew nearer. And nearer.

2 a.m. Rosemary nursed the van into a Bristol suburb, the engine making a sound like two iron pans being clapped together.

Her hand burned from when she'd try to unscrew the radiator cap. But at least after pouring in a couple of litres of Perrier and three cans of Lilt she had managed to start the van and get this far.

Already the temperature gauge was back in the red and steam that now smelled of pineapple had begun to roar out from under the van once more.

She turned off into a industrial estate road lined with warehouses. There she turned off the engine. She sat listening to the hiss of escaping steam and wondered how she could reach Devon by morning.

Richard struggled to break free of the grip of this paralysis. His skin tingled, the pounding came with a slow regular beat as loud as thunder.

Christ . . .

He found himself sitting bolt upright in bed, panting. In near-panic he looked round, seeing nothing but darkness. Christine lay asleep by his side.

He wiped the sweat from his eyes and breathed deeply. Through the open window came the faint hissing sound of leaves moving in a gentle night breeze.

There was no pounding sound.

He breathed a sigh of relief. It had been a dream, a lousy cruel dream.

He walked across to the window to breathe in some of that cool night air.

Outside, a light shone from a downstairs window, illuminating a chunk of lawn. Pacing backward and forward, was Michael. Dressed in black jeans and a white shirt, he looked as if he was rehearsing something he planned to say. His hands moved with those strangely graceful gestures.

"Doesn't that man ever sleep?"

"Sorry, Christine. Did I wake you?"

She put her hands around his arm and squeezed. "Even when

246

I'm asleep I know when you've got out of bed. Are you all right? You're shivering."

"I'm fine. I just needed some air."

"Are you afraid that thing might creep up on us while we're asleep?"

"I think Michael's doing a good job as a guard. Anyway, we put some distance between ourselves and it today."

Christine pressed closer to him; her bare breast cool against his arm. "Michael said earlier it might be another twenty-four hours before it gets here. We should try and get as much rest as possible."

"That's easier said than done."

"I know, love, but you need to relax." Her voice grew husky. "Come back to bed."

He hugged her. Wanting only to feel close to a human being. There was a sense of security in that alone.

Christine kissed him on the lips. He sensed a hunger behind the kiss.

Still kissing, they reached the bed. She ran her hands across his back. Then he felt her hands behind his buttocks, hungrily pulling him into her as her legs came up at either side of his waist.

She whispered. "Do it now. I want to feel you inside me. Don't worry, you won't hurt me. You won't hurt me. You—*ah!*"

He felt a surge run through her body like a wave as he pressed down. Beneath him he saw her teeth and the whites of her eyes glint in the gloom. Her hands were behind his back pulling him firmly into her.

Lust or passion or love, he couldn't give it a name, but something powerful broke through an emotional logjam. He kissed her face, forehead, nose, lips, chin, throat, breasts; her nipples, button-hard. He nipped them.

"Harder," she panted. "Bite harder . . . oh, yes, that's it."

He buried himself deep inside her.

"Don't you stop," she panted. "Don't you dare stop. Harder . . . *harder . . . oh . . .*"

This was sex in the raw. It was animal sex. He rammed every atom of self into the act, forgetting his family, Michael, the dead policemen, the York holocaust; he forgot everything; he forgot himself.

There was only this single reality. And that was to drive himself

247

into this woman. To pound on and on, tasting sweat, feeling the heat, and not thinking about the universe, or what manner of dark things slid behind this surface gloss of reality.

In the back of the VW van Rosemary opened her eyes. Something had woken her, but she wasn't sure what.

She opened her eyes, seeing a square of starry night sky through the windscreen. She lifted herself onto one elbow and the road atlas she had been studying before she'd fallen asleep slipped off onto the floor of the van.

She turned her head to one side as she heard a faint clicking sound. Someone was gently trying the driver's door. It was locked but she'd left a six-inch opening in the passenger door window for ventilation.

Heart hammering, she looked round, trying to think what to do for the best. She could beat on the walls of the van and shout.

That might frighten the thief away. But there was no one else within earshot. What if the thief realized it was a girl alone in the back of the van?

Instead of running away, he might make up his mind to climb in the back with her.

A man-shaped silhouette appeared in front of the windscreen. He'd seen the partly-open window.

Rosemary held her breath. *What now, Red Zed, what now?*

She looked around at the clutter of balsa wood and model airplane parts. There was a box full of screwdrivers and batteries. Silently, she felt through the mess of tools.

As she did so, she glanced back over her shoulder to see a hand wearing a black leather glove moving slowly inside the van, reaching for the inner door handle.

He'd be inside the van in five seconds flat.

Her fingers found spanners, batteries, bundles of wire and a *knife!*

Instinct kicked in.

Without even thinking it through, she grabbed the knife and lunged forward, using her body weight rather than muscular strength to ram the knife into the back of the thief's hand.

The back of the seat hit her in the stomach. The blow winded her. Even so, she clearly heard the loud crunching sound as the blade went clean through glove, skin and meat.

There was a howl of pain.

Then she saw the man's face at the passenger window. He was screaming. A mixture of rage and pain. She saw his wide, blazing eyes looking at her.

Damn. His hand was still on the door handle; he was trying to get in, no doubt to beat her senseless for the pain she'd caused.

Still breathless from the thump of the seat hitting her in the stomach, she scrambled into the front. Then, with her back braced against the driver's door, she used both feet to stamp at his arm.

He screamed again.

But why won't he take his arm out the window? she thought frantically—*take out your fucking arm!*

She switched from stamping at his arm to his face. Only the window was in the way. At the second stamp, it shattered. Then she repeatedly stamped at the man's face.

He screamed and shouted. His brutal eyes blazed into hers. Still he wouldn't move.

Then she knew why.

Jesus, oh sweet Jesus.

She had driven the knife in so hard that it had gone all the way through and pinned his hand to the door like pinning a butterfly to a board.

Taking a deep breath, she planted both feet against his chest, pushed. Pushed harder. Yelled through gritted teeth.

Then something gave.

With a scream that sounded like a pig being castrated the man flew back to sit on the pavement.

Rosemary kneeled up on the seat, ready to punch if he should come back.

She needn't have worried. The man, holding his injured hand to his chest, was making a snotty blubbering sound. As soon as he was on his feet he ran from the van down the road and into the night.

Then Rosemary noticed that the knife still jutted from the inner door panel. A mess of blood pooled on the passenger seat.

So the knife hadn't dislodged, she thought with something nearer to exhilaration than disgust. The blade had simply sliced through the palm, following the lines of the bones in the hand, then exited the hand between the knuckles.

To Rosemary, it felt as if she had passed the final test.

Tomorrow morning, when she stood face to face with Michael, she could do what she had to do with the knife. And she'd feel no remorse . . . whatsoever.

Chapter Fifty-one

Stranger

"Come on, Boys! Follow Rosemary Snow!" Amy was her old self. She stood on the steps of the climbing frame, shouting orders to the invisible Boys.

It was 9 a.m. The morning sun came in shafts through cloud that looked hung like lumps of cotton wool against the sky.

Christine and Michael stood on the lawn watching Amy play. They sipped from mugs of coffee and talked. Richard and Joey were inside the house eating breakfast.

Christine asked, "What happens now?"

"My team are working on the *Codex Alexander* at Norfolk Hall. As soon as they tell us the translation is complete I can re-establish the symbiotic partnership. You'll be free of the infection and can return home."

"Just like that?"

"Just like that." Michael smiled. "Of course, I feel as though I should compensate you for what you've been through."

"Believe me, it'll be more than adequate compensation just to get this nightmare behind us."

Michael sipped his coffee. "I have a farm in the Cotswolds. Why don't you have a week or two there? Amy would love it. There are chickens, cows, sheep, even a couple of ponies."

"Richard has to be back at work next Monday so—"

"Don't say no, Christine." Michael's smile broadened. "I'm making an offer you can't refuse. And you will need time to get over this. You're developing some rings under those eyes."

Lightly he ran a finger down the side of her cheek.

Christine smiled, then shook her head, suddenly confused. "I don't know . . . I'll have to talk to Richard about it."

"Christine. Keep looking at me and nodding."

"Why?"

"Because someone is in the trees on the other side of the fence."

"Who is it?"

"Can't tell. They're hiding behind a tree trunk." He looked across at Amy and called casually. "Amy. Where's your doll?"

"My Rosemary Snow doll?"

"Yes."

"I left her on the swing. Can you bring her to me, please?"

"Right-oh," Michael called. Then, in a low voice, he said to Christine, "Take the doll to Amy and talk to her as if nothing out of the ordinary is happening."

"How do you know it's not just someone out for a walk?"

"Believe me, it isn't. They're watching us."

"What now?"

"Just keep talking to Amy. I'm going to stroll back to the house."

"Why?"

"Because that's where I keep my gun."

Chapter Fifty-two

New Arrival

"Too late," Michael said. "We've got a visitor."

Christine turned round. She saw a man of around six and a half feet tall, heavily built, with hunched shoulders and long white hair tied back into a ponytail.

Michael's reaction to the visitor was surprising.

"Isaac," he shouted, delighted. "What the hell are you doing here?"

The big white-haired man smiled broadly and gave Michael a bear hug. "I've just been checking the other properties and thought I'd drop by to see if you need any help."

"Why are you sneaking about in the woods?" Michael asked, laughing. "You scared me half to death."

"I didn't recognize the car and thought I'd check out who was here before showing myself." The big man's smile dropped. "Are you expecting any more visitors?"

"None, apart from the big boy himself."

"Oh." Isaac nodded. "I saw what happened in York, and put two and two together."

Michael looked grim. "A tragic waste. What you could do for me, Isaac, is get a list of the casualties. We might be able to offer some financial help to the next of kin and the injured."

"I'll get onto it right away."

"I'm sorry, Christine," Michael said. "I've not introduced you. Isaac Herne. He's been with me for . . . what, nine years?"

"Eleven." Isaac's blue eyes twinkled brightly as a child's. "Pleased to meet you, Mrs. Young."

Michael's smile returned. "The young lady on the climbing frame is Amy Young." Michael winked at Amy. "And the doll with the beautiful black hair is Rosemary Snow. Isn't that right, Amy?"

"Sure is."

"Rosemary Snow," Isaac repeated. "Pretty name."

Christine noticed that Isaac and Michael exchanged glances as if one of them had said something significant.

"And don't forget the Boys," called Amy, swinging on the climbing frame like a monkey.

"Who could forget the Boys?" Michael smiled at Isaac. "The Boys are here and there about the garden. Amy sees them but we don't."

Isaac smiled and nodded. "Sounds as if your daughter has a vivid imagination."

"Oh, she has," said Christine, wondering if Isaac's arrival signified that something positive was happening at last.

Isaac said, "I don't want to sound alarmist but you've been here fifteen hours, Michael. Shouldn't you be moving on?"

Michael paused for a moment, head slightly to one side. "I don't feel anything yet. I think our Beastie Boy is still a long way off."

"I had some more vehicles parked up in the barn in case you needed them."

"Good thinking. We could do with ditching the Range Rover. The police may be wanting to eliminate it from their enquiries, as they say, after what happened in York."

"Right." Michael clapped his hands together and checked his watch. "Providing Beastie Boy doesn't get too close, we'll stick around here for another couple of hours, then we'll head off. Come on, Isaac, I'll introduce you to the rest of the family."

Chapter Fifty-three

Isaac

Things had changed since the big man, Isaac, had walked through the cottage door just sixty minutes ago. Richard Young sat at the kitchen table at the calm heart of a whirlwind of activity.

The optimism in the air was so thick you could near as dammit slice it with a knife. Michael hurried backward and forward, fax paper trailing from his hands, taking telephone calls, making telephone calls. Elation electrified him; those downturned eyes sparked with excitement. Richard saw that the man was in gear now; he was like a warrior with the taste of victory running thick across his tongue.

As Richard sat there he watched Isaac take out a harmonica and begin to play a rousing sea shanty. Amy laughed and began to dance to the squeezy-sounding music, her trainers thumping the kitchen floor.

"Richard. Pass the box, love. No, the big cardboard box under the table." Christine had caught the bug, too. Her brown eyes flashed with excitement. "Michael, which books need packing?"

Michael talked as he held the cordless phone to his ear. "All those on the bottom shelf in the study . . . yeah, still there, Harry? Is that the relevant section of the *Codex*? Yeah, the section entitled 'Holding The Beast's Heart.' Does that relate to Alexander's meeting with the oracle in Egypt? It does? Excellent. All the pieces are falling into place . . ."

"Amy," Isaac spoke in a jolly Father Christmas sort of voice. "Do you know the words to 'What Shall We Do With The Drunken Sailor?' "

"Course I do."

"Amy, be nice to Isaac." Christine smiled broadly as she hurried by with the cardboard box.

Christ, thought Richard uneasily, *it's as if they've all been drugged*. Was he the only one not buzzing with the same anticipation? Even Joey was rushing backward and forward with boxes full of computer discs. Twice that morning Richard had noticed Joey sidling across to Michael when he was out of earshot of the others. Then, rubbing his index finger up the side of his nose like a two-bit conspirator, he'd started talking to Michael as if he wanted reassurance about something.

Michael would nod and wink and Joey would move off, looking relieved.

Richard poured himself another coffee. Here he was, faced with his family dancing to Michael's tune—in the case of Amy, dancing literally. They were busily rushing from room to room, then out to the black Ford Granada parked outside. He saw all this, but what came to mind was an iceberg. Because nine-tenths of the iceberg is hidden under water. And Richard couldn't help but think that there was a lot going on that he couldn't see.

Joey said something to Michael as he passed and Richard saw Michael mouth, "Friday."

Was Friday significant? Surely Michael would have told them all if it was. To Richard, it seemed as if Michael was saying "I'll call you Friday." But why the whopping great secret?

Amy still jigged up and down to the notes squeezing from the chrome harmonica. Isaac's Santa Claus eyes were a bright baby-blue, his silver ponytail swung.

Just then Christine came back with the box full of books. Richard saw Michael caught her eye and some understanding seemed to pass between them.

Richard stood up, kicked aside a shoe box that was on the floor by his feet and helped himself to yet another mugful of coffee.

"Hey," Amy protested. "You've kicked Rosemary Snow's van."

Isaac's harmonica playing stopped. To Richard the sudden silence seemed prickly. Static electricity fizzed across his finger when he touched the steel handle of the coffee jug.

"Still want to dance, Amy?" Isaac asked, his baby blues brighter than ever.

"Sure do. I'm just putting Rosemary Snow straight in her van first. Look, Dad, you've knocked her sideways, you bad man."

"Sorry, sweetheart."

"Right," she said. "I'm going to do some more dancing, but first Rosemary Snow's van needs a drink of water."

It all got too oppressive in that kitchen with its low ceiling and fat oak beams. To Richard it felt as if the ceiling was slowly being screwed down closer and closer to his head.

He took his coffee outside, sat on the garden wall and stared grimly out across the valley.

"Shit, double shit, triple shit . . . come on . . . useless bastard!"

She shouted again but the van's engine died on her.

Rosemary Snow stopped the van at the side of the woodland road, jumped out to see steam boiling from the radiator and swore again.

I'm so damn close, she thought. *I can almost smell them.* She breathed deeply. *OK, Red Zed. Don't lose it. Keep in control. Leave the motor to cool, then top it up from the bottles. For Godsakes, it can't be much farther. You crossed over the county boundary ten minutes ago.* She went to check the road atlas. Banwick, near Dartmoor. It didn't look far, but it could only be reached by these narrow twisting lanes.

You'll get there, Red Zed, she told herself. *You'll get there on your feet, or on your hands and knees if you have to.*

She threw open the back of the van, wincing as the still healing ribs and lacerations protested at too much activity, too soon. *Jesus, Red Zed. You're not Superwoman. Just forty-eight hours ago you were still lying in that hospital bed.*

As she pulled out the water bottle she realized that in the last forty-eight hours she'd aged fast.

The Rosemary Snow who once moped around her bedroom, curtains closed, preoccupied with being bullied at school or writing drippy letters to pop stars that she'd never send was dead and buried. Those tormentors at school seemed like little children now. She knew they held no fear for her anymore. If she ever went back to school she'd say in an ice-cold way that would be so dangerous it glittered: "You. Outside. I think I owe you something." Then she'd bounce heads off the school wall.

She gripped the radiator cap and twisted it off. The rage at Michael and the pain caused by her Frankenstein face gave her the energy and determination to finish the job she'd set out to do. And she realized with grim delight that there wasn't a human being on the surface of this shitty planet who could stop her now.

When the steam had stopped gushing from the radiator she

began to pour in the water. In ten minutes, she told herself, she'd be on her way. She had an appointment with destiny.

The harmonica music still belted from the cottage when Michael hurried out.

"Richard. I need your help."

It was the first time Richard had seen the man actually sweat.

"You do?" Richard said coolly.

"If you'll follow me. Please."

Richard shrugged and followed.

"If you agree, I'd like you to drive the second car."

"The Range Rover?"

"No. The police might be looking for that now. There's another car in the barn just beyond these trees."

Richard followed Michael as he hurried up a woodland path.

"Why two cars, Michael?"

"We're so close to getting the Beast back into its . . ." smiling, he tapped the top of his head ". . . harness that I don't want to risk cocking it up by a car breaking down on us."

"So I follow on in a convoy?"

"Yes."

"No. I think we should all stick together."

Michael stopped and turned. "I'll ask Isaac to ride with you."

"Wait a minute." Richard caught Michael's arm. "I thought you said we were all, as you put it, infected."

"You are. But not for much longer, hopefully."

"But that still means if we get separated it might track me down first."

"Really, Richard. Trust me. It's still a long way off. If we leave within the next half-hour or so we can have a steady drive across to Norfolk."

"And that's when that bastard you call the Beast will be back on its leash again, all obedient and making everything in the garden rosy."

"Look, Richard, I don't blame you for feeling bitter. We've been through some shit together in the last couple of days."

"People have died, Michael."

"I know. But we are now so close to stopping it happening ever again." He held his hands apart with an inch between them, fingers trembling. "This close, Richard. Then we can start putting right in this world all that is wrong. Starvation, warfare—"

Richard sighed. "What do you want me to do?"

"Come on, I'll show you." Michael led Richard to where a barn stood in a clearing in the trees. He unlocked a heavy padlock and swung open the door. Inside, he could see the Range Rover, still dented and dusty from York. Beside that, a black Ford Granada that looked a twin of the one parked down by the cottage. The barn itself had been used as a workshop, with shelves containing tools, paint tins, engine parts, even an ancient-looking radio with chunky bakelite knobs.

"I'll just check she's running OK." Michael climbed into the car, started it, revved it for a couple of moments, then switched it off. "Perfect," he announced. "I'll take Amy, Joey and Christine. You follow close behind with Isaac. Trust me, there'll be no problems."

"What if I need to contact you?" He hadn't intended to sound facetious, but that was the way it came out. "Do we work out a series of codes for the car horn, or wind down the window and yell?"

"Neither." Again the forgiving smile. "Look." He pulled a rucksack from the backseat. "Mobile telephone fully charged. I'll have one of these, too. The numbers are preset. Also in the bag is a map showing the location in Norfolk."

"But I'll be following you."

"If the impossible happens and we get split up you'll know how to find Middleton Hall."

"Doesn't Isaac know the way?"

"Yep, but you never know."

"You've taken a lot of precautions for something you say is unlikely."

Michael smiled. "You've heard of sod's law?"

Richard nodded. "If you drop a slice of buttered bread, it's inevitable the sod will fall on the carpet buttered side down."

"You've got it, Dicky Boy, as our roly-poly friend Joey would say."

"OK." Richard found a smile playing on his lips. Michael's charm was starting to work on him, too. Maybe he'd begun to get paranoid about Michael and Christine exchanging glances. *For Christsakes it's not as if they had time—or the opportunity— to become lovers or anything.*

"And in this side pouch." Michael held up the rucksack. "There's a thousand pounds in cash."

"Just in case?"

Michael nodded. "Just in case." Then with a slap on Richard's back he said lightheartedly, "Come on. We'll grab a sandwich before we leave. Oh, by the way. Here are the car keys. Put them somewhere safe."

"Don't worry, I will."

Michael led the way back down to the cottage, chatting enthusiastically. "Christine was saying that you script promotional videos. It's a useful skill; the ability to help people understand new ideas that might otherwise be difficult to take in."

"You mean like the Beast?"

"Exactly." Michael had picked up a stick and thoughtfully decapitated a dandelion clock. "Just for the sake of argument, imagine you were given a commission—money no object—to write a script for a public information film that could explain what the Beast was and how it would benefit humankind. How would you go about it?"

Still talking, they headed down to the cottage below.

Chapter Fifty-four

Crunch Time

For the next thirty minutes they made their preparations to leave. Once Michael took himself off for a walk into the woods to be alone with his thoughts. Five minutes later he was back, saying brightly, "OK, people, let's roll."

It happened as quickly as that. One second Richard was watching Amy wave to him through the back window, the Rosemary Snow doll in the other hand. Christine waving, too. Then, the tires crunched across the pebble yard to the driveway through the trees—and they were gone.

Michael would wait for them at the village service station. It was less than a mile away. Why, then, did Richard feel such a bleak and cold sense of loss, as if he'd just said good-bye to his daughter and wife forever?

"All locked up," Isaac said, pocketing the keys. "Come on, let's get the car and meet up with Michael."

Richard followed Isaac across the garden to a side gate which led to the woodland path up to the barn. The time was 10:58 a.m.

The sound of Michael's car faded into the distance. The sudden quiet that followed increased Richard's unease. He shivered. The strokes of icy fingertips ran down his spine.

Which is absurd, he told himself. They were in the middle of a bloody heatwave. Bees bumbled through the long grass, while sunlight slammed down through the trees in eye-dazzling slabs.

Isaac was making small talk, his silver ponytail swinging from side to side. Occasionally he'd glance back, the baby-blue eyes friendly.

Richard barely heard what the big man said; he put his head down and pushed on up the hill to where the barn stood, its twin doors wide open.

260

"Richard, if you'll drive the car out, I'll lock the barn door behind you."

Richard gave a grim nod and hurried into the barn, its interior suddenly gloomy after the brilliance outside.

The instant he touched the car door handle a fat spark of static cracked across his knuckles.

Isaac stood with the padlock in his hands, saying amiably, "Michael's taken a real shine to Amy, you know. She's a beautiful little girl."

Richard didn't care. He thought: *It's not as if when all this is over we'll be inviting Michael to tea on Boxing Day or to Amy's birthday parties at McDonalds. I'll be cock-a-hoop never to set eyes on the man again.*

He swung himself into the seat.

Then jammed in the ignition key and twisted it.

Nothing.

Not a dicky bird.

Not a click or grunt or squeak.

Richard looked at the key in disbelief. *Has he given me the right ignition key?*

Of course he had. It slipped in easily. It turned easily.

The only thing that didn't happen easily was the motor starting.

"Shit."

He turned the key again. The starter motor didn't turn. There wasn't even the tell-tale click of electricity running through the cables. Dead, dead, bloody dead.

Shit!

He tried the radio. Dead also.

And the dashboard clock.

SHIT!

Isaac sang out, "You're not going to take all day about starting the car, are you, Richard?"

Richard got out of the car and slammed the door with a crash as loud as a shotgun blast.

"What's wrong?" Isaac hurried into the barn. "Why aren't you starting the car?"

"Because . . . *ah!*" As Richard tried to open the bonnet static electricity cracked across his hand again. It felt like a smack from a ruler.

Jesus Christ. Dread . . . a feeling of cold, cold dread shunted through him with enough force to knock the breath out of him.

"Richard. What's wrong. What're you doing?"

"Don't you feel it, Isaac?"

"No, what—"

"Listen!" Richard ran to the old radio with the bakelite knobs, switched it on. Beethoven's Fifth boomed out, sounding like death himself knocking on your front door.

"Just listen to this, Isaac. Listen to what your boss Michael has done to us!" He twisted the saucer-sized tuning dial, taking the radio off station.

Instantly static pumped from the speaker. The sound filled the barn. The regular beat of static. It sounded like the heart-beat of a giant.

Richard's voice rose above the static, "You know what this is?"

Isaac nodded, the baby-blue eyes wide with shock.

"And you know what that means, Isaac? That bastard has just signed our death warrant!"

Ignoring the static shocks, Richard tore open the bonnet of the Ford. Inside the cables to the plugs had been cut.

"Damn, the bastard!" Richard ran to the Range Rover. The keys were still in the ignition. "Isaac. Get in."

Isaac stared as if he'd slipped into a trance.

Richard turned the key.

"Jesus, I don't believe it. The bastard. THE BASTARD!"

Again he opened the bonnet to find the cables cut. Michael had done a thorough job when he'd gone for his supposed woodland walk. He wanted them to be there when the Beast finally came striding invisibly across the Devon landscape.

We're its sacrificial meat, thought Richard with such a huge surge of bitterness that he wanted to scream at the sky and curse God and Michael and the Satanic fates that had brought them together. "That bastard Michael has deliberately abandoned us here."

Sparks flew from his fingers every time he touched metal, the smell of static stained the air, his clothes crackled when he moved and all the time he could hear the old radio that had sedately played music old and new for the last thirty years beating out that terrible, terrible sound. Louder and louder came the beat; that fat burst of static as his Destroyer approached.

Richard screamed at Isaac, "Run!"

Isaac shook his head and sat on the bonnet of the Ford. His

head hung forward, the baby-blue eyes looked down at the ground.

"Come on, man," Richard yelled. "Run!"

Isaac gave a little shake of his head. The baby-blue eyes never looked up.

"You can't just wait here. You've got to—*Christ!*"

Somewhere outside came a tremendous crash. It sounded like a tree falling—*no*, a tree being slammed to the ground.

Isaac took out the silver harmonica and began to play *Greensleeves*. He played it soft and slow; slow as a funeral march.

The man had surrendered himself to his fate.

All the time the radio crunched out the beat of static as the thing got closer. Now the sound was so great the speaker distorted it into a constant pulsing roar of white noise.

Looking down at the ground, Isaac played the harmonica. He'd made up his mind there was nowhere to run.

But Richard ran.

He came out of the barn as if his clothes were on fire, arms windmilling, dragging in choking lungfuls of air.

He didn't know where he was running. Instinct alone guided him. He ran down hill through the trees, leaped over tree roots, fallen trunks, branches—

—thinking: *Please don't let me fall, please don't let me fall, please don't*—

Back in the barn, Isaac played the harmonica, the notes flying through the branches above as gracefully as swallows, the music and the sunlight running together. In a way, Richard felt he ran in a dream. Music. Sunlight. Trees. Long Grass. Dandelions beneath his feet, and—

BANG!

With a roar like thunder the barn was hammered flat.

And the music stopped. Richard snapped out of the trance and ran harder.

Branches whipped his face. A bramble caught his cheek and drew a line in blood.

Crash. He slammed down onto his chest, rolled—rolled again and was back on his feet. Panting, gurgling, trying to draw air into his lungs so he could outrun the thing that followed him.

His Destroyer.

Behind came a series of creaks followed by crashes. It was in the forest now. Crushing a twenty-yard strip of timber as it followed him. Glancing back, he saw trees shiver, writhe as if in agony then explode in a spray of pulp and leaves.

Crack.

He'd run full into a tree trunk. He bounced back, head ringing with pain.

But still he pounded on through the forest, leaping over branches, cutting through clumps of stinging nettles. He felt nothing.

Only the searing need, the burning need to run, and to run faster and faster, until his feet hissed across the leaves and grass as if he flew.

The next time he looked back he saw the sky had turned green.

A million leaves torn from branches and lifted by the updraft of the thing hung in a great cloud between ground and sky, turning even the sunlight that fell on him green.

His chest burned. His heart felt as if it would erupt through his mouth.

Behind, the crashing sounded deafening. By now the tops of falling trees whacked to the ground at either side of him.

It was nearly on top of him.

The ground grew steeper.

He ran down it faster. Perhaps gravity would give him the speed he needed to outrun this thing.

Just another few yards. If he outran it, it would dissipate into thin air; he'd seen it happen before. He'd be safe. It couldn't harm him then. It couldn't—

His foot hooked a tree root. His body whipped forward and down. The ground slammed into him. Winded, he rolled over and over.

That's when he knew he'd run his last step.

Overhead branches sheared as his Destroyer crashed down toward him.

Balling his arms and legs tight to his body, he screwed shut his eyes and with a yell that mated the anticipated agony with rage he waited for the hammer to fall.

Part Three

"Although they rarely realize it, the ultimate ambition of every man, woman and child is to control the uncontrollable."

—John Ducas. Constantinople. Easter Day, AD 1057

Chapter Fifty-five

Ground Zero

At the T-junction a sign pointing left read BANWICK. The combine harvester turned right.

Rosemary hissed, "Thank heaven for small mercies." She gunned the van's dangerously overheated engine and pounded it through the village of thatched cottages. She drove so quickly she overshot the turn-off downhill which was marked with a sign painted on wood that read *Glebe Cottage*.

Again she was following a narrow road with high-banked sides and nowhere to turn round. After another nerve-stripping mile she came upon a cart track. She swung the van off the road, then reversed savagely back, bumping into the opposite bank of the road and leaving a scattering of broken amber indicator lens in the grass.

A bus braked hard, sounded its horn; the driver held out his hands, his mouth moving as he described Rosemary's driving abilities to her. Scowling, she crunched the gear home and lumbered back the way she'd come.

It hit Richard square in the back. A blistering shaft of light pierced his brain.

Then there was nothing more.

He joined the dust of dead worlds that float silently in the void between galaxies. Where there is absolute cold, absolute silence; absolute loneliness.

His lips began to burn. Was that the kiss of eternity itself?

He grunted. Moved his head. His head began to pound.

His lips stung as if they rested on hot metal. He grunted again, opened his eyes.

He lay facedown. The stinging grew worse.

This time he pushed himself up on his hands. He saw the cause of the stinging.

His face had been crushed down against a stinging nettle.

But what was it that had crushed him?

He dragged himself from beneath whatever lay across his back.

For a moment he sat panting, staring at the thing in a daze, allowing the image to take shape in his brain.

He kicked it experimentally with his foot, as if to reassure himself it was real.

A branch, he thought. *A bloody branch*: as tall as he was and as thick as his arm. It had been sheared from a tree overhead and had fallen on him, knocking him to the ground. The leaves that remained on the thing had been ground to a wet pulp. Still in a daze he rolled one between finger and thumb. It left a green stain on his skin.

Why wasn't he dead?

By rights he should be as flat as a hedgehog that had wandered out into the path of a truck.

He stood up, feeling his body—ribs, arms, legs, head. Nothing broken: his back ached where it had been slapped by the branch. If anything, the nettle sting on his lips was worse. He touched them with his fingertips. They'd swollen. And they burned like bloody hell fire. But he felt a damn sight better than he should have done.

His brain took some loosening up. Without understanding, he looked up at the trees. Here, the tops had been sheared off. As he retraced his steps uphill, he saw that the destruction became more savage. Twenty paces farther up the hill the trees had been broken in two, with the top halves lying, bleeding sap, on the ground. While the bottom halves with a few branches still attached stood untouched. As he walked back toward the barn, he saw the trees had been severed closer and closer to the ground until, fifty paces from the barn, there was nothing but knee-high stumps surrounded by sloppy mounds of wood pulp. Another twenty paces and there was nothing but wood pulp. The trees had been snapped off at ground level.

Of the barn itself nothing recognizable remained. Just a half-acre orange dust smear that had once been a thousand or so roof tiles and limestone clippings that had been walls. Beneath that would be tinfoil-thin sheets of metal that had once been two cars and a mess of red that had once been Isaac with the mild, baby-blue eyes.

Richard shook his head. It was too much to take in. If anything, the idea that buzzed around his head was somehow to get to the service station in the village in the hope Michael hadn't gone yet.

He paused, surprised by the understanding that lit up his brain. Michael had planned this. He'd cut the cables when he'd gone out for his supposed stroll around the garden. He'd deliberately abandoned them to the Beast.

Why?

Richard touched his nettle-stung lips. He only knew that Michael had gone now, and taken Richard's family with him. He knew, also, that the Beast had gone with him. Somehow he'd taken it.

Richard pressed his finger against his lips. The burning sting helped clear the fog from his brain. He felt as if he was waking from a trance that had lasted for the last three days. Michael had been lying to them. He understood that now. How much had been lies he didn't know. But he did know the lies had been for a purpose. And as Richard headed up through the trees toward the village at the top of the hill he guessed that purpose had been to get Christine from him somehow.

But was it Christine? He remembered the secretive glances they'd exchanged. But also he remembered Michael's interest in Amy. When York Minster had come down around their ears it had been Amy, only Amy, whom Michael had been interested in saving.

With questions circling in his brain like the rooks above circling the treetops, Richard plodded up the hill.

He half-noticed a yellow VW van come bouncing down the track fifty yards away to his left. But the only idea taking shape in his head now was:

Find Michael. Find him quick.

Because Richard knew as surely as the sun would shine in the morning that something terrible was going to happen. And it would happen soon.

Chapter Fifty-six

Near Miss

"Hallo, Michael. Do you remember me? Rosemary Snow? My face has changed a little since the last time you saw me . . . *you bastard!*"

In goes the knife. *Stick it right through one of those gentle, cow-brown eyes that are as soft as a saint's.*

Drive it hard. Pierce the retina; puncture the orbit. Don't stop there.

Keep pushing, pushing. Push the tip of the blade along the channel occupied by the optic nerve; it'll be soft, pulpy—no resistance there.

With luck you can push the blade deep into his skull. So deep it pierces the frontal lobe of his brain. He will die at your feet.

"Michael dead."

Michael dead . . . she loved the way the sound of the words jingled together like a song lyric.

"Michael's dead, Michael's dead," she sang as she drove the van down the lane through the wood. "Michael's dead, Michael's dead. And I'll bury your bones, hallelujah!"

She giggled. The sound, harsh and loud, drowned even the overheated motor.

Now, terror and excitement filled her with an energy that bordered on the electric.

Above the treetops she could see the red roof of the cottage. She'd seen enough through Amy's eyes to know that this was the place.

This was where her destiny once more intersected with Michael's. She planned nothing fancy. With the knife hidden behind her back she'd knock on the door. When he opened it, she'd say, "Remember me?"

Then stab.

The transmission whined as she coasted down the hill, the van bumping over tractor ruts. The cottage swung into view around the next bend. She switched off the motor and allowed the van to freewheel onto the pebbled yard.

But even as she climbed out of the van, the knife gripped tight in her fist, a gut feeling told her she was too late. There were no cars in the yard; the cottage windows were all shut. The place looked dead.

And after five minutes of pounding on doors and windows with her fist she realized they had gone. She looked through a window. The kitchen looked tidy so they'd not left in a hurry. On the kitchen table was an empty shoe box on which someone had drawn wheels and doors to make it look like a car.

"Damn!" She kicked the door.

Suddenly overwhelmed, she sat down on the doorstep. Her whole body shook. And although she wasn't actually crying, tears streamed down her face. When she wiped them away the scabs came off, sticking to her finger tips in black crumbs.

So close, she thought. *So damn, fucking close. I must have missed them by minutes.*

Damn.

She picked up the knife and looked at the steel blade. The sunlight it reflected dazzled her. She closed her eyes.

For some reason the flashes continued in her head.

"Amy," she whispered. "Amy, where are you now?"

Richard's leg ached. He guessed he must have pulled a calf muscle in the mad run downhill.

Nevertheless, he pressed on through the wood, limping over knots of roots and pushing aside branches. The walk seemed to take forever. His mind spun. The only idea he could cling to was to make for the garage in the village. Perhaps Michael might be waiting for him there.

But he knew he was deluding himself. Michael would be long gone, and he'd have taken Amy, Christine and Joey with him.

That's plan A, he thought grimly. *But what the hell is plan B?*

Rosemary stood where the barn had been. The sun reflected from scraps of metal. The smell of evaporating petrol hung heavily in the hot summer air.

She knew instantly that the thing had been here, too. Running

271

downhill to her right a swathe had been cut as straight as a road through the trees. From what she could see the trees hadn't merely been toppled. They'd been pulped.

A little way off to her left, a swarm of bluebottles buzzed around a stretch of rubble. She'd moved closer to it, waving the flies away. Her mouth turned wet. An unpleasant taste seeped across her tongue.

Someone has died here, she told herself. She knew it wasn't Amy because as she sat on the cottage doorstep a sudden rush of images had come flooding into her head. Not much had been clear. But she'd seen enough through Amy's eyes to tell her that Michael was driving the family along a twisting country road. There'd been the fat man. Repeatedly, he ran his thick sausage fingers through his hair. Amy's mother, looking out of the window, expression serious. But—

Rosemary caught her breath. She stepped back from the patch of rubble where the flies crawled so thickly they created a swarming mat.

She'd not seen the little girl's father, Richard. She looked down at the rubble.

Maybe he was beneath that. Reduced to fly meat.

Unable to bring herself to look more closely, she ran back to the van and drove away.

Chapter Fifty-seven

Adrift

At the same time that Rosemary Snow ran back from the remains of the barn to the van, Richard reached the village. His lips still tingled from the nettle sting.

Market day. Whole families carried bags full of carrots, eggs, bananas, melons.

The normality of it all made Richard feel even more like the outsider. For one insane moment he could have believed he'd become invisible. Couldn't they see terror on his face? Hadn't they heard the thundering roar of the barn being flattened or a hundred trees being pulped?

He paused to look at his reflection in the post office window. What he saw surprised him. After all he'd been through, the panic, the terror, brushed by the lips of death itself he saw, reflected, a perfectly normal-looking man of thirty-something. Expression calm. Clean shaven. He didn't look in any way disheveled. There was a grass stain on his elbow and down one side of his jeans, but as they were black anyway it hardly showed.

Suddenly he was seized by the burning need to jump onto the steps of the war memorial and shout—DON'T YOU PEOPLE KNOW WHAT'S HAPPENED TO ME? I'VE SEEN MEN AND WOMEN DIE! I ALMOST DIED MYSELF! MY FAMILY HAVE BEEN ABDUCTED! WHY CAN'T YOU GUESS WHAT'S HAPPENED TO ME BY THE LOOK IN MY EYES?

People bustled by. All looked so happy and relaxed, every smile on their faces a vicious stab in Richard's heart. Why couldn't they share his pain? Why couldn't they suffer like he suffered?

He wanted to grab people by the arms and tell. He wanted to shout it out in the streets.

But he knew he couldn't. Parents, schoolteachers, society as a whole had conditioned him to behave "normally." He could no more shout the truth from the top of the war memorial than he could strip off his clothes and walk down through the market naked.

Come on, Richard, he told himself grimly. *Pull yourself together. Amy and Christine need you now. Find them.*

He walked quickly along the street, looking for a car rental office. How he'd pay for the car God alone knew. He'd got about three pounds in loose change in his pocket, no wallet—only this . . . this certainty that boiled like molten metal through his veins that he needed to find Amy and Christine and take them away from Michael as quickly as possible. Again the sense of dread and danger rolled through him in great dark waves.

Above the thatched roofs a balloon hung in the sky like a World War Two blimp. Tethered by a line; printed in black along its flank the word THANNATOS.

Possibly it advertised a garage, thought Richard. Anyway, it was a start. As for paying for a hire car, he'd have to cross that bridge when he came to it.

He followed a stream that ran through the village. Two black swans floated midstream.

THANNATOS turned out to be a warehouse-sized store selling antiques. The village's only garage was next door. It had two rusty pumps, one diesel, one petrol. Its core activity seemed to be the sale of animal feed.

"Damn," hissed Richard. Time was running out. Already ideas of stealing a car were running through his head.

Desperate times call for desperate measures, he told himself, flexing a fist as he walked along the pavement. There was no time to worry about consequences. All that was important was that he reached this place in Norfolk. Before Michael did whatever he planned to do to Amy or to Christine.

A hot wind blew down the street. It tumbled a sheet of newspaper against his leg. There was a photograph of York Minister. A headline: DEATH TOLL RISES TO 63.

Richard's blood turned cold and he began to walk faster.

Rosemary Snow took her life in her hands every time she opened the radiator cap. The metal cap came off with a bang. If it wasn't for the fact she'd wrapped the coat around it she'd be sprayed with boiling water. More boiling water squirted out from a crack at the bottom of the radiator, running away down the road in rivulets.

"Heap of shit." She cursed as hot water spat across her bare arm. As soon as she could get near she topped up the radiator from the water bottle. An ominous rumbling followed by a knocking came from the radiator as cold water streamed across hot metal. More steam blew from the cap like from a whistling kettle.

Then, at last, she was back on the road again, hot air blasting through the smashed passenger window.

"Christ, Robbie," she shouted, "I've done you a favor ripping off this pile of junk." She turned into the village's main street. "At least you can claim on your bloody insurance."

She eased the van along the busy street, overtaking a couple of stationary buses, then stopping at the pedestrian crossing as mothers hauled kids across by the hand. Two black swans glided along a stream. Overhead a balloon wrinkled and tugged at the cable.

"Come on, Amy," she whispered. "Show me where you are. Show me pictures, Amy. Show me road signs. Show me names. Ask Michael where you're going. Ask your mummy. Ask—Christ . . . I don't believe it."

Sitting on a bench, at the side of the main road, was the man she recognized as Amy's father.

She felt a sudden surge of relief. At least he hadn't died in the barn wreck. And maybe if he was here so were the others. Perhaps even Michael. She felt across the passenger seat. There was the knife.

Excitement buzzed through her as she pulled the van to the side of the street about fifty yards from where the man sat, then climbed out of the van.

She decided to cross the road and, making no bones about it, tell the man about the danger he and his family faced. Particularly his daughter.

Come on, come on! Traffic streamed by preventing her crossing the road to him.

Then came the unexpected.

A bus pulled up. The man got on it, paid the fare and the bus pulled away before she could even shout.

Damn . . . openmouthed she stood and watched it go. Richard Young sat and even stared over her head as it passed. She waved and shouted but he was so preoccupied he never even noticed.

275

Chapter Fifty-eight

Visions and Nightmares

Snap!

As Richard Young sat on the bus trying to hammer out what the hell he did now, the sound cracked through his head.

He rubbed the back of his neck and rolled his head from side to side.

Snap!

The sound came again. Almost the same kind of sound you get in your ears when you're going uphill or downhill in a car. The air pressure in the inner ear causes a pop as it equalizes with the outer air pressure.

Snap!

Similar but not the same. Anyway, the bus was traveling on a level stretch of road. He yawned, but his ears didn't pop.

Snap!

The sound came from inside his head. Sometimes when people are under prolonged stress they develop a buzzing in the ears. Perhaps this was a similar manifestation. Christ knew he'd been through enough to send him giggling all the way to the nearest psychiatric ward.

He looked out at the trees and Devonshire cottages. They seemed distant and unreal. The other passengers might as well have been images on a TV screen. One woman showed another woman a sweater she'd bought at the market. A child kneeled up on the seat in front of him swooping a toy helicopter. Across the aisle sat an old man with a black dog under his seat. The dog panted in the heat, its long pink tongue dripping spots of saliva onto the bus floor.

Richard thought: *Christ. What do I do now? Where do I go now? Where is Amy? Where is that bastard Michael taking them?*

The bus driver sounded the horn as a VW van overtook the

bus, narrowly missing an oncoming motorcyclist.

Snap!

He closed his eyes. He couldn't chase after them on the damn bus. He'd have to get hold of a car. With luck there'd be a car rental office in the next town. But then again, he had no money to pay for the thing. If he had no money, he'd have no car.

But what was Michael going to do to his family? He had to find them. They needed him. But he would need a car . . .

The conundrum circled around his head. A question with no answer; a damn riddle with no fucking solution.

Snap!

That sound again. Like some frigging numbskull inside his head trying to turn a key in a lock.

Snap!

He clenched his fists; eyes tight shut.

Snap!

There was a pressure growing inside his skull. Maybe his blood pressure was so high one artery after another was giving way under the strain like overinflated tires.

Snap!

Maybe he'd scream and stagger down the bus, blood running like tears from his eyes; blood flowing like snot from his nose; blood bubbling from his ears.

Snap! Snap! SNAP!

The sound of the bus seemed distant. Something was happening to him. He didn't know what. Maybe . . .

Snap!

The passenger behind him was leaning forward so close to the back of his neck he could almost feel their breath on his bare skin. He could sense eyes boring into the back of his head. *Christ* . . .

He looked back, ready to start punching.

No one there.

In fact there were no more passengers sitting behind him.

Jesus, what's happening to me? Here I am, standing on the rock of sanity, but there's a crack appeared beneath my feet, and it's getting wider and wider and . . .

The bus stopped to drop off the old man and his dog.

Richard shut his eyes again, trying to hang onto his crumbling rationality. Again there was a sensation that someone sat behind him almost touching the back of his head.

Snap!

His face felt stiff and numb. But he was sure that was no longer the effect of the nettle sting.

It was as if someone had got their finger inside his brain and had begun to stir. He felt so damn weird.

Snap!

Images bubbled up inside his head. They were so bright and solid he thought for one confused moment that he'd only dreamed he was riding the bus. That he really was sitting between Joey and Christine in the backseat of a car. Joey munched on a bread roll filled with bacon. Mayonnaise slicked his bottom lip white. He looked up at his wife to his right. *Why did she seem so big?* She gazed out of the window, twirling a length of her hair between her fingers as if lost in some problem.

A little butterfly with wings as blue as the sky fluttered inside the car against the side window, then flew forward toward the windscreen. Richard tracked it with his eyes as if it was the most fascinating thing in the world. A hand came up and slapped it against the glass, grinding the beautiful blue wings to crumbs.

Sadness surged up within him with a power that was as inexplicable as it was huge. A lump like an egg squeezed into his throat.

The hand belonged to Michael. He was driving. His brown eyes looked different now. Concentration made them look fierce. He looked like a man who'd decided on some course of action; and he'd follow it to its bitter end.

He looked down at his hands. He saw the Rosemary Snow doll, long black hair tugged by the breeze.

Snap!

He opened his eyes. A muscle beneath his left eyebrow twitched.

The bus stopped. The boy with the helicopter followed his mother off the bus. A girl climbed on the bus. Paid the driver, and sat on the vacant seat in front of him. She had short ginger hair.

Snap!

He closed his eyes. An object felt as if it slipped through his skull. It felt almost the same as when you slide your finger inside your mouth to dislodge a piece of apple from beside your gum.

Snap!

What was this thing he felt inside his skull?

Snap!

A torrent of images erupted. All bright and vivid. But disjointed, making no sense.

One second he was remembering what he saw in York Minster. The walls coming down. A roof timber shattering a statue. But he saw it from a different perspective. He felt the blind terror. But it seemed different somehow. He saw things that he hadn't seen the first time around. A toppling statue of a saint pinned a fat woman to the floor. She writhed beneath it, clawing at the broad stone back in a parody of lovemaking.

Then he saw a figure racing toward him along the aisle out of that boiling mist of dust and debris.

To his astonishment he saw it was himself. As if he was watching a video of what had happened to him on that day.

Or that he was watching through someone else's eyes.

Snap!

Most made no sense. Nighttime. He was in his garden at home. Two brutish-looking men were standing by the house. One struck the other with a hammer across the back of the head . . .

. . . running through a field of yellow flowers. A moonlit night. It follows. The Beast cutting through the yellow crop like a speedboat . . .

. . . a hospital room. A mirror. In the mirror a face surrounded by a mat of long black hair. The face is shockingly wounded . . .

Snap!

He opened his eyes as the bus pulled into the station. This time his head felt clear. He didn't know if he'd actually slept on the bus, but at least the rest had helped.

Even so, his legs were shaky as he climbed off the bus.

He left the station looking for a café. First he'd drink a couple of black coffees, then he'd start looking for a car.

Richard sat at the table in the café. Traffic rumbled by outside. The radio on the counter played "Unchained Melody." The place smelled of freshly brewed coffee. The few customers had occupied the window seats.

Preoccupied, he let his gaze rest on a fly walking around and around on the red tablecloth. The coffee mug steamed in his hand.

"Mind if I join you?"

Almost startled, he looked up. A girl in her late teens with long

279

black hair and a stark white face looked down at him. He glanced around at the empty tables and understood.

He grunted, "I'm not interested."

The audacity of the whore. In a quiet café, in the middle of the day.

As if she hadn't heard what he said, she sat opposite. He began to stand, intending to move to another table.

She grabbed his forearm with a surprising strength that bordered on the ferocious. Then, in a low voice, she said, "My name is Rosemary Snow."

Chapter Fifty-nine

Snow

When he didn't reply straight away, she repeated, "I'm Rosemary Snow."

He stared at her so hard that she broke eye contact self-consciously and pulled her hair across her cheek to hide the crust of scabs that ran down the left side of her face.

At last, he replied simply, "I know."

Her eyes widened, surprised. "Michael told you about me?"

"No. My daughter. My four-year-old daughter." Richard fought to keep the crack of insanity closed beneath his feet. He breathed deeply and took a swallow of coffee.

"So, I did get through to Amy." In something like triumph, she slapped her hand down on the table, causing the café's diners to turn and look.

Richard said, "Amy talked about you a lot; she even named a doll after you."

"Listen. This may be hard to take in, but for the last few days I have been able to see through your daughter's eyes. It started about a fortnight ago when—"

Wearily, Richard held up a hand. "You don't have to explain. I know what happened, or at least I can guess what happened. You've spent some time with Michael?"

She nodded.

"Then that thing that's following him nearly killed you?"

Again a nod.

"Then . . ." Feeling almost drunk, he put his finger to his head. "There were changes in here. You start seeing things. You think at first they're dreams, or . . . or some kind of hallucination?"

"Yes. But they're real. Sometimes it's not clear. But I've seen you riding in a car with Michael, and then there's a heavily built man, lank hair—"

"That's Joey Barrass, my brother-in-law."

"And a woman—your wife?"

"Christine. Yes."

"And the little girl, Amy?"

"Amy." He nodded, feeling a weight against his neck.

"Where are they now?"

Shrugging, he stood up, walked out of the café and headed across a car park. Rosemary Snow followed, limping slightly.

"Wait. Richard. Where are you going?"

"Where am I going? I don't know, Rosemary Snow."

"Wait, just a moment."

"I can't wait any longer. I'm going to find a car."

"Where?"

He shrugged. "Steal one."

"Believe me, Mr. Young, it's harder than you think."

"Any suggestions?" He winced at the bitterness in his voice.

"I've got a van. Use that."

He stopped his furious march through the car park and looked back into her eyes. There was a gentleness and compassion in there, as well as pain. He sighed and let his shoulders drop. "I'm sorry," he said with a faint smile. "Christ, I'm behaving like a right bastard . . . I didn't mean to . . ." He shrugged, words failing him. "Sorry. It's been a hell of a morning."

She smiled, raising her brown eyes to meet his. "It's been a hell of a week."

"I'll see if I can start again. I'm Richard Young." He held out his hand.

"Rosemary Snow." She shook his hand. "When I saw you get off the bus I parked in a side street by the café."

"You've been following me?"

"For a long, long way."

He looked down at the girl who was so slightly built he could have believed a summer's breeze would float her away. "I think we've got some stories to swap, don't you?"

This time her smile was warm. "I think so, too."

Chapter Sixty

Square One

Richard wanted to drive straight to the address Michael had originally given him. But it seemed obvious now, in view of Michael leaving him to be pulped by the Beast, that the address would be false. Rosemary suggested that they find the nearest library, check the telephone directories, then do some phoning.

It would be faster than driving all the way to Norfolk only to find Middleton Hall didn't exist.

As they drove they talked quickly. Rosemary told Richard what had happened to her; that at first Michael had seemed genuinely interested in her, as if she could be of use to him. Then, when the thing had come tearing through the farmhouse to pursue her across the field, he'd realized she was of no use to him after all—and simply abandoned her.

To Richard the pieces of information fell into place. Michael's interest in Amy talking about Rosemary Snow. At first Michael must have assumed Rosemary was dead. But then, when Amy started talking about her, he must have realized that she was still alive. And worse, for him, Rosemary was tracking him down.

Richard guessed Rosemary's aim had been to warn them about Michael. Because now he clearly planned to use Amy in the same way he'd tried to use Rosemary. Just how—and why—wasn't clear. But it must have something to do with his recapturing this entity he called the Beast.

As the realization of this sank in, Richard felt his agitation return and he chewed a knuckle, wishing the damn van could grow wings and fly them to wherever Michael had taken his family.

Rosemary pulled into the library car park, but it was another twenty minutes before they left the van. They sat face to face, talking intensely. Rosemary's eyes flashed in a way that suggested to Richard that finding Michael had become something of a holy quest to her.

At last they went into the library. Richard guessed the quickest way to find out if there was such a place as Middleton Hall was to phone the library nearest to Middleton and ask if anyone had heard of it.

The idea was so simple it was brutal. And Richard was already afraid to hear what the answer would be.

At the same time, fifty miles away, Michael pulled into a garage, telling Christine he would buy some sweets and a drink for Amy.

Once out of sight he pulled the mobile telephone from his pocket and dialed.

"Hello? Spiro? It's Michael. Listen. I'm on my way back to you now. Have the team got everything ready? Good. Because I want to get this over and done with by tonight."

The voice at the other end of the telephone began, respectfully, to protest some point. Michael cut in. "I'm not interested in that. It'll work this time. I know it will. Now . . . I've been staying with the Youngs at Glebe Cottage at Banwick. I want you to get some people across there as quickly as possible. They'll find the area around the barn in . . . a bit of a mess. Tell them to make the place tidy. Got that? Also, have you had any news about the girl Rosemary Snow? Well, keep looking. When you find her, send her to the farm. Right, Spiro, get to it."

He pocketed the telephone, bought the sweets and drink, then returned to where he'd parked the car in the shade of the tree.

Joey was pacing up and down beside it.

"About time, Michael. We can't sit around here waiting for that thing to come back."

Michael smiled warmly. "Don't worry, Joey. It's still a long way off. You've got nothing to worry about at all."

By midday they'd made a single telephone call that had sent Richard to the curbside where he sat slumped with his head in his hands.

A librarian at Middleton and District Library had told them that Middleton Hall had been demolished ten years ago; the site was now a public park.

Rosemary sat down beside him. Hesitantly, she put a reassuring hand on his arm. "Don't worry. We'll find them."

"But where?"

"I was able to find *you*."

"Do you see anything now?"

She shut her eyes. "No. Nothing. But—"

"Try harder."

"I am trying, Richard."

He rubbed his face. "Sorry. But all I want to do is get Amy and Christine away from that man. Before he . . ." He couldn't finish the sentence.

"Come on," Rosemary said, "let's go back to the van."

Richard looked at the passing cars, in a crazy way expecting to see Michael's car with Amy, Christine and Joey in the back.

He stopped suddenly. A sudden idea that was as surprising as it was frightening had hit him.

"What's wrong?" Rosemary asked.

"Michael. When I find him I'm going to kill him. Honest to God, it's not a figure of speech, I'm actually going to kill him."

"No, you're not." She said in a matter-of-fact voice. "I am."

He watched her climb into the driving seat of the van.

"Where now?" she asked.

"Back to the cottage. There might be some clues on how to find Michael."

As she pulled out of the car park, Richard found himself watching her in wonder. She wasn't like any teenage girl he'd met before. Her dark eyes locked onto the road ahead like a hunter's. And there was that matter-of-fact way she said she would kill Michael. And somehow he had no doubt in his mind that was what she intended to do—or die trying.

Chapter Sixty-one

Glebe Cottage Once More

The cottage on the side of the valley was as Richard had left it. He caught sight of where the barn had been and where Isaac still lay, crushed beneath the debris.

As they drove down the track to the cottage he thought the sight would have filled him with horror. But now he only wanted to smash his way into the cottage and pull the place apart until he'd found what he wanted.

"Well, they haven't come back, anyway," Richard said.

"Did you expect them to?"

"No." He gave a grim smile. "I'm just starting to hope for a miracle."

"Do you have a key?"

"No, but it shouldn't be hard to force a lock."

She drove fast, the van crashing across potholes so violently that Richard expected it to crack an axle or at least pop a shock absorber or two.

"Careful you don't wreck your van," he told her.

"I don't care." She shot him a grin. "It's stolen anyway."

First, they walked around the cottage looking for the best way in.

Despite the carnage wreaked by the thing just a hundred or so yards away, the cottage looked like a holiday home waiting for the owners to arrive. The swimming pool at the side was neatly covered by a flexible blue plastic sheet to prevent dirt and leaves from being blown into the water.

"That window up there, above the conservatory." He pointed. "If I climb onto the conservatory roof I could lift you up to it."

He half-expected her to suggest another way but she immediately ran to the trellising attached to the wall and used it like a ladder to reach the conservatory roof.

"Come on," she said, "I'll give you a hand up." She knelt on the glass roof. "Don't stamp your feet or anything like that. It should be toughened glass but I wouldn't like to stake my life on it."

Some of the wooden slats snapped beneath Richard's more substantial weight but at last, panting, he hauled himself onto the glass roof, with the conservatory's wicker furniture ten feet below.

"I see what you mean," he said as the glass made tiny cracking sounds. When he stood he made sure his feet were firmly planted on the steel frame that held the glass.

Gingerly, he edged his way to the wall. The window was in two sections. The lower section was within easy reach but firmly locked. The upper smaller window was open.

"I'll make a stirrup with my hands," he told her, his back resting against the cottage wall. "Step into it; can you reach the window?"

She stepped into his hands and he hoisted her toward he window, amazed at how light she was.

"Easy peasy," he heard her say as she slipped head first through the narrow window.

In seconds, she'd opened the larger window. He hauled himself through to find himself in the bedroom that he and Christine had shared the night before; the duvet still pulled back revealed the depression that their bodies had made. Christ, he just wanted to hold his wife and his daughter close and not let go. Ever.

"Are you OK?" asked Rosemary gently. "You look exhausted."

He forced a smile. "I'll be OK. Maybe we can grab a coffee and a bite to eat while we're here. Come on, let's start looking."

Rosemary whistled with surprise at the sight of Michael's high-tech office.

"From what he told us," Richard said, switching on the computer, "this office is a clone of half a dozen or more scattered around the country from Devon to Scotland. He'd go from one to the other, with that thing he called the Beast following him. When he'd put some space between himself and the thing, he'd come to one of these houses, work on the information his research team were feeding him; then, when it got close, move onto the next house."

Money was no problem then; this set-up must have cost thousands."

"I guess he was on his way to one of these houses when his car broke down and he ended up at my house."

Rosemary pulled a file from the shelf and turned the pages. "Ah, the car," she said in a voice that to Richard sounded remarkably bitter. "You saw it, then?"

"No, he reached my house on foot."

"It was all like this." She dropped the file down beside a pair of fax machines. "No expense spared. A new BMW. It still had the plastic covers on the seats."

"A BMW?" Realization started to burn. "It wasn't by any chance white?"

"It was, actually."

"Hell fire." Richard slammed his palm down onto the desk, making Rosemary jump. "The bastard."

"What's wrong?"

"I saw that white BMW. But it was, let's see, three days before I first clapped eyes on Michael. My daughter Amy found the car in the ditch opposite our house. Damn, *damn* . . . it's all adding up now. It was Michael who opened the gate on Friday night. And . . . and Mark found a patch of blood on the garden path. Michael had a cut on his nose just here. Hell, yes!"

He looked up at Rosemary. She looked confused, almost frightened by the way he was walking up down the room, punching a fist into his open palm, talking to himself.

"It's OK, I'm not mad. Far from it, I'm just beginning to understand."

"You mean that Michael arrived at your house three days before you actually saw him?"

"Yes. And that he was hiding nearby somehow. And watching us. Watching Amy particularly. He's got something planned for her."

Rosemary looked up at him, eyes glistening. "And I'm afraid I think I know what that something is."

Chapter Sixty-two

Plans for Amy

Rosemary said, "I think he plans to use Amy to control that entity that's been following him. He thought I could do it. I couldn't and it almost killed me."

"But Amy? Why Amy? For Godsakes, she's only four years old."

She shrugged. "I think he knows time's running out. Michael's getting desperate."

Richard looked around at the files and books on the shelves. "Then we better start looking. Perhaps one of these will give us some idea where he's taken her."

"You take that shelf, I'll take this one," she said.

Richard pulled a plastic-backed file marked DIRECTORY from the shelf. Listed were names of individuals and organizations with telephone numbers; no addresses. He checked under "M" on the off-chance there would be a Middleton Hall. Nothing. Middleton Hall had been a false address simply to keep Richard out of the picture.

"Listen to this," she said, then read from a file. "This is an extract from something called *The Alchemy of Spirits, Demons And Other Such Beasts Without Flesh*. 'So far, it can be said that only Alexander the Great was successful in carrying the Byzantine Beast beyond the Purple Crescent. Even so, he could not contain it forever and perished young. Constantine the First understood this restriction. Accordingly he transferred the seat and center of the Roman Empire from Rome to Byzantium so that he might benefit from the Beast's vitality.' " Rosemary looked up. "It's underlined in red so I imagine it must be important. Have you any idea what it means?"

Richard nodded grimly. "I think I have. It means Michael has made an almighty cock-up. He should never have taken the Beast away from its home territory in Turkey. Let's have a look at that."

Rosemary handed him the file. Quickly, he flicked over the pages. More areas of text had been underlined. He read them almost at random but the gist was clear enough. "The Ottoman Turks conquered Constantinople in 1453. Presumably they also learned how to enter into that relationship with the Beast. Here it says that in 1596 a certain Sultan Isma'il attempted to take the Beast with him when he marched north in a bid to conquer the whole of Europe, and I quote: 'At the gates of Vienna Sultan Isma'il cried out in agony. His generals watched him die, pressed to death by a grievous weight no human eye could see.' The planned Ottoman Turk invasion of Europe collapsed and they retreated to Turkey."

"So," Rosemary thoughtfully ran her finger down the line of scabs on her face. "What Michael is trying to do is impossible."

"That's what most of these people think. But he knows that Alexander the Great was successful in taking the Beast all the way to India before he lost control of it."

"Then he died very shortly afterward."

"But Michael's confident he can find a solution to the problem. Apparently there's an ancient document known as the *Codex Alexander* which contains instructions how to do exactly that."

"And he's got hold of a copy?"

"In the last few days. His research team have been deciphering the thing. Presumably now Michael is taking my family to wherever the research team are based."

Rosemary pulled file after file from the shelf. Richard watched her, eyes hard with concentration. If the file was of no use she simply threw it on the floor. "Ah, here's something about the *Codex Alexander*. It must have been written before the discovery because it's talking about extracts from it that have turned up in other ancient books."

"Let me see."

Rosemary handed him the file. "I'll make us something to eat and drink. Is there still food in the kitchen?"

"There is, but I'm not hungry."

Again he underestimated her. "You're going to eat something, Richard. If you're going to be of any help to your family you've got to eat, drink and rest when you need to."

He was almost as surprised as her when he felt the grin on his face. "OK, boss."

290

For ten minutes he read the sheets of fax paper bound in the file, his eyes skipping from one red underlined section to the next. His heartbeat faster as he began to understand what Michael intended. At this stage he wasn't sure if it would involve Christine or Amy, or both of them, but he saw that Michael planned to—

That's when the scream came from the kitchen.

Chapter Sixty-three

More Visions

After hearing Rosemary scream Richard reached the kitchen in four seconds flat.

His first thought: *Someone's arrived at the cottage. The police? Michael's people?*

He found Rosemary staring out of the window, eyes bulging, the knife in her hand held so tightly it quivered.

"What is it? What's wrong?"

"Oh." She took a deep quivering breath. "I can see . . . I can see what she's seeing."

"Amy?"

He saw Rosemary didn't respond to what he said but continued to stare out of the window entranced. Every so often her head moved—a little shake, then a nod, as if she was replying to some unheard voice.

" . . . grass, stretching right up there. Lots, lots of it . . . Trees . . . but they are trees in cages. Metal cages around trees. Big house . . ." Her face grew even more pale; her eyes looked enormous. "Road going up. Narrow road. Outside big house people waiting. And flying. Now flying." Rosemary shook her head puzzled. "Amy? Amy, how are you flying? What animals? I don't know what the animals are. Running animals. Running animals and flying. Down below there are fields, houses. Toy houses. Little cars. Now the house. Big house. Big windows. Big chimneys. People waiting outside. Joey, who are those people? Are they waiting for us. Joey looks scared. Joey doesn't like what . . . Hmmph . . ."

"Rosemary. Are you all right?"

She blinked, then turned so she could lean back against the worktop. The knife still tightly clenched in her hand shook, the blade dangerously close to the underside of her chin.

"Hmm? Richard . . . I thought you were in the study. I'm cutting cheese for . . ."

"Take it easy. Here, sit down. It's OK, I'll hold the chair. And you best give me that knife." Gently he took the knife from her and sat her down at the kitchen table. He crouched beside her.

"Rosemary. You were looking through Amy's eyes. What did you see?"

Her eyes still gleamed strangely; she looked as if she was waking from a dream.

"Yes . . . yes, I was. But it wasn't like before. It came so strongly, but all jumbled up. Like she was excited or—"

"Frightened?"

"I don't know." She shook her head quickly, still dazed. "I saw . . . no, Amy saw something moving fast toward her. An animal of some sort."

Richard was appalled. "Jesus, it wasn't that thing, was it?"

"No. It can't have been. It was running toward them. Then alongside them. But it was all muddled up. First I saw they were driving along a narrow road through a grass field that was dotted with trees."

"You said trees in cages? What does that mean?"

She shrugged, her confusion painful to see. "I'm not sure. Trees in cages? I said that? I don't remember." Her eyes were troubled. "Anyway, that doesn't make sense. Who'd put a tree in a cage?"

"Never mind that now. What else did you see?" Richard asked gently. "Any place names, signposts?"

"No."

"You talked about flying. Is it an airport?"

"No. The grass field sloped quite steeply . . . and the word *animals* keeps coming back to me. Amy saw some animals. They excited her. As if they were something new to her. But . . ." She shook her head, forehead wrinkling. "I kept seeing images of the ground as if far below. But when she gets excited she mixes what she's actually seeing with what she's remembering. Has she ever flown before?"

"No, never."

She sighed. "Well, I think she has now. I got the impression it was a small aircraft. I could clearly see fields and houses far below. And I could feel how thrilled she was."

"Damn. If Michael drove to an airport from here then took a

plane they could be anywhere now. The continent, Ireland." He began to pace the kitchen. "Anything else?"

"The house came through clearly. A huge place, like a mansion built out of red brick with tall chimneys at each end."

"It looked new?"

"No. A couple of hundred years at least."

"And there were people standing outside as if there to welcome them."

"Yes. Including some in white coats, you know, the sort doctors wear."

Richard looked at the clock. Five past one. Again the certainty bit into him. *Time's running out.* He had to find them soon.

Rosemary stood up and went back to making the sandwiches. "I don't remember anything else. Only . . ." She looked back at Richard. "The expression on Joey's face. He looked scared. Very scared."

Richard returned to the study. He swept files from the shelves onto the floor, more in pointless rage than in an attempt to find anything. He couldn't access the computer because he didn't know the code. The temptation to put his fist through its stupid screen was enormous.

And why hadn't he been able to see through Amy's eyes? He'd had those clairvoyant flashes on the bus. Why had the ability deserted him now? Why—

Christ, Richard. This is getting you nowhere. Either go the whole hog, tear off your clothes and run screaming down the hillside—or sit down and start reading.

He returned to the *Codex Alexander* file. Michael had taken the latest pages with him, but there were still the earlier notes.

One researcher noted that although Alexander the Great was homosexual he always kept women close to him in his entourage. The researcher suggested that the women were important in the control of the Beast. Over the page, a photocopy of what looked like a fragment of Greek text on papyrus. Beneath that a hand-written translation: ". . . honored and gratified as he is by these gifts of gold and ivory, and pleased though he is with thy bronze likeness, my King requests the provision of girls. These should not be slaves, but girls of high breeding, with intelligence and with charm. My King requests that the girls be sent to him upon your good Majesty reading these words . . ." The same researcher had added a note: "Extract from Alexander's letter to one of his newly conquered kingdoms. It's clear from the letter that he needed women from the aristocratic classes. He needed them desperately, yet one supposes not for any sexual purpose, considering his own preferences."

Richard flicked through the pages, reading fragments here and there. These only reinforced his own fears. *Michael wants Amy and Christine for a purpose.*

Toward the end of the file, another letter written by a Baghdad priest after meeting Alexander the Great: "The conqueror of the world, this great and glorious man, walks everywhere holding the hands of two teenage girls like an idiot boy not allowed from his father's house alone. They say the girls hold the reins of an invisible lion that leaps upon men and tears out their hearts if they disobey what their King instructs. If this is the case, it is a wearying task for the girls. Not yet sixteen, they have the eyes and lips of ancient grandmothers. Gossips tell me that once Alexander orders a girl to hold his lion's reins they grow old in months and die broken by grievous sores and tumors."

Richard's mouth was dry. So that was it. Alexander the Great succeeded in taking the Beast out of its natural habitat. But he didn't take the Beast into himself as other emperors and kings had done. He had used the girls. They had entered into that symbiotic relationship that Michael had told them about, on Alexander the Great's behalf. They controlled the power, but Alexander controlled them. Clearly the strain had been so great that they had withered and died within a few months. Hence, Alexander's demands for a fresh supply of girls.

Michael had Christine and Amy. All the pieces of the jigsaw were flying together at a breathtaking rate.

Richard stood up and kicked the wastepaper basket savagely, sending balls of discarded paper across the room.

Where the hell are they? he thought desperately. *This room must contain a clue. It has to.* He started wrenching drawers from the desk, emptying the contents into a pile. Pencils, pens, notebooks, banknotes bound together by a rubber band, keys. Junk, junk, junk!

Rosemary came to the door and watched him silently as he tore the place apart.

At last she said, "Michael must have been telephoning someone from here. His research team."

"Yes, but there's a file full of numbers there. Which one?"

"You could pick up the phone and press the redial button."

"What? And say, 'Excuse me, has Michael brought my kidnaped family there, by any chance?' "

"I don't know, Richard."

He sighed. "What have I got to lose?" He picked up the phone and pressed the last-number redial. He waited as the numbers clicked through the earpiece.

He reached the speaking clock. Either Michael had genuinely wanted to know the time, or, more likely, he'd simply been covering his tracks.

"What are you doing?" he asked, watching her opening the screwed-up balls of paper that had come from the basket.

"You said Michael had also been sending faxes. These might be the originals he put through the machine this morning."

Richard quickly joined her, smoothing out the sheets of paper.

"My God," breathed Richard. "So Michael's empire was coming apart at the seams."

"What do you mean?"

"Look, these faxes are from a G. Leonard, head of Michael's accountancy and financial team. Leonard says, 'Request urgent instruction regarding restructuring of loans . . . please be advised that mortgagees have repossessed hotel chain . . . two banks have called in loans . . . overdraft facilities refused . . .' Receivers called in at a car franchise and what looks like half a dozen wholesalers."

"So his companies are collapsing?"

"The whole lot's going down the tubes." Richard flicked through more faxes that Michael had obviously filed in the bin, probably unread. "He's a desperate man, no doubting that. In Turkey, when he was cosily cohabiting with that thing, he had power. He made a lot of money and used it to build up business here in Britain. When he came here he lost control of the Beast. So he substituted the power it gave him with the next best thing."

"Money."

"Got it in one. He's like a general throwing his troops into suicidal missions to give him just a few more hours. He's bleeding his companies white. Money's no object, providing it gets him what he wants. Back into bed with the Beast."

"Of course, if he does that he won't need the money. He'll be powerful again."

"So it's a race against time for Michael, too," he said with a savage burst of satisfaction. "I hope this is hurting the sod as much as it's hurting me." He paused, thoughtful for a moment. "There was another file here on the desk. Where did I put it . . . ah, here it is."

Rosemary, sitting on the floor searching through the contents of the basket, looked up. "What is it?"

"It's titled Property Register. Bull's-eye! It lists what I imagine are Michael's properties. Yes, there's the hotel in Wales . . . And, yep, this cottage. There's another, one, two, three, four . . ." He counted quickly, feeling his pulse quicken, sure he was onto something.

"Another fifteen properties—and, thank heaven, they've all got the full addresses."

"And telephone numbers? We could match them with the fax numbers."

"No such luck. A couple have been crossed out with Rs beside them, probably repossessed. Yep, there's a fax at the back from old Mr. Leonard who's beginning to sound frantic. The fraud squad have been asking him why some of the properties have been remortgaged several times over."

"If the property houses a research team and his other staff you'd imagine it would be pretty big."

"You mean like the redbrick mansion you saw through Amy's eyes?"

She nodded.

He glanced down the list. "Most seemed to be rural properties. The Lock Keeper's House, Lancashire. Stable Cottage, Kent—I suppose we can discount those. Hunsway Manor, Cumbria."

"That sounds more promising. It's far enough away from here to make a plane flight worthwhile."

Richard shook his head. "And there's Darlington House in Yorkshire. That could apply to a grand mansion or a house in a suburban street."

"What are those pieces of paper sticking out of the back of the file?"

Richard leafed through them. "Running costs on the properties and values. Not for all of them, though. There's nothing for the Cumbrian house or the Yorkshire one. Wait, look at this. Maintenance funds must have been virtually nonexistent. Again poor old Mr. Leonard had to get Michael to authorize expenditure on every little thing that went wrong. Here's a request for authorization to install burglar alarm here at Glebe Cottage. Scrawled across it, one word: REFUSED. Requests for resurfacing of access to Hunsway Manor, Cumbria. That one's agreed, providing the cost of the work is halved. And an authorization to repair a deer fence at Darlington House. If only these had got the—"

"Wait a minute." Rosemary jumped to her feet and pulled the sheet from Richard's hand. "Deer fence. Authorization to repair a deer fence!" Her face blazed with excitement. "Don't you see? Trees in cages. Amy saw them as they drove up to the big red-brick house. The cages are to protect trees against deer damaging the bark. And Amy saw the big animals that she'd not seen before."

"But we don't know they were deer." Richard didn't really doubt what Rosemary was driving at. He just didn't want to let his hopes rise too far.

Rosemary's eyes shone. "Bet you that crappy old van out there and all its contents that's just what they are. Big deer with bloody big antlers."

"Come on." Richard ripped out the sheet with the address. "It's near Wakefield in Yorkshire so we've got a good five hours' drive in front of us."

"In that van? Make it seven—if we're lucky."

Richard headed for the door, then looked back as Rosemary scrabbled through the balled-up paper on the floor. "What're you looking for?"

Rosemary held up the roll of banknotes he'd thrown to one side. "This might come in handy. There must be a good couple of hundred in—"

Richard held up his hand.

"What is it?" she whispered.

"The fax machine. There's one coming through."

The machine had begun its buzzing as it printed the transmission. Fax paper scrolled from the slot.

Richard tilted his head to one side, reading the fax as it emerged.

"To: All teams. From: HQ. Urgent. All designated personnel to return to HQ immediately." He had to pause as more paper unscrolled. "Transfer is confirmed for 21:00. 19th of June."

"The 19th? That's today."

A cold weight settled in his stomach as he read in a flat voice.

" 'Subject A has been groomed for transfer. Michael is confident of success. Congratulations, everybody. Your rewards will be justly deserved.' " Richard looked up. "Jesus . . . you know what that means?"

Rosemary nodded.

He rubbed his forehead. "Damn, damn. Michael plans to transfer that thing to Amy, like he tried to transfer it to you."

"Twenty-one hundred hours. That's nine o'clock this evening."

"Great," Richard said bitterly. "That gives us less than eight hours to get all the way up to Wakefield, find Amy and then somehow get her out of his hands."

He stared at the sheet of fax paper in his hands like it was a death warrant.

"Richard." Her voice was gentle but insistent. "If we're going we better make a start now."

"You don't have to go with me, you know. I don't think Michael will welcome us with open arms."

"Don't try and stop me, Richard. I'm going to show him what he's done to me." She pulled her hair aside to show him the scabbed wound that dominated the left side of her face. "And this mess is going to be the last thing he sees."

He nodded. "Let's get moving."

But they didn't get far. As Richard headed for the door that led out onto the courtyard he looked out through the window. A car pulled slowly up beside the van and stopped.

He pulled Rosemary back away from the door. "Not that way. We've got visitors."

Chapter Sixty-four

Between a Rock and a Hard Place

Richard saw the red Sierra pull up alongside the VW van in the pebbled yard. The slowness of its approach had set the alarms shrieking in his head.

"Bet you any money these have been sent by Michael," he said.

Two men in their thirties climbed with an unnerving slowness out of the car, heads turning as they scanned the cottage expertly. They were dressed casually in shorts and T-shirts, but they wore them like a uniform and the impression Richard had was that they looked like bodyguards, probably part of Michael's security team.

One man took a pump-action shotgun from the boot of the car, the other opened the van door and reached under the dash-board. The van rocked on its suspension. "I think we won't be using the van again. He's ripping out the wiring."

Rosemary hissed, "Is there another way out of the cottage?"

"There's a side door that takes you out by the swimming pool. Best get out into the woods as quickly as possible."

They cut through the kitchen into the lounge, then into a dining room. Sweat pricked through Richard's skin. Rosemary put into words what he was thinking.

"If they catch us they'll kill us, won't they?"

He nodded, grim-faced, then slid open the patio door and stepped outside. The swimming pool area was enclosed by a seven-foot stone wall. There was access from the pebbled yard by a wrought iron gate. An identical gate at the opposite end of the pool area led into the back garden. Richard planned to leave by that gate, then simply climb over the low fence and slip away into the densely wooded hillside.

They moved lightly toward the gate at the rear. Before opening it, he craned his head over.

Damn.

One of the men had already skirted the cottage into the back garden, perhaps guessing they'd leave the back way.

"Christ, these men are professionals," he whispered. "Back the other way. With luck the other guy's gone into the cottage."

His luck failed him. The second man with the shotgun was walking purposefully across the pebble yard toward them.

Richard hissed. "He's coming this way."

"He's seen us?"

"No. But he's going to be coming through this gate in the next ten seconds."

"Hide."

"Where, for Godsakes?" Richard desperately looked around the pool area. All there was were the pool beneath its plastic cover, ornamental stone benches and a pool surround paved with stone slabs.

The crunch of feet on pebbles grew louder as the man approached the gate.

Chapter Sixty-five

Skin of Tooth

Rosemary whispered, "Get in."

"The pool?"

"Yes. Not here . . . far end. Get under the matting."

Without a word, Richard pulled up the mat from where it lay on the surface of the water and slipped beneath it. After the heat of the summer's day the water felt brutally cold. He held his breath to stop himself grunting at the shock of the cold water rising up over his legs and soaking through his jeans. Rosemary slipped into the water behind him.

The mat fitted the pool perfectly. However, at one end, running the width of the pool, was something like a towel roller that held the pool mat, and one end of the mat was attached to it. When the pool was required all you needed to do was crank a handle and wind the mat back onto the cylinder.

Richard realized that Rosemary had noticed that at this end of the pool the mat left something like a narrow tunnel between the end of the pool's tiled wall and the steep slope of the mat as it came down to rest on the water.

Richard, tall enough to stand in the deep end of the pool, held Rosemary so she didn't need to tread water. Above their heads, the heavy plastic mat allowed a dim blue light through to illuminate their faces and the rippling water around them.

Richard held his breath again as a shadow fell on the mat above as the two men walked by the pool.

He felt Rosemary tense in his arms as she saw the shadow.

His face almost touched hers. Her wide eyes communicated with eye movements alone.

The men began to talk in a way that was cheerful and relaxed.

"The little scrubber can't have gone far. Any sign of her in the cottage?"

"She's been there. Look's as if she's been helping herself to the boss's snap. Breadcrumbs all over the fucking place."

"Filthy little scrubber. Reckon she deserves a good slapping."

"Then she can get her lips around my twelve gauge."

They laughed. Brutal; raw-sounding.

"If she's a good bit of kit I'll toss you for her."

Again laughter.

"Michael doesn't want you to use guns."

"We'll make it look like a pervert took a shine to her. Screw her, bite a chunk or two out of her tits, then stick the boot in until she gets her wings."

Richard saw Rosemary's eyes go wide with shock. He thought she would cry out so he slipped his hand behind her head and pulled her face into the side of his neck. Her slender body trembled in his arms, shaking droplets of water from her hair to drip into the water with what seemed such a tremendously loud sound that he thought they'd hear.

"Pass us a tab, Geordie Boy."

A match scraped.

"Christ, it's hot. When we've done we'll find a bleedin' pub and get bleedin' mortal. If she . . . hey, did you hear that?"

"What?"

"Hell's bells. It's the phone in the car."

Sound of hurrying feet across the stone slabs.

"Geordie Boy."

"What?"

"Get the washing line from the house. When we find her we'll string her up from a tree. Make it look like a suicide."

Again he felt a convulsive shock crack through her arms and back; her eyes screwed shut against the bare skin of his neck.

"Don't worry," he whispered as softly as he could. "I'll not let them touch you."

Richard realized the two men were only looking for Rosemary. Obviously they still believed he was lying mangled with Isaac in the ruins of the barn. That might give him a tiny advantage if they were discovered. But what he could do to hurt them God alone knew. The way they spoke suggested they were ex-military, probably Marines or SAS. They could probably kill him with a jab of a finger.

He waited until the voices receded. One had gone back to the car to take the call. The one called Geordie Boy was probably hunting in the kitchen for the washing line. Then the two would make a thorough search of the place. And that's when they'd find the pair of them.

"Come on, Rosie," he said gently. "We're going to have to get away from here."

In the dim blue light she looked up at him. For the first time he saw she was badly frightened.

He pulled her to the edge of the pool, eased up the matting and looked out.

No one about. *Yet.* Any second Geordie Boy might come swaggering through the gateway, knotting a noose into the end of the washing line. Richard pulled himself from the pool.

Rosemary, he saw, had frozen up with fear. She clearly didn't want to leave the pool. Richard guessed she was thinking it best to stay hidden under the pool cover.

"No, Rosie," he whispered. "We can't stay here. Those guys will take this place apart until they find you."

She held up her arms like a child to be lifted from the water.

The water dripped from them in a way that sounded appallingly loud, drips smacking onto the stone slabs. But there was no way of avoiding it.

Feet squelching in his trainers Richard guided her to the gate that led into the back garden.

What they had to do was keep moving. The two men were pretty nonchalant about finding Rosemary: they'd disabled the van; perhaps they guessed she'd simply gone into hiding under a bed upstairs. A teenage girl would be easy meat. They were probably more used to slogging it out with terrorists in some Arabian desert.

After leaving the pool area, Richard, holding Rosemary's hand, stuck close to the wall as far as the garden fence. There he simply lifted her over the fence before climbing over himself.

Without speaking he pointed into the wood. She nodded and followed as he jogged silently under the canopy of trees.

After a hundred yards, he said in a panted whisper, "You OK?"

She shook back the tangle of wet hair. "Only if I never see those two again. Which way now?"

He pointed a dripping finger. "Downhill. We can move faster."

They ran, their bodies sometimes catching against tree trunks, leaving damp patches on the bark.

He gambled that there hadn't been more men who had perhaps

been dropped off at the top of the track to search the wood. But from the flippant way the men spoke they didn't treat the girl as a serious threat. She was just another of Michael's loose ends to be tied up when they at last caught up with her.

The close encounter with Michael's henchmen back there had taken his mind off Amy and Christine. But the realization came thundering back. He now had something like seven hours to get back to Wakefield. Then, somehow, he had to stop Michael from doing whatever he had planned for Amy.

Richard had never prayed for a miracle before in his life. But as they pounded through the wood, that was when he started.

Chapter Sixty-six

Darlington House

Amy's voice echoed from the brick walls that enclosed the formal garden at the back of Darlington House. Shielding his eyes with his hand, Michael looked to where Christine and Joey stood beside the ornamental pond. They talked intently, as if trying to resolve something that troubled them. Repeatedly, they'd shoot anxious glances back at him and at Amy who sat beside him on the bench.

Michael was pleased with Amy: she had become so happy and relaxed with him. In fact, he'd go further and say she'd become downright affectionate, sometimes scrambling up onto his knee to pull his ears; then he'd tickle her, which would send her into bouts of breathless giggling.

Now she played with the Rosemary Snow doll, talking to herself in that completely self-absorbed way that young children slipped into.

"Rosemary Snow . . . Rosemary Snow. Where do you go? Where do you go? Wet as a kipper; bathroom slipper. Watch out, Boys, here she comes. Stand back, Boys. Bump, bump."

On the face of it, it was a stream of nonsense but Michael listened carefully, nodding as some phrase hit a chord.

As he listened he felt a buzz of excitement. Everything was ready. Everything was going perfectly. He knew the Beast was coming. Moving silently toward them like a shark swimming through the depths of the ocean. It was going to work tonight. He could feel it; by God, he could feel it!

Smiling broadly, he said, "What's Rosemary doing now, sugar?"

"Been swimming." Amy laughed. "Been swimming with her jeans and pants and things on."

"Swimming in her clothes? Bet she got all wet, didn't she?"

"All soaked and yucky." Amy answered his gentle questions but she seemed more interested in moving the doll's legs so it walked along the bench.

"Is Rosemary going to change into dry clothes, Amy?"

"Don't think so. Running—*wheeee* . . . fast as a horse."

"Where to?"

"Don't know."

"Oh."

"Dad does though."

"Your Dad?" He frowned. "Amy, can you see him?"

"Boys! Boys! Out of Rosemary's way, she'll knock you down, *pow*!"

"Amy, can you see your Dad now?"

"Of course, silly. He's with Rosemary Snow."

"Has he been swimming?"

"Yup. And now he's running through the field with her." She didn't look at Michael, just lifted the doll for him to see, then returned to moving its legs so it walked along the bench.

"Whereabouts are they?"

"Oh . . . there." Without looking up, she pointed behind her. She was more interested in the doll.

"The cottage where we stayed last night?"

Amy nodded, then made the doll jump up onto the bench's back rest.

Rosemary Snow jumped down from the fence. "Do you think we can sit down for a while?" She panted and rubbed her side.

"Just another ten minutes." Richard took a deep breath; sweat stung his eyes. "But we can walk now. I just want to put a bit more space between us and those apes."

"We can't walk all the way to Yorkshire."

He looked grim. "Don't remind me. Have you still got the money from the cottage?"

She pulled the dripping bundle of notes from her pocket.

Richard said, "With luck, there'll be enough to get a hire car."

"If we can find somewhere to rent us one. We're in the middle of nowhere."

Richard looked around at the fields and hedgerows. A stream meandered away into the distance. There wasn't even a road. The clock in his head renewed its savage tick. Batting out the seconds that remained between now and nine o'clock.

307

Gritting his teeth, he said, "Come on, if we head downstream we might reach a town before too long."

With Rosemary following Richard set up a hard pace; and he found himself praying for that miracle again.

In the garden of Darlington House, Amy seemed more interested in the doll so, ruffling her hair, Michael said, "I'll just go and get you a cold drink, pumpkin. Oh, and best play in the shade across there, we don't want all this hot sunshine making you poorly." He noticed Christine and Joey shooting him suspicious looks. He pretended not to notice. He'd make sure they wouldn't pose any threat to his plan.

On the way to the house's kitchens he stopped off at the head of security. Mitch Winter, a heavy, diligent man with his bull head shaved to the skull, was speaking on the telephone, a cigarette between finger and thumb of the other hand. On the walls of the office were framed maps of islands. All were small islands; all had, or had had at one time, tiny cloistered communities—Sark, Lundy, Pitcairn, Steep Holm. Interests reflect personality. Sometimes they reflect truths about yourself that even you're not aware of. Ex-Marine, ex-assassin, ex-mercenary, Mitch Winter yearned to become an ex-member of this rat-race life. He hankered for a stone cottage tucked cosily into the fold of a hill that overlooked the sea: solitary cliff-top walks and an easygoing island population; he'd be on first name terms with everyone; evenings he'd spend sipping Guinness in an ancient inn with a dog beneath the table and his hands clean, at last, of other men's blood.

When he saw Michael he hung up and stood respectfully.

Michael snapped out the words. "The girl's father's still alive."

"Richard Young?" The voice was a surprisingly quiet growl.

"And he's with Snow."

"Do you know where?"

"Back in Glebe Cottage in Devon. I want you to get those two idiots you sent down there to go over the area again."

"And when they find them? Make it look like an accident?"

"No," Michael snapped. "Just tell them to kill the pair of them—strangle, knife, gun, sodomize them to death for all I care. I just want Snow and Young rubbed out. Now!"

"But they can't pose a threat. They're only—"

308

"They'll be on their way here. It doesn't take a genius to realize Young'll work out what's planned for tonight."

"I'll get right onto it."

Michael headed off to the kitchen, eyes blazing. He was like a guided missile locked onto its target. He knew what he wanted; he knew he could get it. God help any poor fool who got in his way.

Richard told Rosemary to grab five minutes' rest and try to dry her clothes as best she could before they set off again. He reckoned they'd put three miles between themselves and the cottage so, for the time being, they should be beyond the reach of those hairy-knuckled thugs.

By the stream grew a wild rose bush heavy with white blossoms. He watched Rosemary take out the roll of banknotes and push them one by one onto the thorns like she was hanging out washing to dry.

"How much?" he asked, trying to unlace his trainers.

"Two hundred."

"That'll be enough to hire a car . . . damn." The laces had tangled into a wet knot. He used one foot to push the shoe off. Then he peeled off his socks and shirt. His body ached. Probably more from tension than exhaustion. He noticed a cluster of bruises down his chest and remembered being bounced down the hillside that morning like a tennis ball.

He watched Rosemary peel off her wet jeans: they'd stuck to her legs like a second skin. As she pulled they dragged down her briefs, flashing at him a patch of jet-black pubic hair.

He had to make a deliberate effort to look away. She made no effort to hide herself, as if the events of the last couple of weeks had knocked all the modesty out of her.

Christ, all we need is for a party of ramblers to come along from the Holland-on-Sea Young-At-Heart club, or something, and they'll think they've stumbled on the makings of an open-air orgy.

He draped his shirt, socks and jeans over a branch, then walked by the rose bush with its strange money-fruit and went down to the stream to wash the smell of pool chlorine from his face.

A voice ran through his head: *You've got to reach Wakefield by this evening. You've got to stop Michael. You've got to get Amy and Christine and, yes, even Joey pain-in-the-ass Barrass away from there.*

How? How? How?

Even after walking this far there was still no sign of a town. *What now, Dicky Boy? There might be an isolated house. You find some old dear living alone, take her car.*

Would he break the law, maybe even end up hurting some innocent member of the public to reach Wakefield in time?

He squatted there, gazing trancelike into the rippling water, the stream playing through his fingers; a dragon-fly hovered, electric-blue in the sunshine; a helicopter chopped the summer air high above.

He knew the answer. Yes. This was survival. Deep down he knew he was obeying Nature's rule to the letter. Nature didn't want him to save a four-year-old girl with a passion for Tom and Jerry cartoons and white chocolate and Casper glow-in-the-dark stickers. A little girl who could be so downright bossy sometimes, or who could launch unprovoked attacks on her older brother, trying to bite his nose so hard it brought tears to his eyes. Nature didn't want him, Richard Young, her father, to rescue a little girl called Amy Young. Nature wanted—no, Dicky Boy, Nature bloody well demanded he preserved his and his ancestors' genes that she carried in her body. He was damn well slavishly and blindly obeying a billion years of evolution. Poets and moon-struck teenagers call it love.

I'm obeying the program that must be obeyed. Like that dragon-fly hovers there beating its wings, like that sparrow there on the branch exhausts itself in this heat finding insects to stuff into the greedy beaks of its clamoring chicks. That's not parental love. That's genetic programming. Like a dog or a rat or a human will die for their offspring, so that offspring can breed more and more of the species. *We're not parents, we're damn' postmen.* Children are the envelopes that contain the genes, and humans are slavishly working to make sure the mail arrives safely at its destination. Just to satisfy that untiring, that uncompromising, that pitiless tyrant called Mother Nature—so it can fill the world from seabed to mountaintop with that thing called Life. *What's so bloody good about it? What does life bring but conflict, pain, disappointments, then, ultimately, death?*

"Richard. Are you OK?"

He looked up at her. His eyes stung; all he could see was a blur.

"Must be the pool chlorine."

As he wiped his streaming eyes he felt her guide him by the arm to the banking. There he sat on the grass, his head down. She put her arms around him and held him tight. For a second he sat like a chunk of ice, emotionally blocked until, at last, the feeling broke. Then he held her tightly, too, burying his face into her sun-warm hair and sobbed like a wounded child.

Her closeness was a healing drug. He felt the humanity spread back into his arms, legs, through his whole body like a warming tide.

Was life worth living?

Yes, it bloody well was.

And the lives of his family were precious too. He would win them back, and if he lived to be ninety and sat in his armchair at Christmas surrounded by happy children, grandchildren, great-grandchildren he would remember today. When he felt that great life force, running with an energy greater than a million nuclear generators, greater and more enduring than the stars themselves, when he felt it crackling with a breathtaking power through the willows, through the grass, the rose bush, the bird, the dragon-fly—and through himself; and through this battered and scarred girl that he pulled tight to him, feeling her heartbeat against his arm, her gentle sobbing breath against his neck.

He lifted his head up so he could look into her shining eyes. "We're going to get through this, Rosemary. And we're going to be a team that even Michael can't break."

A smile reached her lips. "Michael doesn't know he's bitten off more than he can chew. We'll show him, won't we?"

"We'll show him, kidda."

And before he could stop himself he kissed her gently on her lips.

The softness of her lips was indescribable. Richard trembled, feeling something of that life force surge in a wave from her lips into his, then back again.

For a moment they stayed in that same embrace, faces a hand's breadth apart, looking into each other's eyes—and reading something there that unrolled a great mystery.

Richard sensed it was time to break the embrace. Rosemary smiled almost shyly now. She felt it, too.

Although they no longer touched physically something had bonded them deeply. At that moment Richard felt closer to this sixteen-year-old girl than he had to anyone before in his life.

As he moved back to find his clothes he noticed a change to her left cheek.

Quickly, he looked again. For a moment he wasn't sure what had caught his eye. Only that it looked different.

Then he knew what was happening.

Chapter Sixty-seven

Resurrection

"Rosemary. Here! Let me see your face!"

Startled, she looked up at him.

"What is it? What's wrong?"

He heard panic drive through her voice.

"Come here." He lifted her hair so he could examine her cheek. "Richard . . ."

"Just a moment." He wiped her face gently with his handkerchief. "I don't believe it; it's coming off."

"What is?"

"The scabs and the stitches. It'll have been that soaking they got in the swimming pool. They're just wiping off."

"The stitches?"

"They're probably made of some kind of polymer. They're dissolving."

He was aware of her eyes, intense and earnest-looking, searching his face as if half-afraid he was playing some cruel joke.

But he could hardly believe his own eyes as that disfiguring ridge of black scab came away as easily as if it were merely dried mud.

After he'd finished she ran down to the water's edge and crouched down to look at her reflection in the water.

For a full minute she stared at it in disbelief. Then she came back up to him, tears filling her eyes.

"It's gone," she said in a voice that was full of wonder.

"The scab would have flaked off naturally anyway."

"No. Not the scab." She stroked her cheek, eyes bright. "I had a birthmark. A big red thing, it was; shaped like a letter Z."

"It's gone now."

She was crying. Richard wasn't sure whether it was relief or sense of loss over something she'd carried since she was born.

"I don't believe it," she was saying and shaking her head. "After all these years. It's gone . . . it's just gone."

Richard realized that the birthmark wasn't as trivial as he supposed. Her whole body shook with relief. For her this had been a miracle. And he'd seen it happen.

She asked him again to look at her face. Was there any scarring? Would it look normal once the pinkness had gone?

"It's perfect. No more scabs; it's not pitted; there's no scar. All there is, is a smooth beautiful cheek."

"But my face was in such a mess. I was a Frankenstein."

"Nature's done a good job healing the wound. Probably with a bit of help from the hospital's plastic surgeon."

He sensed her spirits lift with a surge; her eyes brightened.

Lightly she ran to get dressed. A banknote dislodged itself from one of the rose thorns and floated down to the ground. Cheerfully she picked it up. She had no pants beneath the T-shirt and Richard found himself being mooned.

She realized, pulled the T-shirt back down, then shot him a grin that bordered on the cheeky.

Richard smiled back. He kept the smile on his face as he pulled on his sun-dried socks. The smile felt artificial. Because the truth came thundering back.

The time was 2:15. Wakefield was a solid five hours' drive away: providing they got hold of a car; providing there were no traffic jams; providing there were no unforeseen hold-ups; and providing Michael's apes didn't catch them first.

"The money's dry," Rosemary called.

He gave a nod. Then set off walking across the field. Rosemary Snow had to run to keep up with him.

He was wondering what Amy and Christine were doing right at that moment.

Chapter Sixty-eight

Leaving Michael

At the same time as Richard walked through the Devon field Christine was talking to Joey.

"Well, I have to tell you I don't like it. Where on earth are Richard and Isaac? They should be here by now."

"Michael said they'd make a slight detour to pick up some reports from a researcher."

"But why not fax them? And why did Michael say all along we were going to Norfolk, then suddenly say the venue had been changed to this place in Yorkshire instead? I'm telling you, Joey, something doesn't feel right about what Michael's telling us."

"Nothing's wrong. What have you seen to change your mind about Michael?"

"A feeling. That's all. A feeling deep down that Michael's hiding something."

They walked away from the pond toward where Amy played in the shade of the tree.

"I agree, it's no barrel of laughs." Joey pushed his lank hair back from his forehead. "But it's no different from what we've already been through this week."

"I know . . . well, I *don't* know. Look, Joey, it just feels different. The way Michael's acting."

"It doesn't seem any different to me."

"That's because you don't spend enough time with your children." She looked up at his muddy brown eyes; there was that hurt, defeated look she knew only too well. She sighed. "Joey, he's got the same look in his eye that Mark has when he thinks he's pulled one over on you. You know? He'll be in his bedroom, supposed to be doing his homework and all the time he's watching a wrestling video with the sound turned down."

"What do you think Michael's up to?"

"I don't know, Joey."

"I'll ask him when he thinks he'll get this Beast thing under control again."

"No. Don't do that. But I've been thinking we should do something."

His voice softened. "Like what, Sis?"

She looked at the house, then back at her brother. "We should be thinking of taking Amy away from here. Without Michael's agreement. In fact, without him knowing."

"But how will we get the Beast off our backs? It's—"

"Shh. Michael's coming this way now."

He didn't know the name of the town.

He didn't know the name of the old man.

But Richard Young could have kissed the gritty pavement, then kissed the old man's wrinkled forehead.

"There's one nearby?" Richard repeated, not believing his ears.

The old man scratched the wrinkled forehead. "Bradhall's rent cars, yonder on Church Street."

Richard flashed Rosemary a look of triumph.

"They close early on Thursdays. Bill Bradhall takes his family to Torquay on Thursdays; he's got a sister who—"

"Thank you," Richard said feeling near-overwhelming gratitude to the old man in his baggy gray cardigan.

Richard and Rosemary crossed the street lined with shops and headed in the direction the old man had indicated. The man still talked as they walked away.

"Turn left at Samuel's book shop. Like I said, best be quick. He closes early today."

"Think we're in luck?" Rosemary asked breathlessly as Richard broke into a run.

"By God, we better be."

Richard thought: *The time's coming up to 2:30. If we do get a hire car, and providing the roads are clear we've still got a five-hour drive in front of us. Hell, and it's peak tourist season down here. What if all the hire cars are gone?*

Come on, come on. Bradhall's, the old man said. Bradhall's. Where the hell are they?

The mental clock ticked away the seconds in his head like a time bomb. Little more than six hours left until Michael called in the Beast and made the transfer to Amy.

If it failed. He remembered the crushed policemen, the sheep exploding like crimson paint bombs . . . York Minster. Amy, poor Amy . . .

"Damn. Where the hell is the place?"

"This's Church Street."

"But where the hell is Bradhall's?"

"I can't see a garage. This's all residential."

"Damn."

The old man might be senile, thought Richard, clenching his jaw. *Maybe Bradhall went to the big rental place in the sky in 1963, or some—*

Wait. He'd seen a sign fixed to a wooden driveway gate.

"Bradhall's!" It came out in a whoop. "Come on."

Chapter Sixty-nine

Making Plans for Richard

The wall clock, between the framed maps of the islands of St. Mary's and Barra, said 3:14.

Michael sat on the edge of the desk, his downturned eyes on Mitch. The eyes were coolly confident.

"When did you find out about the hire car?"

"Ten minutes ago."

"Then they've got Snow and Young."

"Not quite."

"As good as. That's what matters."

Mitch pulled on his cigarette, then pointed at an open road atlas. "As you can imagine, in that part of Devon car hire companies are few and far between. My men got lucky the second time they tried. Bradhall Hire, just there; place called Ashton Tracey. The owner was on his way out for the afternoon."

"But he was cooperative?"

"Very cooperative." Ten years ago Mitch Winter would have grinned, enjoying the idea of making men spill their secrets. Ten years on he found the business tedious and grubby. He did what he was told to do competently, but he talked like he was reading times from a train timetable. "Silver Volvo Saloon, model 240, three years old, there's the registration number, green sunstrip running across the top of the windscreen bearing the words BRADHALL HIRE."

Michael said, "If those two guys are pros, and Young's only got about ten minutes start, we'll soon have them."

"I wouldn't be so optimistic."

"These men *are* pros?"

"They are."

"Then they'll catch up with Young and Snow?"

"They are pros. That's precisely why they won't go tearing

across the countryside like something out of a Hollywood cops caper." He spoke slowly, respectfully. "See all those roads between Dartmoor and Exeter? In that maze you could lose the Devil himself."

"But even an idiot would know Young will be heading for where the M5 starts at Exeter; that's the fastest route North."

"Sure. And Young'll be driving that car like a bat out of hell."

"Your men could catch up?"

"They'll not risk being stopped for speeding when they've got a couple of pump action shotguns in the back and . . . no, Michael, don't even think it, please. They're not going to risk jail for pulling a gun on a cop. They know they'd go down for life."

"It's vital Young doesn't get anywhere near here."

"The way he'll be driving might save you a job. He might run the car up a tree."

"I can't risk that."

"Michael. Look. Can I suggest something?"

Michael's downturned eyes were growing icier by the second. At last he shrugged, which Mitch guessed meant was an OK.

"Look, we know he's making a beeline right here. To Darlington House."

"Go on."

"So, I'm suggesting let them come to us. Deal with them when they get here."

"Mitch, I've not told you what I'm doing here, or what I have planned for tonight."

"Damned right, and I don't want to know."

"Good. But what I need is a nice peaceful environment. Things are going to happen tonight—it's OK, Mitch, they won't concern you or your team—but it's vital that little kid out there is in a nice relaxed frame of mind when it does."

"And seeing her daddy get the bullet wouldn't help, right?"

"Right."

Mitch pulled on the cigarette, blew out the smoke thoughtfully, nodded. "Okay. There are only a couple of roads up here from Wakefield. They both go through the urban road system."

"So?"

"So there are plenty of traffic lights. They'll have to stop at least one of them. I'll send my team out on motorcycles and we'll solve this problem Mafia-style.

"I can rely on that?"

Mitch nodded. "But you can't rely on some gossip not reaching the ears of the local village copper; so you might have some explaining."

"As long as they keep their noses out until after nine o'clock."

"Nine o'clock must be pretty special if you can silence the entire British police force."

Michael's boyish grin returned. "After nine o'clock they could show everything that's happened today on TV and there won't be a thing anyone can—or will *want* to—do about it."

"You had something like this going in Turkey, didn't you? I've never known the kind of loyalty you enjoyed across there."

Michael acknowledged the compliment with a nod.

"I've got some good contacts overseas," Mitch said. "They'd pay a lot of money to find out how you managed to win that kind of loyalty."

Michael tapped the side of his nose with his finger. "They couldn't afford it."

With that, Michael left the room, clicking his fingers to a tune that ran through his head.

Mitch Winter cast his mind back six months to when he had first met Michael, in his villa in Turkey. Immediately he'd been transfixed by the man's charisma. Michael had outlined his plans for an extensive business operation in the UK for which he needed Mitch to head a security team.

Mitch Winter had asked no questions. He found himself agreeing enthusiastically to whatever Michael said. He noticed, too, that Michael's staff at the villa looked on him as some kind of god.

It was only when Mitch came back to Yorkshire to set up the team and start recruiting personnel from his old mercenary contacts that he began to wonder what Michael's secret was. People in his presence had wanted to prostrate themselves at his feet. People would have set themselves on fire if he'd asked.

Perhaps he slipped a mickey in their drinks, or was it something more sophisticated? Perhaps concealed apparatus, something like an aerosol, sprayed an atomized solution containing a narcotic into the air.

But were the effects now wearing off?

Mitch Winter's enthusiasm for his work quickly cooled. Michael seemed overly secretive. The research team upstairs, an arrogant lot, were just as bad.

In Turkey Michael looked like a god; here he was looking tacky, even neurotic.

Michael would sometimes ask him to have a Mr. X or a Miss Y killed. Mitch didn't object on moral grounds—all part of the nine-to-five for him—but some of the killings seemed peculiarly pointless.

For instance, the chamber maid Michael'd brought back with him from the airport hotel. Sophie . . . that was her name.

At first there'd been a lot of excitement. The high and mighty upstairs became even more secretive.

They didn't ill-treat Sophie, as far as he could gather from the titbits he picked up from the kitchen staff. All the research team did was talk to her and feed her good meals.

By that time, Michael was away on his mystery tour of Great Britain. However, one day Mitch had a telephone call from him. "That woman I brought in last week," he'd said. "Sophie. I want her taking to the farm."

His code for an execution. Mitch did as he was told with extreme competence, then fed her corpse to the pigs.

And now Michael had something special planned for the little girl tonight. Mitch leaned back, tapping a fresh cigarette against his lips. He studied a framed map of the Scottish island of Coll and he pictured himself walking along the shore from Feall Bay to Calgary Point.

But Mitch couldn't help but wonder what Michael had planned for tonight that was so special. Normally it wouldn't have troubled him. But he'd got curious. Not curious for the sake of it. Curiosity was an integral part of his survival mechanism. He acknowledged he wasn't indestructible.

Not like Mitch's father.

Now that man *had* seemed indestructible. A military "adviser" to foreign governments, his father had walked away from an air force transport plane shot down over Israel when everyone else had gone up in flames. He'd stepped on mines and only lost the sole of his boot. He'd cheerfully run at a T34 tank head-on, then cheekily pop a grenade down the turret. His men had joked that his father's aftershave not only repelled mosquitoes and the ladies but bullets, too. Then, on holiday in Jamaica, he'd carelessly stood on a bar of soap in the bathtub.

Mitch's father rolled off the crematorium conveyor into the

321

flames just forty-eight hours later. Mitch Winter had been twelve years old.

No, Mitch Winter didn't doubt his own mortality. All he yearned for was enough cash in the bank so he could retire to that island cottage in the cleft of the hill, snuggling away from the Atlantic Westerlies, and enjoy a Guinness or two in the cozy bar with the dog at his feet.

He lit the cigarette. Sighed. Then picked up the telephone and told his team to make the necessary arrangements to kill the father of the little child playing outside in the sunshine.

Chapter Seventy

And Yet Faster

3:30. Mitch Winter had just finalized plans to have Richard Young killed. It would take place a mere four or five miles from Darlington House.

Meanwhile Richard cursed a car pulling a speedboat on a trailer. It struggled up the hill, trailer yawing from side to side, the bright pink boat jiggling insecurely on the back.

Damn, all we need is for the thing to come crashing off onto the car.

The voice in the back of Richard's head came back.

. . . up, hurry up, hurry up, hurry up . . . something nasty's going to happen to Amy . . . too slow, Dicky Boy, too slow, hurry up, hurry . . .

The car pulling the trailer turned off into a lay-by. Richard nearly whooped with joy, pressed the accelerator and the car surged forward.

Only to nearly tail-end a tractor that pulled out onto the road in front of him.

. . . hurry up, hurry, hurry up . . . only six and a half hours to go until nine o' clock, hurry up, hurry up . . .

Ahead he saw signs for the start of the motorway at Exeter. *God, it couldn't come soon enough.*

He passed the tractor, swerving away from an oncoming bus.

"Take it easy," Rosemary said gently at his side. "We'll get there. Don't take unnecessary risks."

He knew she was right. He eased off the speed. The needle dropped to sixty. Lips dry as paper, he licked them with an equally dry tongue.

After a moment his right foot increased the pressure on the pedal. The speed crept up again to try and silence that needling voice sitting in the back of his skull.

. . . up, hurry up, hurry . . .

He'd got a dark angel sitting on his shoulder today. Round every corner there seemed to be more delays. A broken-down bus; a traffic light at red; a lumbering truck full of quarried rock; children on bikes; drivers that made tortoises look sporty; roadworks and temporary traffic lights that had a hankering for red, not green.

And every so often Rosemary would say gently, "Take it easy. We can't rush. Once you reach the motorway you can make up time then."

He tried to take his mind off the hold-ups (and the fact that Michael's hired goons might be pursuing them with their shotguns on their laps) by talking to Rosemary.

"Do you know what Amy's doing now?"

"No. I've not seen anything since the cottage. Have you?"

"Nothing. It only happened to me once."

"It's as if you get some kind of psychic charge if you get too close to the Beast. Eventually it begins to fade." She glanced at him with those dark eyes. "I wish I could see what was happening for you, Richard, but I can't anymore."

Rosemary sat looking out of the open passenger window, the rush of air blowing her hair behind her in rippling waves.

The road took them under overhanging trees, the sudden shade a relief. He wished he'd bought a pair of sunglasses; the intensity of the sun would make driving all the way to Wakefield an uncomfortable slog. As they approached Exeter the traffic grew heavier, clogging the roads. He willed it to go faster.

. . . hurry up, hurry up . . . grated the head voice.

. . . time's running out . . . Don't we know it, he thought bitterly as yet another light turned red, bringing the line of traffic in front of him to a dead stop.

As they pulled away, Rosemary said, "Stop at the next filling station you see."

"No need, we've a full tank."

"The car's OK, it's you I'm thinking about."

"I'm fine."

"You're not. Richard, you can't drive five hours straight in this heat, especially after what you went through this morning."

"Believe me, Rosemary. I'm fine."

"Richard. You're going to stop, have a drink, have five

minutes' rest. We'll buy sandwiches and canned drinks for the car."

"No. I'm not stopping until I reach Darlington House. Amy needs me—"

"Amy needs you in one piece; not dehydrated; not so tired you can't think straight."

"Rosemary—"

"Richard," she persisted gently, "it'll take five minutes."

"I can't spare five minutes."

"It's either lose five minutes or lose Amy."

He shook his head.

"I'll pull out the ignition key."

"You won't do that." Then he licked his dry lips and sighed. "But you are right." He smiled wearily. "Again. OK, five minutes."

She smiled gratefully. "Not a moment more. Trust me, Richard, you'll feel better for a coffee."

At the next filling station Richard pulled over. Rosemary bought drinks, prepacked sandwiches and a pair of sunglasses. Richard put them on gratefully as they pulled out of the filling station. Within two miles they joined the motorway and headed north.

Chapter Seventy-one

Joey Sings the Blues

Outside in the garden with the sun blazing down Christine glanced at her watch. 3:45. Ten minutes ago she'd made up her mind to march into the house, find Michael and demand to speak to Richard on the mobile phone. She found terrible images beginning to flash through her head. *Richard's car picks up a nail in the tire. As they're cranking the car up onto the jack that thing comes tearing down on them. They'll run. But the Beast is too fast; it comes rolling down on them like . . .*

With an effort of will she killed the image in her head.

And no, although you want to find Michael and make him call Richard on the mobile, just so you can hear his voice, you're not going to do that. You're going to smile and nod when Michael comes along, hair neatly brushed, downturned eyes all gentle and caring and saying that he's spoken to Richard not five minutes ago and that they should be here within the hour.

Because within the next twenty minutes you and Amy are leaving this place for good.

Casually (because her guts told her loud and clear that someone watched her every movement from one of those windows in the house), she strolled along the garden path to where Joey sat on the grass in the shade of a tree.

Michael had given Amy a bike. Before he'd let her ride it he'd carefully fastened the helmet onto her head, smiling and joking as he tightened the buckle. Then he'd carefully checked the stabilizers. "Don't go too fast, sweetheart," he'd called as she pedaled furiously away. *Christ, he'd sounded like an over-anxious mother.* "And stay on the paths. The grass is too bumpy. Don't want to bang that noggin, do we?"

It all added to Christine's unease. The way he looked at Amy. The same kind of look an antique collector might have on seeing a priceless Roman vase balanced on the edge of a rickety shelf.

Amy came pedaling along the path. Braked hard so the bike skidded to a stop. "Mum. Can I take the stabilizers off?"

"No."

"But I can ride a two-wheeler."

She smiled. "No, honey. Michael wants you to keep the stabilizers until you get used to the bike."

Amy seemed to accept it without the usual grumbles. Michael had certainly won her over.

"Watch me, Mum. I can go fast as a rocket."

She pedaled away along the maze of garden paths, circling around a clump of lavender then pedaling back. The Rosemary Snow doll bounced in the shopping basket fixed to the handlebars.

Christine continued her deliberately casual stroll, occasionally stopping to admire a rose, even going to the extent of lightly stroking the velvet petals. In the back of her mind she could imagine the spy in the upper window writing on his clipboard. "Time: 3:47. Mrs. Christine Young pauses to look at one rose. Pink."

She smiled to herself. *Let the creep make his notes because come 4:15 he'll have nothing but blank sheets after that.*

Eventually she strolled to where Joey sat beneath the tree. He was drinking from a bottle of beer. Two empties lay on their sides in the grass.

"Fancy a beer, Sis?"

"Just give me a sip from your bottle."

"Have you heard when Richard'll be arriving?"

"Yes. Michael said about five-ish."

Joey nodded. "It'll be a weight off your mind when he gets here."

"Except I don't believe Michael for one minute."

"Why don't you ask Michael to call Richard or Isaac on the mobile?"

"I've thought about that, but what I have decided is that I'm leaving with Amy."

Joey sighed. "I hoped you'd have changed your mind about that. Look, Chrissie, it's a bad idea."

"Joey." She gave a grim smile. "I think you've known me long enough to realize you're not going to have a chance in hell of talking me out of it. We are going."

"When?"

"Now."

"Jesus, Chrissie. You know what Michael said. If we get split up, that monster's going to pick us off one by one."

"Why?" She didn't give him chance to answer. "Because Michael says so?"

"You remember York. Those poor bastards; crushed to fuck they were—" Joey's eyes glistened. He took a savage gulp of beer. "Chrissie, love. I don't want that happening to us."

"To you, you mean."

"OK," his voice came low and hoarse. "OK. I'm a tub of lard. I've got shit for brains. I know what you and Richard think. I know it from the look on your faces the moment I walk into your garden. Every time. Every time I walked through that bloody gate I saw it on your faces, 'Jesus wept,' you were saying to yourselves. 'Here comes Joey, sweaty armpits, shit for brains and personality to match.' "

"Joey—"

But he pressed on and she could see the sheer naked hurt in his eyes.

". . . 'Let's see how quick we can get rid of the stupid twat,' you were thinking. But believe me, Chrissie. I thought a lot about you. I love your kids. I wanted to love mine, but when I see them they just look like pint-size copies of me. And I can see in them what people see in me. And it disgusts me."

"Joey," she said gently. "Look, don't start talking about all this now; we have to—"

"Why not now? There might not be a later. I might never get a chance to tell you what I've felt for year after fucking year. But always bottling it up."

"You'll get a chance, Joey."

A fat tear bulged from his eye. "Will I?" he croaked hoarsely. "So I'll get a chance to sit down with you and tell you that I've dreamed about getting Sunnyfields developed, not for the money but just to prove to you that I'm not the family clown, that I'm not the big pork belly with shite for brains? That's all I wanted. To prove to you and Richard that I could do something worthwhile for once, make the Biscuit Billy dream come true so that you'd say 'Oh, we were wrong about Joey; he is an achiever.' "

She guessed he'd been brooding about this for hours and now the words came tumbling out in that hoarse emotional voice. He looked straight ahead, brown eyes glistening, the beer bottle

328

clutched in one hand. She listened to her brother pouring his heart out. It was the kind of speech a drunk might make, but she knew he wouldn't be drunk after only three small beers. The wounds were deep, she realized. Stabs of guilt brought tears to her eyes. She remembered the times they'd avoided Joey or invented some excuse not to meet him socially.

As he talked she sat beside him in the shade of the tree. Amy cycled around the pathways of the ornamental garden, and all Christine could hear was the bitter music of Joey's outpourings.

Eventually she wanted to tell him to shut up, that they needed to talk about getting away from Darlington House but she couldn't bear the look of deep, deep hurt in his eyes if she'd tried to stop him talking.

But the realization paced restlessly inside her head. It was saying, *"Hurry, Christine. Take Amy away. It's dangerous here. Get up and walk away, get up and walk away. Now, now, now . . ."*

Chapter Seventy-two

Speed

The car sat on the hard shoulder of the motorway, bonnet up. A breakdown truck reversed along the hard shoulder to hook up to it, orange lights flashing.

Richard cruised by at seventy. *Christ,* he thought. *If that should happen to us. We'd never make it to Darlington House before nine o'clock.*

Quickly he scanned the gauges, heartbeating a little faster. All seemed fine. Temperature normal. Fuel tank still three-quarters full. But you didn't know what screw was working loose somewhere in the guts of the engine, or if there was a nail on the road ahead.

He pushed the sunglasses up the bridge of his nose and licked his lips.

"Thirsty?" Rosemary reached for the carrier bag between her feet.

He shook his head as he overtook a milk tanker. "Nervous," he said, "very, very nervous. You OK?"

She gave a faint smile and nodded. She ran her fingertips over where the crust of scabs had been. He guessed she still couldn't believe that her face was in one piece and unscarred after all. What did make him uneasy was that after all she'd been through he was driving her to the heart of Michael's lair.

Poor kid had suffered enough. He couldn't risk her getting hurt. After all, Michael wasn't going to just sit back and let him take Amy away. He'd fight tooth and nail for her.

Richard thought of making a stop at the next service station, then, when Rosemary got out of the car to stretch her legs, just driving away and leaving her there. She'd be damned annoyed; but she'd be safe.

His eyes flicked up at a sign. NEXT SERVICES TEN MILES.

Leave Rosemary there? Without a scrap of doubt, it would be for the best.

In the garden at Darlington House Amy still rode the bike, shouting for the Boys to follow her. Joey's bitter outpourings had at last run dry. He sat on the grass with the beer bottle in his hand. He looked tired, deflated, numb.

Christine squeezed his arm reassuringly. Gently she said, "Joey. I want you to listen to me now. In about two minutes I'm going to ask Amy to ride the bike down to the lake at the bottom of the hill. Once I'm behind the boathouse I'll be out of sight of the house."

Joey looked up at her with the hurt-puppy-dog eyes.

"Joey, if you want to come with me I'll meet you there at 4:15. It's best we don't go down to the lake together. It might make them suspicious."

She saw him look up at the house and she guessed he felt the unseen pair of eyes boring into him, too.

"What about Richard?" he asked.

"I . . . I don't know. There's no way I can get a message to him. All I can hope for is that when he arrives here and finds I'm gone they'll let him leave."

"You really think we're prisoners here?"

"I don't want to stay here and find out."

"But this Beast; what if it follows us? We'll be on foot and that thing'll come tearing down on us like an express train."

"Well, I'm going to gamble that Michael's been lying. OK, it did seem to hunt us, too. But then Michael's always been with us. Perhaps it wants only him."

"But if he isn't lying, it'll—"

"Joey, please don't try and talk me out of this. I'm going across to Amy now. She can ride her bike down to the boathouse with me. If you want to risk coming with me meet me there. Remember, a quarter past four."

"What then?"

"From what I can see there's only a deer fence between the boathouse and that clump of trees. We'll cut through there, then across the fields until we find a road."

He nodded heavily, his eyes looking as if they were covered with some slick film.

She stood up. Something touched her as she looked down at

331

his wounded expression. "Joey, I'm sorry we hurt you. We had no idea how you felt."

He looked up and gave a small shrug. "In this age of perfect communications we're still failing to communicate with one another, aren't we?"

"Look, when this is over we'll sit down together, have a real heart to heart."

"Thanks, Sis," he said gratefully. "I'm sorry. I didn't want to—" He shut his mouth quickly, as if afraid of saying too much.

"It's four o' clock. Give me a couple of minutes' head start. Take the path by the tennis courts down to the lake."

He nodded again. She was going to walk away but something made her kiss the back of his neck impulsively then rub the top of his head with the palm of her hand. She'd do that when she had been Amy's age and he was seven. She could even remember herself calling in that same voice Amy used, "Joey here. Kiss and rub of head." Then he'd give that broad delighted smile as she planted the smacking kiss on the back of his neck and rubbed the top of his head before she climbed the stairs to bed, leaving him to watch one of his favorite TV programs, *Star Trek* or *The Man From Uncle*.

As she went to find Amy, despite the heat, she shivered from head to toe and her eyes suddenly filled with tears.

The speed crept up. Richard made a conscious effort to ease off on the accelerator. But again that voice nagged in the back of his mind.

. . . up, hurry up, hurry up . . .

What does Michael plan to do to Amy?

. . . hurry up, hurry up. Not much time left. Still nearly two hundred miles of this Tarmac between you and your family. So much could go wrong. Nail on road; dirt in carburetor; hurry up, hurry up . . .

The speedo reached ninety. He sat in the fast lane of the motorway now, overtaking lines of trucks and cars pulling caravans. Bridges whooshed by. Rosemary sat by his side, long hair flying in long rippling strands from the wind gushing through the open window.

Leave her at the next service station, he told himself.

The service station approached. He needed to indicate, then pull off into the slip road.

But he kept on driving.

. . . no time to stop . . . drive, drive, drive . . . the minutes are flying by. Faster, faster . . .

But that wasn't all of it. That fragile sixteen-year-old girl sitting beside him made him feel stronger. Perhaps that psychic ability hadn't deserted her entirely and she sat there willing him to stay strong and focused.

And right now he needed every shred of concentration and strength he could get his hands on.

He had to get Amy away from Michael. His mind went back to what he'd read in the cottage. About Alexander the Great. How he controlled the Beast through a succession of teenage girls. Yes, they had the ability. But being in that symbiotic relationship with the Beast corroded them from the inside out. They aged quickly. They died young.

Would that happen to his little Amy? The poor kid couldn't win.

If she failed to control the Beast she would be crushed by it.

If she succeeded she might live a few more years controlling that bastard creature according to Michael's instructions. But he imagined her aging fast: the Beast's corrosive presence would dull her hair, teeth would drop out, abscesses would turn her gums into a cluster of yellow blisters; her internal organs would begin to fail one by one; her arms would become twisted, locked tight by muscle spasms. She'd end up lying in a mess of her own drool and diarrhea, tumurs budding along her spine. When she was too weak to control the Beast, what then?

Tied up in a sack weighted with housebricks, then dropped kicking and whimpering into some stinking pond. Drowned like an unwanted puppy. Choking in the . . .

"Richard . . ."

He looked down at the speedo. The needle quivered against a hundred and ten. His hands gripped the steering wheel so tightly the veins bulged up blue through the skin.

"Take it easy," she said gently, her voice nearly lost in the rush of air. "We'll make it."

He managed a nod; his neck muscles achingly tight. He took his foot off the accelerator and allowed the car to slow to eighty. The roar of the tires on the road became a soft rumble and what had been a gray blur flying under the nose of the car became road again.

"Thanks," he said. "I think I'd have managed to kill myself before now if it wasn't for you."

"You don't think I'm too much of a backseat driver, then?"

"No." He managed to smile. "Not at all."

He only wished she could make the voice in his head go away. The one that endlessly repeated:

. . . hurry up, you're going too slow. Time's running out. Hurry up, hurry up . . .

Behind the boathouse Christine waited with Amy on the lakeside path. They were shielded from the house. All that stood between them and the cover of the trees was the iron deer fence. It would be easy enough to climb.

"Can I take the bike with me?" Amy asked.

Christine shook her head. "I'm sorry, sweetheart. It's not ours to keep."

"Where's Dad and that man with the white hair and the music thingy?" She mimed playing the harmonica.

"We'll see Dad soon." She hoped she wasn't telling her daughter a lie. "We're just waiting for Uncle Joey then we're going for a walk."

"Will Michael come?"

"No, hon, he's busy."

"Do you think he'll let me stroke one of his reindeer?" She pointed to where the small herd nibbled at bushes.

"Perhaps. Come and stand by me, Amy."

"Why are we hiding behind this shed for?"

"We're not, we're waiting for Uncle Joey. Whenever he decides to get himself down here."

She looked at her watch. 4:20. She had said she'd wait until 4:15 before leaving. But she knew she couldn't just leave her brother here without giving him just a few more minutes. Although three years younger, she'd stuck up for him at school when he'd been bullied; and she'd sat with her arm around him on the settee when, as a child, he'd cried for his mother.

The minute hand reached twenty-five past. "Come on, Joey," she urged. "Time to go."

She was looking at her watch again, trying to persuade herself to give him another two minutes, when she heard someone approach through the bushes. *At last*, she thought, with a surge of relief. It'd only take seconds to climb the fence and be away through the woods.

"Come on, Amy. Leave the bike. It's . . ." Then she found the words wouldn't come out of her mouth anymore.

"What's the matter?" Michael smiled. "Devil nicked your tongue?"

Chapter Seventy-three

Growing Darker

Christine stared in pure shock.

She'd just not anticipated this.

For a moment the world seemed to rush in at her. The insects in the lakeside flowers buzzed louder, the honking of swans hurt her ears and the sun became a furnace resting just above her eyes.

She blinked.

Amy spoke first. "Have you come to watch me ride my bike, Michael?"

He smiled, the downturned eyes as gentle as a saint's. "Of course I have, sweetie. Shall we ride it back up to the house?"

Christine forced a smile but she felt puzzled. Why should Michael just happen to stroll all the way down here to the lake?

"Beautiful day, isn't it?" Michael said conversationally. "You know, Christine, by tonight all our problems will be over. We've got everything in hand to rein the Beast back in."

"Good . . . I'm glad."

"So, why were you thinking of running away?"

"I wasn't, I—"

"Joey told me everything, Christine."

"Joey?"

"Yes, because he's a caring brother. He didn't want to see you hurt."

Fury snapped through her. "Joey told you? The idiot . . ."

"Joey," Michael called back at the bushes. "Come out, come out, wherever you are," he sang. "Your sister would like a word with you."

At first there was no movement, then Joey pushed his way sheepishly through the bushes, his brown eyes as guilty as hell. He looked down at the ground.

"Joey, what in damnation are you playing at?"

"Chrissie, I thought—"

"You thought? You never did think, that's your damn trouble."

"What are you shouting at Uncle Joey for?" Amy sounded worried. "What's he done wrong?"

Christine advanced on her brother, her voice dropped to a whisper, but she wanted to swing her fist against the bridge of his big nose as hard as she could. "Why on earth did you tell Michael? For crying out loud, what were you thinking?"

"I'm sorry, Chrissie," he said in that small beaten voice. "I really am. I didn't want you to risk getting hurt. Or Amy."

Michael nodded, face serious. "He's right, Christine. If you and Amy took off by yourselves, how far would you get? The Beast would track you down and . . ." He brought the open palm of one hand down into the other.

"How the hell can we believe you, Michael? We don't know if this thing is pursuing us—or is it just hunting *you?*"

"Remember Monday? What happened to the two policemen at the roadside diner? You're infected now. If we split up, it will track you all down, one by one."

Christine shot a look at Amy. Her eyes were big, not really understanding the words, but she was frightened by the tone of the voices.

"Amy, there's nothing to worry about, darling," Michael said softly. "Why don't you ride—"

"Amy," Christine broke in, angry that Michael was always trying to be the one to tell her daughter what to do. "Amy, just ride up to that big tree and back."

Amy pedaled away, the Rosemary Snow doll bouncing in the basket on the handlebars.

"Now what?" Christine sounded cold.

"I . . . I really think it best if . . . if we . . ."

"Shut it, Joey, I'm asking Michael."

"Everything is in hand for tonight, Christine. All we need do is wait until nine. The Beast will come here. This time I know what to do to bring it back under control."

"How will you do that? What's the process?"

"It's really quite complex, so I don't think it's necessary to—"

"You can tell me anyway."

"You're the boss, Christine. The details are contained in the *Codex Alexander*. I told you about the document yesterday. It

337

gives instructions which are remarkably similar to the techniques used by psychiatrists in modern hypnosis."

As Michael explained the process, Christine nodded, her eyes on Amy riding the bike along the track, scattering the small herd of deer, the black hair of the Rosemary Snow doll flying out in the breeze.

Michael explained the details, his hands making those graceful movements as he spoke.

She didn't believe him for a moment. She'd seen the same body language, the same look in her son's eyes when Mark told her some cock-and-bull story about how some teacher or other had kept him late when she knew all along that he and his friends had been getting up to some mischief in town.

Also, she felt the urge to contact Richard to find out if he was all right become a burning need. She wouldn't rest until she heard his voice.

"All right," she said, breaking into Michael's explanation. "I'll stay here on one condition."

"Name it."

"I want to speak to Richard, in person, on the mobile."

He smiled. "No problem, Christine. Come back up to the house. You can call him from there."

Richard switched on the car radio at six o'clock for a time check. The clock in the car said six; his watch, glass still misted from the wetting in the pool, said six; but an insidious paranoia sneaked in. Were the clocks wrong? Had he kept track of the time? Would they make it to Darlington House before nine?

And the voice in his head sang:

. . . hurry up, hurry up, drive faster. In three hours your daughter might be dead . . . hurry up, hurry up . . .

He managed to keep the speed down to eighty. The high-rise blocks of Birmingham, indistinct and ghostly in the heat haze, had swept by on his left a long time ago. Or so it seemed. But now whatever god was master of time and space played cruel tricks, stretching out the motorway ahead.

He found himself half-believing that the same cruel god had run them onto an endless loop of motorway. They'd get no farther. Michael would do whatever he needed to do to Amy. Failure or success for Michael would in either case result in Amy's death. The only question was, would it be quick or slow?

Christine groaned, then rolled onto her back on the bed. Michael looked through the window. Uncle Joey, that plump and stupid man with his lank fringe falling over his eyes, was playing a game with someone more nearly his intellectual equal. Michael watched as Amy cycled along the garden path between rows of pink roses, with Joey loping heavily after her holding the Rosemary Snow doll above his head as if it was flying like Superman.

Michael looked at his watch. Six-thirty. Soon Rosemary Snow would be truly flying. Up to heaven, into the arms of her God.

He shook his head. Rosemary Snow had been one peculiar kid. For a moment back there, a couple of weeks ago, as he'd driven her across country in the BMW, he really had believed she had the ability to control the Beast. In turn, he would have been able to control *her* by becoming her lover. He imagined her lying naked in his bed, her hair spread in a great wash across the pillow, the feel of that slight body in his arms. Perhaps she would have trembled as he held her more tightly. Perhaps crying out the first time they made love.

Then he would have held her, kissing her forehead lightly as she fell asleep in his arms and he would have felt glorious. He would have felt the exultation of knowing that in his arms he held power.

Absolute power to rule absolutely.

He licked his lips, his heartbeating faster. It was strange to feel this excitement again. After losing that relationship with the Beast on his arrival in Britain he'd experienced a peculiar emotional flatness. Nothing now made him feel outraged, or happy, or miserable, or guilty. Just kind of robotically calm.

Once he was reunited with it through little Amy, now cycling around the paths below, perhaps he'd feel emotionally whole again.

He turned back to look at the girl's mother lying unconscious on the bed. The fight she had had with his research team had been extremely undignified. Michael had watched unemotionally until one of his team had been able to push the syringe into her forearm.

He moved closer to the bed. Christine's face, relaxed by the drug, looked far younger. Other men would find that face attractive with its dark eyebrows and pleasantly shaped nose. The lips were full and pink; the skin smooth.

He stroked her forehead.

Dr. Halliwell had removed her clothes, just in case she did wake up and do something so desperately bizarre as to try and hang herself with her brassiere. Whatever happened, Christine would wake up to find the world startlingly different. Because her daughter would be shockingly different.

She muttered as if struggling to escape from the folds of unconsciousness.

Michael saw goose bumps cover her bare breast as if she dreamed of something chilling. The nipples contracted and darkened to a deep rust-brown.

Absently Michael reached out and touched one, marveling how hard the nipple had become. She really was quite pretty. There was nothing coarse about her face. If some of his security team happened to wander in here—the ex-mercenaries and Foreign Legion rejects—he had no doubt what they would do to this sleeping beauty.

Michael heard Amy's voice in the distance, calling her uncle.

He looked back at Christine. Then he sat down on the bed beside her and placed one hand at one side of her head on the pillow, the other hand on the other side. Now on all fours above her, he lowered his face toward hers.

Rosemary looked up suddenly. "Richard. Don't miss it."

"I see it." His spirits lifted. "M1 North. Another twenty minutes and we'll see the signs for Wakefield."

"How long then?"

"Perhaps another fifty minutes. Depends how fast we can push this little beauty."

"Don't push too hard, Richard."

He glanced into her dark, caring eyes. "Don't worry," he said, "I'm going to reach Darlington House in one piece. I can't promise Michael will be leaving in the same way, though."

She gave a grim smile. "Save some for me, won't you?"

As Richard joined the motorway that headed north Michael was bending over Christine, closely examining her sleeping face. Then, turning her head gently to one side, he lowered his face to hers and opened his mouth.

Then slowly, deliberately, he closed his jaws around her ear.

340

He increased the pressure until he heard a faint cracking as his teeth bit into the fleshy part of her ear.

Beneath him she muttered something; but she was too deeply unconscious to stir beyond that sighing mutter and slight wrinkling of her forehead.

He released his grip on her ear, satisfied nothing would wake her now. Not even if her daughter should scream in terror out there in the garden.

He looked down at Christine. A red crescent marked her ear where he'd bitten deep. He searched inside himself, looking for some emotion elicited by biting the unconscious woman who lay naked beneath him. Nothing. Just the same uniform flatness of spirit.

Maybe when the Beast wrenched free of him in that hotel bedroom it had taken part of him with it.

He took a deep breath, feeling a faint tingling across his scalp. Never mind. It was returning. He could feel it rushing like a great dark shadow across the countryside. It sensed where he was now. It was homing in. Like a shark scenting the blood of an injured swimmer.

Coming. Darker.

Now.

With static electricity crackling his clothes, he turned and left his sleeping beauty. There was work to be done. If the Beast came early he must be ready.

Chapter Seventy-four

Assassins

The inexplicable certainty that a perfect stranger intends to harm you might not necessarily be paranoia.

The understanding ran through Richard's head the instant he saw the motorbike pull out of the service station. It followed them, never approaching closer than a hundred yards, always keeping a couple of cars between Volvo and bike, but Richard knew as sure as the sun blazed above Wakefield that they were being followed.

He didn't know if it was some vestigial survival instinct that had been activated by his close brush with the Beast, or whether it had sprung to life over the last few days, triggered by all the mayhem and shit he'd gone through. But there was no doubt, only certainty.

That big Honda with the blue petrol tank followed wolfishly. Careful not to turn his head, he let his eyes flick back and forth to the rearview mirror. Two men on the bike. Passenger sitting up straight on the pillion, white helmet with goggles. Man driving the machine, black helmet with mirrored visor that concealed his face.

Richard licked his dry lips; Rosemary automatically passed him the can. He drank, the cola warm and flat now.

Darlington House was perhaps half a dozen miles away. He knew Wakefield relatively well, and he knew where the village of Spa Croft was. He guessed Darlington House would be pretty close to that.

He left the road that ringed the city and headed out along a main road that sliced through the suburbs in the direction of Spa Croft.

In the rearview mirror he saw the bike. Hanging back behind three cars now. Biding its time.

With one hand he slipped off the sunglasses and wiped his wet forehead.

Deliberately he kept his voice calm as he spoke.

"Rosemary. Do you see where that insect's hit the windscreen? There, directly in front of you."

Puzzled, she looked at the streak of pink on the glass: a bee's wing gummed to the dried blood.

"Yes . . . what about it?"

"I want you to look at it. Keep looking. Don't take your eyes off it for a second."

"What on earth for?"

She sounded even more puzzled, but she did as she was told.

"Trust me, Rosemary." He glanced in the rearview; the men on the bike still thought they'd not been noticed, and hung back in a deliberately nonchalant way.

"Keep your eyes on that mark on the glass in front of you," he said softly. "Because I'm going to tell you something and I don't want you to look at me nor look back. OK?"

"OK."

"We're now being followed by two men on a motorbike."

"Michael's sent them?"

"I imagine so."

"You think they'll try and stop us?"

He shook his head slowly. "They'll kill us at the next traffic lights."

He heard her gasp; sensed she desperately wanted to turn round. But he kept her eyes front.

"I've heard of it before." He was surprised at how calm his voice was. "They'll wait until the next traffic lights, when we're forced to stop at a red light. They'll ride alongside. The pillion rider will fire in through the window into my shoulder. When I look up at him, a reflex action, he'll put the second bullet through my face."

"Oh God."

"It's a classic hit man's gambit. With me out of the way they'll do the same to you, then ride away through the traffic before anyone else can react."

"Jesus, the next traffic lights?"

He nodded.

Ahead the road was long and straight, running downhill. A typical suburban road. Some cars parked at the curb; people walking dogs on the pavements; houses lining the road.

He looked back. The bike kept its distance.

It must be five years since he'd traveled along this road.

Sweet Jesus, where were the next set of traffic lights? He couldn't remember.

She never took her eyes off the blood streak. "What are you going to do?"

"I haven't a clue."

His mouth dried like paper. His stomach felt as if a fistful of moths wanted out; fluttering madly.

"You could turn off into one of those side streets."

"But which ones lead anywhere? They're housing estate roads. Probably leading to dead ends anyway. We'd be a sitting target."

"We could stop the car . . ."

"And run for it?"

"It might be worth a try."

"We couldn't outrun a bike on foot. And there's no chance of outrunning them in the car. That bike'll go a hell of a lick if they open it up. And with this traffic . . ." He shrugged.

"What if you were to try . . . oh no. Oh my God, here it comes."

Richard turned the bend. There, slap in front, a set of traffic lights. They were at green.

He couldn't accelerate because of the sedate speed of the line of cars in front. He could only maintain the same pace and pray the lights didn't turn to red.

If it turns red, jump the light.

Bad idea.

Might not be able to do that if there are cars in front.

If I managed anyway it'd alert the men on the bike we'd spotted them. They'd drive alongside, then at the right opportunity start slamming slugs through the side windows.

And they won't be sporting pop guns. Magnums? 9mm automatics? No doubt loaded with hollow-nosed slugs that pancake inside the body turning brains or internal organs to strawberry pulp.

The light stayed green.

He approached it at an agonizingly slow pace.

If you approach a green light you know as sure as hell it'll turn red. It always does.

Any second now . . .

344

Any second now . . . red would light up. He'd have to stop. The end. He'd be no use to Amy dead.

He sensed Rosemary tense beside him, unblinking eyes on the green light.

Then, before he knew what had happened, they were safely through.

Both let out a huge breath of air.

Hope rising, Richard glanced into the rearview mirror. Now, it must turn red and stop the bike.

Come on, come on . . .

Shit.

No.

The bike accelerated through the lights just as they changed, stopping the flow of traffic behind.

"What now, Rosemary?" he murmured. "For Godsakes, what now?"

The sunglasses began to slip down his sweating nose.

It could only be another mile or so before the next set of traffic lights. Maybe less.

That one had to be red. Sod's law. He wiped the sweat from his eyes.

"Do we stand and fight?" he asked her. He never expected an answer. He was thinking aloud, hoping by some miracle an idea would come sizzling through his head.

He answered himself, "What with? Our fingernails and road atlas?" The bitter laugh he intended came out as a grunt.

"We can't outrun them. We can't fight them. Can we hide?"

He shot her a look. She looked back, eyes glistening.

Poor kid. He should have left her at that motorway station after all. He was driving her to her death.

Any second now there'd be that next set of traffic lights. The bike drives alongside. He could almost hear the crash of the gun; see the side window shatter; feel the tremendous knock as the bullet smashed his shoulder.

Then the bite of a lead slug hitting his face at eight hundred miles an hour.

This is how it ends for Richard Young . . .

Thirty-three years old. Wife. Two children. Promo video script writer.

Christ, what have you done with your life, Richard . . .

Will people even remember your name in twenty years . . .

What made him most bitter was failing even to reach Amy. He imagined her playing with the doll, singing some made-up song, then looking up at him, that smile of delight when she saw her Dad was there to play.

His eyes stung.

He found himself imagining all the difficult periods of his life. School examinations. The endless revising. The exams seeming months away. Then suddenly you're sitting in that great bleak hall, desks running in lines at either side. A big clock ticking away the minutes beside the notice board. The teacher handing out exam papers. In front of you is a pen, pencil, ruler and fresh packet of Polo mints. Here it is: crunch time.

Instantly, another memory flashed into his head. That grim November day of his granddad Jack's funeral. Richard had been thirteen years old. A wind had swept rain down onto the mourners as they left their cars and walked across to the chapel entrance to follow the coffin inside.

Richard had hung back. So far he'd been able to avoid actually seeing the coffin. He'd seen the hearse, though, leading the cortège. A monstrous black thing that scared him so badly.

Don't let me see the coffin, don't want to see where they put Granddad Jack.

. . . he's in there? What does he look like? What do dead people look like?

He'd fought back the questions.

Don't think about it. Don't imagine what it's like in that cold box . . .

. . . don't . . .

Then they'd stopped at the chapel. Richard had prayed that the day of the funeral would never come. He'd willed time to slow.

But the day had come.

He'd loved his granddad Jack. The stories the old man would tell him as they walked to the park to fly the model plane.

Then came the time Richard had to actually look at the coffin. He'd climbed out of the car at the chapel, his mother and father walking slightly ahead of him.

He looked in any direction but the one where the coffin lay on its chrome trolley. He'd looked at a tractor plowing a field half a mile away, he'd looked at cars on the road, he'd stopped to tie his shoelaces.

They'd approached the chapel doors. He knew he'd vomit. And

he knew that when he saw the coffin he'd pass out. He could barely breathe.

The idea of seeing the wooden box that contained his dead grandfather was so terrifying he knew there'd be no life beyond that moment. Inside a part of him would die.

"Dad," he'd said suddenly. "I've forgotten my coat. Give me the car keys. I'll go back and get it."

His Dad had looked at him, irritated for a moment. Then he must have seen the look on his son's face. He'd given a little smile. "Come on, Richard," he'd said gently, putting his arm around him. "Don't worry, it'll soon be over."

He'd seen the coffin then. A cold-water sensation ran through his stomach. It was unpleasant to see that wooden box, and to know that Granddad Jack was inside the polished woodwork. But it wasn't as bad as he'd thought.

The car went over a poorly surfaced hole in the road. The jolt brought him back. Ahead, a stream of cars. A road sign for temporary traffic lights. Behind, two men on a motorcycle, whose single goal was to take his life and that of the teenage girl at his side.

And he'd been down Memory Lane, down fucking Memory Lane, recalling shit from his fucking past . . .

No. That wasn't it. His hands tightened on the steering wheel, heartbeat quickening.

The coffin.

His fingers tingled.

The coffin!

He'd been terrified of it. But he had confronted that fear and got through the experience. In fact, it had awakened some hidden aspect of himself. He'd felt more grown-up after meeting that fear head-on and beating it.

Just a week after the funeral he and Steve Gossman had gone into town by themselves and sneaked into the cinema to see a Dracula double bill. They'd never done that before. But now he felt as if he was mature enough to take on new challenges.

Now came the biggest challenge of his life.

A road sign said: TEMPORARY TRAFFIC LIGHTS. 500 YARDS.

He must make the decision now.

If it was the right one, he and Rosemary would live.

The wrong one, they'd be dead within the next forty-five seconds.

Chapter Seventy-five

The Hit

Richard knew what he had to do.

If he was to have any chance at all he had to kill the hit men on the motorbike.

That wasn't going to be an easy thing to do. They were professionals. They must know every trick in the book.

He eased off slightly on the accelerator, dropping the speed down to forty. It couldn't be more than four hundred yards to the traffic lights at the roadworks.

The road ahead curved to the left. The lights probably wouldn't be much beyond that bend.

He glanced back. The bike still sat back a hundred yards behind, two cars and a bus between him and the bike. When they rounded the bend ahead for a few seconds, the men on the bike would lose sight of them anyway.

"Rosemary." He licked his dry lips. "When I say 'down' take off your seat belt and crouch down on the floor."

Her voice, although small, was trusting. "OK."

He swallowed. *Christ, this isn't going to work.* He wished he were anywhere but here.

The road curved gradually to the left; he glanced quickly from rearview mirror to road. When the motorbike disappeared behind the curve of the road behind him he said:

"Down."

He followed a line of traffic. Ahead he could see the road works. His arms tensed. Rosemary shrugged off the seat belt and crouched on the floor in the well beneath the dashboard where the passenger's legs rested.

A baker's delivery van approached head-on.

He braked savagely and U-turned the car in the road, tires screeching. A driver sounded his horn.

"Christ!" Rosemary cried, looking up at him from the car floor.

Now he was following the baker's van back the way they had come. Still the bike hadn't rounded the corner. He accelerated until he was just an arm's length from the back end of the baker's van. With luck it would hide them just long enough for what he'd do next.

What *would* he do next?

The sudden temptation came simply to hang onto the tail of the van, hope the assassins wouldn't notice them and keep on riding.

But he knew that was impossible. They couldn't miss seeing them. And when they came speeding after them and the pillion passenger drew the handgun, he wouldn't miss when he fired.

The van ambled along at thirty-five. Around the corner came the bus behind which the motorbike cruised. Richard saw the man riding the bike look up.

He'd noticed straight away that Richard's Volvo was no longer in front of him. Richard eased the car nearer to the curb, trying to put the van between him and the bike.

He only needed the rider not to notice him for another three seconds.

He gripped the steering wheel. His teeth clenched. His concentration nailed to the road ahead.

Keep focused, he thought. Don't let it slip. Here he comes; Jesus, here he comes . . .

The rider eased the bike out past the bus, perhaps guessing their prey had tried to make a run for it. The bike accelerated savagely. Richard saw its front wheel lift clear of the Tarmac.

Do it, the voice yelled in his head—*DO IT! NOW!*

As the bike overtook the bus, engine screaming, Richard yanked the steering wheel hard, stamped the accelerator. The car surged forward, overtaking the baker's van.

The bike, overtaking the bus, came head-on. But Richard was overtaking, too, filling the gap between bus and van. There was nowhere to go but forward.

Richard watched with feelings of horror and a fatal curiosity as the bike seemed to glide in slow motion toward them.

There was nothing the biker could do. He saw, too, that he was speeding head-on toward the car. No way back, no way left, no way right.

Richard saw the man's head jerk up in surprise.

Yes, you know who I am now, Richard thought with a wild surge of satisfaction. *You know who I am! YOU KNOW WHO* . . .

The impact was tremendous.

The sound of the crash blasted through the car, through his head and into eternity.

This image burned into his brain: the front wheel of the bike hitting the front bumper of the Volvo, the force whipping the back end of the bike up into the air so it went somersaulting clear of the car roof to land in the road behind. The pillion rider went with it in a lazy somersault. The man hit the road at seventy miles an hour, bouncing like a rubber ball in a straggling mess of breaking arms and legs to roll under the wheels of a passing car.

Next an explosion.

The windscreen flashed white as if drenched with milk.

Then the laminated glass ripped inward in a single piece.

Dimly he realized Rosemary was screaming.

He shut it out; the wind blasted into his face; horns sounded; he focused on keeping the car on the road.

He yanked the car into another skidding U-turn. Then hammered that great chunk of steel and rubber and hammering pistons back the way they'd come. He weaved around the mangled Honda; around the baker's van; around the torn wreck of a thing that had once been the pillion rider.

Where the rider of the bike had gone, God alone knew. Probably thrown fifty yards into someone's front garden.

Chapter Seventy-six

Preparations

Michael said: "We haven't much time."

The tension in his voice sent a rash of shivers down Joey's spine. As he followed Michael out of the walled garden and onto the path that led around the house, he looked across the meadows as if fully expecting to see some huge shadow-beast come striding across the horizon.

Joey almost needed to jog to keep up with Michael. "Michael . . . Michael . . . you sure this is going to be OK?"

"Everything's going to be fine, Joey."

Joey sensed the man's confidence. Christ, he hoped it was well placed.

"Where's Christine and Amy?" he asked.

"In the car, out front."

"Maybe I should join them."

"Not yet, Joey. I'll need your help in a minute."

Christ, he should be in the car, just in case all this went pear-shaped. What could he do? Sweat dribbled down Joey's chest beneath his shirt.

"Whereabouts are they, exactly?" Joey wiped the sweat from his eyes. "If this goes wrong again, I need—"

"Oh, Joey, ye of little faith." Michael shot Joey a caring smile. "They're in the red Ford by the stables. Now, don't worry, we've plenty of time."

Joey felt uneasy. He wasn't sure why. Did he believe what Michael told him? Were Christine and Amy sitting patiently in the car ready to run again? Would that thing run amok and start rolling across that huge house like a road roller?

He wiped his dry lips. *Christ, a drink.* Brandy, vodka, anything, but he needed one *now*.

They were now at the back of the house. Half a dozen members of the research team were there, rushing backward and forward, carrying files and walkie-talkies. They all had their jobs to do and as far as Joey could tell they were doing them efficiently.

Michael headed for the raised terrace, stopping twice en route to give orders.

Joey looked uneasily across at the horizon where the setting sun now dropped in a crimson splash of flame.

"Michael . . ." *Shit:* Joey felt fear eating into him. "Michael. Which direction will it come from?"

Michael pointed. "See those two clumps of trees on the hill? Over there, about half a mile away?"

Joey nodded, mouth dry.

"It'll come through that gap in the trees—straight through like an express train."

Joey's eyes swiveled in the direction Michael pointed. The setting sun seemed to be sinking into the hundred-yard gap between the two clumps of woodland. Hell, it all seemed too close for comfort.

"Then," Michael continued, "it'll roll down the grass fields to the lake at the bottom, down there; then up this side, up through the field where those deer are grazing, through the fence, up this lawn. Then right up to the terrace."

"Hell . . ." Joey breathed out. "And that's . . . where you and it come together again?"

"In that symbiotic relationship. Yes. And all that happens in just a shade under forty minutes."

"But it's not even eight yet. You said nine."

"So it's going to be early, Joey. Sooner we get it over and done with the better, eh?"

Joey nodded quickly.

"Come up to the terrace. We're just finalizing the arrangement . . . Tina, you've got the spare power packs for the laptop, just in case?"

Michael moved off like a commanding officer giving orders to his troops just before the battle.

Joey stepped onto the terrace, his eyes big with astonishment at its transformation.

In the softening light of the setting sun he looked around the terrace. As big as a pair of tennis courts, it adjoined the back of the house where a set of large French windows opened onto it.

The terrace itself was paved with stone slabs and ran at waist height above the lawn that surrounded it on three sides. Along the perimeter of the terrace ran a low stone wall, topped here and there with stone urns that contained red and yellow flowers. The wall fronting the terrace opened to a flight of stone steps that led down to the lawn itself.

Joey saw that Michael's staff had cleared the terrace of the usual patio furniture. Now it was bare, apart from a long wooden table that had been brought from the dining room. That stood in the center of the terrace. Big enough to seat thirty people, it had a solitary straight-backed chair so whoever was seated at the table would look down across the lawns to the lake and the hillside beyond with its two clumps of trees.

Joey found it hard to take his eyes from the trees now. Nevertheless, he forced himself to look back at the terrace, trying not to imagine what would soon be darkly approaching.

The table itself was bare apart from a laptop computer. Even from here he could see the blue illuminated screen and columns of white text.

Between the table and the steps that led down to the lawn stood a carefully positioned armchair, angled slightly toward the clumps of trees on the hill. Anyone sitting in it would be able to look toward that hill and still talk to whoever sat at the table without awkwardly twisting round.

There were too many questions oozing around Joey's head. He was scared, sure; but there was more than that. He began to suspect that Michael was keeping him in the dark.

"Who's going to sit there?" He nodded at the chair as Michael walked by, carrying an open document file. "I thought you were going to be here alone when—"

"Just a moment, Joey. I'm just having a last run-through with the team."

Michael, dressed in a white shirt and black trousers, sat at the table, keying commands into the laptop, his eyes glued to the screen. A dozen men and women split into two groups to stand at each side of him, leaning toward him to see the screen. For all the world it looked like the painting of Christ and the Last Supper, with the Disciples at the long table, leaning toward Him to fasten onto every word He spoke.

Joey looked anxiously toward the horizon. Sunset would be early because of the hills. Streaks of high cloud as red as blood

353

looked like claw marks torn across the sky. Behind him, the windows of the house turned that same deep red.

Joey shivered. The minutes were ticking away.

Christ, I should be in the car with Chrissie and Amy. Maybe if I go to the car I won't be missed. I can sit in the driving seat. Maybe with the engine idling.

Maybe . . .

The idea hit hard, taking him by surprise.

Jesus, yes. Maybe I can just drive out of here, taking Chrissie and Amy with me.

That's what his sister wanted. He wiped the sweat from his nose. Unease now mixing with guilt. He felt convinced he'd done the right thing, telling Michael about Christine's plan to escape. If she'd been running across those fields with Amy, hand in hand, and that thing had come rolling across the fields, they'd be dead.

That's right, he thought trying to convince himself he'd done the right thing. *You've saved the life of your sister and your niece by telling Michael.*

Michael's voice startled him.

"Joey."

"What's wrong? Is it here?"

"No, we've plenty of time."

"You want me to go to the car?"

"Soon, Joey. First I've got something important to show you."

Chapter Seventy-seven

Off Road

"Hell . . . if I'm not careful this is going to end in disaster."

Richard passed an old white milestone at the side of the road. *SPA CROFT 3 MILES.*

"Richard. It'll be OK." Rosemary's voice was gentle and reassuring.

"We can't be certain that those guys were alone. There could be another pair of them on a bike around the next corner."

"We'll handle it," she said firmly.

"Will we?" He was still shaking from head to toe. "I think we were just lucky that time."

"Hold on, Richard. We're nearly there."

He looked out through the open windscreen, scanning the road ahead. Nothing but the odd oncoming car. But who knew who the occupants were. That red van approaching now. Maybe its driver cradled a sawn-off shotgun on his lap, waiting until he was close enough to . . .

The van passed by.

Richard looked back quickly through the rearview mirror.

He's going to U-turn, thought Richard, heart drumming. *He's going to come after us.*

The van kept on going.

He glanced at Rosemary.

Without speaking, her eyes met his; her long hair rippled in the air blasting in through where the windscreen had been.

A motorbike roared by.

Richard almost cried out. But it carried on speeding away into the distance.

Richard made a decision. "This's close enough."

"Where are you going?"

"See these woods? They go for miles. And if I remember

rightly they're criss-crossed with trackways." He peeled off to the right, driving hard along a dirt lane that took them deep into the wood.

"You know this area, then?"

"I used to come up here years ago. Just pray my instinct for direction holds out."

The tracks were baked concrete-hard by the summer sun. What they weren't were flat and the car jolted violently over the ruts.

"Hold on," he said. "This isn't going to be a comfortable ride."

The car bumped along; occasionally the underside would scrape the track when dropping down into a particularly deep rut.

"Thank God for Volvo," Richard said grimly, "they build cars to last."

Hitting the bike head-on hadn't done as much damage to the car as he would have imagined. The bonnet curved in slightly where the hit man had slammed into it; the windscreen was gone, of course. The real damage seemed to be to the car's steering. The car had taken a heck of a whack in the front end; probably the tracking had been knocked out; now even on the smoother sections of track the car pulled to the left and Richard had to keep compensating so they didn't end up wrapping themselves around a tree trunk.

How far to Darlington House? Maybe another two miles?

But maybe cutting through the woods was a mistake. The trees closed in so much he couldn't see any landmarks. Just hundreds of damn trees. For all he knew he might be driving *away* from Darlington House. After all he'd never set eyes on the place before.

Damn.

A gray-haired woman walking her dog was slap in the middle of the track.

Not slowing he slung the car to the right of her, crashing through the bushes at the edge of the track.

He glanced at Rosemary. She looked calm, eyes on the woodland track ahead. She trusted him; and he could almost feel her willing him to find a way through the wood.

"Joey. This way. I've got something for you."

Joey followed Michael across the terrace, then down to the path where the motorbike stood.

Joey licked his dry lips and nodded at the bike. "For the quick getaway if anything goes wrong."

Michael smiled. "Believe me, Joey, it won't go wrong. We've cracked the *Codex Alexander*."

"Why the bike, then?"

"We're going for a ride. Don't worry, Joey, you won't fall off."

"But where—"

"Hop on, Joey. I'm going to show you something . . . don't bother about the helmets, we're not going far."

Joey, shaking his head, puzzled, climbed onto the pillion behind Michael. Michael revved the bike lightly and kicked off.

Shouldn't Michael be back on the terrace making preparations? What was so important that he had to show it to Joey now? Joey repeatedly looked across the lake to where the two clumps of woodlands bulged from the hillside. The setting sun actually seemed to rest in the cleft between them.

Christ, he wanted out of this. He didn't know if his heart could take anymore. And why the hell was Michael taking him down here?

"First stop," Michael said almost lightly as he pulled up by the boathouse.

Joey looked up at him as he climbed off the bike. The man actually seemed to be getting a kick out of this. Yeah, there was tension there, too, but Joey sensed the man's excitement.

"Don't hang about, Joey. We haven't much time."

Joey followed Michael into the boathouse. It looked as if it wasn't used much anymore. A couple of windows were broken; bird droppings spattered the brick floors in a white crust.

Joey watched Michael unlock a metal cabinet and pull out a shoebox-sized package wrapped in white plastic.

"Joey. This is for you."

For a chilling second Joey thought it was a gun.

"What is it?"

"Don't be so nervous, Joey."

"I think we should go back to the house."

"Remember at the cottage? I told you I wanted to invest in your property development."

Joey was stunned. "You want to do that now? Can't it wait until—"

"Events are going to move very quickly after tonight, Joey. I

357

want to give you the cash now. I'm very grateful for the way you've helped me over the last few days."

Joey rubbed his forehead, confused. "Hell of a strange place to keep your cash."

"Call me paranoid, but I can't always trust it to the banks. I've had to squirrel away cash here and there in case I couldn't get access to the house."

"But we need to draw up written contracts, and you—"

Michael looked straight at him, the downturned eyes unblinking. "I trust you, Joey. Do you trust me?"

"Of course I do. But there must be ten thousand—"

"Fifteen thousand. Come on, Joey. I'll get you the rest. A hundred thousand should be sufficient for my deposit. I have your bank account details so I can transfer the balance in a few days."

"Sufficient . . . a hundred thousand? Yeah, fine . . . great, I mean—"

"Come on, then, Joey. We can't waste anymore time."

Michael walked quickly back to the still-idling bike.

"Where now?" Joey asked, fear turning to excitement. *Cash up front for the Sunnyfields development!* He couldn't wait to see Christine's and Richard's gob-smacked faces.

He climbed back onto the pillion behind Michael. This time Michael left the lake path and cut across the field, scattering the herd of deer.

Joey realized they were heading away from the house. And when he realized the direction they were headed in the feelings of panic came back hard.

"Michael," he shouted above the roar of the bike. "You're taking us up to the trees. That thing'll come through there any minute."

"We're not going that far. Only as far as the drive."

"Why?"

"You'll see . . . and don't worry. We've got plenty of time."

Joey clutched the parcel of cash to his stomach. This thing was tearing him in two. He wanted to get back to the house and wait in the car with Christine and Amy. But he also wanted that money.

"Nearly there," Michael shouted.

Joey looked ahead, his eyes watering from the slipstream. *Where the hell was the cash?* All he could see was the grass slope rising before him; the driveway, deer fence, then those two clumps of trees with the sun going down between them.

He chewed his lip. Maybe even a hundred thousand wasn't worth all this.

Michael pulled the bike up just before the driveway passed through the gap in the deer fence.

"Where is it?" Joey looked around as if expecting to find the bundle of cash lying in the grass.

"Right under your very nose, Joey."

"Huh?"

"Cattle grid. Where the drive comes through the fence."

Joey watched Michael walk the ten paces or so from the bike to the cattle grid set into the driveway. Michael crouched down and tugged at the steel bars. He pulled again. Shook his head. "It's sticking, Joey. Can you give me a hand?"

Joey carefully rested the parcel of money on the bike's seat, then moved to where Michael crouched on the grid.

Joey's sense of uneasiness increased. *Hell of a weird place to keep all that cash.* Basically all it was was a wide trench that ran across the road, covered by a steel grid. Vehicles and people could pass over easily enough but the bars were too widely spaced for hoofed animals so it kept cattle and deer where they were supposed to be as effectively as a gate.

"Are you sure the money's down there?" Joey asked.

"Put it there myself three weeks ago." Michael pointed down at the grid. "I had a section cut so it lifts like a trap door. It's sticking, though. You'll have to give me a hand."

Joey peered down through the bars. All he could see was shadow.

Michael crouched down again. Joey heard a metallic scrape and a clunk as if he was maybe releasing the trapdoor's locking mechanism, but he couldn't see properly because Michael had his back to him.

"Joey, just get a hold of the bars there and pull."

Joey crouched down beside Michael. Again the uneasiness wouldn't leave him. He glanced back at the redbrick house. It seemed a long way away.

And the two clumps of trees looked far too close for comfort. Probably less than two hundred yards separated him from them.

"Hold tight, Joey . . . That's it. Perfect."

"Hey, what the hell are you doing? Stop it. Michael . . . *Michael! Stop it!*"

Chapter Seventy-eight

Nearly There

"For Christ's sake, Michael . . . What are you playing at?"

Michael rose and walked back to the bike.

"Michael. Take them off me . . . *please*."

Michael slowly shook his head.

Joey stared down in horror and disbelief at what Michael had done. The handcuff around his wrist gleamed pink in the setting sun. He tugged hard. He managed to lift his hand no more than five inches before the chain pulled tight, rattling the other cuff where it had been clamped around one of the cattle grid's solid steel bars.

Why's he done this to me? thought Joey, panicking. *Why's he handcuffed me to the cattle grid?*

That thing's coming . . .

. . . it's coming soon . . .

Time?

What's the friggin' time?

He tried to look at his watch. His hands shook so much he couldn't pull back his shirt sleeve with his handcuffed hand.

"Want to know the time, Joey? I make it . . . let's see. 8:15."

"Michael . . . Take off the cuffs now . . . please, Michael."

Michael stood with his hands on his hips, gazing thoughtfully up at the gap that ran between the clumps of trees.

As if only just registering what Joey had said he replied, "Why should I do that, Joey?"

"Because I helped you."

Michael shrugged. "It's a cruel world, Joey."

"Let me go . . . please I'll do anything you want."

He nodded. "You would as well, Joey. But . . ." He sighed, pretending to sound regretful. "But you're more use to me here."

"But what on earth for? What good am I up here?"

Michael walked up to the cattle grid, checked the handcuffs were holding, then, straightening, rubbed Joey's head as if he was rubbing the head of a dog.

Chained so he couldn't straighten beyond a crouching position, Joey twisted to face Michael. The man's face was expressionless.

Joey was sobbing now. "Michael . . . Why are you keeping me up here? I've done nothing wrong . . . I . . . I told you about Christine. I told you all about what . . . Michael, unlock it. *Please, unlock it . . .*"

Every so often Michael would give the tiniest hint of a smile. Then Joey's hopes would soar. *He's testing me,* he'd think frantically . . . *just testing me. Any second now he'll unlock the cuff, smile and say "Just joking, Joey."* Then they'd be back on the bike and heading back to the—

"Michael . . . Where are you going? No . . ."

Michael had climbed back astride the bike. He revved it. Blue exhaust swirled around his legs.

Then, letting the machine idle softly, he looked back at Joey with his downturned gentle eyes.

"Michael." Joey's voice dropped into a low plea. "Why are you leaving me up here?"

Michael smiled. "Bait."

Joey's heart gave a thump and seemed to stop. He froze there, crouched on the grid, not even blinking as he stared at Michael rocking the bike off its stand.

Michael looked back at him, smiled again and said, "What's wrong, Joey? Devil nicked your tongue?"

Then he accelerated downhill, back toward the house.

Joey shook his head. Why couldn't he breathe? Why couldn't he speak?

Then it came blasting through in a long full-blooded scream. *"You can't leave me here! You can't! Bastard . . . BASTARD!"*

Michael's white shirt stood out against the grass. A single speeding white spot that flew down the hillside, by the lake, then back up across the lawns to the house.

Joey sobbed like a bullied child. "You can't leave me here . . . I'll tell, I'll tell . . . *I'll tell!*"

"When is this forest going to end?"

Richard crashed the gears as he followed the track uphill.

"Do you know where the house is?" Rosemary asked.

"No. But I know roughly where the village is. It can't be that far away." He shot Rosemary a look. "You think you'll recognize the house when you see it?"

"Positive. Very big. Three stories. Red brick with tall chimney stacks."

He checked the time. "Twenty past eight. Christ, we're cutting this fine. We should be there by now. Amy's . . ." He shook his head. He didn't know how he'd do it, he only knew, somehow, he'd take his family away from Michael.

If only he could find a way through this endless wood.

Michael arrived back at the terrace as Mitch Winter brought Amy out of the house. She carried the Rosemary Snow doll in one arm as if it was a baby.

Mitch was smiling and talking to her. He looked more like a favorite old uncle than a battle-scarred mercenary. Amy appeared happy enough in his company and Michael watched her explaining something to Mitch that involved a lot of gesturing with her free arm.

"How we doin', sweetheart?" Michael said, holding out his arms. She ran happily toward him and held out her arms to be picked up, dropping the Rosemary Snow doll.

"Oops," Mitch Winter said, bending down to pick up the doll. "Nearly lost little Rosemary Snow there."

"What's Rosemary been doing now, sweetheart?" Michael gently brushed her hair from her face.

She shrugged. "Don't know, don't care." Then she grinned, her eyes twinkling. "Michael. I want to whisper you something."

"Whisper away, Amy."

He carried her toward the armchair. She whispered, excited and breathless, into his ear. "Mitch has told me you've got a surprise for me."

Smiling, he whispered back into his ear, "Sure have."

"What surprise is it?"

"Wouldn't be a surprise if I told you," he whispered.

Again her hot breath ran into his ear. "Is it a surprise for later . . . or for now?"

"Now."

He felt a tremor of excitement run through her. "Where is it?"

"You'll just have to wait a minute."

"Just one minute?"

"Yes."

"What's the big chair outside for?"

"So you can sit and wait for the surprise, Amy."

He sat her down in the chair. "Just stay there a second. I want to tell Uncle Mitch something."

"Uncle Mitch." She giggled, her hands over her mouth.

"How long now?" Mitch asked.

"Until what?"

Mitch glanced around the terrace at the unusual arrangement of the armchair and long dining room table with the laptop computer placed in the center. "Until you do whatever you've planned?"

"I thought you didn't know anything about tonight."

"I don't and I'm happy for it to stay that way. All I want to know is when you want me to make myself scarce."

"You can go now."

He nodded. "Oh, by the way. You ought to know that . . ." He glanced at Amy and dropped his voice. "Young and Snow. They've just gone and spread Murten and Kramer all over the Tarmac."

"I thought you said those guys knew how to handle themselves."

"Even they can't handle being hit head-on by a Volvo."

"*Richard Young?* He did that?"

"The word we're picking up from eyewitnesses is that Young turned the car around and rammed it into them head-on."

Michael rubbed his jaw. "You promised me they wouldn't be a problem, Mitch."

"And they won't. I've men posted all around the perimeter of the grounds. They'll pick them off if they get too close . . . and don't worry, Amy won't see a thing from here."

Michael nodded. "I can rely on them not to screw up?"

"You can."

"OK. See you later, Mitch."

Mitch started to walk away, then something occurred to him. "Michael," he said in a low voice. "What you've got planned for tonight. It doesn't involve hurting the little girl does it?"

Michael smiled, but his eyes were hard. "Go check your men, Mitch."

Mitch Winter, stone-faced, walked away.

Chapter Seventy-nine

Static

Michael crouched beside Amy, smiling and chatting. The sun had all but set; already the sky was turning darker.

A tiny earpiece linked to the radio in his pocket relayed streams of information from his team in the house. He knew they would be watching the two clumps of woodland from the upper windows. No doubt they could see Joey Barrass tugging at his handcuff chain on the far hill. Michael could even draw a mental diagram of Joey's position between the house and those clumps of trees through which the Beast would pass.

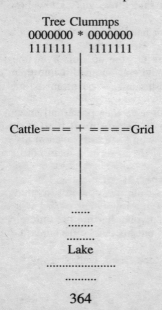

```
                 Tree Clummps
             0000000 * 0000000
              1111111   1111111
                      |
                      |
                      |
                      |
                      |
     Cattle=== + ====Grid
                      |
                      |
                      |
                   ......
                  .........
                  ..........
                   Lake
              .......................
                  ...........
```

Terrace

———

House

And from here, no one could hear Joey's screams.

Amy pointed at the tiny black radio mike clipped to Michael's shirt pocket.

"What's that?"

"Oh, just a little badge."

"Funny-looking badge."

"Would you like me to take it off, Amy?"

"No, it's OK." Amy gave a sudden grin and knitted her fingers together. "What's the surprise, Michael?"

"Oh, but as I said a minute ago, if I tell you it won't be a surprise."

"Tell me . . . please." Her eyes shone brightly in the last rays of the sun.

"Well," Michael whispered, leaning closer toward Amy. "It's a . . . oh, I don't know if I dare tell you."

"Go on, please."

"It's a . . . puppy."

"A puppy?" Her face blazed with happiness. "A real puppy?"

"Yes."

"One to keep forever and ever?"

Michael smiled broadly. "For ever and ever. Amen."

"Oh, I've got to ask my Mum if it's OK to keep him." She wriggled toward the end of the armchair, ready to rush inside the house.

Michael gently laid his hand on her arm. "Tell your Mum later. She's having a sleep at the moment."

Amy's face fell. "But she might not let me keep the puppy."

"Oh, she will, Amy. I've already asked her. She says tomorrow we can buy the puppy a basket, and food . . ."

"And some toys. Puppies like rubber bones and things."

"Of course we can."

"And a blanket to sleep on."

"And a collar, and we—*oh* . . . Amy . . ." Static cracked

through his earpiece. "Amy, I think I can hear that puppy. He's on his way."

She twisted around in the armchair so she could look down onto the lawn. "Where, Michael? I can't see him."

"Now, Amy. This puppy is very special. In fact, he's a magic puppy."

Amy's eyes went large.

Michael smiled. "So, we have to play a special game to make him stay. Do you understand?"

She nodded, grinning excitedly.

"Now, Amy, listen to me and do exactly what I tell you."

Joey tugged at the handcuff. He screamed as he tried to snap the chain that held him to the cattle grid by his left wrist.

The chain links weren't even bending.

He paused, chest heaving. Sweat ran down his face.

Something rattled through the branches of a tree.

He shouted in fear, looked up the hillside toward the trees.

A pigeon flew from a chestnut tree. Another followed, wings clacking against the twigs.

Jesus . . .

He breathed deeply.

Getaway-Joey-getaway-Joey-getaway-Joey . . . The head-voice rattled . . . *getaway-Joey-getaway-Joey . . .*

He wiped the sweat from his muddy brown eyes with his free hand. The sky was growing darker.

Shit, Joey . . . Get away from here . . .

. . . getaway-getaway-getaway . . .

He braced his feet against the cattle grid bars and heaved, trying to snap the chain.

. . . bad thing coming, Joey . . . bad thing coming . . .

Static electricity crackled through his hair. The fillings in his teeth tingled.

He tugged until the skin broke on his wrist. Blood flowed. He shook his head, like a bear caught in a trap. And he screamed and screamed . . .

Then something terrible happened.

On any other hot summer's evening it would have been welcome.

Not tonight.

A breath of air moved down the hillside.

It ruffled his hair and chilled the sweat on his face.

Joey stared, eyes bulging.

THE BEAST WAS BACK.

Deeply unconscious on the bed, Christine felt it too. She moaned. In the drugged dream she had dreamed she'd been looking for something important. She'd searched her home from garage to attic.

Now something in the dream found *her.*

Something dark.

A great coldness swept over her. She moaned and struggled to wake.

As Richard drove the car along the woodland track he heard Rosemary moan.

"Oh, did you feel that?" she whispered, her eyes wide with shock.

Richard nodded. It had been like some great dark star passing in front of the sun. He shivered. Ice points pricked his spine.

The engine began to miss. The digital clock blanked.

He switched on the radio, then stabbed at the presets until he hit free space between radio stations.

Static squelched from the speakers. It came in great slow fat beats. Like the sound of some dark and monstrous heart.

A wave of pure horror ran through him.

"Oh, God. It's here." He shot Rosemary a look. *"We're too late."*

Chapter Eighty

It's Here

Bursts of static erupted into Michael's ear through the earpiece. The voices of his team distorted. Above the terrace the sky had turned deep blue; a thin silver crescent of the moon showed.

His mouth turned dry but still he maintained the gentle smile.

"I think the puppy's here, Amy."

Too excited to sit still in the armchair, she knelt up to bounce on the cushion.

"Now remember what I said, Amy. You must do everything I say or that magic puppy just won't come."

"Where is he? Where is he?"

"Now, stay in the armchair, Amy. And do everything I say."

Michael stood up and moved quickly back to the table on the terrace.

In a low voice he spoke, knowing the mike would relay what he said to his team. "I'm back at the table now. Laptop functioning OK, despite heavy static. And Amy's as good as gold." He looked up toward the skyline. The two clumps of woodland looked like dark mounds now in the dusk.

"Stand by, everyone. Here it comes, ladies and gentlemen. The Beast is back."

He looked at Amy and said, more loudly, "Amy. He's going to be here any minute now."

"Where is he?"

"See over the lake? There're two big clumps of trees on that hillside. He's coming from there."

"All that way away?"

"That's right. He's going to have a long run to get here, isn't he?"

"He'll be puffed out."

"He will."

"Can you see him, Michael?"

"Not yet. But I know he's there. Right, Amy. He'll come down the hillside, across the lake . . ."

"He can swim?"

"Oh, he can do anything. Then he'll come running right up across the lawns, and up here onto the terrace where you're sitting."

"Will he jump up at me?"

"He'll want to jump up onto your knee and sit there, Amy. He's been waiting a long, long time to meet you."

She looked out across the lawns in the direction of the wood.

"Make him come now, Michael. I can't wait."

"Oh, don't worry, Amy. He's on his way."

"Shall I do it now, Michael?"

"Yes, Amy. Close your eyes. And whatever you do, don't open them. Got that?"

"Yes."

"Eyes tight shut?"

"Yes, Michael."

"Keep them shut tight until I tell you to open them. Then you'll see the puppy. Now, Amy, listen carefully. I want you to imagine the puppy's running through the trees. He's all black and furry. With floppy ears . . . shiny brown eyes." Michael scrolled up the text, reading from the screen now. "Keep imagining him running through those trees. He's a lonely puppy, and he knows you'll love him and you'll look after him. That's why he's running so fast. He'll want to play when he gets here, but be careful. He can be a naughty puppy sometimes. He might even want to jump up at your head. So, you keep telling him to sit on your knee . . . and to sit very, very still. Got that, Amy?"

He saw her nod, her hair glinting in the sunset.

"Now picture that puppy running. He's getting closer . . . and closer . . . and closer . . ."

The transfer had begun.

8:30 p.m. Joey stopped tugging when he heard the groan.

It sounded human.

But it sounded impossibly loud.

The groan came again. So deep and so loud that it rumbled through the ground to rattle the cattle grating beneath his feet. It sounded like the dying song of a lost and long-forgotten god.

He couldn't breathe. Sheer terror cracked through him like blasts of electricity.

He looked up, neck muscles twitching, eyes watering.

The grassy slope and the two clumps of trees still appeared the same, except that the trees themselves looked almost black in the dusk now that the sun had gone, leaving a deep red afterglow above the horizon.

The groan came again; the cattle grid vibrated. Eyes still fixed on the gap in the clumps of trees, Joey yanked harder at his bonds. He tried to slip the steel cuff off over his hand but his wrists were too plump; the cuff bit deeper into skin.

"Go away! Leave me . . . leave me alone!"

The Beast was coming. He knew it. He could feel it. He could even taste it. Static filled the air; his tongue felt as if a hundred pins pricked it.

". . . leave . . . leave me alone . . ." His voice was raw with terror. ". . . leave . . ."

Rooks flew suddenly out of the woods in panic; black flapping wings beat the air above his head.

Rabbits and foxes ran by. Behind him the deer herd stampeded toward the far end of the field. There they jostled against one another in terror, held from running farther by the deer fence.

"No . . . Michael! Let me go . . . please . . . *PLEASE!*"

It came.

A shape rose above the two clumps of trees. At first Joey stared in fascinated horror, believing that he actually saw the Beast.

It was a dark smoky figure, undulating, shape-shifting, moving forward, inexorably, tirelessly forward. Unstoppable.

Like the hammer of God.

The dark shape rose and fell above the trees.

Then Joey realized that what he was watching were millions of leaves torn from the branches by a savage updraft of air.

They only looked black in the dusk. Around the edges flashed a red halo where the final glimmer of sunlight reflected from the leaves.

God, no . . . this isn't happening to me. I'm dreaming . . . I'm not here. It's not happening. I won't die, I won't die . . . oh, God! Chrissie! Chrissie! I'm sorry . . . I'M SORRY!

Shadowlike it rolled through the gap in the trees. Trees at the edge of the cleft fell beneath it, shattered from tip to root.

Solid timber cracked with explosive force.

It gathered pace.

Joey, chained into a crouching position, watched it roll toward him, still sucking a plume of leaves after it in the vacuum it created.

Grass flattened in a twenty-yard-wide swathe.

Joey couldn't take his bulging eyes from that flattening grass. It ran toward him like an invisible wheel, crushing everything in its path. A lone tree standing on the hillside exploded into a spray of white splinters.

"No, Christ, please, no . . ."

Joey gave one last massive tug.

A chain link snapped with a crack. That adrenaline-fueled pull had been tremendous, its force threw him onto his back across the cattle grid's steel bars.

Christ, I've done it! For Godsakes get on your feet . . . run . . . run . . .

He tried to stand.

He could not move.

He looked up. His eyes bulged. He could not breathe. His heart hammered against his chest wall.

There was nothing up there. At least nothing he could see.

But he felt it . . .

. . . pressing . . .

. . . pressing down.

An incredible weight on his chest, arms, face, legs.

He lay there, flat on his back across the cattle grid, held tight there by the Beast.

He tried to scream out his agony and frustration and his terror.

But the pressure wouldn't let him whisper.

The weight increased. The steel bars of the cattle grid dug into his back. Ribs crackled; skin split.

Like the hammer of God, it came down.

And Joey felt no more pain.

Chapter Eighty-one

Darker

As Michael kept up the steady flow of instructions to Amy, his voice low and relaxing, he saw the approach of the Beast.

Distantly he heard the rumble of trees crashing earthward. A smoky pall of torn leaves gushed up into the darkening sky.

Even from here, sitting at the table on the terrace, he heard the distant creak of the cattle grid collapsing.

Poor Joey . . .

He shook his head.

An excited voice crackled above the static now raging in the earpiece. His team had seen it, too.

He kept speaking. Low, relaxing.

"The puppy's on his way, Amy. Keep those eyes closed. Imagine him running down the hill; his tail's wagging; he's looking forward to seeing you. Remember, he can be naughty. But he'll do what you tell him. So if he jumps up, tell him to sit still on your knee . . ."

Across the lake a willow tree bent like an archer's bow, then snapped at the root.

The boathouse flattened with a distant *crump*.

"Nearly here, Amy."

He saw her shiver with excitement.

Now the lake churned and boiled; the water, once almost black in the approaching night, turned white as milk, fizzing and creaming like beer from a shaken can.

Momentarily the waters parted; even Michael felt a burst of astonishment as the lake split into two halves. Then it was through the lake and the two halves rushed inward to slap into one another again in a burst of spray.

". . . almost here."

Static crackled in his earpiece. The laptop screen snowstormed.

Not that it mattered now.

He knew the text by heart.

In any event, it was too close now to stop.

As he spoke to Amy, who knelt there on the armchair twenty paces away, he shot a glance at the motorbike parked alongside the terrace.

And for the first time doubt sneaked into his head.

Maybe it wouldn't work tonight after all.

Maybe it would roll onto the terrace crushing the girl.

If it did, could he make it to the bike and ride away before it crushed *him*?

Still talking in that low voice, he watched the grass flatten as it rolled up the hill. Halfway up, it hit a post-and-wire fence.

The wires snapped like overtightened guitar strings, breaking one after another to create an unearthly music that shimmered back from the house and the hills.

"Don't worry about the noise, Amy. Nothing to do with us. Just keep imagining that puppy, that black, furry puppy . . ."

Michael's voice dried. The ground shook beneath his feet.

He shot a look at the bike. And he realized it was too far away to reach in time.

Because the Beast had, at last, arrived.

Chapter Eighty-two

Darkness Comes

The time: 8:45.

Richard nearly plowed head-on into the white Transit van as it careered around the bend toward them, its tires tearing up clouds of track dirt.

He swerved to the right, slamming into the saplings that lined the woodland track. Leaves torn from branches fluttered into their faces through the open front of the car. The trunk of a tree appeared through the bushes; the car clipped it, shaving off bark. Then he bounced down to the track again.

"You all right?"

Rosemary nodded, her face grim.

"The van . . ." He nodded back over his shoulder. "He's after us."

He knew the van driver would turn around as fast as he could to follow them. He guessed, also, there would be more of Michael's men nearby. The crumb of good news was that Darlington House couldn't be far away now.

"See that?" she called above the noise. "The clock's gone crazy."

"Engine's acting up, too. Electrical interference."

"Has this thing—the Beast—had that effect before?"

"No. Perhaps it's getting bigger . . . more powerful . . ."

"So we can assume it's here?"

He nodded. And he knew that they were too late.

All he could hope was that somehow Christine and Joey had found a car and driven Amy away in time.

That bastard, Michael . . . I hope he's been crushed to shit.

"At last. It looks as if we're coming out of it." The trees began to thin.

"There!" Rosemary stabbed her finger forward. "See the house."

"That's Darlington House?"

"That's the one, all right. I remember those tall chimneys."

It was still a good five minutes' drive away. He only hoped the motor would hold out. The revs would suddenly fade before kicking back in again, surging the car forward.

He glanced in the rearview mirror. The van must surely appear any moment now.

On the dashboard the digital clock flickered, numbers scrambling insanely.

"Look out!"

Rosemary's voice punched his ear. Standing in the track ahead was a man with a rifle at his shoulder.

He aimed it. Biding his time for a clear shot.

To Richard's left the trees broke, leaving an expanse of rough pasture running down toward a lake.

And in those trees to his left, walking their way, a man with a submachine gun.

Machine gun or rifle? You choose, thought Richard desperately.

"Rosemary!" he yelled. "Down on the floor."

Christ. He gambled the machine gun fired handgun ammunition. Probably fairly low muzzle velocity hollow-nosed slugs. Stop a man dead in his tracks.

But, Richard staked his life on it, the machine gun ammo wouldn't have the clout to penetrate the thick steel skin of the Volvo's door.

With Rosemary crouching down on the floor, Richard aimed the bucking car in the direction of the lake and lay on his side on the passenger seat.

If his luck held out Machine gun Man would still be too far away to fire down into the cabin of the car. The man'd have to aim at the car's flank as it tore by.

Richard, pressing down into the passenger seat, saw nothing but darkening sky. He steered with one hand, the other shielding his face.

The wait was agonizing. The engine roared, the car bucked and accelerated downhill. There weren't many trees now: he prayed the car wouldn't find one of the few that dotted the grass between here and the lake; Christ knew, he didn't want—

Then came the sharp snapping sound of bullets slamming into the side of the car.

Side windows shattered; hot metal bored holes through the air above his head.

Then it was over.

He whooped.

They were past the machine gunner. Behind him the van was only just chugging out of the wood. Ahead was clear grassland down to the lake, after that a driveway would take them up to the house.

Then something solid knocked the back of the car. At first he thought the back wheels had gone over a branch, but suddenly it felt as if a weight dragged the car down at the back.

"What's wrong?" Rosemary called pulling herself back onto the passenger seat.

"I don't know; it could be—*Damn.*"

He saw what had happened: a man strolled almost leisurely from behind the cover of a tree trunk, a shotgun in his hand.

"He must have blasted the back tire."

The man aimed again, not even hurrying.

"Down." Both he and Rosemary ducked. But the man wasn't aiming at them. Expertly, he hit the front tire, tearing rubber to shit. Now the car slewed sideways.

The speedo needle dropped back to twenty.

Richard thrashed the engine.

"Come on, come on!"

But with two tires gone the car moved crabwise, throwing off what remained of the two tires, leaving two steel hubs to buzz like circular saws at the turf, throwing up dirt, shredding grass. No traction now. The car slowing to a stop. And there was not a damn thing Richard could do about it.

He looked up to see armed men walking slowly toward them from every direction.

With a final bump, the car slid sideways to stop against a tree.

Chapter Eighty-three

Dark

"It's not what your years of experience fighting all those dirty wars in the Middle East and Africa have prepared you for, Mitch, but I'd like you to baby-sit Amy for me."

Mitch Winter stood on the terrace, a radio handset in his hands, and tilted his head to one side which clearly meant: *Would you mind repeating that?*

Michael nodded toward Amy who sat staring at her knees as if they were the most fascinating thing in the world. "I know she likes you, Mitch, and I need to spend a few minutes with my people upstairs."

"You're the boss."

"I am now. Yes." He smiled.

Mitch hid his puzzlement and watched the little girl. He found to his surprise that he was relieved she'd not been hurt but she seemed different somehow. Perhaps it was the expression on her face. Happy, but . . . just different. Mitch shivered.

"By the way," Michael said in a low voice. "The Youngs have a son, called Mark. He's on a camping holiday with a friend. I'll give you the details later but I want him dead."

Again Mitch said in a flat voice, "You're the boss."

"And what's happening to Rosemary Snow and Young?"

"My men have them surrounded on the hillside across the lake. They'll be out of the picture any minute now."

"Good."

"You want them fed to the pigs?"

"Frankly, I don't care. You can leave them to rot in the grass for all it matters."

Mitch, even more puzzled, watched Michael walk back to the house. He looked like a man who'd just been made king of the world.

* * *

"Rosemary . . . out of the car . . . keep your head down. Stay by the door."

"What are we going to do?"

"Run for it."

Richard switched the headlights on full beam so they slashed through the gloom into the faces of the men approaching the front of the car. Maybe they'd be dazzled enough for their aim to be spoiled.

But as soon as he crouched beside Rosemary between the car door and the main body of the vehicle he realized there was nowhere to run.

All around them was a closing ring of men armed with rifles, shotguns, machine-guns.

Rosemary's eyes met his. "Hell . . . we're sitting ducks, aren't we?"

He nodded.

The men inched their way forward. *They're professionals, all right*, thought Richard; *they're moving like they're out for a stroll in the park.*

He lifted his head just above the window frame to see how close the men at the far side of the car were.

Damn close.

He could even see they wore headsets with microphones so they could whisper instructions to each other by radio.

As he watched, one of the men paused and lifted his hand to the mic fixed to the headphones: obviously relaying instructions.

In the next second Richard knew only too well what those instructions were.

A clattering of sharp cracks came from all directions. Bullets whined around them, slamming into the car, shaking pieces of safety glass down onto them.

Richard put his arm around Rosemary and pulled her more tightly into the corner where the car door hinged to the body of the car.

More gunfire. *Christ* . . . he even saw the bullets glow red hot against the darkening sky as they whipped by.

In a tiny voice Rosemary repeated over and over: "Jesus, get us out of this . . . get us out of this . . ."

Chapter Eighty-four

Amy Says . . .

"What's wrong, Amy?"

Mitch crouched beside her. She still knelt on the armchair. It was nearly dark now and she was only illuminated by the lights shining through the windows of the house.

"Amy, what's the matter?" he repeated. Her face had become serious; her eyes glistened but for some reason she could not take her eyes from her knees.

"Puppy's frightened?" she said, troubled.

"The puppy?" Mitch frowned. "What puppy?"

"Puppy on my knee. He's frightened by all that noise."

Mitch could hear the gunshots echoing down the hillside. *My God*, he thought, lightly rubbing the walkie-talkie against his chin, *if this little girl only knew. That was the sound of her daddy dying.*

Instead, he forced a smile and started to talk about the imaginary puppy she pretended she could see on her knee.

"He's frightened," she insisted, "I can feel him shivering. Mitch, tell them to stop making the noise."

He was going to say, *Don't worry, Amy, it's only fireworks.*

But even as he opened his mouth to say the words a sudden weight pressed hard against his chest; he could hardly breathe; a throbbing ache ran up through his neck into his head.

Don't worry, Amy, it's only fireworks.

The words wouldn't reach his lips. The pain in his chest became a spike, driving through his ribs. His eyes watered.

"Mitch Winter . . . this is Mitch Winter. You are to cease firing immediately. I repeat. Cease firing immediately."

Heart lurching, he looked at the radio in his hand as if it had sprouted rose blossoms.

Hell's bells, what am I saying? he thought, bewildered.

A voice crackled over the speaker. It sounded puzzled. "Confirm order, please."

He intended to say: *Ignore last order. Finish the job.*

Instead, to his astonishment, he found himself saying, "Order confirmed. Do not, I repeat, do not fire another shot. Now, confirm the order!"

"Order confirmed, sir. What action should we take now?"

Mitch licked his dry lips. His heart thudded. Dizzy, his mind spun in a way he'd never experienced before.

"Who are you talking to?" Amy asked, smiling back down at her knees again.

He was going to say, *No one important.* Instead: "The men who were making the noise."

"Naughty men. They were frightening the puppy."

He looked down at her bare knees. It seemed absurd but he knew he would have to ask the question. "Those men who were making the noise. What shall I tell them to do now?"

She looked up, annoyed. "Puppy's still shivering. Tell them to go home."

Mitch spoke into the radio. "You must . . . *must* do as I say."

"Fire away, sir."

"You must go home."

"Home?" The voice sounded even more puzzled.

"Home. Yes. *Go home.*"

On the hillside, Richard waited for the first bullets to shred his stomach and chest. He and Rosemary curled in a ball together, sheltering from the glass spraying from the car.

Then . . . it stopped.

It came as suddenly as that.

One second bullets screamed around their heads, then there were no more bullets.

The echoes of gunshots crackled into the distance.

And then there was only silence.

This is it, he thought. *They're going to rush us.*

But no one came.

Cautiously, he looked over the bullet-chewed door.

"What's happening?" Rosemary whispered.

"I think you should take a look at this."

Richard saw the men were slowly backing away from the car. Some shook their heads as if they'd heard something they didn't believe. Then, one by one, they began running back to the house.

"Why are they leaving?"

Richard shook his head. "I just don't know. They could have killed us easily."

"Perhaps it's because the Beast has arrived. Look. Down there, by the lakeside."

Even though it was nearly dark he could see the crushed remains of a building by the lake and a snapped tree. No doubt about it. It had been here. He wiped his mouth. *Or, worse*, maybe it was still here.

"Come on," he said. "It's time we called on Michael."

Chapter Eighty-five

Puppy

Christine rolled over on the bed. Even though unconscious, a sense of dread rolled through her. She moaned and tried to sit up. Her body felt it had turned to concrete. Why couldn't she wake up?

She forced her eyes open. A bare room. Windows without curtains. It began to turn around her.

Was she drunk?

No, she remembered . . .

Amy.

Something about Amy . . .

But where *was* Amy?

Again dread pealed through her like the clanging of a huge and terrible bell.

Dread and danger. She sensed it hovering nearby. She had to find Amy.

Arms and legs like foam rubber, she struggled to rise from the bed.

Mitch had been running across the dark lawns for ten minutes now. He carried Amy piggyback style on his back. All the time she giggled and told him to follow the puppy. She'd shout instructions to it:

"Puppy sit. Puppy jump. Puppy run up the steps. Puppy run down the steps."

He choked the air into his lungs; his chest felt as if a great weight crushed it.

"Run faster, Mitch, run faster." It was agony but he had to obey.

He ran through the blocks of light thrown on the grass from the windows of the house. Sometimes he thought he could even see Amy's imaginary puppy. A dark bundle of shadows that moved fast across the grass, somehow always avoiding the light from the windows.

At first he tried to frame the words to ask Amy to let him rest. But something had taken over. He only knew he had to keep running, with Amy riding on his back. Maybe forever.

His lungs crackled.

"Puppy jump over the flowers." The giggling sounded manic now.

At last he heard Michael's voice. "Amy, come back up to the terrace, sweetheart."

"Mitch up the steps."

Still carrying her on his back he lumbered up the stone steps to the terrace. Sweat poured down his face.

"Mitch is looking a bit tired, Amy. Can he go inside for a sit down?"

"OK." She bounced back into the armchair. "Puppy! Puppy! Come on. Knees . . . on my knees. That's a good boy."

Suddenly the control was over. Mitch turned his back on Amy and he walked back into the house.

He was scared.

No, he wasn't.

He was terrified.

"What do you think to your new puppy?" Michael asked. "Do you like him?"

"I love him," she said firmly. "He's beautiful . . . aren't you beautiful, aren't you beautiful?" she sang.

Michael watched, smiling. It had worked. Now he stood shoulder to shoulder with the emperors of ancient times. Not just the Byzantine Emperors. They hadn't the guts to seize control of the Beast and take it anywhere in the world. No, he ranked alongside Alexander the Great. Conqueror of the world.

He smiled. "Thirsty, honey?"

Amy nodded.

"Come on, let's have a walk to the kitchen and get you a nice cold drink."

"Can I bring the puppy?"

"Oh, yes. You take him everywhere now. In fact, don't let him out of your sight."

"Can he sleep on my bed?"

"Of course."

"I can't wait for Mum and Dad and Mark to see him."

Michael led Amy by the hand through the French windows, through the dining room and into a hallway that was big enough to comfortably park a truck inside. A wide flight of stairs guarded by a stone balustrade swept up to the next landing; the stone balustrade continued running the full width of it in a grand classical style. At the end of the hallway, where a doorway led into the kitchen, was a high-backed wing chair.

"Oh, look," Amy sang. "Mitch is asleep in the chair." She put her fingers to her lips and shushed, then tiptoed through into the kitchen.

Michael noticed Mitch's eyes. Half-open, they stared at the floor without seeing. One hand rested on his chest; the fingers were turning blue.

"Poor Mitch," he said softly. "All you ever wanted from life was to retire to an island."

But even now, Michael mused, smiling, poor Mitch was sailing out to some dark island, across a very much darker sea.

Christine had covered half the distance between the bed and the door. The walls were distorted. Dizziness came in great sluggish waves. One second she'd be on her hands and knees. The next she'd open her eyes to find herself facedown on the carpet.

Danger and dread.

The words pealed through her head.

Danger and dread . . .

She knew she must reach Amy. Something terrible was going to happen. And time was running out.

Mitch Winter's men found Michael in the kitchen.

Both he and Amy were drinking milk; there was a saucer of milk on the floor.

They didn't beat about the bush.

"What happened to Mitch?" asked one, the shotgun raised diagonally across his chest.

Michael smiled at Amy. "He's gone to sleep."

"He's fucking dead and you fucking know it."

"Watch your language. The little girl's not deaf, you know."

"Fucking shut it."

The man aimed the shotgun at Michael's chest.

"He's scaring the puppy, isn't he, Amy?"

She nodded, her eyes around with fear.

Michael smiled. "Silly, noisy men, aren't they?" He glanced round, counting them. Twelve. All the surviving members of security were here. For what good they were.

"Amy, let's play a game."

She looked at the armed men, unsure what do.

"Don't worry. Those are nice men, really. They'll join in."

They looked at one another, obviously wondering what Michael intended.

"Amy, turn and look at the men. Now, Amy . . . repeat after me: *Amy says put down your guns.*"

They lifted their guns. Michael heard the bolt of a submachine gun being pulled back.

Amy sounded frightened. "Amy says . . . Amy says put down your guns."

The guns rattled to the floor. Michael felt a solid burst of satisfaction as the men's eyes widened, their faces flushed red. And he saw fear in those widening eyes.

"Repeat after me, Amy. *Amy says put your hands on your heads.*"

Amy giggled, enjoying herself. "Amy says put your hands on your heads!"

The sound of palms slapping against scalps filled the kitchen as the men obeyed. Eyes wide now; Adam's apples jerking in their throats.

"Now." Michael grinned. "Amy, I'll whisper in your ear what to say next."

The men didn't move their hands from their heads, or move an inch—only their eyes flashed alarm.

Michael whispered into Amy's ear.

She giggled. Then she took a deep breath and said in a voice that was loud and clear:

"Amy says . . . *go hang yourselves!*"

Chapter Eighty-six

Strange Fruit

Ten minutes later, Richard entered Darlington Hall by the main entrance. Rosemary followed, moving silently, expecting any moment to meet the gunmen.

Although lights shone from the upper part of the house, those in the lower part of the house were unlit, leaving the entrance hall a gloomy shadow pool.

Richard glanced back at Rosemary. She was a silhouette now apart from her eyes that gleamed white out of the near-darkness.

They moved deeper into the house. Above, a crystal chandelier twinkled faintly in the little light that did filter through the tall windows.

Every so often, Richard would pause, listening. But no sound came from the house. Perhaps it had been abandoned. The way the gunmen had run suggested that they'd been warned the police were on their way.

With luck the gunmen might have run for it.

Or perhaps they might be waiting beyond the next door.

They were.

On her hands and knees Christine reached the bedroom door. She pulled herself into a sitting position. Her head swung loosely forward, smacking into the door frame.

She felt nothing.

The drug numbed her from head to toe.

She tried to call Joey's name but only a dry whisper left her lips.

Dread. Danger.

The words still rang inside her head, driving her to turn the door handle. Amy needed her. She knew it.

Slowly, she dragged herself into the corridor.

* * *

Christl

The men filled the hallway. Richard clenched his fists, ready to aim a punch at the man nearest to him.

The man turned to look at him.

No, not look at him. He *kept* turning. In a weirdly smooth way that suggested he was rotating on a turntable.

He felt Rosemary grab his arm. She, too, had seen the dozen or so men standing there in the gloom. But some were impossibly tall, their heads reaching halfway to the ceiling.

Silence. Absolute silence.

Richard shivered. Why didn't they react; why this strange turning around on the spot like some weird waltz?

Rosemary's voice was a whisper. "Look at them . . . look at what they've done."

His eyes adjusted at last to the heavy gloom. The men hung by ropes from a series of small stone pillars that formed a safety balustrade that ran up the stairs then across the upper landing.

For some reason all these men had tied ropes around the stone pillars, then slipped a noose over their heads and jumped.

Most had dislocated the spinal vertebrae, their necks obscenely stretched. Blood trickled from nostrils.

The ropes were so long that many of the men's feet almost, but not quite, touched the floor.

And there they turned silently on their ropes. Hanging like man-shaped fruit from a tree.

Rosemary touched his elbow. "Look." She nodded back toward a high-backed armchair. Richard recoiled, thinking that a man sat staring at them.

That man didn't move either.

"I think he's dead," she whispered. "Look at the eyes."

Ice-cold shivers tremored through his body. "Christ, what happened here?"

"Mass suicide?"

His mouth dried. "Come on, I want to see if Amy and Christine are still here."

On the floor lay a revolver. Richard picked it up. Then he pushed open the door beside the seated corpse.

The sudden brilliance of the kitchen lights dazzled him.

The first thing that happened was that something hit him hard across the forearm; the pain shot like a bullet up his elbow and into his neck. The gun, knocked from his hand, rattled onto the tiled floor.

He was aware of two men at his side, but it was the man standing in front of him that caught his attention.

Rosemary gasped.

"What's the matter?" Michael smiled, downturned eyes gentle as ever. "Devil nicked your tongues?"

Chapter Eighty-seven

Showdown

"Don't worry, Richard," Michael said, sitting on the kitchen table, legs casually swinging. "Christine and Amy are safe."

"Joey?"

Michael shook his head. "Sorry."

"You didn't have to hurt him, you sick little bastard."

"I don't hurt people for the fun of it, Richard. And I don't do anything without a good reason."

"So, there was a reason for leaving Isaac and me up at the barn when you knew all along that thing was coming?"

"I still can't believe you got away from the Beast, Richard."

"Well, it helps you move quickly when you know some poor guy has just been mashed flat and you're next. You deserve to be—"

"I deserve what? The same?"

Michael's eyes twinkled. *Why, the bastard's actually happy*, Richard thought, a bitter taste flooding his mouth.

"My, my, Richard. I didn't think you were so naive. A general doesn't go into battle believing he won't lose at least a few of his men."

"You're a mean bastard."

"And what do *you* think, oh-so-sweet Rosemary Snow? Not saying anything? My, the Devil *has* nicked your tongue, hasn't he?"

Richard stood there, hardly believing what he heard as Michael began to lecture them on how the world would be a better place now.

Out of the corner of his eye he now saw three men. One, wearing a white doctor's coat, carried a pistol. One carried a shotgun; the other a submachine gun. If anything, these seemed more dangerous than the professional gunmen. They sweated nervously. Richard didn't think it would take much to startle one of them into pulling the trigger.

". . . remember I told you I would have the power to inspire all men to become heroes. To work for a common goal with total dedication, total enthusiasm. I can inspire them to eradicate famine. I can inspire them to work and work until we've turned the deserts green again. This is a new world order. Peace will be—"

The snarl sounded as if it came from an animal. Then Rosemary leaped at Michael like a hell-cat, knocking him backward across the table, fingers ripping at his eyes.

Someone fired the shotgun.

They fired it deliberately high: the buckshot rattled against the copper pans hung above the worktops. A glass jar full of pasta exploded on a shelf.

Richard felt a gun barrel stab into his back. Reluctantly, he raised his hands.

The man in the white coat lunged after Rosemary, twisted her long black hair around his fists and pulled her back as she swore and kicked.

Michael sat up, blinking. A trickle of blood ran from the corner of his lips. When he opened his mouth Richard saw his teeth stained red with more blood.

"Nice one." Richard smiled at Rosemary. "I wish I'd got the guts to do the same."

Shock turned Michael's face so white it looked as if it'd been dusted with flour.

"My God, you've come out of your shell since I picked you off that roadside, Rosemary Snow." He spat blood.

"Where's Christine?" Richard demanded.

"Upstairs. She's fine."

"Amy?"

"Playing in the dining room."

"She's all right?"

"Top of the world. You should see her."

Rosemary snarled, "We know what you've done. We've seen enough of that *Codex Alexander* to know how you've got the Beast back under control again."

"You're using Amy to control it." Richard's voice dropped. "You've got to get rid of this thing, whatever it is."

"Why on earth should I do that after all the trouble I've gone to to rein it back in again?"

"Because it'll kill Amy, then it'll kill you."

"No, Richard. You'll find we've learned a lot since old Alexander of Macedonia's day."

Rosemary spoke in a fast low voice. "You know nothing. That Beast you're so fond of corrodes people from the inside out."

He shook his head. "You're the ignorant ones. The Byzantine Emperors lived to ripe old ages."

"Yeah, and you should've seen them. They were shriveled and twisted up by the Beast," Rosemary said. "Crippled; driven mad by the pain of enduring it possessing their bodies."

"Possessing? You make it sound like some low-life demon, Rosemary Snow."

"Constantine the First was the first Byzantine Emperor. The Beast drove him so paranoid he had his wife and eldest son executed."

"In any case, Rosemary," he smiled, "it doesn't possess my body, it possesses Mr. Young's daughter."

Richard wanted to punch that smug face. The smile. Those eyes that were so gentle; that said they cared for people in trouble. *Like shit they did.*

Michael sat on the table, his fingers knitted together. Again he managed to give the impression that he was the one who'd been hurt. As if proffered kindness had been dashed back in his face.

"The thing is, I admire you both. You've gone through hell and high water to reach here. But you understand the dilemma I face now. I can't allow you to influence Amy." He smiled. "You see, to all intents and purposes, *I'm* her daddy now."

Richard felt the cold creeping over him. Soon something was going to erupt inside. "You think so?"

Michael nodded. "She controls the power. I control Amy."

Deep down inside, although Richard didn't know why, a tiny spark of hope flickered. "So, you control Amy. Good for you, Michael. You know something? She's only four years old but I've never been able to say that." He smiled. "She's got a will of her own."

He saw the smile on Michael's face falter briefly. Then it came back and Richard realized that Michael had chosen to ignore him. "Nevertheless, Richard. Rosemary. If you were in my position, what would you do with two people who jeopardized your plans?"

Richard felt the shotgun barrel dig harder into his back.

Chapter Eighty-eight

Power

Richard did the first thing that came into his head. He knew the man pushing the muzzle of the shotgun between his shoulder blades was going to pull the trigger on Michael's nod.

He spun round, aiming to knock the shotgun barrel up with his left hand while punching the guy with his right.

He succeeded in pushing the barrel up at the ceiling, but his punch went wide. Although a scientist, the guy was fit. Richard didn't even see the gun barrel coming down until it was too late.

The twin barrels came down like a club; with a shockingly loud crack they smacked into the side of his face. Richard went down hard. His head rang like a bell and the room pitched around him. Groggily, he pulled himself up onto one elbow.

He saw that the white-coated man, holding Rosemary brutally by the hair, had forced her head over the sink. In his free hand he held a revolver which he pointed at the back of her head. The white-coated man looked away from her, his face screwed tight with tension. He didn't want to see the mess he would make when he finally pulled the trigger.

Richard shook his head, still dizzy; his face throbbed. Then he heard a rapid murmuring.

It's Rosemary, he thought, *poor kid's praying. She knows this is it.*

Then he heard the words: ". . . into the kitchen; Amy, come into the kitchen. Your daddy's hurt. Amy, come into the kitchen. Amy . . ."

Then he heard Michael's voice. "Shut her up."

White-coat replied, "There still might be some residual telepathic link . . . you can't stop her thinking."

Michael replied in a low voice, "Oh yes, you can."

White-coat tensed, holding Rosemary's head at arm's length

over the sink. His gun hand trembled as his fingers tightened.

"Now?" he asked.

Michael nodded. "Now, Dr. Lane."

Richard waited for the *crack!* of the bullet leaving the barrel to smack into the sixteen-year-old's skull.

A wave of black engulfed him; he blinked; shook his head, groggy. *I must have blacked out*, he thought, *I didn't hear the shot.*

But here comes the blood. Rosemary Snow is dead . . .

He couldn't bear to look across the floor to where the body must lie.

Instead, his eyes fixed on the trickle of deep red, as thick as syrup, rolling across the white tiles toward him.

Poor kid. I should've left her at that service station. Now I've brought her here to die. Her brains blown out into a kitchen sink.

The blood reached a drain set in the tiled floor and rolled over the chrome rim, then began to drip, drip, drip . . .

. . . into the waste pipe.

And now here comes mine, Richard thought, a bitter taste in his mouth. Shotgun blast to back. *Then my blood runs with Rosemary's down into that plug hole, mixing, mingling, then flowing to the river . . . then some distant sea . . .*

Already his mind had detached itself from the center of his brain. The kitchen seemed unreal, as if he already floated away from the life he'd held down here on Earth for these last thirty-three years.

The thick blood, red-black, almost purple, continued its drip, drip, drip into the drain.

Bang.

He blinked. It wasn't a gunshot. It was the sensation of him suddenly being snapped back into the real world.

Why hadn't they fired? Why was it so quiet?

His eyes followed the trail of blood.

From the drain, across the white tiles. But not toward the sink where Rosemary had been held. The blood trail led into the gap between a line of refrigerators and long food preparation tables.

His eyes focused on a pair of white trainers. They glistened red with blood. More drops of blood splashed into a small blood puddle beside the shoes.

He allowed his gaze to track up the yellow trousers; up the sweatshirt.

"Amy?" he whispered, his mind clearing. *"Amy."*

Then he saw the carton in her hand hanging loosely by her side. Blackcurrant juice still trickled from the straw hole; it pattered onto the floor, swelling the trickle that fed the floor grate.

"Amy . . ."

She looked straight through him, her eyes glassy. She did this when she was sleepy; as if that tired four-year-old mind couldn't quite synch itself with the real world. But there was something more. The eyes, although glassy and fixed, had changed. As if she'd seen something stupendous.

Something shocking.

"Amy, are you all right?"

When she didn't respond he glanced to his left. The guy in the white coat still held Rosemary over the sink. But she'd managed to lift her head to look at Amy. Michael himself moved very slowly as if not wishing to startle the four-year-old.

"Amy, darling," Michael said in a low voice. "Take Puppy back into the dining room. I'll bring you some supper. There's a video we—"

"Amy—" Richard began but felt the stab of the shotgun muzzle in his back.

Amy looked at the guns, her eyes still glassy, trancelike.

"Don't frighten Puppy."

"We won't, darling," Michael soothed. "We're just . . . playing."

"Puppy doesn't like guns."

"Go back into the dining room, Amy."

Richard sensed a sudden unease among the three members of the research team. Their eyes flicked anxiously from Amy to Michael, then back again.

Amy, glassy-eyed, still stared at the bare kitchen wall as if her eyes were focused on something beyond it.

"Don't like guns," she said in a faint voice. "People with guns should . . ." She cocked her head to one side as if listening to an inner voice. *"People with guns should run away."*

Richard heard the men behind him gasp.

He looked up, almost recoiling from the look of shock and the fear, the absolute fear in their faces.

"People with guns should run away."

They gasped again; a deep, throaty sound which Richard imag-

394

ined a human would make if a heavy boulder had been lowered onto their stomach.

Michael began to speak. "No, Amy. That's naughty. Don't tell the men to—"

"Run, run, run away." Amy's voice was barely a whisper.

Richard flinched at the sudden commotion behind him.

"No, Amy!" Michael shouted. "Stop it!"

Richard climbed to his feet, expecting to be clubbed by the shotgun again.

But the three men had got something else on their minds.

They'd got somewhere important to go.

They didn't know where . . .

. . . but wherever it was, they were going to hurry there and they wouldn't pause until they reached their destination. All three nodded, as if eagerly obeying orders; their eyes blazed.

"No, Amy . . ."

Her eyes were glassy. She still stared at the wall.

Richard watched White-coat drop Rosemary. Then he followed his two colleagues, through the door, through the hallway decorated with the hanging men—*bang*—through the main entrance doors and away through the night.

Richard's head snapped back to look at his daughter. He realized the significance of her power now . . . the Beast's power that she wielded. The absolute power over men. The power to command them to die for you. And for them to go willingly to their death, joyously crying out your name with their final breath.

Immediately he knew why the gunmen had hanged themselves.

And he knew that White-coat and his two colleagues would gladly—would passionately—run until an artery ruptured under the pressure.

Michael moved quickly. He picked up the dropped shotgun, then the submachine gun, slipping its strap over his shoulder. Then he pointed the shotgun's twin barrels at Richard and said, "The buck stops here, Young. I'm finishing the job."

Rosemary pulled herself to her feet by the sink. "Amy . . . Amy. Stop Michael hurting your daddy . . ."

Still staring, still glassy-eyed, Amy said, "Stop it, Michael. Stop it."

He looked at her sharply. "Go into the dining room, Amy. Go there, now."

Amy murmured, "Men with guns should run away."

Richard looked at Michael expectantly.

"Don't raise your hopes, Richard." Michael smiled. "It won't happen to me. Remember, I've lived years with the Beast in Turkey. I'm immune."

"Michael!" Amy's face turned red; her eyes snapped wide. "Don't hurt my Daddy, don't hurt my Daddy, don't—"

"Amy!" Michael shouted. "Amy, out of here. *Now!*"

A sound started in Amy's throat. Like a motor starting. A low growl rising, louder, louder, morphing into a scream; her body shook as if bolts of electricity cracked through it.

"Amy . . ." Rosemary ran to her as the four-year-old shut her eyes and dropped backward, hitting the tiles with a soft thumping sound.

Richard's stomach lurched. "Is she OK? Rosemary . . ."

Rosemary picked her up and held the little girl like a baby, head on her shoulder.

"She's breathing . . . she's OK." Rosemary's voice tremored.

Michael pointed the shotgun at Richard. "Rosemary. Take Amy into the dining room. Do as—"

He stopped speaking as the brass pans jingled together. A white towel, hanging from a wall hook, moved as if blown by a light draft.

Michael shook his head as if dismissing the draft as unimportant, then looked back at Richard. All pretense of the calm confidence had gone. The smile vanished. His downturned eyes were hard. Not taking those eyes off Richard, he said again, "Rosemary. Take Amy into the dining room. Through that door, first on your right."

The pans jingled again; the white towel fluttered.

Frowning, Michael glanced at where the draft had seemed to come from.

And then the draft came again. Only this time it wasn't a draft. It was a hurricane. The pans clanged together like bell clappers; the towel ripped from the hook and flapped above Richard's head. Rosemary's hair blew out behind her in rippling waves.

Richard scrambled to his feet. He saw Michael gesture to him with the shotgun to keep back.

"What's wrong, Michael? Did you expect this?"

He didn't reply; the tension turned his face ugly now, as if it revealed what had always lain under that smiling mask.

"It's Amy," Rosemary shouted above the blast of air, "she's dreaming . . ."

"It'll soon stop." Panic cracked through Michael's voice. "Wake her."

"I can't. I think it's some kind of fit."

"Come here," Michael yelled. "I'll wake her."

The wind howled around and around the kitchen like a tornado, ripping sheets of paper from a notice board. Cutlery flew like shrapnel. The pans crashed against the refrigerator doors.

The kitchen door opened. Briefly, Richard saw more of Michael's people beyond it, carrying guns. A man in glasses started through the door.

Then the door closed with thunderous slam—

—opened a split second later. The man was rocking back on his heels, his glasses smashed into his face. Another tried to come through the doorway, a revolver held high in his hand. The door slammed shut, trapping his arm between the door and the frame. Then, in impossibly quick succession, it slammed open-shut, open-shut, open-shut, smashing the man's forearm. Richard heard distant howls of pain. Then the door crashed shut.

And stayed shut.

Richard sensed that tremendous strength in the room. The door forced shut, as if a bull elephant pushed against it.

This was the power of the Beast he'd seen earlier; the same power that had killed the policemen, wrecked cars; brought down York's thousand-year-old cathedral.

It was in here with them.

But this time it was controlled by his four-year-old daughter's dreaming mind.

He found himself remembering the dreams she'd told him about. The scary dreams, faces at windows, gurgling monsters in the toilet, the Boys pulling her, crying, out of bed . . .

The Beast was interacting with those dreams now.

He sensed that power pushing at the walls, at the floor, at him; a leaping electric power, sending flashes of blue light cracking and sizzling along the metal work surfaces to spark from cooker to dishwasher to sink and back again.

"You must make her stop." Michael sounded as if he was pleading. The fluorescent lights flickered, went out.

But there was no darkness now.

The kitchen wall that Amy had stared at with those glassy

entranced eyes glowed milky white. It filled the kitchen with its cold glow. He saw Michael looking about the kitchen, frightened now. Rosemary stood and stared at the glowing wall, her hair still flapping about her, Amy still held tight in her arms.

Michael pointed the shotgun at Rosemary. And for the first time Richard realized he might fire at Amy if he thought his own life was threatened.

Taking a deep breath, Richard thought grimly. *"Here goes."* Then he lunged forward at Michael.

Chapter Eighty-nine

Where Shadows Stalk Darker

Michael's concentration was so fixed on Amy in Rosemary's arms that he didn't see Richard spring at him. Until it was too late.

Richard saw those downturned eyes snap from Amy to him as he closed the gap across the kitchen floor. Before Michael could react, he swung his fist as hard as he could into the middle of Michael's face.

Christ, Richard never expected it to feel that good. There was something both savage and sweetly satisfying at feeling his fist hit the bastard.

With a grunt Michael fell back onto the floor. Blood bubbled from his nose.

Then the winds hit with explosive force. Torrents of cabbages, potatoes, apples streamed over Michael as he lay flat out on his back on the tiled floor.

Richard heard a yell as the force of the gale threatened to hurl Rosemary against the wall that now glowed weirdly; flickers of rainbow colors raced across it.

Richard dragged himself back through the maelstrom, caught Rosemary in his arms and pulled her and Amy back, away from the shimmering wall.

Rosemary tried to shout something but the wind tore the words from her mouth.

Now he sensed there was more than the wind tearing through the kitchen. That force he'd sensed earlier seemed to run through the very fabric of the walls, floor, worktops, cookers and refrigerators. He was beginning to see . . .

No. He closed his eyes. He knew he wasn't really seeing this; it was some kind of illusion transmitted by Amy's sleeping mind.

When he next opened his eyes, he tried to ignore what he thought he saw.

As cupboard doors swung open so fiercely that hinges tore, woodwork splintered, he saw the . . . *no*, he told himself, *I'm not seeing them. They're not real.*

But he found himself recalling pictures of totem poles. And now in that kitchen in Darlington House, it seemed he saw those same totem-pole faces with hooked beaks and overlarge eyes. And those totem-pole faces stared at him from every cupboard, every refrigerator as the doors tore open one after another. He shook his head—*an illusion*, he told himself, desperately . . . *nothing but a damn illusion*.

But the faces wouldn't go away.

The kitchen wall glowed more brightly. He couldn't see the wall tiles now, only the milky light and flash of rainbow colors shimmering outward from its center.

And then he sensed that something moved just beyond the wall. Something shadowy and huge and very, very dangerous.

He sensed it wanted to come into the kitchen.

It wanted to join them.

Richard felt a huge jolt of fear.

He sensed . . . *no*, he didn't . . . he *knew*; he knew: like it was absolute fact; like he knew he had two arms, two legs; he *knew* that the shadow-thing beyond the wall wanted to come through to their world.

It paced: backward, forward, backward, forward . . .

And all the time Richard knew it stared in at them; its eyes (and there were oh-so-many eyes) fixed on the little people in that kitchen; it found them fascinating.

And Richard felt its want; its hunger; its need to join them there.

When the gunshot came it sounded strangely flat, as if the shotgun had been fired outside in the middle of a field.

Richard looked round, dazed by the ceaseless rush of totem face images and blasts of the hurricane.

Michael lay on his back on the floor: trying to aim the shotgun one-handed, while holding onto the table leg with the other, as if afraid of being carried away by the force of the gale.

Richard pulled Rosemary behind one of the huge stainless steel cookers as Michael fired the second shot. A light fitting shattered.

He looked over the top of the cooker. Michael aimed the shotgun again. But it was only a double-barreled shotgun. He'd had two shots. Richard glanced back to where Rosemary crouched with the unconscious Amy, trying to protect her from the debris being whirled by the winds.

Richard looked back at Michael who was trying to fire the gun, but was either too dazed from Richard's full-blooded punch or the effects of the whirlwind to understand why nothing happened when he pulled the trigger.

Richard moved on all fours toward Michael. He couldn't stand. Potatoes and cabbages cracked against his arms and legs, driven before the blast of air.

He looked at Michael who was now looking at the floor for more ammo. Then Richard saw he'd seen the submachine gun that had fallen to the floor. Michael, too, climbed on all fours and struggled across the floor toward it.

Richard tried to move faster: sometimes the wind caught him and tugged him backward across the slippery tiles.

He shot a look over his shoulder. The wall glowed. The rainbow colors moved more quickly.

And so did the shadow behind it. It paced faster. Backward-forward-backward-forward . . .

As if growing more excited at the thought of breaking through.

. . . backward-forward-backward . . .

Richard felt pure dread run through him. Was this the Beast itself?

Or perhaps, all along, the thing they thought was the Beast was only some *part* of the creature, reaching in from some alien dimension. Perhaps the part they'd encountered had been the equivalent of a boy's finger as he experimentally probes beneath the surface of a pond, carelessly prodding his finger at tadpoles and water snails.

The main part of it was the huge and dreadful shadow that paced beyond the wall. Wanting . . . needing . . . *lusting* to come inside.

Faster now, he scrambled after Michael who clawed his way toward the machine gun.

The cupboard doors crashed open; bags of sugar cascaded onto the floor, bursting; the hurricane caught the sugar, whipping it up to turn the air white. The crystals driven by the force of compressed air stung Richard's face; he inhaled, tasting sweetness.

Gritting his teeth, he forced himself to stand and leap forward as Michael's hand stretched out toward the machine gun. Richard landed on the back of the other man's legs. Hooking his hand inside Michael's shirt collar, Richard tried to pull him back from the gun.

The wind blasted; sugar swirled in the air; potatoes and cabbages rolled by in a lunatic race.

Richard pulled as hard as he could, trying to drag Michael back. Now Richard found it hard to breathe. He was weakening, and he realized this mad tug-of-war would only end when Richard had managed to haul Michael away from the gun. Or when Michael's outstretched hand reached the gun.

And, all the time, Richard sensed the shadow moving faster and faster behind the wall, ready for the second the barrier between this world and its own came tumbling down.

Chapter Ninety

Beastworld

Rosemary Snow opened her eyes to see the life-and-death struggle taking place at the far side of the kitchen: Michael trying to stretch out his arm and reach the gun, Richard trying to pull him back. The gale shrieked, whipping the mist of sugar hanging in the air into swirling whirlpools like dwarf tornadoes.

"What's all that noise for?"

She looked down at Amy in her arms. Amy's eyes opened sleepily.

"Don't worry, Amy. You're safe."

"But it's frightening my puppy."

Rosemary glanced around at the vegetables skittering across the floor. "What puppy, Amy?"

"Puppy Michael gave me. Here." She held out her cupped hands. "Puppy's in there. He's frightened."

Rosemary nodded, understanding. "He's a lovely puppy, Amy. Can I hold him?"

"OK."

Rosemary took a deep breath. She realized that Michael had somehow made Amy see the Beast as something nonthreatening, as a puppy, so that she wouldn't be frightened.

"Amy, you have to give the puppy to me."

Amy looked puzzled for a moment. "But he's frightened. Maybe I should keep holding him."

"I know he's yours, Amy," said Rosemary gently. "But it's tiring holding him all the time, isn't it?"

Amy nodded sleepily.

"Give me the puppy . . . just for a moment. There. I've got him."

Instantly Rosemary felt a crushing weight in the base of her skull; pains shot down her neck. She gasped.

As gently as she could, she sat Amy down on the floor. Then she pulled herself to her feet.

God, this is killing me . . . I can't do it . . .

The pain in her head and neck was more than she could endure.

The weight was settling on her chest; she couldn't breathe. She couldn't carry this thing anymore. She'd have to let it go.

But if she did that she knew it would crush them all.

Through the mist of swirling sugar she could see Michael reaching forward for the gun. He'd caused all this. He'd caused all those deaths, he was to blame . . .

Sheer hatred for the man erupted inside her, filling her from heart to fingertips with an incandescent rage.

Suddenly she could breathe again; the weight on her chest lightened.

In an instant, that fire of hate for the man forced her mind into focus: a hard brilliant focus she'd never experienced before.

"MICHAEL!"

Her voice shocked her; it thundered through her lips, deep, almost masculine.

Michael heard it and turned back, his eyes wide with shock.

The wind died in that moment. The vegetables stopped their mad rolling. In the kitchen all was still and quiet. Behind the wall that glowed white as milk the shadow moved faster; backward-forward . . .

"MICHAEL."

And then, from the look on Michael's face, she realized he now understood what had happened to her.

"Rosemary. I knew you could do it." His voice sounded small. "I knew . . . you're beautiful . . . beautiful. Rosemary, come back with me. We can make the world—"

As a glassy calm crept over Rosemary her lips and neck began to tingle. She looked Michael full in the face. And whether she spoke the words or just thought them she didn't know:

I KNOW YOU, MICHAEL. YOU WERE A LONER AT SCHOOL. YOU TRIED TO IMPRESS THE CHILDREN BY INVENTING WAYS TO BE CRUEL TO ANIMALS. REMEMBER THE KITTEN AND THE FIREWORKS, MICHAEL? REMEMBER THE DUCKLINGS AND THE LIGHTER FUEL? HOW YOU LAUGHED. BUT EVEN THE TOUGHEST KIDS WERE SICKENED.

SO YOU CHANGED.

NOW YOU WERE KIND TO ANIMALS. AS LONG AS THEY SEEMED GRATEFUL. IF THEY STOPPED BEING GRATEFUL, YOU STOPPED BEING NICE.

"Stop it, Rosemary." Michael begged.

THEN YOU FOUND THAT POWER IN TURKEY. BOY-OH-BOY, YOU DISCOVERED YOU COULD *MAKE* PEOPLE LIKE YOU. YOU'D GOT POWER, YOU'D GOT ALL THAT SEXY POWER. YOU COULD HURT PEOPLE AS MUCH AS YOU LIKED UNTIL THEY CRIED TEARS OF BLOOD BUT THEY'D STILL BEG FOR MORE BECAUSE YOU TOLD THEM TO. AND THEN YOU DREAMED ABOUT MAKING THE WORLD A HAPPY PLACE.

ON ONE CONDITION.

WE'D ALL HAVE TO BE GRATEFUL ALL OF THE TIME.

YOU WANT THAT POWER SO MUCH, DON'T YOU, MICHAEL?

SO I'M GOING TO LET YOU HAVE SOME OF IT. A NICE BIG PIECE THAT WILL KEEP YOU GOING FOREVER.

"No. Rosemary. You can't do this to me! Rosemary . . ."

IT'S WHAT YOU WANTED, ISN'T IT? YOU AND THAT THING YOU FOUND? TO BE REUNITED.

"No!"

GET READY, MICHAEL. HERE COMES THE POWER. HERE IT COMES.

NOW.

MICHAEL. LISTEN TO ME. YOU FEEL THE POWER RUN INTO YOUR BODY, INTO YOUR LEGS. NOW YOU HAVE THE POWER TO RUN FOREVER ON LEGS THAT WILL NEVER TIRE, NEVER WEAKEN. YOU'LL NEVER STUMBLE. LEGS LIKE A MACHINE. LEGS THAT WILL NEVER DIE.

NOW ON THE WORD *GO* YOU WILL RUN—

"No, Rosemary! Don't! You don't know what you're doing to me. I can't—"

. . . YOU WILL RUN FOREVER MICHAEL. THROUGH THERE.

She pointed at the glowing wall where the shadow paced.

IT'S TIME, MICHAEL. READY. STEADY. *GO!*

Richard watched Michael's face. The eyes were huge and terrified. The man's face ran with sweat, muscles in his throat and face convulsed.

"Nooooo . . ."

The word became a howl.

Then Michael looked at his legs as if they'd burst into flames; a mixture of shock and agony.

He moved in one convulsive lurch to his feet.

And then he ran.

Richard watched him run straight for the wall of white light. He hit it at a run. And he disappeared.

Richard didn't know how long they sat there. There was no strength left in his arms and legs. He couldn't move.

The light had gone from the wall. Now, it was just a kitchen wall again, like the rest, with blank white tiles.

At one point he heard Rosemary talking to Amy in a low gentle voice.

"Where's the puppy, Amy?"

"I've taken him back. I wanted to hold him."

"Amy, do you know something?"

"What?"

"Michael took that puppy away from its home. He shouldn't have done that because it made the puppy sad and lonely."

"Where does he live, then?"

"A long way away."

"Can't I keep him?"

"It wouldn't be nice for the puppy, would it?"

"Suppose not. How can we take him home?"

Rosemary said gently. "He's a magic puppy. Just tell him to go home."

"And he will?"

"Yes, Amy. He will."

"OK, puppy. Home you go."

Richard, exhausted, opened his eyes. There was a sudden swirl of displaced air. Then nothing. Apart from, that is, a sense of emptiness, as if some great presence had departed. Everything in the kitchen was still . . . quiet. Then he noticed that, falling from the ceiling, were specks of white. They drifted slowly down onto his hands and face.

He heard Amy's delighted voice calling him. "Daddy. Look! It's snowing! It's snowing."

Amy, arms straight out, turned around and around, catching those impossible snowflakes on her tongue. Despite Richard's ex-

406

haustion, a warm bubble of happiness rose up inside of him. Smiling wearily, he heard Amy singing over and over, "It's snowing, it's snowing, it's snowing . . ."

And Richard knew it was all over.

Chapter Ninety-one

Sunrise

Friday

Rosemary Snow stepped down from the train in her hometown.

The town seemed different now. The buildings didn't look so ugly, or so intimidating. In fact, the town didn't look that bad after all. She slipped the strap of the bag over her shoulder and walked confidently along the platform. She looked forward to going home. There was nothing to fear there. She smiled to herself. *She* was the strong one now.

Rosemary Snow left the station, joined the shoppers thronging in the streets, and allowed herself to be carried away into the heart of a town she'd be content to call home.

Saturday

Mark Young ran up the drive, the rucksack swinging on his back. He unlocked the door and pushed it open with his foot.

"Anyone home?" he called, his voice echoing from the hall walls. He dropped the rucksack and pushed open the kitchen door.

"Hall-lo! I'm back! Anyone home?"

He shoved open the living room door. It was empty.

He went back to the kitchen, opened the back door and crossed the sunlit lawn to the patio. Then, as he'd seen his father do in the past, he stood on the brick walls of the barbecue and used it as a look-out.

Beyond the hedge lay Sunnyfields. There, in the sunlight, he saw his mother and father and Amy; a blanket spread out on the grass. They were eating sandwiches and drinking orange juice.

Happy to be home, Mark pushed his hands into his pockets, then, whistling in a carefree kind of way, he headed for the gate, ready to tell them all about the adventures he'd had on his week away from home.

Chapter Ninety-two

Forever Darker

Michael. You run beneath a black sky that has never known a single star.

You run across a plain; gray dust beneath your feet.

You can never stop.

Because close behind something pursues you; you can't see it, but you sense its dark and pounding presence.

Michael, you run by clumps of willow trees. They shiver as you pass; the leaves hiss coldly.

As you run you are clear-headed, you are aware of your surroundings. As you are aware of your breath jolting in-out, in-out through your arid lips.

Your legs hurt; the pain bites deep.

You must run.

You can never stop.

Feel it, Michael. It is close behind you . . . darkly pounding.

You thirst. But how can you ever stop to drink?

Never stop, Michael. Never stop.

So you run on across the talcum-dry plain that stretches into forever. The monotony of dust and willows excruciating.

Michael, you grow hungry, brutally hungry. You scream in pain.

Now your mouth is dry; your belly swollen.

Thirst and hunger. Twin suns burning in your screaming sky.

But still you run.

And run.

And your eyes still see this world of dust and willows. And you feel the agony gnaw your legs.

And you know that, even though you began this endless race through the arid dreamscape a man, what runs through it now is a man no longer.

YOU KNOW: That the arid air blows through your ribs; that the skin has peeled from your skull; that your heart is dry as a stone; that two plump eyes stare whitely out from the sockets.

And, Michael, you know: That you will run on . . . and on . . .
FOREVER **DARKER**.

THE END

SIMON CLARK

Darkness Demands

Life looks good for John Newton. He lives in the quiet village of Skelbrooke with his family. He has a new home and a successful career writing true crime books. He never gives a thought to the vast nearby cemetery known as the Necropolis. He never wonders what might lurk there.

Then the letters begin to arrive in the dead of night demanding trivial offerings—chocolate, beer, toys. At first John dismisses the notes as a prank. But he soon learns the hard way that they're not. For there is an ancient entity that resides beneath the Necropolis that has the power to demand things. And the power to punish those foolish enough to refuse.

___4898-1 $5.99 US/$6.99 CAN

SIMON CLARK

Blood Crazy

Saturday is a normal day. People go shopping. To the movies. Everything is just as it should be. But not for long. By Sunday, civilization is in ruins. Adults have become murderously insane. One by one they become infected with a crazed, uncontrollable urge to slaughter the young—even their own children. Especially their own children.

Will this be the way the world ends, in waves of madness and carnage? What will be left of our world as we know it? And who, if anyone, will survive? Terror follows terror in this apocalyptic nightmare vision by one of the most powerful talents in modern horror fiction. Prepare yourself for mankind's final days of fear.

__4825-6 $5.99 US/$6.99 CAN

NAILED
BY
THE
HEART
SIMON CLARK

"One of the year's most gripping horror novels . . . Truly terrifying." —*Today* (UK)

The Stainforth family—Chris, Ruth and their young son, David—move into the ancient sea-fort in a nice little coastal town to begin a new life, to start fresh. At the time it seems like the perfect place to do it, so quiet, so secluded. But they have no way of knowing that they've moved into what was once a sacred site of an old religion. And that the old god is not dead—only waiting. Already the god's dark power has begun to spread, changing and polluting all that it touches. A hideous evil pervades the small town. Soon the dead no longer stay dead. When the power awakens the rotting crew of a ship that sank decades earlier, a nightmare of bloodshed and violence begins for the Stainforths, a nightmare that can end only with the ultimate sacrifice—death.

___4713-6 $5.99 US/$6.99 CAN

Dorchester Publishing Co., Inc.
P.O. Box 6640
Wayne, PA 19087-8640

Please add $1.75 for shipping and handling for the first book and $.50 for each book thereafter. NY, NYC, and PA residents, please add appropriate sales tax. No cash, stamps, or C.O.D.s. All orders shipped within 6 weeks via postal service book rate. Canadian orders require $2.00 extra postage and must be paid in U.S. dollars through a U.S. banking facility.

Name_____
Address_____
City_____State_____Zip_____
I have enclosed $_____ in payment for the checked book(s).
Payment <u>must</u> accompany all orders. ❑ Please send a free catalog.

IN THE DARK

RICHARD LAYMON

Nothing much happens to Jane Kerry, a young librarian. Then one day Jane finds an envelope containing a fifty-dollar bill and a note instructing her to "Look homeward, angel." Jane pulls a copy of the Thomas Wolfe novel of that title off the shelf and finds a second envelope. This one contains a hundred-dollar bill and another clue. Both are signed, "MOG (Master of Games)." But this is no ordinary game. As it goes on, it requires more and more of Jane's ingenuity, and pushes her into actions that she knows are crazy, immoral or criminal—and it becomes continually more dangerous. More than once, Jane must fight for her life, and she soon learns that MOG won't let her quit this game. She'll have to play to the bitter end.

___4916-3 $5.99 US/$6.99 CAN

Dorchester Publishing Co., Inc.
P.O. Box 6640
Wayne, PA 19087-8640